Copyright © 2022 by Maddison Cole

All rights reserved. No part of this publication may be reproduced, stored or transmitted in any form or by any means, electronic, mechanical, photocopying, recording, scanning, or otherwise without written permission from the publisher. It is illegal to copy this book, post it to a website, or distribute it by any other means without permission.

This novel is entirely a work of fiction. The names, characters and incidents portrayed in it are the work of the author's imagination. Any resemblance to actual persons, living or dead, events or localities is entirely coincidental.

Maddison Cole asserts the moral right to be identified as the author of this work.

Maddison Cole has no responsibility for the persistence or accuracy of URLs for external or third-party Internet Websites referred to in this publication and does not guarantee that any content on such Websites is, or will remain, accurate or appropriate.

Designations used by companies to distinguish their products are often claimed as trademarks. All brand names and product names used in this book and on its cover are trade names, service marks, trademarks and registered trademarks of their respective owners. The publishers and the book are not associated with any product or vendor mentioned in this book. None of the companies referenced within the book have endorsed the book.

First edition

Ebook ISBN Number: B09V3WFLFC

Paperback ISBN Number: 9798429692678

Editing & Proofreading: Mom Loves Book Editing

Cover Design: Jessica Mohring at Raven Ink Covers

Formatting: Emma Luna at Moonlight Author Services

AUTHOR NOTE

The writing in this book is the Queen's English, but please don't hold the fact I'm a Brit against me! I can't help it, but I have worked hard to make sure you understand what I am talking about. If anything does confuse you, give me a shout!

Also, I feel the need to point out that Hamish ran a bit rampant in this book, more than usual. I am not responsible for anything he says or does, and any offence he causes the Scottish Nation is solely on him. I cannot be held responsible.

TRIGGER WARNING

The 'I Love Candy' series features a feisty female lead and her broody harem. Candy is spontaneous, impulsive, and reckless, which makes this book inappropriate for anyone under the age of 18.

She gives as good as she gets, causing chaos and usually leaves you wondering who is bullying who!

Expect excessive amounts of steam, violence, and cursing throughout.

This series is an RH trilogy with a HEA…eventually!

DEDICATION

To Claire Douglas and your Army of Gummy Bears!

May they have a long and prosperous reign, full of jiggly-spanks and candy-embellished tanks.

Smashin' Candy

I Love Candy Book Two

Maddison Cole

CANDY

"Throat punch the cunt," Angus's gruff voice declares. I roll my eyes over the rim of my cocktail glass, ignoring him in favor of people watching across the bar. He's still pissed about the revelation of Malik's motives in the woods last week, but just like I told Malik before he stormed upstairs, never to reappear, I'm not going anywhere. There's a reason I like the bad guys. Because they do bad shit. Comes with the territory, so I'm never surprised when they do just that. In all their broody bullcrap, they're still as predictable as anyone else.

Take Mr. Pensive Peenhead further along the bar, for example. He may have been my type once; dark hair swept low over his eyes, tattoos leaking from the neck of his oversized hoodie. The whole 'I only care about the bottom of my beer and not the women fawning all over me' vibe. Now though, he just looks like a jerk who came out on our busiest night of the week to act like he wants to be alone. What a douchebag.

He glances up to meet my eye, and I yawn before returning to my cocktail from the Ejaculating Unicorn collection we have on display. The good shit's out back. Tipping the contents of the glass down my throat, I beckon Gabriel over for a refill. Now here's a handsome guy. His dark contacts barely swing my way as he takes the glass, shakes up a new glittery cocktail and places it back in front of me.

"Ah-hem," I fake a cough. "Forgetting something?" Raising his head to the sky, Gabriel's chest heaves with a sigh, and he tugs on the cuff of his pale blue shirt. A party of thirsty women grab his attention across the other side, and he strides away, completely ignoring me. It's all part of the act. Despite Malik having been the only Gambler's Monarch to return home in the past several days, the bartenders are still working hard to imitate their bosses, as per their iron-clad contracts. It comes as no surprise Gabriel is Malik's lookalike.

Pushing my drink aside, I use the rungs on the stool to hoist myself over the bar. Men immediately catcall for me to pour them drinks, to which I stick my middle finger up and lick the length of it. Retrieving my own damn umbrella, like some sort of slave, I decide to lean along the length of Gabriel's back while he's uncorking a bottle of wine.

"How long did you have to study him for?" I ask, slipping the umbrella behind his ear. "Malik, I mean." Gabriel gives me a warning glare over his shoulder to shut my face in case anyone is listening in. Except the music is booming, and no one is stupid enough to eavesdrop on me after some whore caught me halfway through a conversation with Angus the other day. I've never seen someone's back bend so far after I shoved her over one of the low sofas and gave her a quick titty slap. Besides, it seems like the only one interested in me within a mile of here is Peenhead.

"Get off of me. I'm working," Gabriel shoves me away and spins on his dress shoe heel. "I need to fetch more champagne for this hen do. Hold the fort." He leaves via the connecting door to the rest of Malik's home without waiting for a response. Still had that umbrella tucked behind his ear though, bringing a chuckle to my lips. One that's soon drowned out by the desperate punters screaming drink orders at me.

I look over their sea of heads to Nick, Ace's lookalike. He's also spending a lot of time trying to please the extensive hen do, although, without a tray of drinks in his hands, he seems to be having a little too much fun. I shove my gum into the pocket of my cheek to stick my fingers in my mouth and whistle at him. The sound slices through the crowd, gaining his attention, and I raise my arms in a 'what the fuck' motion. Not because I'm jealous, but because I made a vow with myself the moment I swore not to become a stripper like mommy dearest. I'll never serve anyone.

With my attention averted, Peenhead moves to stand directly in front of me across the bar, whipping up the front of his hoodie to flash a lazy six-pack of the skinny variety and a gun nestled into his waistband. Oh, look at that. He is rather interesting after all. I cock a brow, lowering my arms with a hard slap against the PVC catsuit I'm wearing. Clinging to my curves like cellophane with a tear drop cleavage reveal, the one-piece is quickly becoming a favorite of mine. But nothing has quite topped the knee-high boots I treated myself to with Malik's credit card. It's been lonely as shit around here lately, and online shopping is soooo addictive. They lace up in a criss-cross pattern and of course, they're hot pink-

"Are you fucking listening to me?!" Peenhead screams, pulling my eyes back up from the mini fashion show I was giving myself, to the gun that's now being brandished at my face. Noticing at the same time, the hen party begins to squeal and run in all directions like brain-dead chickens. Rolling my eyes, I slip a hand beneath the bar to grip my faithful bat, the Candy Crusher, in my palm. With the other hand, I lean over the bar to settle the gun between my eyebrows.

"Honey, if you're going to point a gun my way, you'd better be nine inches deep in me because gunplay gets me off. Sadly, beneath all that hair, your face looks like you've been hit with a shovel. It's like anti-viagra. I'm anti-hard for you-" Swiftly, although with an unsure wobble, Peenhead shifts the gun to over my shoulder and shoots. The two-way mirror behind the bar shatters, causing everyone else in the club to notice and start fleeing for the door. Me, however, I can ignore my newly burst eardrum in favor of softly chuckling in his direction.

"I'm serious. Open the cash register, or you can say goodbye to your pretty face."

"Aww, you think I'm pretty?" I mock with a wide grin. This twat-muffin just played his weakest card, proving he doesn't have the balls to shoot someone outside of whatever video game started him on this quest. Unhooking my gum from where I stashed it inside my cheek, I blow a large, pink bubble and pop it in his face. Peenhead jerks back as my gum creates a web over his eyes, and I remove the Candy Crusher from her hiding spot. Hello girl, I greet in my mind and place a kiss on her varnished pine. Then, I swing with the might of Joe DiMaggio. Eat your heart out Marylin Monroe. At least three teeth shoot from Peenhead's mouth on contact, a spray of blood covering the bar top.

Hoisting myself up, my next hit connects with the hand holding the gun, snapping his wrist. After that, it's mostly a blur, but the message is clear. Don't fuck with me if you aren't going to back up your actions. That's like committing to a porno when he knows he can't last more than a few minutes. Very disappointing.

Hands grip me from behind, yanking me off the limp body that strangely looks better, all battered and bruised. More interesting, at least. Now he can get the sympathy vote when he goes home empty-handed crying to his mom.

"You're welcome," I say, spitting my gum onto his blood-soaked hoodie. I shrug off the hands yanking me away, throwing a warning glare at Gabriel for coming between me and my fun. Except it's not Gabriel standing there, but the real deal himself.

"Oh, hey Malimoo!" I shout, dropping my beloved bat in favor of spinning for a tight hug. Then I remember Malik isn't a big fan of being touched, and since when the fuck was I a hugger anyway? Pulling back, I spot Angus sitting on the bar with one angry eyebrow cocked.

"What the hell is going on down here?" Malik roars over my shoulder at Nick. I attempt to take a sly side-step until I realize

Malik's hand is still on the small of my back, holding me close to him. The bartender starts to splutter, which is just painful all round, so I tilt Malik's chin back my way.

"Well, there's good news, bad news, and good news. In that order." I nod, matter of factly. Malik's expression doesn't shift from dangerously tense, so I carry on. "Good news is you still have all of tonight's takings safely in the register. Bad news is you need to pay for a new glass divider." I risk a glance at the shards that have rained down all over the expensive whiskeys and smashed a high percentage of those too. "The other good news is that you've finally left your tower Rapunzel, so now we can make love on the bar amongst the carnage and blood of our enemies." Peenhead uses that moment to cough, and I shove my boot into his stomach for fun. Malik, though, doesn't seem all that impressed.

Releasing me, I frown at the sweep of coldness not only from the missing contact of his hand but also the general way Malik regarded me before turning to leave. That's when Gabriel returns, bumping shoulders with his lookalike in the doorway. He doesn't share Malik's cool façade, his eyes bulging at the sight of the bar and his mouth dropping open like a horse waiting for an apple. Too bad I left my bridle upstairs.

"Less gawking, more tidying stable boy," I double click in Gabriel's direction before exiting. I manage to catch Malik before he ascends the staircase back to his self-declared prison.

"Hey," I tug on his arm, pulling him back down the step to face me. "What's wrong?" A sharp inhale is the only warning I get that his voice will be raised, and his temple vein is going to have a pulsing party in his head.

"What's wrong is that you have absolutely no regard for your own safety. Anything could have happened in the time it took me to see the CCTV footage and run my ass down here. Haven't I lost enough people I care about to have to worry about you getting into fucking gunfights in my bar?!" My eyebrows raise, and a smile plays about my lips.

"You care about me," I singsong. Winding my arms around a

stiffened Malik, not holding back on the burning need for physical contact, I press a light kiss on his jaw. "I think you're underestimating my capabilities, and if you don't want to run down the stairs, maybe you should be on hand for supposed gun-wielding fanatics looking to get their asses kicked." Unable to resist, and thanks to my hot heels, I lean into Malik's firm body and run my nose down the length of his.

Man, I didn't realize until now that I've actually…missed him. All of them really. Maybe that's why I downloaded the weird voice notes I found on Ace's computer and loaded them to the Alexa's in each room. Even found some motion-sensor attachments as well. Every time I pass the gym, Jack's voice rings out with Beyonce's 'If I Were a Boy'. Possibly stuffing his pillowcase and hanging it from the pull-up bar for a little boogie was a step too far, but it smelt like him, and Angus spurred me on.

"I'd be a fool to underestimate you, but one day you might pick a fight with the wrong person. Not like that woman you chucked over the sofa a few days ago." There's a playful twitch in Malik's brow, which is rare for him. Maybe I'm not the only one who's missed our conversations.

"Aww, you were watching me the whole time like a proper stalker." Walking backward, I pull Malik with me until the backs of my knees hit the poker table. Then I spin us to push him to sit down and climb aboard. Malik shifts himself back onto the table so my thighs can rest on the green felt, his hands winding around to hold my ass. "Besides," I go to chew my gum before realizing it's missing. Dammit. "Picking fights is what I do, and beating on big tough guys is my specialty. If one happens to get the better of me one day, that's a decent way to go out. Should earn me a warrior's burial over the edge of a cliff." The memory of freefalling from Big Cheese's limo springs to mind, and I smirk. Yeah, that would have been an epic way to die.

"I really wish you wouldn't talk about yourself like that," Malik frowns. He reaches up, tugging a strand of pink hair behind my ear. Once he's done, I shake it back out on a humourless grunt.

"And I really wish you'd shove your dick into my throat, but here we are, chatting like old ladies," I grind my hips against him. Malik's hard stare doesn't budge, and I shrug on a sigh. "Thanks to my seventh foster father, I've been to my fair share of pedo parties to know self-respect is a wasteful resource. Life's simpler and better without a deluded sense of dignity getting in the way." The frown deepens into a full-on scowl, so I quickly push my hand over Malik's mouth, halting whatever pitiful spew I don't want to hear. For the first time, now the adrenaline of his closeness has eased, my eyes drag over his appearance. Scruffy hair, a baggy t-shirt with a white stain dripped down the front, the scrape of a premature beard against my palm. Not the Malik I'm used to.

"How about I promise to work on valuing myself whilst I'm bringing the Monarch's home? As long as you promise to take a shower. What is this; toothpaste, mayo, or cum?" Gripping his t-shirt, I rub my tongue back and forth over the stain, hinting at a minty taste. Toothpaste, how boring. Prying his t-shirt back, Malik pulls me plush against him and runs his fingers down the length of my exposed back.

"Now who's the one caring," he mutters into my ear. Lowering back, I'm drawn over the length of Malik's body and reminded of just what I saw in him. Or rather, felt. The evidence of his hard-on against my core does sweet things to my libido, but I don't want sweet. I want hard and raw. To be used and bruised and left limp with a bitter taste oozing across my tongue. I wonder if I slip enough Toxic Waste sour candy into Malik's food, his cum might start to taste like it? Not sensing where my mind has gone, Malik halts my hips from grinding over his rock-hard cock and draws my gaze back to his face. "Why does it even bother you if the Gambling Monarchs are back together or not?"

"Because you made me your Queen. I've got the jacket to prove it and everything." I jerk my chin towards the leather jacket I've basically lived in, slung across the sideboard from earlier. I'd been working my way through the rum when I saw the hen-do arrive at the bar and figured I could have more fun out there. One way or another, I was sure by the end of the night, I'd have been joining or fighting them. Wins either way in my books. A pleasure-lacking groan vibrates through Malik's chest.

"Haven't you been paying attention? It doesn't mean anything. This doesn't mean anything," Malik gestures to the bar through the shattered hatch. "I…." He drowns himself out with a sigh.

"Well, it does to me." I look away from his jet-black eyes that see too much and hide even more. Jeez, the tension in here is stifling. "You can't tease me with five cocks and expect me to settle for just your pencil dick." We share a look, both knowing that was bullshit, but Malik lets it drop. Moving us from the poker table, Malik links his fingers in mine and leads me towards the stairs. I catch Nick's eye through the hatch, throwing him a wink before disappearing from view. I should have insulted Malik's dick ages ago if I knew it'd spur him to prove me wrong.

Instead of bypassing the middle floor like I thought, Malik draws me into the hallway I've walked alone for the past week. Every door is closed as if I could trap the essence of those who so recently lived here inside and stop them from escaping. Opening the door to my Barbie-inspired room, Malik gestures for me to enter first.

"Team Stefan all the way!" Spade's slurred voice shouts as I pass under the motion sensor hanging over the top of my wardrobe. I keep my eyes forward and spine straight, not wanting to have the creepy voice note conversation with Malik. Spade's wrong anyway, and I've had many conversations with the cupboard door about just why Damon deserved to win the girl, even if Elena got on my tits. Unlike her, I encourage men to bite me on a regular basis, despite their lack of vampire abilities.

Striding past, Malik heads straight for the bathroom to switch the shower on, beckoning me to join him. Only when we're naked and beneath the warm spray do I let the bravado I've been relying on fade away. Malik washes my hair with pink-tinted shampoo before running a soapy loofa over my body. He pays particular attention to my nipples, making me moan against his lips.

"Four, by the way," he mumbles as I'm about to tongue-fuck the living shit out of him.

"Huh?" I jerk back in confusion.

"You said you were teased with five dicks. There were four of us." This time, I do ravage his mouth but not because I couldn't resist the pull drawing me closer and closer. It's to hide the sly smirk that threatened to spoil this moment. I haven't finally drawn Malik out of his shell, just to shut him down with my intentions to bring Jasper back along with the others. Sure, holding us at gunpoint in the woods isn't typically followed by sitting around a campfire to hold hands and sing Kumbaya.

But I've been with Jasper enough to know he's just as misguided as the rest of them. His intentions are weak; his plots to bring down those he once called brothers are ineffective. If he'd really wanted to destroy them, it would have been done already. Call me an optimist, but I reckon there's a reason he holds back, which can only mean there's still hope for him yet.

JASPER

"Where the fuck have you been?" I bellow when Oscar finally walks through the front door. Granted, he looks like a sack of shit, but that doesn't quell my temper. The mess of black hair on his head is matted, covering the top half of his bruised and swollen face. His hoodie is stained with large, dark spots that will never come out of the cream fabric. But more interestingly, one of the armholes is swaying freely.

"The hospital," Oscar spares a glance my way and heads for the staircase. Diving into his way, I glower, already anticipating bad news. He might be just some kid I picked up scamming the elderly, but if I offer decent money for a job, I expect it done.

"For three days?!" I slam a hand on his shoulder, causing him to cry out. As I suspected, there's a knot hidden beneath the collar of his hoodie, concealing an arm sling. "I've been sitting here with my dick in my hand waiting for news from you."

"Well, that's not entirely true," Tanya walks around the corner in a satin robe. Her brown hair is pinned up from a recent shower, the ends that caught the spray dripping down her back. I refrain from rolling my eyes at the unnecessary sway of her hips, but only because she's the reason I've been able to make Leicester's old mansion my current home.

Without any family to speak of, the estate was sitting here unclaimed, and thanks to his long line of criminal activity, none of his formal crew could legally claim it. Tanya, however, had done some legit work on the books and provided me with an in. As long as I keep letting her believe I'm besotted by her pussy, she's granted me full access. The moment I find a loophole to get the mansion in my name though, she's as good as dead. Oscar makes a move to leave again, and I squeeze his shoulder.

"At least tell me what I want to know, and then I'll let you go. Did it work? Did Malik come to Candy's aid and for the love of fuck, tell me you got a clean shot in before he evidently kicked your ass." I hunt for Oscar's eyes between the swelling, finding the slits of brown barely open. His dry laugh quickly turns into a pained cough.

"During my briefing, you left out the part that the girl is a fucking psychopath. Sure, I heard Malik's voice, but she'd already broken my arm in two places by then. I'm doubling my fee as compensation. Next time you want to get her attention, do it your damn self." I let Oscar leave this time, mostly because the anger that's been riding me ever since I watched Candy leave with my enemy in the woods has finally cracked. A slow smile spreads across my face as he limps up the staircase. I should have anticipated Candy wouldn't roll over like a good bitch and let Malik take the fall for her but damn. She's vicious, and that does all kinds of things to my psyche.

Tanya winds an arm around my waist which I immediately dislodge, making my way towards the kitchen. It's barely ten in the morning, yet something tells me I'll be needing a stiff drink if I'm going to get through today. Having taken the shorter route around the lower level, Tanya is already at the island by the time I stroll in. She reaches for the elaborate whiskey decanter and pours me a double measure. Accepting the glass, I head outside and drop into the lounger facing the pool. This is the exact spot I held Spade at gunpoint, threatening to kill the man I once considered a brother. I don't reckon I could have gone through with it then, but now, I couldn't care less about family ties. It's all about the vengeance, baby.

"Let's do something today," the high-pitched voice comes from the sliding patio doors. This time, I release the groan I've been holding in. I wasn't surprised when Tanya came crawling back after 'our break up.' Her words, not mine. That would imply we were ever more than wasting time together. It's a shame because she's not the dumbest crayon in the box, yet she only cares about improving her position of power.

"I'm good here," I respond, trying to stop her from coming any closer. Of course, she never takes the hint and drops her slender ass on the wicker bench to my left.

"Oh, come on, we've been stuck in this mansion for almost two weeks. If we left now, we could spend the afternoon at the beach. Sipping margaritas with our toes in the ocean during sunset. Doesn't that sound romantic?" I down my drink and loll my head to the side. How long has she been cooking that one up? Yet, she's kinda, right. What else would I be doing other than staring at this pool again, brooding over what Malik and Candy might be doing right now? I don't need much of an imagination to envision exactly what that is. At least I've kept tabs on the other guys, and I'm satisfied to know they haven't run home like good little pups.

"Fuck it," I half-shrug. Tanya squeals, making me instantly regret my decision as she shoots up to get ready. After a couple of minutes, I sigh and make my way back inside. Taking the long way around the lower level, my feet stop moving of their own accord beside the billiard table. This happens every time, hence why I normally take the shorter route to the main staircase. The rough felt scrapes against my fingertips as I trail a hand over the surface, remembering all too well the view I had on Malik's pool table. Snapping myself back to reality because there's no use drowning in a fantasy that can never be, I head directly towards the bedroom

I've claimed. All to myself, I might add. Having my own space was non-negotiable.

Straight out of a luxury show home magazine, dark wooden beams arch across the ceiling. A statement fireplace rests against the textured, grey feature wall, which also holds a huge flatscreen. All the furniture is chocolate brown to match the ottoman, broken up by shades of cream splashed across the walls, bedspreads, rug, and a sofa pushed into an alcove of large windows. I catch sight of myself in the TV's reflection thanks to the sun's glare from the outside. Or, more specifically, I catch sight of the hideous scar rounding the side of my face. Raising my hand, I stop short of touching it before turning away on a scowl. After changing into a pair of floral board shorts, the tag drives under the crease of my ass, threatening to steal my V-card. I rip it out and toss the rapey tag across the room before dropping onto the sofa. That's me ready, but no doubt Tanya will be at least an hour yet.

True to typical fashion, I've run out of new trends on my Tiktok feed by the time Tanya appears in the doorway. Sunglasses tilt over a mound of back brushed hair, trailing into symmetrical curls on either side of her exposed cleavage. A tiny, sunflower dress flows from just above her nipples to the top of her thighs. The thing that really makes me quirk a brow though is the Instagram-perfect, full-face of make-up beaming back at me.

"You do know I'm going to dunk your head in the ocean as soon as we get there, right?" I ask, forcing myself up to my feet. Tanya gasps, placing a hand across her chest.

"Don't you dare! I'm only going so I can brush up my tan."

"Let's hope the sun can find you under all that gloop on your face then," I mock. Yes, I'm being a dick, but clingy girls rub me the wrong way. Pushing my phone into my pocket, I near Tanya, and she holds out a straw beach bag expectantly.

"I packed for you too," she complains, and I take the damn bag. Turning in her glittery sandals with a smug smile, I follow Tanya down the length of the hallway and down the grand staircase. Debating with myself whether I should ditch her at a gas station or on the beach itself, we make it all the way to the exterior garage when Tanya halts me with a hand on my bare chest.

"I forgot my bronzing spray! Start the car; I'll be right back!" I wait for her to disappear back into the mansion before cursing under my breath. The things I do for a decent place to stay. At this rate, I'm seriously contemplating moving back into my locker if it means a day without her hanging off me like a deranged sloth. Using the key fob, the garage door slowly rises of its own accord, and as I take a regretful step inside, I stop in my tracks.

"Hey Boo," calls the pink imp I've been picturing each time I let Tanya squat on my dick. Candy is sprawled across the backseat of the Lamborghini convertible, wiggling her fingers and popping her gum. Taking in my swim shorts and beach bag, she sits up to lean over the driver's seat. "Ooohhh, this looks fun. Are we going on a road trip?" I throw one look at the upstairs window where Tanya can be seen rooting through one of her vanities, and my mind is made up.

"We are now." I smirk, tossing Candy the bag and dropping into the front. Her fingers dive into my hair, drawing a shudder from my shoulders. My instincts are screaming, but I lock them all away in favor of whatever adventure Candy has in store for me today. Sure, she's declared herself the enemy, and yes, she'll have a thousand more reasons to hate me tomorrow. But like I said earlier, fuck it.

CANDY

Leaning back in the seat, I shove the final Cheeto from the bag in my mouth. "Sheee! Aye tol you aye ka'oo ihh!" I grunt around the mouthful, celebrating my victory. Jasper watches me in the rear-view mirror, humor shining in his green eyes. He really should know better than to challenge me by now, and when it comes to how much I can fit in my mouth, there really is no competition. Swallowing is a whole another issue, and I end up choking before spitting all over the side of the Lambo. The rapid-fire of cheesy bullets rain over a cyclist who waves his fist and shouts curses at me. Wow, some people just really need to chill the fuck out.

With the exception of our brief snack stop, because no trip is complete without road snacks, Jasper has gunned us towards Roughstone Valley. Probably not the official name, but that's the only clue my driver for the day would give me on our destination. He winds through the back roads with clear knowledge of the area, parking up around the back of someone's beach shack. Around the side of the patio, a narrow walkway hidden by overgrown bushes leads to a set of rickety, old steps. Winding an arm around my waist, Jasper leads us towards the beach below with too much swagger for someone who hired a hit on me three days ago.

I'd had an inkling even a stupid kid wouldn't openly fire a gun on the busiest night of the week simply for the cash register's contents. That's what gas stations are for. I hadn't, however, expected the happy-go-lucky gunman to lead me from the hospital straight back to Big Cheese's old mansion, or Jasper for that matter. That's the joy of not living by a schedule or unnecessary set of rules. Every day is an adventure, and I never know where I'm going to end up.

The humidity is just this side of uncomfortable, with almost enough breeze cutting through the balm to make it tolerable. The sun beats from a cloudless sky, brushing over a shimmering ocean. It's enough to make even me turn into some English Poet, searching for the right words to describe the landscape.

"Wow, this place is even more surprising than Angus in his Rocky Horror phase." Jasper raises an eyebrow and smiles widely. His dimple winks at me, and I hold back from dipping my tongue into it. Don't want to show all my cards before we've even started this….date? No, that's too serious. This is an unplanned, blasé day out. Reaching the bottom step, I pause to untie and remove my fabulous, knee-high boots. Once my legs are bare, I can pretend the Denim booty shorts and crop top I'm wearing was totally intentional for the seaside. Thanks to its secretive location, the sand is only playing host to a few other couples and one family. Yuck, who would bring kids to such a relaxing location? It's as if they want me to pick a fight about their tantruming brats. If I had my way, there would be steel-bar cages at every location to lock them up and let the adults enjoy themselves, as nature intended.

Jasper draws me far away from all others, brushing clear a spot in the golden sand and gesturing for me to sit. I step in between his legs and settle myself down on his crotch, wriggling my ass to find the comfiest spot. A guttural groan meets my ears, and I throw him a cheeky look.

"Problem?"

"Not at all. You've just put on so much weight since you were last in my lap." I chuckle, calling his bullshit by attempting to move, but his hands clamp me in place. Thought so. Leaning back into Jasper's body, slotted together like two jigsaw pieces, the scenery is picture-perfect. The gentle roll of waves, a fluttering dance of gulls across the open sky, laughter from the children building a sandcastle a little distance away. Makes me feel rather nauseous, to tell the truth.

"So, you've got me here all to yourself, love. We gonna talk about…anything?" Jasper asks after a long moment. I tilt my head sideways, much preferring the view behind me.

"What do you want to talk about? We could discuss the weather or how, innocent or not, Steven Avery is a key example of police corruption and evidence manipulation?" My snark earns a jerk from Jasper's crotch, and I snicker. "Fine, let's get the nitty-gritty over with so we can go back to enjoying our day. You want to know why I left the woods with Malik, why my ass is pressed against your dick instead of a gun after that Walmart-version of a hitman you sent my way, and why I'm here with you when I should be chasing down the rest of the Monarchs."

"Well…except for the hitman part. He was only meant to draw old grumpy boots out so I could get intel on how tortured he is without his minions. Bet he's bloody miserable," Jasper grins. I let the conversation drop, reaching for the floral beach bag nestled into the sand at our side. Not the type of accessory I'd have expected Jasper to carry but I can't deny it suits him. Rooting around inside, I find a hair tie and throw my hair up into a high knot. A pair of firm hands slide over my shoulders, massaging the point between my shoulder blades to my neck.

"Fair enough," I dodge the topic of Malik's mood scale. "The answer to the other points are simple and the mantra I live my life by. Because I can, and I don't give a fuck about appearances." My shrug is suppressed by Jasper working his magic on the kinks in my upper back. Further down the shore, a motorized boat pulls in, and two older men jump down from the deck. With a cooler box in each hand, they meander our way, offering out a range of drinks and ice creams. Spotting a fancy leather purse poking out of the beach bag, I fish out a note for two cokes and two mini tubs of Haagen-Dazs.

"Keep the change," I salute them on their retreat.

"You know that was a fifty, right?" I drown out Jasper's question with the pleasured moaning of my first, creamy mouthful. Cookies and cream for the win. Besides, I can be rather generous when it's not me paying. Companionable silence falls over us again, the time away from civilization is utterly refreshing. Maybe it's because I barely use gadgets, but there's nothing worse than being around those who are glued to their phones. They can't walk straight, can't talk without abbreviating absolutely everything and the drama. Fuck me; *the drama* is never-ending when no one is held accountable for their comments. I prefer the trusty penknife in my boot, always on standby for bitchy remarks.

Tossing our rubbish aside, I twist to push my head into the crook of Jasper's neck. The saltiness of the air mixes with the woodsy scent of his skin, flooding me with all kinds of strange and naughty thoughts. Malik has wrung orgasm after orgasm from me over the past few days, and then again this morning, but I never promised to be a one-man woman for a reason. That reason being... I'm just a bit of a slut, really, and I like all the flavours in the ice cream parlor. Why settle if no one is asking you to? Using one of my nails, I toy with Jasper's nipple, scraping back and forth over the bud. His hardness beneath my thigh jolts, and a strangled moan vibrates through his chest.

"I'm sure Tanya would have packed a bikini or two in that bag for selfie purposes if you fancy joining me for a swim."

"Ew," I shoot upright on a cringe. "As if I would break my no-underwear rule to come in contact with Tanya's discharge."

"Her what now?" Jasper cocks an eyebrow, glancing towards the bag as if something contagious is about to spring out. I roll my eyes, taking his can of coke for a quick swig and passing it back for him to down the rest.

"Discharge, aka vagina mucus."

"Fucking hell Candy," Jasper chokes on his drink, spraying all over the place as he splutters. "Don't you keep anything in?"

"Life is better without filters," I say, throwing up two fingers and pouting like a duck. I saw that slogan on a billboard once with the model to match. "Anyways, if you think I need a bikini to enjoy myself, you clearly haven't been paying attention." I jump to my feet, wriggling out of my shorts and stripping off my white crop top with red hearts over the nipples. I streak butt naked across the beach with my arms pumping, and Jasper's not far behind. His laughter is drowned out by screaming children after the crazy, naked lady diverts from her path to trample all over their sandcastle.

I wave off their cries, my feet breaching the water before I dive straight in. The coolness is a welcome wash over my skin. I move my body like a mermaid, fighting against the resistance of the incoming waves until I make it beyond the barrier to calmer seas. Breaching the surface, I look around for any sign of my British companion. A hand wraps around my ankle, dragging me below once more. A pair of lips smash against mine, hiding our kiss from the world above. A string of bubbles leaking from my mouth is the only evidence we're even down here. Hooking my legs around his back, I use Jasper as my anchor to keep us beneath just a few more moments, finding him gloriously naked too.

"Do you really need to?" Jasper asks as we resurface, breaking the spell of the deep. I hang from him still, tracing the droplets along his collar bone.

"Need to what?" I torment, rolling my hips over the soft head of his cock, teasing my entrance.

"Find the others. I've done them a service, setting them all free from Malik's rule. Leave them be." The rare glimpse of seriousness in his gaze tells me he truly believes his words. Jasper can hide his intentions from everyone else, but he hasn't cut all the ties he believes he has. Maybe it's because I'm on the outside, sad times, but I seem to be able to see this whole cockfucked mess so much simpler than they can.

"Yes, I have to find them. And you're going to help me," I flash a full-toothed grin.

"Ha!" He splashes water at my face. "Yeah, right. I'm definitely going to reunite the group I've finally managed to destroy." I grip a handful of his blonde hair, tilting his face for our eyes to meet directly.

"Yes, you are. Because this time, you're not going to be shunned or cast aside. You had no issue with Malik's rules until he sold you out. Instead of confronting him, your revenge scheme escalated, and now everyone is hurting because they're all separated, even me." Something flashes behind his green eyes, confusion maybe. Keeping him held in place, I stop resisting and plunge my tongue into his mouth. No hiding, no reservations. I take what I want and mouth-fuck it. Simple. By the time we break apart, Jasper's laugh is breathless, and his smirk holds no conviction.

"Ahh, I see. This is more about you finally having a family, so you want to reunite mine," Jasper nods, but there's no malice in his words. Just truth. "Aside from the fact you'll never get Malik and me in a room without my hands around his throat, how exactly do you propose to bring the lads back together again?" This time, I tilt my hips at the perfect angle and draw Jasper towards me with my locked ankles at his back. Thanks to both mine and the ocean's wetness, I sink down on the length of his shaft with ease, and we share a glorious moan.

"That's the easy part," I wink. "With my magical pussy, of course."

SPADE

A meaty fist slams into my jaw just as the last whistle blows, but I'm not leaving it at that. The deal was whoever was still standing at the end wins tonight's haul, and I'm not sharing my winnings with this bulky bastard. Launching myself forward, I grab his throat in both hands, using my momentum to swing him to the stony ground. Punches land on my kidneys as I drop on top of his chest, wringing his neck like yesterday's laundry. The whistle goes again, and I slam his skull back into the ground, forcing him to tap out.

"You'd better stay down," I threaten. Hopping up on the third whistle, I raise my hands to the crowd, drinking in their cheers when Meathead swings out his leg. He sweeps my ankles out from under me, and I crash face-first into the ground. The wetness of spit slaps across my cheek just before a barefoot connects with my gut. Motherfucker.

The crowd's efforts double as their 'reigning champion' takes his walk of victory and the pile of cash handed to him by the referee. It comes as no surprise; from the corner of my eye, I spot Meathead drawing a small stack of notes from the top of the pile and stuff them into the ref's pocket. It's all corrupt with underground fighting, but that's the whole point.

Jumping to my feet on a slight sway, I run full speed into his mid-section. Tackling him down again, the cash flies all around, and I grab for the notes while punching him in the face. By the time I'm hauled off, he is no longer recognizable and my pockets are stuffed with mula. I repay the favor by spitting a wad of blood onto my lesser opponent, fighting against the several hands dragging me backward. The bouncers from the main club wrangle me up the stairs, through the club, and throw me on my ass out the front door. Jokes on them, I think to myself, as I dive onto my bike and ride into the night. My torso is a mess of bruises and sweat as I pull a wheelie down the street, forcing pedestrians to jump out of the way screaming. What a night to be alive.

My smile lasts right up until I skid to a stop behind a florist, and I push my hands in my pockets to find them empty. The money must have slipped out while I was gunning it down the sidewalk, compensating my nearly crushed victims with an instant pay out. Fuck! I hang over the handlebar, measured breaths sawing in and out of me from both exertion and anger. I suppose I should be thankful I feel alive at all, after a week of numbness. Taking my small win, I rev my engine and use the road this time to make my way back to the motel out of town. It's only a matter of time until the sleazy owner, that definitely stalks his women occupants realizes the card I put on record is going to bounce.

The lights are all out by the time I get back, but I shut off my bike and push it into the parking lot just in case. Leaving it hidden between two 4x4's either side, I creep back to my designated room as quickly as my high-tops allow on the gravel. Producing a key from the sole, a trick I learned from Candy, I let myself in a sigh. What has my life become? I head straight for a shower, washing my body free of the grime caked across my skin. The substances on the secret fight club floor are questionable, to say the least, and a pain to scrub off. Soon enough, I drop onto the bed in a thread-bare towel and resume my latest hobby of staring at the wall.

I'm surprised Malik hasn't come looking for me yet, not that I'd be hard to find. Yet every time I just sit here, I wonder if it'll be the moment the door is kicked down, and he orders me to return. And fuck it, I would in a heartbeat. The solitude of this dank motel room has given me plenty of sleepless nights on a rock-hard mattress to think. And think. And give up thinking.

Sure, Malik is a cruel bastard, playing with people's lives for his own gain. But my grievances are nothing compared to the others. I discovered I had a knack for counting cards straight out of college and quickly grew addicted to robbing casinos blind. The adrenaline rush was like no other, and at some point, the money didn't even matter. They were just figures on a tally I kept while the notes sat untouched in a train station locker. I was staying at a motel much like this one at the time, so trusting the mini safes or door locks wasn't an option. The point is, I would have got caught sooner or later. Malik sped up the process, gave me a place to stay, put me to work, and used my skills to pull off a bunch of heists. Talk about a new adrenaline rush. And I got a family out of it.

Which brings me back to the present. It's clear if Malik wanted me to return, he'd have sought me out by now, and I'm too stubborn to crawl back of my own accord. Talk about pathetic. So, my other option is to rebuild, and rebuilding takes money. Screw it. Pushing upright, I stalk over to the duffle bag I'm living out of. I swung by the Devil's Bedpost before exiting Malik's life for good, stuffing as much as I could into my bag before he returned and then snuck out the back. Donning the only shirt and slacks I brought, I pair them with my high-tops and take a look in the bathroom mirror. The facial hair lining my jaw has entered the itchy stage, and my braids appear deflated.

Smoothing it back the best I can with a wad of coconut oil, I vow to get something done about the coarse locks soon. I turn my attention to my face, shaving and rubbing some lotion into my skin in an effort to brighten my sunken blue eyes. I look exactly how I feel like I haven't slept in a week and been beaten the shit out of numerous times. My lip is swollen, and there's a lump on my eyebrow, but for the most part, I'm in better shape than I should be.

After a mental pep talk that my appearance isn't going to get any better than this, I leave the room without bothering to lock it. There's nothing of value to steal anyway. Striding towards my bike, a light flicks on in the main building, and a shout travels through the cracked window.

"Tyrell!" I curse under my breath at the sound of my birth name, ducking and running the rest of the way to my bike. The pervert motel owner's shouts follow me, becoming loud enough to hear over my bike's engine. I swerve out of the lot, laughing as he takes chase after my twenty-inch wheels. Obviously, I lose him as soon as I hit the main road and gun it south, but a part of me considered stopping to see what his scrawny ass would do. Instead of heading back the way I came from earlier, I set my sights on the city in the distance. Its glistening skyscrapers stretch towards the starry sky, coaxing me closer.

The wind on my face draws a smile from me, the tight ball in my chest easing. I may not have a handle on what to do with my life, and that's okay. As long as I keep smiling, keep laughing, no day is wasted. Arriving at the Blue Moon casino in no time, thanks to doing 120mph most of the way here, I pull up to the archway entrance and toss my keys to the valet.

"Er, Sir? We don't-" the spotty teen starts, and I silence him off with a hard stare. My biceps strain against my shirt sleeves, and I snarl my cut lip, making him turn impossibly paler. "Uh, I'll just wheel it down the end of the sidewalk so I can keep an eye on it," he mutters, handing me a ticket stub. I wink, promising to slip him some of my winnings on the way out. I step inside the grand casino, inhaling the flowery aroma being pumped from the vent systems, along with underlying scents of pink grapefruit and disappointment. The automatic doors close behind me, sealing me inside without a window or clock in sight. Heaven.

A cocktail waitress in a tiny skirt approaches me with a swing to her hips. Offering me a bottle of beer from her tray, she welcomes me and points out the direction of the cashier's booth. I thank her, ignoring the way she lingers, and sip my beer as I casually walk around the tables. A few security guards clock me while I roam but mostly because they're frowning at my high-tops. Luckily, the rest of my attire seems to appease their dress code, and they hang back, letting me find my mark. My eyes fall on a frail, old man being used as a cling station by a pair of busty, blonde twins. They giggle at every word he says in between blowing on his dice and cheering through a game of craps.

Falling into the crowd gathering around them, I cheer along with his consistent row of wins, wondering if he too is cheating or if he's just that damn lucky. Bodies shove in an effort to get a clear view, the press of expensive satin and diamantine dresses irritating me. Widening my stance, I cross my arms and use my bulk as an unmovable shield. I wrinkle my nose at the mix of perfumes and colognes, holding my head high to avoid sneezing. A flash of fuchsia pink catches my eye, and I freeze, hunting for the origin. An alarm bell rings in my mind, but as a woman with a pink feather boa steps back into view, my chest deflates.

On the table, stacks of chips are pushed in the older man's direction when he's had enough, allowing for some others to have a turn. The first loss causes the crowd to groan and disperse, although I'm too focused on the twins loading up a wooden caddy with the old man's winnings. Once finished, he takes a hold of the gold handle on top and makes his way towards the men's restrooms. Perfect.

"I can hold your chips for you while you're in there," Bimbo number one offers when they stop outside. I step behind a fake potted plant the size of me, listening in to the exchange.

"Will you fuck," the old man gruffs, and I immediately like him more. He disappears into the bathroom, caddy in hand. As soon as the girls are distracted by another seemingly rich man, this one in his 50's in a pinstripe suit, I sneak by unseen and slip into the men's restroom. I spot the caddy first, sitting alone on the side of the basin while a series of grunts come from the urinal further around the dividing wall. I could snatch it and run, although it would be too obvious to anyone paying attention. Maybe I just take a few off the top while washing my hands. Yet the grunting becomes pained and gets the better of my curiosity, so I step around the wall and into view.

"Everything…okay in here?" I ask the old man's back. He jerks, sparing me a look over his shoulder.

"Damn zipper's stuck," he bites out, hunching over in an effort to free himself from his slacks. "Would you mind? Before I piss myself." My eyes widen, flicking from the man to the chips and back. The gentleman in me takes over, leading the way over to the urinals. No matter what age, walking through a high-end casino with piss all over your trousers is just too demoralizing. Crouching down, I wave his hands away so I can see what we're dealing with. A minuscule amount of the cotton has become pinched between his zipper, and that's all it takes to trap a poor elderly man in his pants. Trying to pry the zip down myself, I hold his belt to stop the rest of his junk from moving too much.

"You really got it jammed in there," I say, jostling his junk around like a loose pocket of change. A bang from behind distracts me as another guy walks in. Short cropped hair makes his face look fatter than it is, although his green uniform is struggling to contain his oversized gut. With widened eyes, he halts and slowly retraces his steps at the sight of me kneeling in front of the old man. I roll my eyes, and on one more tug, yank the zipper free over a pair of tight, white briefs.

"Oh, thank you, thank you," he praises, patting me on the head, which makes the situation so much worse. He turns to do his business in the urinal while I wash my hands, then wet and scrub the patch of my hair he tugged. OAP germs, gross. He joins my side within a few minutes, having no problems doing himself back up.

"Here. Let me give you something for your trouble." He picks up his wooden caddy, squinting at the chips filled all the way to the brim. "Which one is the five hundred?" he asks. My conscience urges me to tell the truth, but then the little devil hops up on my shoulder, daring me to take what is truly owed for what's gone down in this restroom. My knuckles grazed his old man dick through the cotton, a memory I need compensating for.

"The blue and white one," I point. He pries the chip out, placing it in my palm with a withered smile.

"Don't spend it all at once, young man," he coos, and I step away before he tries to pat me again. Looking at the $50,000 chip in my hand, I close my fist around it and smile.

"Oh, I won't." Exiting the bathroom, there's no sight of the blonde twins as I head for the cashier's booth to get my chip divided into smaller amounts. The shrewd, stout woman regards me curiously until a familiar face tells her it's time for a shift change. Dropping in her seat, the doughnut-lover in his green uniform widens his eyes on me, the same way he did while interrupting me getting my hustle on in the bathroom. Okay, maybe it wasn't as smooth as a hustle, but I got what I needed. He doesn't question how I acquired the chip, splitting it into a handful of thousands and sliding them back to me.

"Enjoy your time at Blue Moon, Sir," he nods. "You've certainly earned it." I scowl at him, no longer in the mood to play right now. Instead, I walk through the lobby and excitable crowds to enter the bar area. Dropping onto a bar stool, I order a double whiskey neat and lean on my threaded fingers. I could cash up now, take the money and go, but there's no fun in simply being given or stealing money. I want to either win, fight or earn it. The best currency in my mind is the thrill, not the cash. Although even sitting here, I feel something's missing.

"Your drink," the bartender returns, sliding the glass towards me. "And this was left for you." Handing over a cream envelope, I frown at the name scrawled in fancy cursive. Spade. The bartender walks away before I can ask any more questions, and I twist in my seat, looking for who could have left me a private note in a random casino. No one knows me here because that was my intention. To be anonymous.

Scooping my finger beneath the seal, I pop the envelope open and pull out the letter inside. It's folded yet padded, and I take a moment to feel the weight of it in my hand. A thousand thoughts spin around in my mind in question to its contents. After all the shit Malik has pulled came to light, maybe there's been a lawsuit taken against him. But then again, the delivery and name are too informal. No, this has something dodgy written all over it. Giving in to my curiosity, I quickly unfold the paper.

BLAM. An explosion goes off in my face but not the painful kind. Unless a ton of pink glitter is considered painful. The shimmering confetti hits me full force, coating my skin and dripping down my shirt. Gasps and bubbling laughter erupt all around while my attention is on the note in my hand. It's an invitation from the glitter pixie herself. Through my glittery veil, a light flashes, and as I look up, there she is. Unable to hold her phone still enough to get a good picture from the hysterical laughter spilling through her gum chewing. I vault out of my seat, causing her to scream and run. Oh, she'd better fucking run.

Skidding through the casino, a trail of glitter is cast behind me like some kind of sugar plum fairy as I barge people out of the way. Candy slithers through the crowds with ease, something my size won't allow, but with my fists clenched and chest heaving, I don't mind tackling onlookers out of the way. She makes it out of the main door and into the darkness before I can see which way she went. Diving through the automatic closing door, the valet flinches at the sight of me —menacing, furious…and pink.

Headlights burst to life, forcing me to cover my eyes with my hand as Candy speeds past on her quad bike. The one we all gifted her the day she became Queen of the Monarchs. I watch her go, listening to her cackle disappear in the wind and exhale. Despite what came before, we did that. We let a psychotic chick take over our lives and even crowned her for it. She united us, changed us, and improved us. That's the life *I* agreed to live. Not because Malik said so, but because it's what I wanted. Now it seems like Candy wants her minions back together, and with an invitation like that, how the fuck could I refuse?

ACE

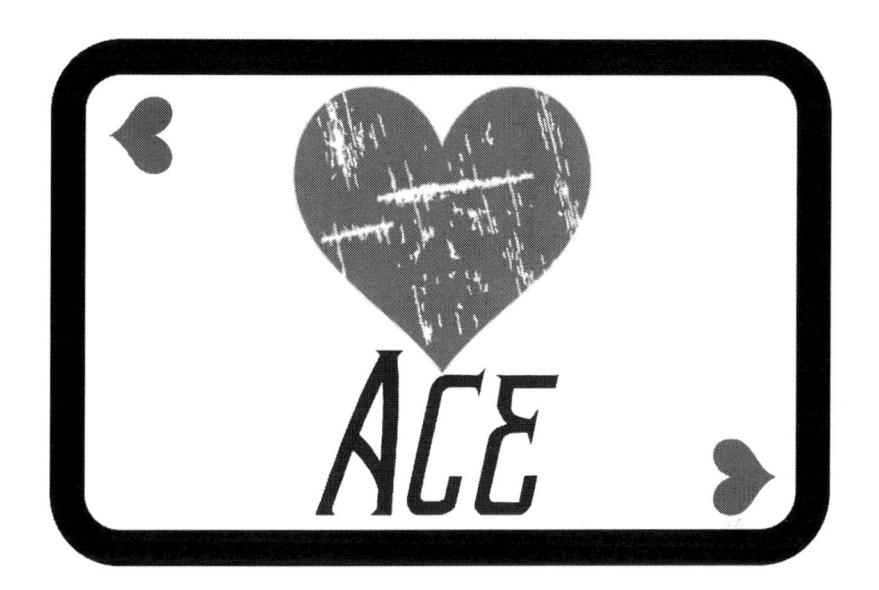

I follow the routine like clockwork. 6 am workout, 7 am shower, leave the hotel by 8. Grab breakfast to go and get across town before she leaves for the morning school run. From there, it's the usual. I go where she goes; soaking in what makes her smile, what makes her eyes sparkle with life. So many nights, my thumb hovered on the emergency call button, ready to turn myself in. I've punished myself to the point of insanity spent years drowning in regret over her. The woman I thought I'd killed with my bare hands.

Beckoned by the call of a shrill voice, the blonde runs across the length of the play area with another toddler braced on her hip. Her hair is tied into a high ponytail, her body clad in athletic lycra. With the multitasking nature only a mother could have, she hoists the screaming girl into the swing she's been hanging off for the last five minutes. Placing the other girl with matching red curls in the swing adjacent, the woman begins to sing while pushing the swings in turn. There are only a few other families in the play area, yet with her lot, it's at full capacity.

"Oooo, Parent or Pedophile! I love this game!" a familiar voice chirps. Candy throws herself down on the bench, pressed right against my side. I'm positioned across the green, beneath a large oak. Not close enough to pry but not too far away either. Sighing, I lean into the pink imp who has somehow found me at last. I knew it would come eventually, and if I'm being honest, I'm glad it didn't take too long.

"There she is," I point in the blonde's direction. There's no point pretending I'm not lurking around, spying on this woman. Especially since Candy seems to see straight through me. In the playground, the boy in the pushchair has awoken, so the blonde calls for her older children to take over pushing their siblings in the swings while she rocks her baby back to sleep.

"Mmmm, you're right. Definitely suspicious. No one has that many kids for the fun of it. What do you think we're dealing with here? Human trafficking, rearing drug runners?"

"Harmony Garfield," I continue, ignoring Candy's skewered view of the world. "She wanted to be an actress until she met her photographer husband. They traveled the world, shooting various magazine campaigns until he ran off with a waitress. Returning home, Harmony didn't want to wait for a man to start the family she'd always wanted, so she used the stash of Malik's money she'd been saving to have IVF. Two sets of triplets and a surprise pregnancy with her new boyfriend."

"Flaming Fajitas, Ace. Stalker much? That couple over there are probably playing a version of Parent of Paedophile with us, and right now, you look like you're in the latter. Leave the damn woman and her family alone." I balk at the elderly couple staring directly at us from a bench across the green, quickly diverting my eyes.

"I didn't know what else to do with myself," I rush to say in defense. "I've spent years punishing myself for killing her. I thought if I got to know her....or maybe if I understood why she would fake her death for money...." A small hand slithers up the inside of my arm, drawing me back from the dark path my thoughts were about to take me down. Again. Assessing her easy smile, I have to wonder if Candy is ever a victim to her demons.

Her pink outer layer is a ruse for the true extent of her ruthless, cold-blooded nature. She could slit a throat as if it were as common practice as a handshake and not lose a moment's sleep over it. I'm envious of that trait, but I also know it comes from a place of trauma that I most likely wouldn't have survived.

"You thought seeing her would wash the guilt away, but it hasn't. Has it?" Candy lays it all out there. The words I was struggling to come to terms with myself, yet she got it in an instant. I shake my head on a sigh, running a hand over my overgrown brown hair.

"I was so sure I was born this way, so the times I hurt you were because I couldn't help it. But then I find out I never was that person, and my actions were in my control the whole time, yet I didn't reign them in. That's what makes me a true monster," I groan. Clenching my fists until the length of my knuckles crack, I wish I were alone so I could turn them on myself.

"Does it always have to be so…" Candy flaps her hands around in the air when words fail her. I get the point, though. I only wish I knew how to shift the weight from my shoulders and press restart. To unlock the crushing restraints banded around my chest, or silence the voice in the back of my mind. 'You don't deserve happiness.' 'You aren't worthy of a fresh slate.' I know whose voice it is; my mother's. Although I've never felt an ounce of sympathy for putting her in a well-deserved grave.

"There's something I want you to see," Candy breaks the heavy silence. "But first, you have to promise me something."

"What's that?" I quirk a brow her way and realize her face is right beside mine. Her breath smells sweet like bubblegum, and I become trapped in her chocolate brown eyes.

"You have to leave all this," she gestures at all of me, "right here on this bench. If I think someone deserves punishing, I make it my personal mission to do Karma's dirty work. But you've punished yourself enough, so here's your liberation. I forgive you of your sins, Ace. The world forgives you. Now do us all a favor and live a little." Standing and offering out her hand, I take it without reservation. After all, I've been waiting for a sign of what to do with my life, and she's here giving me a solution.

Candy forces me into a power walk and then a quick sprint over the road to catch a bus about to depart. Taking care of the tickets, she ushers me into a tiny bench seat by the window. I watch the landscape go by as far as the end of town, then turn my attention to the marvel on my left instead. Pulling a stick of gum from in between her cleavage, she tosses the wrapper aside and pops it into her mouth. How she was able to appear in a small suburb and already know the bus schedule is beyond me. Was it blind luck, or is she just that resourceful? I suppose surviving has become a force of habit on her part.

We pull up some time later in a new town, at a recently up-cycled high street still emanating the stench of paint. Nightclubs fit for students line either side of the street, marred by vomit stains on the pavement by last night's lightweights. Dragging me off the bus, Candy stands before a disguised building at the end corner, holding her arms wide to shout 'ta da!' There's nothing distinguishable worth noting. Blacked-out windows with vibrant red paintwork across the header. Candy draws me towards a building labelled 'Adventure Land,' which wraps around the side and stretches back the length of three blocks.

Despite the sign clearly saying closed, Candy pushes her way inside and holds the door open for me. Air conditioning hits me first, the smell of liquor second, and the overwhelming color palette third. An indoor climbing frame stretches from floor to ceiling, encased in black mesh. Sponge mats line the ground between a ball pit and curling slide, swinging ropes, and hidden tunnels. The most jarring aspect other than the saturation slamming a headache into me, is the sheer size of the equipment. This play area isn't for children, but I take a glance down at all 5ft 11, bulging muscles and intimidating tattoos of me. There's no freaking way.

"What exactly are we doing here?" I ask tentatively. Candy whips a wide grin my way, smacking the gum between her teeth and prods a finger into my chest.

"We're looking for the little boy inside of you that forgot how to have fun. Then I'm going to use the big boy you've got locked in your pants to have some fun of my own." She winks and twirls away to the bar posted against the opposite wall. There's someone already fixing drinks across the wooden countertop, moving with the skill of a practiced bartender. Shaking up a cocktail, complete with an umbrella, he turns to pass the glass over to Candy, and my eyebrows shoot to my hairline. Dazzling green eyes, deeply ingrained dimples, blonde spiked hair poking out from his designer hoodie.

"You sought out Jack before me?" I ask, slightly offended. Surely I was the easiest to sway since, other than the lies, I had no issue being under Malik's rule. It saved me wandering around without a purpose. The blonde's smirk widens, although hidden by the tilt of his head, as he retrieves two whiskey glasses and a bottle of Johnnie Walker.

"Guess again," he chortles. I halt my approach, a trickle of unease slithering through me. Looking at me properly now, I note the crescent-shaped scar that runs from his eye to the corner of his mouth.

"Wait, Jasper? What…what's going on here? Is this some sort of anti-monarchy rebellion because I'm not interested-"

"Woah, hold up!" Candy races over to grab my wrist as I try to leave. "We're not trapping you or asking for anything beyond today. We just want to have some fun." I snort, knowing that's exactly what Jasper wants to do. It's his M.O. Fun now, seriousness never. Looking over Candy's pretty face, I see a hint of vulnerability flash behind her brown eyes. She really wants me here for some reason. Drawing her around so I can block Jasper's prying eyes out of view, I lean down to talk with her privately.

"Be honest. Why him? You could have brought any of the others along for this…" I look around at the foam obstacle course, which I must admit has perked my interest. Malik would never have staged this type of intervention; this is all her. Candy's arms snake around the back of my neck, pushing up on her tiptoes to meet my stare.

"Look. He was one of you before and gifted the nickname Jester. You can't tell me you guys didn't have some good times. All I've heard since I crashed into your bar was how Jasper took the fun when he left. Isn't it time to put the bullshit aside and just…be brothers again?" A small voice in my mind wants to give in to the plea in her eyes, but this time, she's really pushing it. Too much has happened just to forgive and forget.

"You're right," I sigh on a nod. "He did leave." Twisting out of her grip, I head for the door when a handful of cocktail umbrellas hit me in the back of the head. Scowling over my shoulder, Jasper rounds the bar to get up in my face.

"To protect Jack. Once Malik cut me off, it was impossible to return, so I focused my skill set on proving to you guys what he really was. If anything, you could have located me with one click of your computer, but instead, you took his word for it. You abandoned me, not the other way around."

"It was a confusing time," I look away from his green gaze. "But this isn't on me. If you'd just picked up the phone, I would have listened-" I'm cut off by the static of the tannoy system. Candy is leaning over the reception desk, holding a microphone to her mouth.

"It's simple Ace," her voice echoes around the entire building. "Stay, drink, play, enjoy yourself. If you still want to walk away at the end, I won't stop you. But I do want you to come home." Home. Not only does the notion of belonging rile up conflicting emotions, but warmth also spreads through my chest at Candy's acceptance of it. This isn't just about me. It's about all of us rebuilding our family, cementing a place to call home. And Candy wants me to be a part of it. Barging past Jasper with a hard knock to his shoulder, I grab both whiskeys on the bar top and down them, one after the other.

"Better make mine triples," I grumble. Candy bounds over to throw herself at me, and I fight the creeping smile threatening to unfold. I can do this, just relax and have a good time like all other guy's my age. I'm done regretting what I could have had. It's time to be the best version of myself otherwise what's the point of continuing on at all?

"On your marks, get set," I slur as Candy shoots forward. I lunge to grab her waist, but she slips through my fingers, and I topple forward on my chest.

"Easy, Champ. Can't have this insane chick showing us up," Jasper chuckles, helping me back to my feet. There's a stupid smile stretched between my ears as I slap Jasper's back. Candy kept up with us drink for drink; there's no way she can be so spritely while I'm ready for a fucking nap. Jogging into the play area, I grab a hold of the foam pole and take stock of our surroundings.

"Here, pussy pussy pussy," Jasper coos, hunting for our prey. I can't remember who suggested the game, only that it's a take on 'tag' and the person still up at the end of the hour is to receive a forfeit. Thanks to drawing the short straw, I'm currently tagged, but as I sway on my feet, I can tell I'll need a minute.

"Here, take this. You'll be able to find her quicker than me," I grumble, slapping Jasper's hand. He shoots off too, making my head spin with the quickness of his movements. Dropping down onto the edge of the ball pit, I listen to the sounds of screaming and laughter echoing around the climbing frame above my head. Heaving out a few sharp breaths, I give myself a slap across the face and jump to my feet. Come on Ace, man up and dominate this oversized play gym.

This time, my socked feet managed to move one in front of the other. Due to the rigidity of our jeans, Jasper and I decided to strip down to our boxers and t-shirts while Candy is running around in her underwear to 'even the playing field.' Thumping footsteps bang overhead, giving me a sense of direction to re-join the fun that's left me behind. Except for needing to use my hands to ascend the spongey stairs, my mental pep talk seems to have worked, and I'm on the upper floor with a clearer head in time for Candy to collide with me.

"Tag!" she giggles, zooming off. I'm more ready this time, gripping her tiny waist and hauling her off her feet. Striding across a rope bridge, I take the brunt of her wriggling to level my mouth to her ear.

"You can take that tag straight back." Without waiting for the sharp-tongued response I'm sure she had ready, I throw Candy into the mouth of a curling slide.

"I'll get you back, asssssshooooole!" she screams. Through two layers of black mesh, I spot Jasper on the other side of a rope swing. He drops down beneath a lowered platform, effectively disappearing from view. I grumble at the slender fuck, hunting for a hiding place of my own as I hear Candy already on her way up the steps.

Zigzagging through a series of distorted mirrors, I dive into a tunnel, careful to avoid an acrylic peek hole in the center. Trying to cram my bulk in the floating tube isn't easy, but it gives me the reprieve I need from the adrenaline flooding my system. As ripped as I am, I'm not as experienced in confrontation as my fellow Monarchs. Even on heists, I was the guy that controlled the drones or sat behind a screen. Movement to my right jerks me back to Jasper skidding into my hidey-hole. I grunt, shoving my feet into his side in an effort to push him out.

"Hey! Hey!" Jasper whispers, pushing my legs aside to wriggle his way back inside. "We need to team up Ace; corner Candy at the last minute so whoever is tagged can get her before the time is up."

"To what end? You just want to make sure you don't lose," I narrow my eyes. Call me competitive, but even in a child's game in a play area, I'm not being tricked by him yet again.

"Loser has to do a forfeit, remember?" Jasper knocks on my head, making me wince. "She'll have to do whatever we want." I frown at his dancing eyebrows, my sluggish mind not catching up quick enough for his liking. He punches my shoulder and then clicks his fingers in front of my face. That's it; I'm going to beat the shit out of this condescending shithead. Right after I find out what he's insinuating. "We're going to fuck that chick," he deadpans. This time it's my turn to punch him.

"She's not just some chick. She's…" I trail off, lost for words.

"Ours," Jasper finishes for me with such resolve in his green gaze, I can't argue. "She's ours, Ace. And we're going to win this game so we can fuck her."

"Together?" I ask in a tiny voice. I've shared her before with the others, but doing so with Jasper seems like a whole new level of betrayal to my gang. Or rather, former gang. Malik may have made us, but he also ruined us. He lied to me set me up to think I *killed* someone. So maybe I should take my vengeance in a way I know that would really hurt him but really please me. I'm going to give myself this, give myself in to her. Every moment with Candy is a wild ride, and I'm on board.

With a sharp nod, I pull my legs back and shove him out the other side before exiting myself. To make this work, I need to find the minx that's turned our worlds upside down. I don't have to look far since as soon as I pop out of the tunnel, she's there to crush me in a headlock —a surprisingly strong one.

"Done having your bum fun? Thought we were playing a game here." Candy wrenches me along the spongey floor, ignoring my protests at her insinuation. Jasper doesn't help by chuckling, following right behind.

"It's all in the curling finger action. I warn you, though; Ace is prone to squealing when his prostate is being milked."

"My fucking what?!" I roar, twisting out of Candy's grip. She pops a gum bubble in my face, hiding the frustrated flush flaming my cheeks. Her chocolate eyes are focused on Jasper through the other side of the netting, sparkling with mirth.

"You obviously didn't do it right then. I heard no such squeal. You're up, by the way." The haze of exasperation causing me to shake my head clears to realize Candy is now talking to me. She's gone in the next moment, her ass cheeks bouncing deliciously on either side of a hot pink thong. On lithe feet, she's able to prance across the foam platforms with little noise, disappearing downstairs. Jasper isn't so fast though, his dirty chuckle drowned out as I throw myself through the tunnel in a flash. Leaping, my hands lock around his ankles and drop him on his front like a sack of shit.

"As if I'd be the bottom out of me and you," I grit through clenched teeth, crawling up the length of his body. This seems to entertain him just as much, so I 'tag' him via a punch to the cheek. Jumping to my feet, I slam a heel into his gut as I make my getaway. He hisses about not being a team player, then Jasper's right behind me, slamming my head into a yellow sponger pole.

"Meant to be on a team here, fuckface," he grunts, shoulder barging past. If that's the way he wants to play it, I'm game. From shoving, kicking out legs, elbowing, and punching, it seems nothing is off-limits as Jasper, and I barrel towards the lower level. I twist his arm back in an effort to jump down the last step first, and he bucks me into a hanging block that resembles a punching bag.

Spinning and walking back to slam Jasper into a rock climbing wall, the game fades as our fight turns semi-real. Weeks of anger and frustration power my blows, the opportunity to vent impossible to refuse. Getting in a lucky hit, Jasper's ring catches my eyebrow, causing a thin line of blood to trickle past my eye. My head pounds, my stomach is roiling with the liquor threatening to come back up. Pushing a step away, I hold up a finger and bend over to dry heave.

"How long has it been?" Jasper's British accent seeps through the thumping in my ears. I shoot him a 'I'm not in the mood for your questions' type look, but he continues anyway. "Since you last took out your anger on someone? I know Malik was your go-to when the aggression got too much, but even without that release, you used to be able to handle your whiskey better than this." I push myself upright, reigning back the rage that I let slip.

"I'm fine," I grumble. Catching sight of a giant clock hanging over the bar, the minute hand ticks into our last ten minutes. Shit.

I'd gotten so caught up in besting Jasper I'd forgotten all about Candy's forfeit. Where the fuck is she anyway? Jasper catches on to my shift in mood, hunting for a sight of her fuchsia pink hair or peachy ass.

The base level is much more open than upstairs, each section divided by the same black netting. The vibrant colors may be the perfect place for someone like her to hide, but I had no idea Candy could remain quiet for this long. Sharing a nod with Jasper, we move stealthily in different directions. My socks press into the spongey floor as I knock low-hanging climbing ropes out of my face. Greeting a pair of horizontal rollers I'm never going to fit through; I'm forced to turn back and try a different route. Each time, Jasper and I keep circling back to the massive ball pit sitting in the center.

"Surely not..."Jasper tails off, tilting his head at the multicolored balls. I risk a glance at the clock, spotting only a few minutes to spare.

"Worth a shot," I shrug, diving headfirst into the pit. It's deceivingly deep, the plastic balls encasing my large body as I wriggle like a fish on a hook to find her. A body too heavy to be Candy's collides with mine, and I surface to see Jasper throwing himself high in the air and back down like he's probably seen whales do on TV. He even shouts 'Free Willy' each time, puffing lungfuls of air out like he's spouting water. I roll my eyes, fanning my arms out to search. Even if Jasper does find her first, he'll give her a concussion doing that. The untouched balls across the far side shimmy, and I zero in on the tiny hand reaching up to grip the side.

"Oh no, you don't!" I wade across the pit, smacking away the balls in my way. Jasper notices the object of my focus, attempting to quickly hoist herself over the edge before we manage to grab an ankle each. Dragging her back in between the middle of us, I glance over her head to see the clock hand stroke on the hour.

"Tag," Jasper and I shout at the same time with menacing grins glued to our faces. Candy isn't affected by the pair of predators leering over her. In fact, she slips a hand beneath each of our t-shirts and around our waists to draw small circles over our hips. A shudder rolls through me, although why is anyone's guess. Her touch is the most human contact I've had since leaving the Devil's Bedpost. Not that I'd wanted it before, but in the short time Candy has encroached all over my space, I found I didn't entirely hate it.

"If you guys weren't so busy butt-fucking around, you'd have caught me much sooner. Good game, though. Ready for another drink?" I feel Jasper's grip around her tighten, and a sudden flare of jealousy is drawn to the surface, causing me to copy the attention. Her body shifts under my grip, turning to face my old friend, so her ass is crushed against my dick. Blood rushes south, and in no time, I'm hard and aching to slam the slender waist encased in my hands down all nine inches of me.

"Nah-ah," Jasper slowly shakes his head slowly, oblivious to the images flashing before my eyes, none of which include him. Not taking his green eyes off her for a moment, his head dips within a breath of claiming her mouth. "You lost against the pair of us, love. It's time to receive your punishment."

CANDY

With his grip on my sides, Ace hoists my body up, spinning me at the last moment to seat me on the edge of the ball pit. The heightened wall, efficiently wrapped in plastic, puts the boys at eye level with my crotch. Jasper's next to pull himself up, taking care to roll his boxer-covered dick across my face. I lash out with my teeth, causing him to jolt aside.

"Oi, you little minx," he chuckles, although the fear in his green eyes was real. Dropping down onto his knees behind me, the clasp of my bra is flicked open. Ace's large hands take care of my thong, peeling it down the length of my legs. I lean back into Jasper, propping my feet on Ace's shoulders, and sigh contentedly. If I were president, I'd make it the law for everyone to be naked. It's the best way to be. But then I imagine my old landlady, Mrs. Smithers, with all her lumpy bits hanging out and shudder. Okay, scratch that - all hot people must be nudists. The rest will be on house arrest until they're toned up enough to join the hotties.

"Something about that cruel smile tells me I don't want to know what you're thinking," Jasper comments. I roll my head across his shoulder, meeting his mouth in the middle. His tongue sweeps in with an open invitation, coated in the smoked fruity tang of whiskey. My own will taste the same from the few sips we had just before the game began; the rest of the time, we kept refilling Ace's glass and topping ours up with apple juice. It's a wonder he's even standing at all, considering he had most of the bottle to himself.

A pair of strong hands lift my feet, dropping them back over his bulky shoulders. Edging closer, I feel the scrape of Ace's trimmed beard across my inner thigh. His hot breath sawing in and out over my primed cunt, open and waiting. The first lazy lick tears me apart, and I groan into Jasper's mouth. Ace does it again, savoring my taste from ass to clit and back again. All the while, Jasper takes ownership of my breasts, reaching around to tease my nipples on that precipice of pain and pleasure.

I take their torment for as long as I can before Jasper's tongue is no longer sufficient. I need something thicker, sturdier, and able to handle the scrape of my teeth. Without disturbing Ace, now he's picked up his pace, I draw Jasper up onto the spongey block beside me. The mirth in his eyes tells me he knows where this is going and tugs his boxers off in preparation. The moment he's kneeled beside me, I take his girthy cock into the back of my throat. Saltiness smooths a path, the taste of his arousal striking a chord with my own. Harmoniously, I fall into a rhythm with Ace.

He licks, I lick. He sucks, I suck. And when he spits to shove two fingers inside of me, Jasper got one hell of a surprise. The strangled cry that left his lips wasn't completely out of outrage, though, leading me to believe there's no way these men have all been locked up in Malik's tower, denied sexual contact, and given unlimited access to alcohol without a little experimentation going on. Saving that line of questioning for later, I ease my hand back around to Jasper's balls, scratching my nails over his sac and thighs.

"Fucking hell, Candy, you're something else," Jasper groans. His fingers sink into my hair, holding my head in place for him to fuck my mouth. I didn't let myself get caught for this 'forfeit' to be over so quickly, so I yank my head away, releasing him with a loud pop. They really should work on lowering their voices next time they're plotting against me, but when the punishment works in my favor, it's worth the sacrifice.

Jasper's glazed eyes flare with frustration and curiosity as I turn my attention to Ace. Spreading my legs wide, I give him full access and a silent demand to make me cum. He obeys, thrusting his fingers into me while his tongue does sinful things to my clit. Flicking, sucking, scraping. My toes curl, and with my hand squeezing the base of Jasper's shaft, I cum on a satisfied scream. The tremors twitching through me haven't fully subsided when Jasper yanks me upright and tosses me over his shoulder. Bare ass in the air, the coolness washing over my clit prolongs my post-climax bliss. As does the jostle with each of his steps and rumble of a barked order at Ace vibrating from Jasper's chest into my thighs.

Dropping me onto the plastic-wrapped floor, a pair of large rollers like I'd imagine seeing at a car wash are suspended around a foot above ground level. Ace appears on the other side as Jasper wrenches my arms through the rollers, and I'm yanked into the middle. Halting me halfway, the wonder that is Ace's cock has been released, and as he kneels, springs to attention in front of my face.

"Open wide," he grips my jaw, and for once, I allow myself to be dominated. My lips curl around his purple head, the softness too tempting to not smooth my tongue back and forth over it like a cat. Ace shakes my jaw again to open my mouth, and then I find out why. With only the warning of Jasper's hands spreading my ass, his dick slams into my dripping wet pussy. I jostle forward, taking Ace all the way down my throat. Thank fuck for my lack of tonsils.

United groans sound from either side when Jasper thrusts into me again, hitting all the way home. Balanced between the rollers, I'm unable to do anything but steady myself on Ace's thighs. His gentle hold on my jaw must be able to feel his dick jostling back and forth, and although I feel his fingers twitching to get rougher, he manages to restrain. Jasper, on the other hand, doesn't relent his vigorous pounding. Something tells me he didn't like being left on the edge of emptying his sack earlier, and I make a mental note to do it every time from now on.

"Jest," Ace grunts, his tone tight. There's a clear warning to slow down as the first drops of precum sweep along my tongue. The message goes unheard. Gripping me tighter, Jasper's hand drags upwards for his fingers to tease my asshole. When the shift in my breathy moans grow to a higher pitch, I wrap my legs around his back and lock my ankles, forcing him to slow it down for all of our sakes. We've only hired the play area for today, and after the mess that's going to need cleaning, I doubt we'll be invited back anytime soon. And trying to get Jasper in a room with any other of the Monarch's seems unlikely, so the here and now is all we have.

With an intense climax already on the verge of slamming through me, Jasper's long strokes from my opening to my G-spot push me over the edge in no time. His hips grind, caressing that sweet spot inside while I mewl around the girth of Ace's dick. Arching between the rollers, my core explodes, and a kalcidoscope bursts behind my closed eyelids. Every color of the rainbow beats in time with the pulsating pleasure raking through my center, drawing one groan into the next. I release my suction on Ace in favor of wriggling, suddenly feeling too restrained. Twitching wildly, my nails tear into the plastic covering below.

The come down turns my body to liquid, and this time, when I'm manhandled, it's with the care of a gentle giant. Ace slides me through the rollers, despite Jasper's grip trying to hold my thighs in place, and draws me into his arms. I flop against his hard chest, thankful for the reprieve as he leads me away. His eyes, a shade darker than my chocolate ones, regard me with surprise and conflict, although I'd bet my last stick of gum neither emotion is aimed my way. Ace prefers to have his control limited as if the monster in him might attack at any moment if given the chance. If nothing else, I hope today gives him some insight into who he really is. What he really is.

Setting me on my feet in a dimmed stretch of padded floors and net walls, Ace's mouth finds mine. He's slow at first, savoring the taste of his precum on my tongue and packing too much emotion into one kiss for me to decipher all at once. Then the heat kicks in, his cock grinding into my abdomen as his grip turns punishing on my hips, and I continue to spur him on. Harder. Rougher. Deeper. Ace has the knowledge that he won't hurt me now, but he also needs to know when I want him to. Breaking away with his chest heaving, those brown eyes hunt around for our missing Brit. Sliding a hand between us to cup his stubbled jaw, I turn him back to face me.

"You're a part of this three-way too, Ace. What is it you want?" His mind ticks in time with the clock in the distance, the silence stretching on. I don't pressure him though, reaching down to grasp his dick. Still slick with my spit, I pump my hand firmer up and down his shaft, watching the scene play through his emotions with unrestrained amusement. Using my other hand to cradle his balls, he finally cracks.

"I want my dick to be the one making you fall apart. I want to hear you scream my name.

"Then take those things." A flicker of uncertainty crosses his features as if taking me while Jasper isn't here is going against some sort of newly re-established bro code. Then it's gone. Gripping my sides, Ace hoists me up with impressive strength. Above us, hoops of rope hang through the elongated space with the intention of hanging from. Well, if the play area insists. I push my hands through the hoops and grab onto the rope above, effectively pushing my chest into Ace's face. His mouth closes over my nipple, biting down hard before licking the bud better. I arch into him, coaxing him to do it again and again. All the while, with my legs clinging around his middle, I'm tilting my hips to the perfect angle to settle down onto Ace's dick. A sharp groan is pulled from both of us, and his head drops into my cleavage on a relieved exhale.

"Nice choice, bro," Jasper slaps his hand on Ace's back. My head lolls aside to see his free hand running the length of his slickened cock. Wasting no time, he rounds to the back of me. "I take it you've done this before," he pokes his dick at the entrance to my ass. I snort, not even dignifying that with an answer. On each roll of Ace's hips, Jasper slides further into my ass, bit by painstakingly slow bit. I grumble in frustration, needing both of them fully seated in me and now.

"So...tight," someone groans, possibly even me. Pressed between two firm chests, we move as one. Ace slides in and out rhythmically; I roll my hips, and Jasper remains nestled in my back passage, groaning with me. It's a toxic combination of lust and power we all grow heady on instantly. Moving one of his hands from my ass cheeks, Ace thrusts inside whilst pressing down on my lower abdomen. I moan in shock as the head of his cock and the pressure of his palm effectively lockdown on my g-spot. Twice more, and the sensations building within threaten to blow my fucking mind.

"I'm not gonna last," I whimper despite rolling my hips to increase our pleasure.

"We're right there with you, Babygirl, don't hold back," Jasper soothes in my ear. I lean my head back on his shoulder, the sheer exhaustion of being so thoroughly full causing sweat to break out across my forehead. I feel like I'm going to burst but not until I feel both of these giant cocks pulsating inside of me. Winding his arm beneath my breasts, Jasper takes my weight so I can release the ropes, and I settle impossibly further into him.

"Take it home for us, Ace," he grunts, struggling to hold off himself. Ace obeys our pleading moans, clamping his hands on Jasper's shoulders for stability. Then, he fucks my cunt like the world is about to come crashing down. No holding back and definitely no mercy, his thrusts are bruising, and his dick is all powerful. I even scream 'All hail Ace's cock' amongst a string of curses, my nails biting into Jasper's arm.

"Yes, Ace!" I cry as the tremors crumble into a body-shattering orgasm. My pussy spasms, tightening around Ace so firmly, he explodes inside me just before Jasper does.

"Holy fuck!" Jasper grinds out, the three of us jerking and writhing together. It's dirty as fuck, but also beautiful. A perfect moment of unison, crashing through more barriers than any words would have been able. Hot cum leaks between us, and a delirious laugh is torn from my throat.

"I don't care how or when, but this is going to be a regular occurrence," I decide. Grunts come from both of the heads collapsed on my shoulders which I'll take as acceptance. It's sweet they thought my statement needed their approval as if I don't always get what I want. No exceptions.

MALIK

Candy slides out of the yellow cab, taking her sweet time to thank the driver. I remain posted on the porch of the Devil's Bedpost, my arms crossed and temper flaring. If finding the house empty and the takings from that night missing weren't insult enough, her general disregard for the 37 voicemails I've left over the past few days is plain rude. She knows my control issues are as deeply ingrained as my trust ones. On that thought, I'd better call off the search party I assembled this morning.

After a small taunting wave, Candy leans back into the open door, her ass sticking out and her laughter ruining the peaceful ambiance of a clear sunset. I usually enjoy this in-between period, where the day drinkers have faded out and the evening crowd's arrival is imminent. A simple moment where I can catch my breath, away from keeping up the pretense of the bar. Rumors of the men who reside here are whispered through the local towns, adding to our allure.

When my temper has flared enough and my patience has officially worn out, I stomp down the front steps. The untied boots on my feet are possibly Spade's, with the laces flicking over the tongue hanging out of my trouser leg. As a distraction, I'd planned to be present for business tonight, but now my plans are centered around a peachy ass and my stinging palm. Pulling back, Candy's eyes twinkle in the dying sun as a much larger body follows her out of the vehicle. My steps pull up short, my mind stuttering to a blank.

"Ace?" I ask tentatively, catching sight of his dark eyes beneath a furrowed brow. His hair is the same, cropped at the sides and longer on top, the sideburns leading into a neatly trimmed beard. Standing tall in his dark jeans and t-shirt, his arms are shadowed by the veins trailing down to the duffle bag clasped in his hand. He says nothing, keeping his attention focused on Candy by his side. She, however, seems oblivious to the tension rippling through our stand-off.

"Come on boys, we've got a bar to run." Linking her fingers through Ace's, she catches hold of mine on the way past and leads us back to the building. I try to catch his gaze over her bobbing pink head, but he ignores me. Everything I've been practicing to say if I ever saw one of them again has fled from my mind anyway. Inside the club, Candy deposits the pair of us onto stool's and uses the middle one to hoist herself over the bar.

"Should have been a delivery for me this morning - did it arrive?" she asks me, grabbing a couple of bottles from the Ejaculating Unicorn collection. I really need to cancel the standing order to stop the truck from showing up with fresh stock. Fascinated by the knowing smiles she continues to share with Ace; I forget to answer until she prods me in the chest.

"Huh? Oh, yeah. There's five crates by the basement door with your name printed all over them. Care to enlighten me on what you've been ordering this time?" My reference to the many, *many* clothing packages doesn't go unnoticed as she glances down at the stunning number clinging to her body. For anyone else, there would be a specific time and place for such an outfit, but for Candy, it just fits. With boned breast cups, the gold leotard reminds me of something Wonder Woman would wear. From a waist belt, panels of black netting flow to the bottom of her intimidating spiked heels.

I narrow my eyes, noting the extra care spent on curling the ends of her hair and the hint of make-up causing her eyelashes to flick in thick strokes.

"Did I miss something? What's the special occasion?" Instead of answering, Candy turns to busy herself, and Ace's head rolls my way.

"She's been at the hairdressers all day, getting her roots touched up. Made me sit and wait, and that was before the shopping started," he grumbles. I nod, concealing the relief that he's just talking to me again. What I did to Ace was unforgivable, I know that. The fact he has refused to look my way once shows he's only here for her, but that's good enough. Now he's mentioned it, Candy's hair does look a little brighter in the spotlights above the new two-way mirror. She returns with three tall flutes, all containing a suspiciously neon liquid and swirling specks of glitter.

"If you really must know, we're celebrating." Lifting her glass, Candy waits for us to toast with her before downing the lot in one gulp. So much for savoring the flavor. I take a sip, surprised the taste isn't as overpoweringly sweet as I prepared myself for. More and more, where Candy is concerned, I find that even if the drink had been disgusting, I'd have drunk it to keep her happy. I'd do a lot of things to keep her happy, and that thought is utterly terrifying. If I don't regain some sense of control, I can see myself becoming too dependent on the wildness she brings and less able to center myself. All of which cannot happen.

"What are we celebrating exactly?" I place down the glass and thread my fingers on the bar. "The fact you're not dead after disappearing for two days with a bagful of cash? You didn't even take your bat. What if-"

"We're celebrating my birthday," she sighs. "Well, the day I chose to be my birthday since my birth records got lost somewhere between foster homes three and twelve. Truth is I've never...I mean, usually I..."

"You've never had a birthday party before?" Ace fills in what she doesn't want to say. A rare glimpse of vulnerability flares in her cheeks, and her brown eyes slide further down the bar. Tightening her eyebrows, she mumbles something under her breath I can't quite make out. As quickly as it started, her gritted teeth relax, and she's back in the present, taking back Ace's drink to down.

"Not with others invited," Candy shrugs. "And there's only so many times I can listen to Angus impersonate Marylin Monroe to sing Happy Birthday Mrs. Poonani Pits, all breathless like a chain smoker." Ace and I share a confused look, showing he also has no idea who's she's talking about but silently decides to drop the subject. This woman, although she could have left a note, has been out looking for my boys. Clearing up my mess. And somehow, she's managed to convince Ace to return, even if only for tonight. She damn well deserves a birthday.

"I have some calls to make. I'll be back soon." Using the rung on the bar stool, I stand tall enough to lean over the bar and drag Candy in for a quick, demanding kiss. My hand holds the back of her neck in place, relishing the contact I've missed. Spending all the time locked away in my room was a waste, even if I'd been trying to do the right thing by her. I hurt those I keep close. I clipped their wings in fear they would fly away, never stopping to allow myself to fly alongside them. Whatever noble part of me was left would rather suffer alone than crush her spirit. She's too wild to be tamed, too precious to be contained. But that didn't stop me from watching her on the surveillance cameras day in and day out.

Breaking apart, I leave the bar without a look back. My cell phone is already out of my pocket before I've made it into the kitchen, my thumbs twitching to get started. It's about time I used my money for a valid reason instead of blackmail. I'm going to give her a night she'll never forget, and then she'll want to stay. No, fuck that. Then, she'll have to stay.

Not even I can believe what I've managed to pull together in the space of a few hours. Word has spread through the nearby towns that the party of the century is happening at The Devil's Bedpost tonight, and we have the turn-out to prove it.

After diverting the incoming cars to an overflow car park down the dirt path that leads here, a dance space has been created with interlocking ground mats. The DJ who was already booked has moved his booth onto one end of the porch, while a makeshift bar corners the other. Although the black covers are just for show, giving a few bartenders a place to stand while taking orders on their phones. The reinforcements inside will make the real drinks, and the waitresses will ferry back and forth.

Decoration-wise, I sent the employees out to buy everything neon, bright and pink they saw, and they didn't disappoint. Illuminated flamingos stand around the dance floor with matching string lights hanging from the porch. A huge lightbox spells out 'Happy Bday Candy' for all to see from the top of a speaker. Performers on stilts and animated clowns greet tonight's guests, while bars extending out from a mobile circus truck provide large hoops for two women to balance inside high above the crowd. It's about as spontaneous as I get, and I hope she appreciates it. Right on cue, Candy steps out of the bar, and Ace slips the blindfold I passed him off her face. Pure shock and delight cross her features, sparking an unfamiliar warmth within my chest.

"Looks like I'm just in time," a deep voice jars me from my thoughts. I hunt for the source, settling on a pair of piercing blue eyes directly behind me.

"Spade." My eyebrows shoot upwards. "You came back." My voice is a little too hopeful. Showing emotion is like showing weakness; that's something Candy and I agree on. But I know my errors and have spent every day in my suite thinking back on my faults. I need to change if I have any hope of holding onto the family I once made.

"I was invited," Spade shoves an envelope into my chest and

walks on by. A smattering of glitter washes over my black shirt, and no matter how much I try to brush myself down, it only gets worse. Slender arms wrap around my middle, Pressing the sparkles further into the cotton.

"I have to go change," I growl, spinning in Candy's hold. She frowns until I point out the mess on my front, earning me a wide grin.

"Nah ah, I like you like this. Except, hold on." Unbuttoning the cuffs of my best Ralph Lauren shirt, which I put on for her, I might add, Candy rolls the sleeves up to my elbows one by one. Loosening my tie, she then slides it away from my neck and drapes it on her arm before popping my top few buttons. I stand still, suppressing a shudder of fury as she continues her assault on my clothing. I don't remember too much of my father, but I recall he was always sharply dressed. 'Dress for the day you wish to have,' he would say. Exhaling sharply, I briefly close my eyes in a bid to restrain my impending outburst.

"Aaaaaaaand, done!" Candy shouts over the heavy bass. Her hand smooths through my hair before I can stop her from smearing the glitter from my shirt through my carefully styled quiff. The vein in my head pulses, and my teeth are clenched hard enough to crack. A pair of bellowing laughs wash away the red mist ascending over my vision, giving me a focus aside from how ridiculous I must look. Noticing Spade for the first time, Candy reaches up to loop my tie around his neck and fastens it over his t-shirt.

"Nice to see you, hot stuff. You gonna just stand there, or are you coming to dance with me?" She finishes tying the worst knot I've ever seen, holding a hand out for him. Without a moment's pause, he obeys with a flick of his wrist to twirl her around. The dance floor has grown packed around us, with more than a few women trying to grind against me. Spotting Ace's retreating back, I slip through the crowd after him.

"Hey, Ace," I call out. He comes to a stop on the edge of the dancefloor, crossing his arms and staring over the sea of heads to keep Candy in his eye line. "I appreciate you coming back." Ace gives no reply, no flicker that he's even heard me. Freezing me out is his typical way to deal with uncomfortable situations, but the blow-out will come. When I least expect it, I'll find Ace sneaking up on me with a knife to my neck and murder in his eyes.

"Look, I know I've got a lot to explain and apologize for. But I hope you'll stay and give me the chance. I'll let you take your payback however you see fit." I huff out a breath, knowing I'm asking too much. The fact I'm asking at all and not demanding is a reflection on how much I've been trying to change for all the good it will do. Slowly, Ace turns to put his back to the music, his size shadowing us with the illusion of privacy.

"Thanks to you, I have no one and nowhere to go. This is my home as much as anyone else's, but that has nothing to do with you: your bullshit rules, your heists, your blackmail. I'll have no part in any of it. As far as I'm concerned," Ace swings his puppy-dog brown eyes on me with a coldness I've only seen him express in the mirror. "You're dead to me." Striding away, I'm faced with standing alone to watch Candy grind against Spade in the center of the dancefloor. Sure, it's great to see another one of my men home, but the dry-fucking display in front of me isn't my idea of easy watching.

Striding away, I pick up the pieces of my morale that Ace stamped on, and rightly so, to approach a group of staff members standing around. I'm thrown by their casual attitudes and relaxed uniform since I usually run such a strict business. Clad in black with clean-cut looks, I sought for only the utmost professionals when hiring.

The women can choose between black trousers like the men or black skirts, and for tip's sake, they choose the latter. Some go as far as wearing patterned tights, from fishnet to see-through with black bows embroidered into the back of their thighs. I don't mind too much, as it keeps business alive, but I had to provide the men with extra training on workplace sexual harassment. Then, there were the NDA's and regular martial arts classes the staff had to complete with the instruction to remain vigilant of impending attacks. Which right now, they are not.

The tallest of the bunch waves me over before realizing I'm not Gabriel. I had to send my lookalike home this evening to avoid confusion. Wide-eyed, he quickly stomps out the cigarette perched between his fingers and makes a hasty exit before the others spot me.

"Is everyone having a good time?" I ask rhetorically in a clipped tone. Many jolt, spinning to conceal the drinks in their hands I've already spotted. I take a long breath, steadying myself. It's not their fault I'm struggling with the loss of control, but pushing my boundaries right now is not a wise idea. "How about we all get back to work before I not only dock these drinks from your pay but replace you entirely." The group splits in a rush of heeled boots and dress shoes, except for the three men I whistle to hang back.

"We could do with some of the heightened tables and stools out here. Grab some others and set them up around the edge of the dance floor."

"Yes, sir," Jack's lookalike, Max, nods. The brown roots are starting to show amongst his dyed blonde hair, and he's forgotten to put in his green contacts. I'll let it slip tonight, considering enough of the real monarchs are here to front an attack should it happen, but tomorrow I'll be coming down so hard on my staff, I expect the need to replace half of them. Weeding out the weak suits me fine. If they want to be paid twice the average bartender, they need to live up to expectations.

A hand slides into mine, and it's only then I catch the heavy rise and fall to my chest. My jaw is bruisingly tight, and my hand is shaking slightly with the need to hit something. I know Ace's words have hit me deeper than I want to let on, but I deserved every single one. Lashing out will only make me more of a dick than I already am.

"Hey," Candy cups my cheek and turns my head to face her. Using the height of her spiked heels, her mouth is on mine before I'm fully facing her way. The surge of adrenaline already coursing through me shoots upwards, centering on the places where Candy's body leans into mine. Her curves press into my palms as she gently rolls her hips to the beat of the music. Before I realize what's happening, we're fully making out and dancing like two lovers lost in the crowd. I'm no longer Malik, the King who trapped his pawns in a pathetic attempt to not be alone. I'm just a man being pulled along in the crazy world that follows Candy wherever she goes.

Swept away with the sweet taste of her tongue, the surfacing rage disappears in favor of lust. Hot, hard lust projected to the base of my cock until it's pressed into her, aching to hit home. I could whisk her upstairs right now, let the party continue while I make the guest of honor scream with pleasure. Easing herself away from our kiss, Candy remains crushed against me and drops her hand onto my shoulder. With my arms wrapped around her, afraid of the cold that will sweep in when she has to move away, I catch sight of Ace and Spade standing at one of the newly-moved tables a few feet away. Their eyes are trained on my movements, curiosity filling their darkened gazes. Ducking my head into her neck, I let the world sink away for just a little longer.

"Oh," Candy giggles as she raises her head, catching sight of my face. "You have some…" Pointing from her lips to mine, she notes the smeared pink lipstick across her face. No doubt mine matches. Licking her thumb, Candy attempts to clean my mouth, but I dodge her touch. Not because being groomed by her salvia is fucking disgusting, but because I'm damn well proud of what I've managed to do here tonight. I've let loose, and I want everyone to see that she is ours —one of the Gambling Monarchs. I'll wear her mark like any servant would of his Queen.

With a satisfied smirk, Candy winks at me and drifts back into the middle of the dancefloor. I stand, staring after her until a beermat whips me in the side of the face. I don't even react aside from assessing it by my feet and then heading over to the table where I'm presuming Spade threw it from. Whipping out my phone, I shoot a message to the bartender to keep the drinks permanently filled on this table before sliding it back in my pocket. The same brown and blue eyes are still staring at me, waiting for my next move. Then Spade bursts into a fit of laughter.

"Have you seen the fucking state of you?" he chuckles, and Ace cracks a smile. "Glitter in your hair, lipstick across your face. Do you know she stuck a 'Kick me' sign on your back? Anyone who doesn't know you would think you're a regular guy on a night out." I twist in all directions, unable to reach the square of paper I can now spot in the center of my back. The tightness of my shirt pins my arms from reaching, and I give up on a huffed laugh.

"I suppose you're right. Good thing everyone here knows me, and my reputation is officially fucked." The words don't sound as bitter as I expected them to and, as the first round of whiskeys arrive, I take the bottle and down a large swig. Handing out the glasses before the bartender retreats, I pour out a huge dose for each of my brothers and lean on the table to watch Candy dance. Neither moves, so I push the glasses directly in front of them. "Drink, please. You might as well enjoy my downfall in comfort."

Spade breaks his stoic stance first, shrugging and taking the drink. Songs bleed from one into the next, as do the drinks until the bottle is empty. A bubbly waitress with her black shirt open and pulled tight around her cleavage skips over, replacing the empty bottle with a purple-tinted version of unicorn spunk champagne. She lingers, smiling sweetly in the hopes of being noticed.

"Move the fuck along while you still have the intact shins to do so," Candy bumps the waitress's hip out of the way. In the short time, my eyes had been averted to take the champagne flutes from the tray, I hadn't noticed Candy leave the dancefloor. Her impeccable timing tells me she was watching me as closely as I had been watching her. Pulling a penknife from a concealment in her waist belt, she pries off the wrapping around the seal with surprising care. I watch in fascination as Candy carefully scours a line around the neck of the bottle with her knife and then smashes it on the side of the table. Purple liquid and glass shatters in all directions, not that I even try to dodge it. I'm already a mess; a spillage and tiny lacerations on my forearms aren't going to make it much worse.

"No one's ever thrown me a party before," Candy beams, leaning against my shoulder. "Occurs to me that you all have yet to give me a gift, though." She smirks over the rim of her flute, daring Spade with a twitch of her eyebrows.

"And what is it you want, Crazy Girl?" he smiles, full of bad intentions. I brace myself for the reply but what follows has me spluttering on the glittery drink more.

"I want you to forgive Malik so we can go back to destroying his pool table. In fact, we can gangbang over all the surfaces around his suite. Tie him down, make him watch, gag him so he can't give orders." A purely evil side-eye comes my way, but I'm still catching up with the mental images she's provided. Heat floods to my dick while my mind is screaming to put an end to the suggestion right now. Spade, though, glances over the party, contemplating her offer. Would he forgive me so easily? Or would he agree for her while always resenting me? That's no way for a family to live; I need to earn his trust back and rebuild my foundation with all the guys.

"My grievances aren't as serious as the other's," Spade ponders out loud, and my eyebrows shoot up. His piercing blue eyes swing my way, causing the rest of the party to drop out in favor of my attention hanging on his next words. "But nothing you did was okay. Being alone doesn't give you the right to fabricate your own family by whatever means necessary. I returned because curiosity got the better of me, and I've decided to stay. But you're not forgiven." Candy turns to me, her face so full of satisfaction; I would agree to just about anything to keep that smile there. The day Candy falters, we're all doomed.

"I understand," I nod, raising my glass. "A toast to making me suffer for my bad judgment?" It's a cop-out, but despite everything, everyone around the table lifts their champagne flutes to clink with mine.

"To sticking around while Candy pushes you to your limits,"

Spade agrees, and Ace grunts. "Any type of torture she dishes out will be much more entertaining than what we could come up with." Candy taps a finger on her chin, clearly thinking what to do to me next and to tell the truth, I'm worried. I can take physical pain or shouted words, but Candy will fuck with my psyche. Tear apart my convictions, reconfigure my ideals, and put me back together again. I just hope she and everyone else likes the end result. Spade catches me swallowing thickly and chuckles again, lightening the mood.

"I have a condition," Ace suddenly pipes up. He's remained quiet this entire time, slowly sipping his drink while a range of still-filled glasses surround him. Dipping his head, I only hear him because the song bleeding from the speakers ends with a few precious seconds until the next begins. "The twins need to come back. Both of them."

I should have known it was coming, and of course, Jack was my next port of call. But there's so much bad blood between Jasper and me. Even if I wanted to, he hates me. Yet without needing to consider the logistics, I find myself nodding. I may have built our family, but I did so on broken foundations. Fixing my bond with Jasper is the only way to feel complete again. Leaning across the table, I hold out my hand in front of Ace.

"I won't stop until we are *all* back together again. I promise," I nod. Without much faith, Ace takes my hand and gives it a firm shake. Candy's arm winds around my middle, bolstering me with her strength. She got her birthday wish, and I make a mental note to thank her for it over and over until her voice is raw.

Without even trying, Candy has awakened me to the truth and allowed me to see things clearly. I'd become so cold I cut off those I was trying to keep close. I lost sight of what all my rules were in place to prevent. My biggest downfall, though, was sacrificing Jasper. I cut him off told the others he abandoned us out of fear they'd leave with him once they learned the truth, which they did. But this time, I have something I didn't have before, something precious which will unite us all.

As if she can read my mind, Candy's head tilts into view with a smirk. She beckons me with her towards the dancefloor, and like a magnet, I'm drawn to her. Incapable of thinking about disagreeing. When I think of what I could have had, or what I almost lost, Candy's the shining beacon in the centre of it all. Holding onto her was my last saving grace but now I want more. I want her to unite us. To be the missing link in our bond. So even with the various kicks to my calves from random members of the crowd, I put my future in her hands and damn the consequences.

CANDY

An announcement made by the DJ has all of the dancers moving aside, allowing the entertainers to take center stage. I take a position at the front of the barging crowd, throwing out a few death glares to those shoving from behind. The three men stepping into my sides seem to do a better job, earning us a wide berth to watch the show. With Ace standing protectively at my back, I link fingers with Malik and Spade, giddy with excitement. The stilted men carry a coffin into the middle, placing it down as gently as they are able from their height. One of the aerialists swans across the mats, swirling a rainbow-striped ribbon and, in a flourish, pops the coffin open. From inside, she draws out a can of fuel and a stack of juggling pins tightly bound in flammable cloths.

"Yes!" I gasp, releasing the boys. Running into the fold, the DJ announces me as the Birthday Girl, and the crowd cheers excitedly. Three sets of eyes watch me steadily, but I ignore them, asking the aerialist if I can have a go. A little reluctantly, she hands over the pins and fuel, and I give her a wink. "Don't worry babes, I've got this." Kicking the coffin closed, I jump up on top and pop off the fuel's cap. Luckily the hole is big enough to dip the cloth end of the pins straight in, and as I do so, I prop the dried ends one by one in between my thighs.

"Candy," Malik's voice seeps out of the crowd in a warning. I roll my eyes, sick to death of these guys still underestimating me after everything we've been through. Lifting the can, I pour a healthy dose into my mouth and wipe my chin with the back of my hand. Then, taking three pins in each hand, I smack them together steadily to get the crowd clapping. The atmosphere picks up as much as the fear bleeding from Malik's eyes does, and I make sure to hold his gaze. Holding the pins in a cross in front of me, I blow the fuel out to ignite them in giant gulfs of fire. The heat radiates back on my face, spurring me on to toss the pins up in turn and juggle for all to applaud. I work the crowd so well; I reckon I might have made a good stripper after all.

For my big finale, I catch three pins in each hand again and do a flaming front flip off the coffin. With the biggest smile on my face, I throw the pins up to the stilts men who take over for me and take a bow. I'm on cloud nine by the time I skip back over to Malik, whipping the residue of fuel from my face across the chest of his shirt. I could have used the towel one of the waitresses had brought over, but where's the fun in that? I want to see just how far Malik will let me push his appearance before he explodes.

The aerialist has gone a little ashy as she lifts the coffin lid once more, bending over to pull two more scantily clad performers out of the base. Both heave and gasp but manage to pull themselves back into the routine soon enough. I suppose there wasn't much oxygen in there while I was standing on top, living my best life. Oops. The truck backs up for the metal hoops to hover around 15 feet above the ground. Using silky ribbons hanging down, they twist themselves up to the safety of their hoops, continuing on as if they didn't almost suffocate. What professional performers; I'll make sure Malik pays them double for a job well done.

"Where did you learn to do that?" Spade tips his head, brushing a kiss against my cheek. Winding an arm around my waist, he draws me towards the back of the crowd with the others in tow. The view from here is terrible, but we're away from the majority of the noise and hidden enough for Spade to run his hands all over me. It occurs to me that, unlike Malik and Ace, Spade hasn't had to chance to reconnect with me physically. Sure, we barely knew each other before, and it has only been a few weeks, but we had something solid that needs reconciling. Tonight.

"Ran away with a bunch of circus rejects once," I shrug, remembering his question. "They had a freak show that frequented strip clubs and brothels. Turned out to be a bunch of opium addicts that were spiking me. The comedown was a bitch, but I lost my virginity to the world's most endowed dwarf and learned a few tricks along the way, so it wasn't all bad." I reach up, winding my hands around Spade's neck. Ace steps closer, brushing the hair over my shoulder to run his thumb over my neck.

"Opium is nasty stuff. What made you decide to get yourself sorted out?" His hooded puppy brown eyes hold way too much concern for a Friday night.

"Not me - Big Cheese. Hunted me down all the way across the country and forced me into a fancy rehab the celebrities use. I worked for him exclusively after that, more to pay off the long list of debts he decided I owed rather than loyalty." With Malik joining the fold, some silent communication is passed between the three of them, just like old times.

"Had you run jobs for him before that?" Ace asks.

"Uh, yeah. He bailed me out from my first arrest wanted me to join his ranks. It took me a while to submit to being owned, but he was relentless. Why'd you ask?" Instead of replying, Ace grunts and continues his exploration of my neck. He's probably marveling that he can be so bold and not have the intention of choking me out. I make a point to remind him a good choking gets my nipples harder than an icicle in winter. Malik responds, trailing his knuckles over my hip.

"It just seems a little strange that Leicester would go to such lengths to find you and bring you back. He could have picked up a new crew member from the same town easily enough. I made it my business to keep an eye on him, and he was never lacking for new recruits."

"Well, he's dead now, and we'll join him soon if we waste our time hunting for answers that aren't there. Besides, the real show is about to begin." I point upwards just as the first golden light shoots into the sky. This is the part of the night I've been waiting for. Malik doesn't seem surprised as the light explodes across the night sky in a burst of orange and yellow. No doubt he had a good snoop in my delivery crates and saw the production-worthy fireworks I'd ordered in. Members of the crowd who had been lingering on the outskirts of the parking lot rush in to watch, closing us into the group of sweaty bodies. However, there's only three bodies I'm concerned with right now, and the way Spade spins me in front of him; he knows exactly what's on my mind.

"No birthday of yours is complete without a public spectacle," he mumbles into my ear. Here I was thinking Ace would be the easiest to bring home, the lost puppy that he was, but it's Spade I should have sought out first. Twisting my head, I'm captivated by his stark blue eyes, so full of mystery and amusement.

"What made you come tonight?" I ask. I know what fairy-tale me wants his reply to be, but Angus is right there, clinging onto my arm like a koala to tell me his answer. Free drink and easy pussy. Both of those things are true, so I shoot him yet another glare, mouthing for him to shut his tiny, gummy mouth.

"Well, it wasn't the invite, that's for damn sure," Spade replies, oblivious of my distraction. Winding his arms around me, he rests his chin on my shoulder and sighs. "It kills me to say it, but Malik got exactly what he wanted. I don't have anywhere else to belong in this world, so even if it's harder to be here, it's where I need to be. You were a key factor in returning, though."

"Oh yeah? Why's that?" I tease, grinding my ass back against his fly. Spade pushes back against me with equal arousal, a rumble from his chest vibrating into my back.

"Something tells me as long as you're around, the days won't be as long, and the nights won't be as quiet." To prove his point, another firework cracks against the dark blanket overhead. I suppose he's right - subtle isn't my scene. If life's not interesting, I find a way to make it so. Luckily, I've stumbled across a group of guys who had a Candy shaped hole in their dynamic, begging to be filled with a whole load of excitement and a shit-ton of sass.

As the next firework shoots up from behind the Devil's Bedpost, followed by a reel of many more, Spade slips his hand through the slit in my skirt and beneath the crotch of my gold leotard. I grow wet instantly, relishing the cool breeze toying over the surface of my skin. His other arm winds around my chest, delving into my bra cup. Grabbing my breast firmly, his teeth sink into my shoulder, and I melt beneath him. Fucking, yes. His coarse fingers search roughly for my clit, finding it in no time. Applying pressure, I gasp into the silence between the sky's echoing cracks, drawing attention to myself.

"You got a ticket? $100 a minute for this live porno." I smirk at a prude in front, her face the image of shock. Ace and Malik catch on too at that point, quickly moving to block me from view, and I chuckle deep in my throat. I quite enjoy a public spectacle, and it seems they don't. That's their problem. I'm fine with my own sexuality and the need to exploit it. Spade joins me in my laughter, playing my body like his own personal fiddle. Plucking at my nipple, gnawing on my neck, circling my clit. Spade has me writhing at his touch, and with each deafening crack from above, my own climax is building, threatening to explode.

Prying the leotard open with his thumb, I widen my stance for Spade to spear me with his fingers. The evidence of my lust is clear for all to sense, and it doesn't go unnoticed that Ace and Malik have taken a step backward in an effort to get closer. Ace's hand reaches back to brush my bare thigh between my billowing skirt.

Spade doesn't relent his assault, drawing me towards the ledge I desperately want to jump off without a parachute. I'd fall into the abyss for the pleasure building inside of me, causing trembles to take over my legs. As the fireworks come to their big ending, the colors meld from one to the next as my eyes un-focus, and on one sharp twist of his fingers inside me, I shatter. My scream is silenced by the thunderous cracks piercing the night air, and as everyone cheers, I could swear it was for my climax.

JACK

Tonight's the night; I grin to myself in the lengthy mirror. The glow across my skin is thanks to the peel-off face mask I did in the bath, and the perfectly smooth shine to my slicked-back hair took an hour of work —only the best when I've got a date. I had to do something because sitting around staring at my toes was driving me insane. Nothing held my interest long enough to be considered a hobby, and then it occurred to me. I'm in my prime; I should be out there, loving life and breaking a string of hearts. Jump straight on the horse's back and ride that baby into the sunset, thoroughly sated and finally fulfilled.

I forego a tie, leaving the top button of my powered blue shirt open. Tanned braces stretch over my shoulders, clipping onto a pair of beige slacks over my freshly-polished dress shoes. Fuck yeah, this is the me I always should have been. If my life wasn't hijacked by a kleptomaniac, I'd look exactly like the man smirking back in the mirror: dimples, sparkling eyes and all. Slipping on my suit jacket, I head for the door. A light tap sounds on the other side just as I open it, finding my date for this evening ready for the night of her life. Drinking me in, her smile grows as she squeezes her tits closer together in a tiny black dress.

"You look delicious," she coos, settling into my body. Sliding her hands up my shirt, she pops my collar to frame my neck.

"Not looking so bad yourself," I smirk back. That's an understatement. Her flame red hair and matching lip, a smattering of freckles and wide chocolate eyes. She's everything the regular guy would go for, and tonight that's exactly who I'm going to be. Regular. "Ready to go?" I don't get an answer in favor of her biting her bottom lip, and I agree with the sentiment. With the mix of coconut bath crème and extortionately expensive cologne clinging to my skin, I'd fuck me too.

Heading for the elevator, we travel in a comfortable silence towards the lobby arm in arm, all sly smiles and flirty looks. Passing the lobby bar where we met last week, I open the door for her to exit the hotel first, where I then hail a taxi. My bike is safely stashed in the underground parking lot, but there's no chance I'm returning tonight without needing assistance to walk straight, never mind being sober enough to drive.

Our destination pulls into view in no time, a quaint little place I found on a morning jog last week. Honestly, I'd thought it was a trick of the mind, but as I circled back day after day, it's still here — a fully authentic English pub. Large brass letters hang over a wall of windows and the small canopy to create a smoking area. Punters are already draped over the tables standing outside, thoroughly smashed, and heavily involved in an arm-wrestling match.

Inside, dusty patterned booths and that memorable smell of mid-life crisis take me back to my childhood. Our dad frequented a pub just like this one, where Jasper and I would play hide and seek amongst people's legs or sit to do our homework at the bar. Those were the days before money became more important than family, and we were sent away. My date's arm slinks into the crook of mine, bringing me back to the present. I haven't thought about my childhood in a long time, and it's probably for the best that I don't. Not thinking of myself as a sole child is too painful, especially when Jasper and I were closer than close. Picking a secluded booth in the back corner, I pass a copy of the food menu to the redhead sitting beside me. This is nice. This is normal.

Falling into a light conversation about our days and her job as a freelance photographer, a passing waitress takes our order. Records from the 80's play softly overhead, and the chatter around picks up to a sociable level. The evening crowd is lively for mid-week, a group of men laughing by the bar, drawing my attention more than once. By the time our food and drinks arrive, I'm full-out staring at the group, trying to figure out the dynamics. Who's the boss, who's the funny one, the quietly stoic one? Did they all make the decision to go out together, or did someone take charge?

"Is there...anything else I can get you?" the waitress asks, frowning in the direction I'm staring.

"Oh, no, this is perfect. Thanks," I mumble, glancing at my triple-stacked burger, dirty fries, and onion rings. Pub grub is the best. The gorgeous woman pressing her leg against my thigh has the spaghetti bolognese with an extra serving of garlic bread. Carb city - my kind of girl, I grin to myself. The waitress bobs in a half-curtsey, leaving us to enjoy our meals in peace. Still, I can't bring myself to stop looking over at the group of men every time they burst into a fit of laughter. I wish it could have been that natural for us.

"Hey, I've always wanted to do this. Just like I've seen in the movies," my date beams. Picking up a lengthy piece of spaghetti from her plate, she bobs her eyebrows, holding one end out for me. I see where this is going; she's wanted my mouth on hers since I stepped out of the hotel room, but I'm game. Taking the spaghetti strand, I lean over the table to put one end in my mouth. She copies, her cleavage fit to burst over her dinner. Once I feel the gentle tug her red lips provide, I draw the pasta into my mouth, pulling me further across the table until we are a few inches apart. Her eyes tilt at the corners, and my eyes drift close, desperately wanting to live out that fairy-tale romance for myself, just once.

"High-yah!" a voice shouts over the chatter, and I open my eyes in time to see a hand fly through the center of my date and me. Not having the intended effect of karate chopping the spaghetti in half, the strand slicks back out of my mouth and drops onto the table between us. A wet, soggy strand of salvia, utterly ruining the moment. I don't have to look for who's responsible as an all-too-familiar voice rings in my ears. "See, told you I knew karate."

"You don't know karate," Malik answers the pink bombshell I'd forced myself to forget. But now she's here, in the authentic pub I found, ruining my date. Pushing to my feet, I huff through my nose before swinging my gaze to hers. Candy fucking Crystal. As perky as ever, her hair radiates with a sweetness she can't compare with. I see the irony now, between her approachable appearance and her dark soul that's rotten to the core. She's just another ploy from Malik to control us after being selected as the *chosen one*. The only one we're allowed to involve ourselves with emotionally or sexually. Well, not me, not anymore. I choose my own destiny, and I choose for her to be nowhere near it.

"What are you doing here?" I seethe, struggling to contain my temper. Any pretense of calm I'd found whilst being on my own has vanished. Even before Malik, I always had Jasper attached to my hip. For once, I had the chance to be just…me. But it seems my break from the Gambler's Monarchs has ended, and it becomes apparent that's all it was - a break. A temporary vacation before life crashed back down on my shoulders.

"Saving you from yourself," Candy clicks her tongue. Her brown eyes flick to my date, who's moved to stand beside me. The two women stand nose to nose, evenly matched in height. Their profiles glare at each other with similarly colored chocolate eyes and a slight upturn to their noses I hadn't registered before now. The comparisons stop there though since Candy is in a full, glossy black catsuit paired with chunky, studded boots. Not your typical night out attire, and it's drawing enough attention from those seated around us. Malik steps into her side in his pressed navy suit and winds a protective arm around her waist.

"I know you're pretty, Jack, but whoring yourself out is never the answer," Candy smirks, twisting her head to openly ignore the woman at my side. I mimic Malik's move, pulling her in closer whilst a layer of red mist descends.

"I'm not whoring myself out; this is my...new girlfriend." I say, throwing an apologetic side-eye in her direction. Introducing a woman as your girlfriend after just a few nights out is not the best dating etiquette, but the shocked smile on her face says she's not totally against the idea. Cozying up against me, I drop a casual kiss onto her cheek as if it is a regular occurrence between the two of us. It's not, but it could be.

"Does your dog have a name?" Candy scrunches up her face, still preferring to look at the ceiling. I bristle, puffing out my chest on a growl.

"If you must know, this is Cherry. Cherry, this is the maniac who ruined my life and his new pet project." Bringing her focus back to us, Candy gives Cherry an up and down look, full of disgust.

"Ew." She turns out of Malik's grip and strides away. I take a step after her before remembering I'm not a part of their bullshit anymore. Holding Cherry even tighter in fear she'll notice how much baggage I have and make a run for it; I allow my gaze to fall on Malik for the first time. The self-proclaimed King of a world he manufactured.

"I'll ask again," I drop my voice. "What the fuck are you doing here?"

"I've come to bring you home. I tried to lock Candy in the car, but I made the mistake of cracking the window for air, and she slithered out," he shrugs one shoulder beneath his jacket. Holding my eye while he smooths down his tie, Malik shifts his whole body to face Cherry and puts on his fakest, charming smile. "Allow me to introduce myself; I'm Ma-"

"Save your breath. I'm making a home for myself from now on. One without you in it, so if you can fuck off, I have a date to finish." Malik's eyes remain on Cherry, assessing her too closely for my liking. Briefly looking down, there's a slight lift of his eyebrows as he mumbles something like *'interesting'* under his breath. I want to ask what the fuck that was about but somehow resist, not wanting to fall back into the trap of caring what Malik thinks.

"I understand," he nods, returning his dark stare to meet my gaze. "You know where I am if you change your mind." With that, he leaves, and I swear a piece of my heart tears off and goes with him. Unlike before, where I got to be the one walking away, watching Malik retreat seems to hurt so much more.

"Wow," Cherry takes a long exhale. "There's definitely a story here. Feel like sharing?" Her expression is naturally curious as she draws me back into the booth, where we resume our seats. So much for an enjoyable date. We haven't even gotten to dessert, and the drama has washed over us like a tsunami.

"That was…for lack of a better description, my family. Although Candy is just some nut-job that latched onto us and refused to let go. It doesn't make for great conversation. I'm sure you don't-"

"No, please. I'm interested," Cherry coaxes with a smile. Her body is angled to me, her squashed cleavage pressing into my arm. When I hesitate, she reaches out to take my hand in hers, interlocking our fingers. "Besides, you just introduced me as your girlfriend. You owe me," she winks, and I huff out a laugh. Yeah, she's right on that front. Running a hand through my hair, I push my plate aside, having lost my appetite strangely enough.

"You're right – and I am sorry about that. It's hard to know where to begin. I suppose first off; you ought to know I'm a twin. My brother and I were sent over here for an *'enriched boarding school brimming with culture,'*" I finger quote, relaying the sales pitch we were told as excited young boys. "Aka, our parents decided rearing twins wasn't all it was cracked up to be and wanted to reclaim their old lives. Didn't matter anyway; Jasper and I became orphans whilst over here, so we had no reason to go back."

Cherry gasps, expressing her sympathy, but I wave it off. "Don't worry about it; I've come to understand shit happens, and there's nothing I can do about it." I take a long sip of my beer, wishing I could have been completely shitfaced for this conversation.

"Anyways, when we graduated, we did what any guys who have been imprisoned in the same building for several years would. We partied. Hard. Got ourselves in a bit of trouble caught the attention of the wrong crowd. Or so we thought." Cherry is molded into my side now, hanging on my every word like she's binging a sitcom, and I don't want to disappoint. "I recently found out that man you just saw; he orchestrated the whole thing. Blackmailed this particularly rough gang to chase and beat us every time we stopped long enough to get caught. All so we'd see his helping hand for the lie it was and buy into the false family he created."

Cherry's eyes grow wide, looking in the direction Malik left in. "When you say family, you mean there were others he did that to?"

"Not with the exact same tactic but yeah, he conned the lot of us." I shrug to pass off the emotions I've yet to deal with. Burying until they disappear is more my style.

"Hot damn. That's some heavy shit," Cherry breathes, nibbling on a piece of garlic bread. "By the animosity, I'm guessing this was all quite recent. What did your twin say when he found out? Is he staying at the hotel too?" Her questions are innocent enough, but my gaze slides away, unable to speak past the bitterness that rises in my throat. That's the worst bit. Jasper knew for so long and didn't say anything. Cherry must realize I don't want to speak anymore, as a small 'ahh' comes from her vibrant, red lips, and she scoots back to give me some space.

"I'm sorry you had to go through all of that, but is it entirely selfish to say I'm glad I bumped into you last week – regardless of the reasons you're staying in a hotel? Finding a handsome guy that's single, straight, and interesting is unheard of these days." A rumble of laughter escapes my chest, and the weight that was threatening to crush me lightens.

"I did warn you, not great conversation. Enough of that, let's get back to our date. If you still want to continue, that is..." I duck my head, hiding the blush crawling up my cheeks. Why am I so terrible at this? I can charm a woman into a quickie behind the dumpster with a click of my fingers, but this whole dating thing is a mystery to me. Keeping someone's attention beyond physical attraction coming up with captivating things to say it's a minefield to me. But I want to try. Even if I already know by today's cameo, Candy won't leave me be anytime soon.

CANDY

It was late when we got back last night, or at least that was my excuse to go straight to bed. No drink, no nightcap in someone else's room. Just me, writhing around in a fit of rage between the covers. Don't ask me what I was, and still am, so angry about — returning without Jack probably. Definitely not the dreaded 'J' word Angus has been suggesting. *Jealousy*.

Stomping downstairs at some ungodly hour that shouldn't exist, I head straight for the fridge. The chaos of half-opened packets and greasy takeaway boxes I left inside have disappeared, and once again, the shelving hierarchy has been reinstated. I roll my eyes from Malik's organized top shelf, all the way down to Spade's protein shakes and Ace's meat and cheese platters. Crammed into the bottom drawer, all of my shit that is still edible has been neatly compartmentalized into plastic tubs. Fucking Malik and his OCD.

Out of spite, I grab for his fancy oat milk over the standard cow-piss and go in search of his cereal collection. The grey hoodie I'm wearing rises past my bare ass as I reach up, plucking out a box from the highest cupboard. My actions are as hostile as my temper, slamming a bowl down and shaking the cutlery drawer viciously until a spoon magically emerges. Turning, I find the sarcastic little prick sitting at the dining table; his pink grin stretched wide in amusement.

"It's not Malik's fault Jack has replaced you," Angus taunts, baring his pointed teeth in a rare, mocking smile.

"Who's fucking side are you on?" I growl back.

"Whatever side will see you spilling blood before eight in the morning." I groan at the mention of the time, glancing at the kitchen clock to confirm Angus' statement. Ten to fucking eight. I used to party from one night into the next without stopping, snorting cocaine for breakfast, and taking Molly for lunch. Now, look at me - a bitter hoe who is vindictive in her milk choices.

Preferring not to sit beside my so-called best friend, not when he's been pondering the most inventive ways we could deal with *Cherry* all night and therefore reminding me of her every five seconds, I hop up on the kitchen counter and cross my legs. Shoveling the first spoonful into my mouth, Ace arrives with a ding from the elevator, rejuvenated and smelling of eucalyptus after his routine workout and shower.

"Where's Jack?" he demands, the tension in his voice faltering as he spots my naked pussy nestled between my legs and the hoodie's hem. I'm not even sure who's it is. Aside from Malik's, all clothes returned from the launderette seem to become fair game, and I've taken a stash to hide at the bottom of my wardrobe. Munching on my cereal, my mind travels to who could have purchased the jingle-bell Christmas thong until Ace snaps his fingers in my face. "I've checked Jack's room, and it's empty. I thought you went to retrieve him - so where is he?"

"Balls deep in a crimson-Candy lookalike," Angus chortles to himself. I blow out a harsh breath, my nostrils flaring, and I toss my half-empty bowl into the nearby basin.

"Take it down a notch, Steroid Ken." I push at Ace's firm chest to let me slide off the counter. This puts me at a height disadvantage, though, so I kick over a stool and hop up, placing my hands on my hips. "Either you're on board with coercing fully grown men here against their will or not, pick a side." Ace's puppy dog brown eyes falter, his stance weakening.

"This is different. No matter how we came about, I refuse to live here without all of the Monarchs under this roof. We're a family; we need to be together." A patronizing look bleeds from my eyes as my finger trails the edge of his shadowed jawline.

"Hmmm, you're right - that is totally different from what Malik tried to do," I drawl. Soothing down the chest of his beige t-shirt, I flick Ace's nipples through the cotton and sigh. Usually, I'd have jumped his bones just for the distraction, but for the life of me, I can't figure out why I'm not in the mood. Hopping down from the stool, I flip off Angus on my way towards the bar. A day like today needs plenty of unicorn cum cocktails. When I reach the door, I pause and throw a curious look at Ace over my shoulder.

"I wonder, does having all of your Monarchs under one roof include Jasper?" Ace's following steps draw to a stop, his brow creasing. We haven't spoken about what happened at the indoor play area since Jasper hugged us both goodbye and left without a word. Not a promise to return, any mention of how right the three of us being together felt, nothing. Silence passes between us, and although the answer is clear in Ace's eyes, he still doesn't want to voice it. Jasper belongs here, more than I do anyway.

"Well, how about you think about that while I drink myself into a coma? If you're so desperate to get your boys back, you go get them." I push my way through the metal door dividing the house from the bar without waiting for an answer.

We both know Ace won't be leaving the Devil's Bedpost anytime soon - for the same reasons he won't turn his computers back on. He doesn't want any part of the real world. These walls are all he needs, but I'm not so easily contained. Tropical birds don't do well in small cages. I need to go where the wind takes me, jump off buildings in the hope of flying, and shit on people's ice creams. Ace isn't very bird-like; more of a cowardly lion. All gorgeous, golden skin and muscle, but scared his own shadow might take over. I decide there, and then, if Ace won't leave with me to find some fun, I'll have to force him.

The smell of disinfectant doesn't hit me like I was expecting. Lipstick-stained glasses line the bar top, and the stools are toppled over amongst sticky spillages across the lino floor.

"Wow, the cleaning company sucks," Angus voices my inner monologue. He yanks himself up the side of the bar, the stretch of his elastic skin squeaking loudly. I nod in agreement, though. Even if the cleaning company took the night off or whatever, the bar staff are going to get in deep shit for leaving the place in this state. Flicking on the lights, Ace grunts at the same sight and heads for the hidden safe beneath the cash register.

"Hmmmm, it's all here," he mumbles to himself. I shrug, helping myself to a bottle of gin.

"You see a mess and immediately jump to a robbery? Loosen up, Ace. The staff had some fun after hours, probably were bought a few too many drinks. You can't expect them to be so robotic all the time."

"They're not paid to have fun," Malik's voice comes in hard and sharp behind me. He plucks the bottle from my hand, placing it back on the glass shelf. If I didn't know better, I'd think Malik has a time machine upstairs because the tension in his shoulders and flawless suit pressed against his body are elements of the old him. Not the man I got to dirty grind against me to Eminem's top hits at my birthday party.

"Aww Malli-Moo, you didn't have to get all dressed up for me," I stroke the length of his teal tie. His laser-sharp gaze is too focused on the destruction around the room, so I grab his dick through his grey slacks and squeeze hard. Jolting back to me, his gaze softens ever so slightly as he pries my fingers free of his crotch and holds my hand between us. "I dig it though; the whole big, bad boss and sexy secretary routine," I wink, and this earns me a small smile. Big win in Malik terms.

"I'm concerned with which role I'm supposed to be playing in that fantasy," he replies deeply, giving me plenty to think about while he addresses Ace over my head. "I have a meeting with one of the bar's vendors. Tedious paperwork, really, but if we're going straight, I need to make sure this bar is enough of an investment to support us all." I don't miss the way his dark eyes flicker my way, and my heart flutters. He included me in his 'us all'. Although, the notion that I'm some damsel in need of supporting is laughable. Maybe what he really means is they can run the bar while I pickpocket the punters. Yeah, that sounds better.

"Going straight?" Ace echoes, drifting into our personal space. I remain in place, sandwiched between the two, continuing to play with Malik's silver buttons and tie pin.

"Isn't that what you wanted? No more heists, no more danger, and no more rules." I glance up in time to see the tell-tale temple twitch and slight strain to Malik's neck that betrays how uncomfortable that last notion makes him. But he doesn't call backsies, so credit is given where it's due. Ace winds his arms around me from behind and pulls me away from ruffling Malik's fancy pocket cloth.

"We'd better not keep you then," Ace says. "I'll be on Candy duty." I frown, elbowing my way out of his grip. Unless Candy duty includes doing 69 on the roof, he can get fucked. I don't need babysitting. Malik thanks Ace for the offer and briefly closes the gap between us.

"Don't get into any trouble while I'm gone." He places a kiss on my forehead, and I glower at his back all the way to the door. I read this word once, and it seemed to stick because every time I think it, Angus bursts out laughing. Oxymoron. Malik being gone and me *not* getting into trouble definitely sounds like a moronic suggestion because now that's all I plan on doing. Diving out of Ace's grip after he tries to grab for me again, I run for the dividing metal door. It swings open as I reach it, and thanks to the momentum, I slam straight into a topless Spade.

"Woah!" he cries, falling a few steps back before he manages to catch me. "Where's the fire, Crazy Girl?" Strong hands close around my arms, and I thrash around, kicking and cursing like a woman possessed. "Hey! Take it easy. What's happened?" Spade tries to calm me, taking a step back and holding up his hands.

"You can't control me," I grit out, fists raised and ready for a fight. I'm all up for having a good time and sex until none of us can walk, but I didn't sign up for being caged or tamed or any of that shit. Spade's stance relaxes, and an easy smile plays about his lips.

"As if I'd even try." Slowly Spade shuffles towards me, and despite my fight or flight instincts still being in full swing, I let him pull me into a hug. "Take it from the guy you shot and then sucked off a few days later; I wouldn't dare try to control a wild spirit like yours. These days, I love waking up, wondering what rollercoaster adventure you're going to bring. Today's as good a day as any to be alive. So tell me, Crazy Girl," Spade gently tilts my head up to look at him. "What do you feel like doing today?"

Before letting me answer, Spade's mouth brushes over mine. His fresh toothpaste breath tickles my lips a second before he ravages my mouth for an explosive peppermint make-out session. I let myself go weak, being held up by Spade's strong arm banded around my back. His tongue strokes mine with expert skill, drawing out my delayed anger at Jack and diluting it in lust. Another body moves in behind, but this time, I don't feel trapped but empowered. Like how it was with Jasper and Ace inside of me, our bodies slick with sweat. I'm the center of their attention and the focus of their attraction and damn if it doesn't feel good.

Withdrawing from our kiss, Spade's lips skim over my skin and gently press on the end of my nose. My eyelids flutter open, finding Spade's stark blue eyes already waiting for me there. Against his bronzed skin, his irises gleam, and I wish I could dive into their ocean-like depths. An idea comes to mind, and a wicked grin grows across my face.

"Grab your trunks, boys; we're going swimming." I whoop, sharing a high-five with Spade, but I can already feel the hesitation at my back.

"But…we don't have a pool," Ace points out. I tsk, slipping out of their holds, and make my way towards the stairs. Angus is right by my ankle, sharing my devious smile.

"One of us does," I shrug, getting ready to dart away to get ready. "He just isn't here yet."

JASPER

Planting my sneakers on the countertop, the teenage assistant yawns widely. Ginger hair is plaited into long French braids; both sides of her freckled face wobble as she chews a piece of gum between thick, metal braces. Taking one look at the Nikes that aren't usually my style, she carries them out back and returns with a pair of striped bowling shoes.

"Have you booked a lane?" she shouts in a nasally tone over the booming music of the bowling alley.

"No need. My party's already started without me." Peering over my shoulder, I spot my lookalike lining up with a teal-colored ball. Pussy lightweight choice. Skidding the ball down the polished maple wood, it veers left and slams into the gutter. I smirk to myself, slipping the shoes on beneath the matching dark denim jeans he's wearing. It wasn't hard to mimic his entire outfit since I stalked him and his side chick around a range of designer outlets all morning. He only bought one polo top, these ridiculously priced jeans, and the Nikey's. Someone else may have questioned their sanity around the $400 mark, but no fun ever came from sitting at home, and this is sure to be fun.

Frustrated with his terrible aim, Jack scuffs up his hair, tugging at the blonde ends. Kissing his date on the cheek, he excuses himself, and I duck my face behind an arcade machine until he's passed. Heading towards the bar, I edge around a party of middle-aged women and make a beeline for the lane. The woman with vibrant red hair, a floral blouse, and the tightest skinny jeans hugging her long legs bends over to collect her ball of choice. Striding towards the bold, black line printed in the wood flooring, I slip in behind her, purposely looking over her right shoulder, so she doesn't see the damn scar on my opposite cheek.

"Back so soon?" she giggles, pressing her ass back into my crotch. Smirking her way to showcase a dimple, I momentarily pause at the face beaming back at me. Large, chocolate brown eyes. Slight upturn to her nose. The faintest specks of freckles in the flashing disco lights. She's the image of Candy. Right down to the red piece of gum visible between her teeth, framed by red lipstick to match her hair color. A real chuckle escapes me this time as I hold her hand around the ball and tilt her hips ever so slightly, taking aim and bowling directly down the center of the lane. The pins ricochet in all directions, earning her first strike of the night.

"I couldn't stay away," I mutter in answer to her question. Leaning her cheek into me, I inhale the pomegranate scent clinging to her skin. She even smells like Candy. A harsh shout behind gives me a second's warning to release the clone before Jack rams into the side of me. Slamming me into a pillar, he lands a punch in my mouth, and I instantly taste blood.

"Temper, temper," I laugh, shoving back at his chest. Many of the people bowling nearby and even some assistants from behind the counter have frozen at our display, unsure of what to do. I wave them off, slinging an arm over my brother and walking him back to his confused date. "Your date bears quite the resemblance to someone else we're both rather familiar with. Seems like you've found yourself a clone, little brother." I chuckle into Jack's ear. He nudges me away from him, standing between his date and me.

"We're the same age, cunt-features."

"I was born first; I'm older," I wave my hand in the air. Jack's lady friend clings to his back, assessing me in the colored lighting. She takes a particular interest in my scar before frowning at the way I'm dressed. I pull at the polo collar, wishing I could have kept up the rouse a little longer after going through all this effort. What's the point of even having an identical twin if I can't impersonate him once in a while? "Well, Jack, don't be rude. Introduce me to your date."

"I'm Cherry-" she extends her hand around Jack, and he quickly takes hold of her forearm to wind it around his body instead.

"Don't bother; he's not staying." I take in the scene with a heavy dose of amusement. The way Jack is clinging onto the pretense that he really feels for this woman, or how she's pretending not to notice the hostility between us. Their living in a bubble of their own fiction, one that won't withstand bursting as soon as a particular pink-haired psycho gets her claws into it. But I'll let them keep up their façade, for now.

"Is it so bad I wanted to join in with you? A little sibling rivalry is healthy," I smirk. Jack's temper flares, but his grip on Cherry's hand loosens, and she mistakes that for acceptance. Clapping excitedly and whispering in Jack's ear she'll be right back; Cherry heads off to the main reception. Sweet of her to think I was referring to their game, as the board resets with my name included. I suppose Jack has already filled her in on my existence, and here I was thinking he was trying to forget about me.

"Ladies first," I call with a flourish on my hand. Cherry's chest bobs wildly as she skips back, her floral blouse barely concealing a deep-set cleavage. Amazing body, bubbly personality, a beaming smile. In any other world, she probably would be perfect for Jack, or hell, any of us. But we've had our taste of Candy, and I've no doubt, like me, Jack has developed quite the sweet tooth. Taking her ball in hand, Cherry restarts the game as I fall back into the safety zone.

"So..." I say when Jack moves close enough. "Daytime date, huh? Serious stuff." My twin rolls his eyes, favoring weighing up different balls rather than answering me. There's only one way Jack will warm up to me when he's in this mood, and it'll have to be alcohol-induced. Slipping to the bar, I grab a round of drinks and return just as he balls another gutter ball, never one to learn his lesson the first time around. Putting a beer in his hand, I scoop up an indigo ball from the roller and plant myself in front of the black line: Aim central, slight turn to the right, power from the shoulder. The ball glides over the wood, crashing into the pins and earning me a single split on either side. Damn it.

"Smooth talk your way out of that one," Jack smirks, lifting his bottle in the air. See, alcohol and a touch of failure on my part work every time. I go for the left side, tossing a ball down the lane without watching for the end result. The crack of impact reaches my ears as I drink my own beer, and Cherry high-fives me on her way past.

"Okay, I'll give it to you," I join Jack on the bench and swing my arm over his shoulder. He does not like that. "She seems pretty cool." He doesn't like that even more. Bristling, Jack's chest puffs out, and his grip tightens on the glass bottle in his hands. "Relax, baby bro," I mock, slapping his thigh. "I'm not interested in your date. But you can't deny the resemblance to Candy. Take it from me, no matter how much you want to, replacing her isn't going to work." Slumping back, Jack sighs. It's his turn, but Cherry announces she's popping to the bathroom, so he remains by my side a little longer.

"Candy is just…some fricking weirdo that crashed into the bar and never left. She means nothing to me."

"You can lie to yourself, but you can't lie to me," I grin, tapping my temple. Twin telepathy is real, and my instincts are blaring with everything Jack is trying to hide. "Some fricking weirdo wouldn't have managed to unite a completely shattered family bond in a matter of weeks. I was hellbent on destroying the Monarchs because I didn't see a future where we could all be together again. I thought once we were free, me and you could hit the road again, find our place in the world." I pause to drink, kissing that dream goodbye with my next words.

"But while I was impersonating you, I saw something I wouldn't have believed if I didn't witness it myself. She was breaking Malik's control, remedying Ace's demons, and easing Spade's constant foul mood. All without even trying. She's something special, Jack, and I think you at least should be there to benefit from it."

"Seriously? After you were intent on breaking us all up, you're suggesting I go straight back?" Just then, my phone vibrates in the jeans pocket. I pull it out as Cherry returns, reminding Jack to take his turn. I smirk, watching him comply like a whipped puppy, and peer at my phone's screen. 'Motion detected,' the notification reads. I frown, sitting upright. Leicester's surveillance system around the mansion was seriously outdated, so I had new cameras installed for as long as I'm staying there and linking it to my cell. Unlocking the screen, the trepidation building in my chest flees, and my eyebrows hit my hairline.

Who else would I find strolling around the backyard than Candy herself, heading directly for the pool. A tiny bathing suit that might as well not exist just about covers her breasts. The rest of it gapes around her sides, tying at the back while the thong bottom-half dips into the valley of her perfect ass. My cock twitches at just the memory of what I did to that ass, how she clenched around me and screamed like we were performing an exorcism. Fuck.

Trailing just behind, Ace is carrying a huge, inflatable lounger while Spade shoulders a bag bursting with towels. For a moment, I simply watched in curiosity at what they're up to. Spade sets down the bag on a tabletop, riffling through it. His hair is braided back into a ponytail that trails the length of his bronzed, bareback. Like Ace, he's wearing a pair of bright boardie shorts, which must be Candy's choice, and sneakers that he kicks off in favor for the sliders he pulls out of his bag. Smart - can't ride the bikes in sliders.

Spade lifts his foot to push into the slider when Ace, on Candy's orders, barrels into his side. The pair fly into the pool together, splashing and fighting for the upper hands. Flashes of teeth and boyish smiles pierce through the grainy surveillance cam, spearing my chest with a unusual feeling. One I felt while Ace and I were playing hide and seek with Candy in the play area. Hope, joy, unity. A mix of all three perhaps. Amongst the chaos, Candy eases the neon pink lounger into the water and lowers herself. A pair of heart sunglasses I vaguely recognize shield her eyes from the sun as she drifts across the pool, kicking Ace and Spade away when they go for her ankles. I can practically hear their laughter buzzing around my mind, drowning out the bowling alley speakers.

"Hey," Jack kicks my shoe. "You playing this thing or what?" I look up at the scoreboard, seeing Jack is still on zero and is offering me a turn for his own gain. Standing, I glance to my phone and back, finding that crashing Jack's date has lost its appeal. Cherry appears at my brother's side, sipping on a J20 and curling her hand into his.

"I have a better idea," I smile so widely it tugs on my scar. Flashing my screen at Jack, his brow furrows, and I already sense his head shake before it happens. "This is where I'm staying for now, until I figure out what to do with myself. You can stay there too if you like, it beats living out of a hotel." Cherry's eyes widen, whether from the sight of Candy on the screen or my knowledge of their living arrangements; I'm not sure. Jack also gives her a half shrug, knowing I make it my business to keep track, but she begins to ask the question anyway.

"How did you-"

"It doesn't matter. Jack, can we...talk in private for a moment?" The earnest in my eyes must persuade him to detach the woman hanging onto his arm and tell her to give us a minute. Cherry nods with an understanding smile, finding a ball to take my turn. Goodbye, high score. Taking Jack aside, he shrugs my arm away but stays close to hear what I have to say. It's a start. "I've been waiting to speak to all of you without Malik lingering around. This is my chance. What do you say we make this gate crash into a real party? Light up the BBQ, drink and soak up the sun like old times. I...kinda need this Jacky boy." I bob my brows, putting on all my charm until he relents.

"Fine. But Cherry's coming with us." My eyes slide to the redhead who's continuing to take turn after turn, bowling each ball as if we're not conspiring behind her. Jack's serious about including this girl in all aspects of his life, even the ones that will put her in danger.

"On your head be it," I sigh, although a selfish part of me perks up at the idea. Cherry seems nice enough, and I'm sure she means well, but seeing Candy in action is a sight to behold. Semi-stable Candy, who holds all the cards, is one thing, but intuition tells me in full crazed mode, she's magnificent. Sorry to sacrifice you, Cherry, but this, I've got to see.

CANDY

The click of high heels shatters through the daze of sunbathing. The pink lounger beneath me wobbles on the surface of the water, and I tilt down the heart-framed sunglasses I found in Tanya's room. I was doing her a favor; they're not her style unless she's trying a little too hard to be me. Standing side by side, the twins would be identical if it weren't for the scar claiming the side of Jasper's face. They place down carrier bags on the glass table, and Jasper turns his focus on lighting the BBQ, falling back into place within the group as if he never left. Jack winds his arm around the waist of a tall bimbo with tomato red hair, easing her in our direction.

"Jack!" Ace pipes up first, diving under the surface and swimming beneath my inflatable. He comes up too prematurely, knocking me aside, and I take a dive of my own, cocktail glass and all. I swim over to the ladder, clinging onto one of the rungs in favor of staying beneath the water for as long as I can. Seems like the safest option when my fingers are itching to snap some necks. Whether Jack is a double-crossing douche canoe or not, I sort of, an itty bitty tiny bit care about him, and his death would be a shame.

There's so much life left in that tongue of his one that I've laid claim to in my mind so it's a done deal. He's mine.

My lungs begin to burn, and I relish it. Anything beats going up there. A flash of pink wriggles into view, and I glare at Angus. He's fashioned his gummy feet into a mermaid's tail and is wearing the heart sunglasses over his chest like a bra. Rolling his body like a fish, he grins and pulls a sign out of his ass with 'Jealous' written across in black marker. I scream an underwater curse at him, causing precious bubbles to escape my mouth. Diving forward, I snatch my glasses back and then kick my way up to the surface. I'm having some serious second thoughts about the promise thirteen-year-old me made to always keep him around.

Back in the world of the dry, Jasper has managed to get the fire going already, and the rest are all crowding around Jack's uninvited guest. How fucking dare he anyway; this was my surprise takeover party. One that was supposed to end in a four-way by the pool when Jasper returned home to find us already slippery and wet. I never agreed to whatever gang-bang porno that is about to take place here, not if I'm sharing the spotlight at least.

Using the side, I drag myself out of the water and pace away across the green. No one notices or calls to me, so I slip into the garage. For some reason, despite my knack for always doing the opposite, of what I was told, Big Cheese entrusted me with his secret hideouts. More importantly, with ways to protect myself if his mansion was ever under attack. Well, my pride is under attack, and I can practically hear his voice telling me that's the same thing.

Opening the fake fuse box, I locate the black button that will allow the whole unit to pop off the wall. A keypad sits behind it, the passcode my fake birthday, and inside the hole in the wall, I pull out my favorite weapon —an archer's bow. I've been waiting for the day Cheese wouldn't be around so I can use the silver-tipped arrows on something bigger than pesky pigeons. Withdrawing the arrow bag, I sling it across my back. The strap cuts through my cleavage in the tiny, pink swimsuit while my hair drips a puddle around my feet. Placing the bow on the hood of the

Lamborghini, I wipe my hands over the seats in an effort to dry them for a better grip. Then, with a steady exhale, I emerge with my bow primed with its first arrow.

Closing one eye, I watch for the moment Cherry's forehead comes into view. She's laughing at something; her red lips stretched wide of gleaming white teeth. Her hair is an offensive shade of tomato red, and I have to wonder if the blood will even be visible once it seeps into her hairline. At the very least, I want access to enough to draw two bloodlines on either side of my cheeks, so I tilt my bow downwards and line it up with her eye instead. Syncing with the rhythmic pound of my heartbeat in my ears, I pace myself for the moment she looks my way, draw the bowstring back and release the arrow.

It sails through the air with a whistle as I take a step back to assess my good work. Right up to the point, Spade steps in to pass Cherry a hot dog, and the arrow spears his shoulder. Shit.

"Ahhh!" he screams from across the yard. I quickly toss the bow and arrow into the garage, slamming the door shut. All eyes turn my way, and I look around, holding my hand over my eyes in search of the shooter. It's no use, though, as Jack bellows my name, and I trek over with stomping footsteps. Spade is kneeling on the ground; his fists braced on the ground. Ace stands over him, counting down from three when he snaps the length of the arrow so just a little more than the head is embedded in his skin. Kneeling down, I slap Spade on his other shoulder, and he grunts in pain.

"How you enjoying that adventure you wanted?" I smirk. His blue eyes flash my way with fury and a trace of misery.

"Why's it always me?!" he whimpers, and despite the big, tough guy routine, he flops down into my lap for a hug. Running my fingers through the lines between his braids, I block out Cherry's panicked voice, offering to call an ambulance.

"Don't worry about it, love," Jack tells her, and I see red all over again. "Ace is fetching his bike to take Spade to the ER. Meanwhile, we can eat, and then how about a few rounds of strip poker?"

"Oooh, I love a bit of strip poker," Jasper joins Cherry's other side. "Not usually with my brother, though." Their shadows block the sunlight from my eyes, and as I glance up, I'm sure there's a sly smirk on Cherry's face. She planned this. I don't know how or why, but she knew I'd act out and surrounded herself with my men as a contingency. Wheels skid around the corner of the mansion, screeching over the paving slabs and leaving thick tire marks in its wake. Ace hops off his bike, rushing over to ease Spade up.

"I called Malik," he announces, and we all freeze. Shit, Malik isn't going to be happy I went all Happy Gilmore with a bow and arrow at a pool party, and he's totally right, of course. If I wasn't being dramatic, I'd have grabbed the handgun from the Lambo's glove compartment and just shot the bitch. Oblivious to the held breaths around him, including Jasper's, Ace continues. "A private practitioner owes him a favor. Spade will be seen straight away and home by dinner. You're okay making your own way back, right?" Ace questions me while Spade swings his leg over the bike.

"Is that a joke?" I raise an eyebrow. I know he's only living up to his promise to be on 'Candy duty', but I'm a fully grown woman. A clingy one when I've found a decent place to stay, so obviously, I can find my own way back unaccompanied. Satisfied, Ace climbs onto the bike behind Spade, both in just swim shorts and sneakers and carefully revs the engine without touching his friend's shoulder.

"Well, that was different. Oddly exciting, though. I don't think we've properly met - I'm Cherry," the redhead holds out her hand to me once the bike's sped off. Taking a step forward, putting us eye to eye, I scan her face closely for the first time. There's a slight upturn to the tip of her nose, a faint smattering of freckles. Her eyes are the same velvety brown as mine beneath thick lashes and defined brows. The red waves framing her face fall just past her shoulders, where illustrative tattoos pattern her arms. As she waits for my reply, I see a wad of red gum pass between her teeth. Hell fucking no.

"Candy," I roughly take her hand at an awkward angle between us. With a sharp tug, Cherry is yanked chest to chest with me, close enough for my lips to graze her cheek as I speak. "You've picked the wrong family to fuck with. I promise next time; no one will be around to take the arrow, bullet, or even cheese knife I throw in your direction." With that, I shove her backward so hard Cherry stumbles on her ridiculous heels and trips into the swimming pool with a huge splash.

Jack barrels forward and dives into the water to be her personal lifeguard, and Jasper grabs me from behind. Not in anger, but to protect me from Jack when he's finished rewriting the ending of Titanic. Using my pink inflatable as his aid, Jack eases Cherry on top and swims her back towards the edge. All the while, Angus jumps up and down across the pool in a skimpy cheerleading outfit, pom-poms and all, spelling out letters with his stubby arms.

'J-E-A-L-'

I twist in the arms holding me, turning my back on Angus' chant, but Jasper mistakes my action for needing a hug. I don't resist as he starts to stroke my hair though, and when he reaches into his pocket to produce a cube of pink bubblegum, I almost squeal. Unwrapping and popping it into my mouth, Jasper pulls me over to the bench seat, not breaking our hold as we lower down on a sigh. Against the cotton of his white vest, his heart beats a steady rhythm whilst Jasper gently whispers into my ear.

"Jack's just acting out. Let him get it out of his system; then he'll realize he's just as crazy about you as the rest of us." Tilting my head upwards, Jasper's green eyes hold enough sincerity to banish most of the murderous thoughts from my mind. I can't respond through the wad of gum I've chewed on so furiously it's become a sugary gum shield. Damn *Cherry*. Who the fuck is Cherry anyway?! A whore? A gold digger? An assassin? All I know is I immediately hate her. The scowl is back in full force as I spot Jack cradling her in a towel by the edge of the pool. Again, something Jasper mistakes for a sense of insecurity.

"Ahh," Jasper chuckles lightly, brushing my hair behind my ear. "I can see you don't believe me. Well, I'm going to say it one more time because I reckon you haven't been told this enough, but afterward I'll let my actions do all the talking. I'm fucking psycho for you, Crazy Girl." An uncomfortable feeling surges to life in the pit of my stomach, working its way to my chest. I've heard people describe it as butterflies, but my mind conjures an image of razor-blade wings slicing me up from the inside. Either way, I wind my arms around Jasper's body and rest my head on his shoulder for a while. The coughing and spluttering from behind is music to my ears. Along with the smell of food cooking on the BBQ, this is about as romantic as it gets for a girl like me.

"I think you need to work on controlling your temper there, sugar," Cherry half-chokes, staggering on one heel nearby, and the razor-tipped cutterflies die a sudden death.

I feel Jasper's hold tense around me, although it's too late. If this bitch wants to see my temper, she'd better have her gravestone picked out. Launching myself in her direction, Jack and Jasper try to act as our shields, but it's no use as my fist connects with Cherry's temple. Ironically, it turns out Spade was right after all; today is a good day to be alive.

SPADE

Shattered shoulder blade. Six weeks to heal. A stupid sling and a physiotherapy course to attend. Once again, I'm rendered useless in the face of an attack. Not that we're expecting any, now that Leicester is dead, but one can never be too careful. My non-strapped arm is slung over Malik's shoulder as he walks me through our back door. I told him back at the medical practice, when he insisted on being present, I can walk just fine on my own, but he insisted. Probably a sense of delayed guilt or unfulfilled need to take care of us all.

Easing me into the chair of our poker table, both he and Ace fuss over making me a drink and taking off my shoes, but I wave them away.

"Seriously, I'm fine. I'm just going to sit here until I know Candy is back safe, then I'll go to bed." Malik's eyes darken the way they did when he found out we'd left Candy at her old boss' mansion with Jasper, Jack, and his new arm-piece. I'm not sure which one was the deciding factor that got his temple vein pulsing, but I can hazard a guess. Candy told me Jasper would come running once we triggered the alarms to the house, but I wasn't expecting him to be so at ease. It was hard to take my eyes off him, manning the BBQ, drinking a beer, smiling at the sight of us together like one big happy family.

The back door crashes open beyond my view, the sounds of a struggle filling the kitchen next door. Instead of running to help, Ace's mouth drops open, and Malik simply pulls out a chair for Jack to manhandle Candy into. Her body is bound with a lengthy hose pipe, and there's a black strip of tape covering her mouth. Throwing her down into Malik's provided chair, Jack ushers Cherry through the room and into the elevator, giving us all a pointed look as the doors slide closed with her inside.

"What did you do?" Malik sighs, ripping the tape off Candy's mouth. Ace tackles her restraints, freeing her arm enough to wipe the redness now covering her lower face.

"You don't have to sound so disappointed," Candy groans. "I may have daddy issues, but I'm not a kid."

"Then stop acting like one," Malik snaps. It might be the meds I'm on, but I swear a coldness sweeps through the room, emanating from the icy stare on Candy's face. She doesn't speak, which is even worse for someone who never usually keeps her mouth closed. Finding herself freed of the hose, Candy stands calmly and reaches up to tie her wavy hair into a high ponytail. I share a one-shouldered shrug with Ace, as worried as I am intrigued about what's coming next. Securing her hair tightly, Candy spins around for her ponytail to whip Malik across the face.

"Childish enough for you?" she glares back at him. Whatever Malik was going to say is cut off by the heavy footsteps running down the stairs, and Jack appears. Someone pass the popcorn; this is about to get good.

"Yeah, thanks for your help, guys," Jack drawls, barging his way into the center of the room. "Jasper was about as much help as a chocolate teapot, and I couldn't leave this one," he sticks a thumb in Candy's direction, "unattended long enough to get Cherry back to the hotel. No doubt if she saw the location, I'd be seeing a new arson report on the news by morning."

"I thought I said stay out of trouble," Malik says with a tight jaw. Ace wisely sidesteps away from the stare-down between Candy and the pair of dickheads approaching this all wrong. He slides into the seat beside me; his knuckles clenched on his thigh.

"Look," Jack huffs, circling around the back of Candy's chair. "I get it must be hard coming to terms with the fact you mean nothing to me, but tackling Cherry down and the mud fight was truly unnecessary." He leans over her shoulder to toy with a strand of her hair, narrowly avoiding the backward head butt Candy throws his way.

"She smirked at me," Candy grimaces. Must have been one hell of a smirk.

"You shouted 'it's Britney Bitch' whilst trying to drown her in the soil." Jack retorts, re-joining Malik's side. The boss himself may appear impassive, but there's a deep-rooted look in his eyes that says he's plain disappointed.

"You might not see it right now, but I happen to pride myself on my intuition," Candy starts until Jack cuts her off with a spiteful laugh.

"That's a joke, right? You have the worst intuition I've ever known. The world around you is all cupcakes and rainbows, where you think leprechauns play, and your actions don't have consequences. What you are is damn lucky you haven't wound up dead already."

"That's just ridiculous," Candy tuts, popping out her hip. "Leprechauns don't have time to play; they work damn hard making shoes, protecting their treasure, and granting wishes."

"I don't have the time or patience for this," Jack groans, pacing away. He sweeps a hand over his hair, mimicking what Jasper would do in the same situation. Once this is dealt with, I need to have a chat with Malik about Jasper. Even Ace seemed comfortable in his company, and he's a tough nut to crack.

"Okay real talk," Candy holds up her hands. "My intuition might not always be on point, but right now - that bitch is tingling like a hippy with crabs. She's up to something, and no good can come of having her here. She *smirked* at me." Candy catches my eye, silently begging me to believe her.

"Yet, Jack is a Monarch, and I vowed to bring my men home," Malik steps forward to take Candy's hands in his. I wince, preparing myself for her snapping his wrists, but it doesn't come. "I promised there would be no more rules, which includes only sharing you. If Jack likes Cherry, then we all need to get on board - for the sake of our family." Behind Malik's back, the tension eases from Jack's shoulders, and he looks curiously in our direction. I nod, along with Ace, showing our support. I may not like it, but I see what Malik is trying to do here.

He promised things would change, and since he ordered the only girl we could be with is Candy, that rule has to drop too. Ace, Malik, and I no doubt will continue to for personal reasons, but I understand Jack wants to branch out. He and Jasper were the youngest of us when they were brought here, and while Jasper's been doing whatever or whoever he wants for the past few years, Jack's been left to stew. He needs a chance to live a life of his choice, even though I reckon he'll come back around to our way in the end.

After placing a light kiss on Candy's forehead, Malik gestures for Jack to join him in the bar so they can talk in private. Just before the door shuts between the two sections of the building, Malik stops to address Candy's stoic back.

"For the record, from what I understand, you've been reconnecting with Jasper as well. The next time you see him, you can pass on from me that our door is open. It's time all of the Monarchs returned home." The door closes, and my brothers make their way around the bar through the two-sided mirror. We, however, sit in stunned silence.

"Okay, 'fess up.' Did he have a brain transplant while we were away?" I ask Candy, pathetically trying to lighten the mood. It's impossible Malik has altered himself so much in such a short space of time, so how he's venting his frustrations in other ways is anyone's guess. Deep down, he's still the boy that lost his parents and built an empire from nothing. Bruce Wayne, eat your heart out.

Sighing, I push myself to my feet and wobble slightly — damn meds. Ace is there to steady me, and together, we make our way over to Candy, where she still stands stock still. Her breathing is a little too steady as if she's fighting against the urge to lash out and break every piece of furniture nearby.

"Hey," Ace says first. Reaching up, he gently eases the band from Candy's hair, letting the pink locks fall around her shoulders. "What's going on with you?" Candy's unfocused eyes slide to us, blinking away the daze as she realizes we're right in front of her.

"So that's it," Candy says quietly. "She's staying." I've never seen Candy rattled. Not when she's being shot at, chased, hunted. Not once. But this situation has burrowed its way beneath her skin and drawn out a side to her I need to work out how to handle. Surely it's not all because Jack doesn't want to join in the harem she's creating. But at this stage, I have no evidence to go by that Cherry has an ulterior motive. Sliding her brown eyes to my worried look, her shoulders sag. "I don't....play well with others."

"Come on gorgeous; Doc says I need to rest, and I can only do that knowing where you are. Stay with me tonight?" I ask. Candy glances at my sling, noticing my injury for the first time since I left the mansion. Frowning, her fingers trail over the knot on my shoulder, and she looks at me thoughtfully.

"Hmmm, if you insist, that's best for your recovery. No hanky panky, though. You need to rest." A slow, mocking grin appears on her face, and Ace chuckles beneath his breath.

"Woah, hold up, menacing Cupid. My shoulder took your arrow, not my dick. And you owe me for that stunt, big time." Ace laughs, but I'm deadly serious. I'm at least getting a blowjob for this. Linking her fingers in my free hand, Candy leads me up the stairs with Ace at my back in case I fall. Reaching the second floor, he bids us both goodnight, but Candy is quick to grab his wrist, halting him in place.

"Erm, who excused you? Spade wants some action, but he's not fit to take part. Live porno it is," she grins, forcing Ace to skip down the hall with her to my room. "You coming hot stuff?" Candy calls back when I remain in place with my jaw slack.

"Apparently not," I grumble, dragging my feet after them. I suppose a show is better than nothing, I tell myself, flexing my left hand to warm it up. Looks like an awkward jerk off it is.

CANDY

Wiping down the bar, I toss my damp rag into the trash can. Leaning my cheek on my fist, I sigh, watching the rest of the staff set up for opening. I've been down here keeping busy since sunrise, scraping gum off the underside of the tables, replenishing the bar snacks. The staff have been side-eyeing me since they arrived, but as I warned them, the first person that calls me domesticated will find the bar messed up again, with their blood coating every surface and their organs hanging from the lights. I'm not doing this shit out of goodwill, but rather as a way to keep busy. Bumping into Cherry will only end up bad for her, and I don't want to strain Malik and Jack's freshly mended relationship. Ugh, it's true. I am fucking domesticated.

"Ay yo Candy," Nick pops his head around the connecting door. Floppy brown hair jostles above matching colored eyes. His skin is a little too tanned to match Ace's, not that anyone looks too closely. I purse my lips, waiting for him to say whatever has got him bouncing on his toes, looking towards the kitchen. "There's a package outback you need to sign for."

"Ooh, saucy. I hope he's hot." I slide from the barstool, a refreshed skip in my step. Passing through the bottom level and into the kitchen, I spot a blacked-out car through the window. He has parked over three spaces with the driver's side window left open —Dick move. Unfortunately, my package is the opposite of hot. One yellow eye glares at me through the metal mesh of a cage being shoved in my face, his wrinkly rolls of skin making me cringe.

"Miss Crystal?" The delivery man holding the cat carrier asks. "I'm sorry to have to inform you, but Pearl Smithers - your landlady - has died. In her last will and testament, she decided to leave her beloved Sphinx to you."

"That fucking whore bag!" I shout, and the slick blonde man in front of me goes pale. Now that I'm looking at him properly, I haven't seen many delivery dudes suited and booted with official lanyards on. Weird.

"Sh-she was 87 years old," he stutters. I raise a brow, looking down at fancy his clipboard.

"And? You don't think 87-year-olds can be whore bags? You clearly haven't been to a care home for ex-Naked Tease employees then. All the stewards take care of is screwing the patients. I've already booked my mom's place for when she retires from the strip club with all her whorey friends." The man's eyes have gone freakishly wide now, and he looks around for assistance. Groaning, I grab the carrier from his grip and narrow my eyes. "What you waiting for, a medal? You made your delivery, off you fuck."

Slamming the door in his face, I wait until the delivery guy has returned to his car and driven away before opening it back up again to stand on the back step. Shaking a fist in the air, I yell towards the sky.

"I bet you're having a great laugh at my expense, you old bat!! Jokes on you because I'm going to put your cat in a fucking stew!" Sphinx starts banging around in his cage, making a weird mewing sound as if he's possessed. Oh, that's just my shitty luck. I'm here shouting at the sky when bitch-face Smither's spirit is in the damn cat. Holding the cage up, Sphinx hisses at me, and I hiss right back.

"We'll see who's laughing when the coyotes have had their way with you."

Placing the cage down on the back step, I pop the latch and shake the hairless creature out. He looks up at me with a one-eyed spiteful stare, and I shove him down the steps with my boot. "Go on, get lost." Without waiting, I stride back towards the stairwell and pause. Puffing out my cheeks, I flail my arms and spin around again. What am I supposed to do with myself? If I go upstairs, I'll no doubt bump into Cherry; then I'll lash out for the squealy sex noises I had to listen to last night. She knew I could hear through the adjoining bathroom, and yet, she taunted me even so. That's practically permission to remove her voice box in itself.

Instead, I make the smart choice for once. I walk away. Within an instant, a flash of a shadow curls around my sneakers before I trip over Sphinx. We hiss at each other as I open the connecting door to the bar, shoving him out of the way.

"Awww," Cherry coos, and my stomach rolls. I literally can't catch a break this morning. Her red hair is tied in a messy bun, and, like me, she's kitted out in lycra workout gear. The only difference is I dressed this way for the attention, not the chance to burn calories. Hopping down from the barstool I'd recently occupied, she makes her way around the bar to get a better look at my inherited burden. "You got a puddy tat." Bending over, a string of kissy noises follow in a bid to get Sphinx's attention. Weirdo.

"Don't get too attached; I'm going to make him into a katsu curry," I snort, drawing a shocked look from her brown eyes. "Get it? Cat-su." My hysteria doubles until I'm bending over, holding myself up with my hands on my knees. Cherry ignores me, edging closer in an attempt to stroke the feline version of a mangled penis. Sphinx makes a screeching sound I'm pretty sure cats shouldn't be able to make, arching his back and remaining close to my ankles.

"Huh," I wipe the tears from my eyes. Scooping him up, Sphinx flails and tries to bite my hand until he's in the cradle of my arms. "Actually, he seems like a pretty good judge of character. Maybe he'll have his uses." We lock eyes, well mine with his yellow one, a moment of understanding passing between us when he screeches again.

"But..." Cherry stands, seeming confused. "He hissed at you too?"

"Exactly. Amazing judge of character," I nod. Setting Sphinx on the bar top, I slip behind and pour myself a tequila. Knocking it back in one, I welcome the burn as Cherry slowly eases herself back onto the stool opposite. First, a backhanded inheritance and now a chit-chat with the whore banging my fourth Monarch. The fates must be against me today, and to think, I've been doing karma's work for years. You'd reckon she'd sway in my favor once in a while.

Cherry doesn't speak while I pour another shot, just watches me carefully with judgey eyes. She must want something, or she'd still be in the safety of Jack's suspended bed. Blowing out a harsh breath, I drop my hands onto the bar and lean over to address her face to face. "What are you doing down here?" Cherry shifts back, crossing her fingers in her lap and pulling a tight smile.

"I think we got off to the wrong start. I didn't even get to introduce myself properly, so I thought maybe I could join you on your jog." Frowning from Cherry's lycra vest to my crop top, she mistakes my expression for confusion instead of the insult that I would waste my time jogging. "I saw you in your sportswear through the adjoining bathroom doors and figured it would be a chance to get to know you and the area. Jack warned me to stay away, but what he doesn't know won't hurt him," she winks at me. *Winks. At. Me.*

"Here's what I just heard," I say, climbing up on the bar top. Sitting on my knees, I hover so far over Cherry; she has to grip the bar to stop from toppling backward. "You spied on me in my personal space, snuck out so you can survey the area in a bid to get me alone and take your revenge for shooting at you. After which, you'll dispose of my body on some hidden, dirt track." On a gasp, Cherry hops down and takes a few steps away.

"Is it possible I just want to be your friend? You're a part of

Jack's life, and now so am I. We should try to get along." The bar staff in the background have paused setting up, watching carefully for what I might do next. Grimacing, I set back on my heels.

"Friends are for those who want to be betrayed. They're not trustworthy."

"Friends, or females in general?" Cherry quirks a brow. She bravely takes a step forward, her hands raised. I don't give her question much thought as she nears close enough for me to bat her hands away. I'm not some raging bull that can be tamed with a simple gesture. "You have no problem trusting the men around here."

"Men are fickle," I snort. "They're under the spell of my body, and I've claimed them. *All* of them," I put emphasis on the 'all' as an open threat. Cherry drops her hands, slapping them on her thighs with a sigh.

"Look, I've tried to make amends, even though the issue is all in your head. Jack was right; you're not open to being reasoned with." Grabbing the bottle of tequila, she strides away with her head held high and a satisfied grin on her face. Pausing in the doorway, she stops abruptly with one bony finger held in the air.

"Oh, and technically, you only have three Monarchs since Jack's mine, and the last one isn't even here. You should get used to being happy with what you have or prepare to watch your back." I sit on the bar long after she's trotted away. Ignoring the thinly-veiled threat I'm sure worked in high school, it kills me to say that she's right. Without all of the Monarchs here, I have no chance at officially getting them back together for good. Dropping down onto my feet, I make quick work of the stairs with only one thought in mind. I need to talk to Malik.

Ace

"Meeting in the games room," Candy swings her head around the doorjamb to my room. Her pink hair swishes over the one-shouldered black jumper she's donned. From the waist down, the baggy hem hangs over tightly fitted jeans with a pair of black Uggs on her feet. When I hesitate at the sight of her being so covered up, she pops her gum bubble in frustration. "Now, Ace! Get up!" I rise from my bed, having sat down after my morning shower and not gotten back up, following her into the hallway. Candy has already disappeared, although I can hear her snapping the same order at Spade next door.

I don't wait for the pair to join, although Candy is right behind me on the staircase as I descend. Her rushed shuffling footsteps urge me to move quicker, entering the games room in no time.

"Holy shit," I mutter under my breath, coming to an abrupt stop. Candy crashes into my back, peering around to see Jasper sitting at our poker table. Smirking at Jack across the other side, it almost feels like old times except for the red-headed lookalike hanging off Jack's every word. His green eyes slide my way, a question in his hitched eyebrow. It shouldn't be awkward being around him after we shared Candy so openly, even if I didn't get the chance to speak at the mansion before Spade took an arrow to the shoulder. But something about him being *here*, smiling like nothing's gone down, unnerves me.

And the surprises keep coming as Malik appears through the connecting door from the bar in a pair of designer jeans and a t-shirt. My eyes nearly pop out of my skull as I wonder if I truly woke up this morning or if I'm still asleep. Spade arrives by my side, wolf-whistling and causing Malik to blush.

"Don't you look…normal," Spade grins, using his free hand to smack Malik on the back. Jasper grunts in his throat, and we all shuffle around to take a seat. All except Malik, of course, who stands at the head of the table.

"Right. Now that everyone is here," his dark eyes slide to Jasper and promptly away again, "Time for business, so everyone listen up." A collective sigh rings out around the table. Here we go, back to bossing us around. I knew a change of clothes and a few weeks in Candy's company wouldn't be enough to change a person with issues as deep-rooted as Malik's. Candy leans back in her chair, planting her boots on the table. She shares a small smile with Malik before he carries on.

"Firstly, I want to address the most pressing issue—my apology. The actions I took were unreasonable, but it's not bringing us together that I'm truly sorry for. It's the way I treated Jasper. If only I'd listened or given you all the chance to choose for yourselves, so much heartache could have been avoided. Words aren't my forte, but I hope this is enough of a start until my actions prove the same."

No one speaks; no one moves. The air of change settles upon each of us, all eyes settling on Jasper for his response. His gaze is fixed in his lap, although the outstretch of his arm would suggest Candy's taken his hand beneath the table. For years, I never thought I'd see the day we all sat around this table again but fuck me; she's done it. In a few short weeks, this insane girl with a bad gum habit and no regard for her own life has bulldozed through our lives and reconnected us in ways I can't fathom. We're together because of her, and something tells me we'll be even stronger from here on out. We have an anchor now.

Sensing no one is going to speak, Malik clears his throat uncomfortably. From his back pocket, he withdraws a stack of cue cards and flicks through them. On my left, Spade's snort turns into a chuckle which sets us all off. Even Malik cracks a smile and tosses his cue cards onto the table.

"Fuck it, let's drink," he grins, heading for the sideboard. Returning with a stack of glasses and the delicate glass decanter of his fanciest red wine, I help in pouring and serving until we all have a filled glass in hand. Pulling up a chair, Malik finally sits down, cementing his place amongst us at long last. No hierarchy, just…brothers. Well, and the two females glaring daggers at one another. Candy swirls the red liquid in her glass menacingly, narrowing her eyes over the rim.

Raising my glass to my lips, movement out the corner of my eye doesn't register until something jumps in my lap, clawing at my dick. I spit out the wine, spraying an even layer of red over the ghost of a witch's cat sitting in my lap. It glares one yellow eye at me, hissing, and I shove it onto the floor. Landing with a thud, since it didn't even try to catch itself, Candy calls out the name Sphinx across the table and it obeys, disappearing from view.

"Come on then," Jack claps, oblivious of the mini seizure I just had. I don't like cats on the best of days, never mind a fugly naked one that looks like it's been run over by a truck. "Finish the speech. I'm sure you spent all night on it," he smirks, downing the contents of his glass.

"Well…yeah, I did, but it seems a bit pointless now," Malik half grumbles, but I don't miss the humor dancing across his dark eyes. He smooths his hair back neatly and tugs at his t-shirt, clearly missing the usual tie and collar he prefers.

"Alright then, I'll read it," Jack jumps up to grab for the cards. Malik dives forward, scuffling most of them his way but not before Jack swipes a few for himself. Twisting himself away from everyone's reach, Jack rounds the room behind my chair and puts on his best impression of Malik.

"From now on, we're a team, so where we go next has to be a group decision. In respect of us going straight, I've broken off all ties with the crime families who used to hire us regularly and buried any trace of evidence we've ever been anywhere we shouldn't. On paper, the bar is our sole income, and I'm happy to treat it as such. However, there could be a chance for expanding this venue or looking for a second site, but it is to be discussed another time. Together."

Jack finishes off strong, bowing when Candy applauds. Spade whoops, slapping his free hand on his thigh, and I can't fight my laugh. Malik doesn't seem all that impressed, his focus trained on a pensive-looking Jasper.

"See, here's the issue," Jasper leans forward, killing the jokey atmosphere as he links his fingers together on the felt-covered table. I glance to Spade with a look of dread at Jasper's next words. "When you called me last night, you didn't say anything about a *team*," he mocks.

I hang my head and blow out a breath, knowing this was all too easy to be true. It's a wonder his stubborn ass even came; never mind remained around this table long enough to reconnect and start again. I glance up just in time to see Malik's brow furrow, the devastation on his face clear for all to see. None of us are able to simply forgive and forget what Malik's done, but it's clear how hard our ex-leader is trying to change for us.

"No," Jasper shakes his head. "What you said was - we're a family. This bar isn't just a job but our legacy. Regardless of who's name, this building is listed under, we built this place from the ground up. We did the renovations, built the furniture, hung the stag's head over the mirror. And it was us who originally worked behind the bar when we first opened. This place is all of ours."

"So...that's it? You'll come home?" Jack asks, clearly not expecting Jasper to forgive Malik so easily. To forgive all of us so easily. Jasper nods slowly, his arm tensing from where he's holding Candy's hand beneath the table.

"I think I've been hurt enough, don't you?" The question goes unanswered for more reasons than one. Whereas Malik's damage was emotional, I was the one to physically hurt him, and I'll have to stare at the scar lining his cheek, feeling a personal wave of guilt every day from now on. Candy breaks into a smile first, throwing her arms around Jasper's neck and drawing him in for a quick kiss. His resulting grin is everything, easing the tension around the table in a split second. Well, I'll be damned. Jack walks over to his twin, pulling him up and throwing an arm over his shoulder.

"Welcome back, Jester," he smirks. Spade leans over the table, fist-pumping Jasper, and I do the same. There's no falter in his movement, accepting my look of apology with a simple nod. That's it; he's finally home. It's Malik's turn to stand, awkwardly making his way over to hold out his hand. Jasper smacks it away, pulling Malik into a bear hug.

"No more friction. It's time we get this family back on track for all of our sake's," Jasper raises his glass. A ripple of excitement passes through the room, a palpable giddiness of what's going to come next.

"So we're all in agreement then? The Devil's Bedpost is our sole business venture?" Collective nods are shared around the table, and Malik breaks into the biggest smile I've seen from him in years. "Ace, would you mind taking care of your hard drives? Delete anything illegal and withdraw us fully from the dark web." I double blink at the request, accustomed to orders being barked at me. Nodding, the tension visibly leaves Malik's shoulders, and he sighs in relief.

"Great. Good, okay then. Let's…get on with our days then. I need to get the fuck out of this homeless get-up and into something a little more rigid for a start," Malik grunts, giving Candy a side-eye glance. She giggles, stroking the front of his t-shirt over his chest. Bringing her hand to his lips, Malik kisses her gently before leaving and not looking back. The meeting is officially over, yet we linger, not fully sure what to do with ourselves.

Cherry hops up on an unnecessary pair of tall heels, trotting over to Jack in a tiny mini skirt and vest. Her red hair is wavier than usual and slick with product, her lips a vibrant red. Candy's smile is instantly replaced by a scowl, her eyes glued to Cherry's chest bobbing up and down in a push-up bra. I have to wonder how much impact Cherry's outfit choice had on Candy's new baggy sweatshirt and full-length jeans vibe today.

"How about you show me around, Jackikins? Particularly what's on the other side of the garage door," Cherry purrs, draping herself all over Jack. He nods reluctantly, seemingly not wanting to pull away from Jasper when he's so recently returned. Candy bristles, popping her hip and folding her arms.

"If your pet whore so much as breathes on my bike, I'll mount her lips on the seat so she can kiss my ass every time I ride it." Jack chokes on a laugh before he manages to cover it up.

"She's joking," he reassures Cherry. "But she's also a crazy bitch, so just don't go near her quad bike, and we'll be all good. I don't want to wake up to you with a shaven head," he half chuckles, but the fear in Cherry's face is real. Over Jack's shoulder, Candy mimes buzzing a razor over her own head, and Jasper swoops in to distract her.

"Come on, hot stuff. I reckon it's time I saw what pink version of hell you've unleashed in my old room," he says, coaxing her towards the stairs. Reaching the bottom step, Jasper pauses to look back at us all and smiles. "It's sure good to be home at last, boys," he winks, pulling Candy away. Jack makes a quick exit with Cherry as well, leaving Spade and me to sink into our chairs.

"Well, that was…different," Spade blows out a chuckle. I nod, having no better words myself. Through the two-way mirror, the bar has just opened for business, and a string of day drinkers have already arrived. To them, this place is just a hangout. Little do they know behind the glass, this is our home. Full of stress, arguments, and too much big dick energy for our own good, but our home nonetheless. Bumping Spade with the back of my hand, I jerk my chin towards the elevator.

"I'm gonna sort out those hard drives. Care to sit in with me for company?" Spade grunts a reply, rising to make his way to my room while I trail behind. Following the latest session of physiotherapy he shouldn't be doing yet, Spade still has to change out of his workout gear, never mind the overriding manly stench that implies he needs a shower, but I also don't want to be alone again. Especially not when I've been avoiding turning on my computer. Everything I did on there was to follow Malik's orders and unknowingly help cover up the secrets he held. But it's different this time; it has to be.

I find Spade already flopped on my bed by the time I enter, exactly where I knew he'd be. They all complain I have the most comfortable bed but never do anything to change their own. Especially Jack because he won't forfeit his hammock bed for anything. Switching on the computer, I head for my mini-fridge and grab out two cans of red bull. I didn't touch the wine Malik prefers, no matter what time of day it is. He could drink from morning through night and still not be affected.

Rounding back after giving Spade his can, I drop down into my seat with a heavy sigh. Typing in my password, I start on erasing the hard drives first. Spade hums a tune and soon is singing the entire Greatest Showman soundtrack from start to finish. I huff as if I hate it, but really, it's nice not to be sitting in silence. Now we can have some input in the bar; I might throw myself into a hobby. Try out blacksmithing or carpentry, maybe. That way, I can still vent any pent-up anger and see if I can use my hands for something worthwhile for a change.

Finishing with the hard drives, I toss them into the trash can and quickly jump into the dark web. It won't take long to find our old clientele and withdraw our services before deleting my user status for good. As soon as the window loads, a poster image I'm all too familiar with pops up in the center of the screen. I frown, closing it, but two more take its place. Again and again, the more I close, the more reappear until my own screen is filled with the image I can't avoid. After taking a look closer at the information underneath, I gasp in realization. Spade stops singing and sits up, looking over my shoulder and coming to the same conclusion.

"Shit. That's not good."

CANDY

"And then we slide the hatch back into place, and voila," Jasper whispers into the darkness. I reach my hands out, holding onto his crossed legs as he switches on a wall-mounted LED light. By wall-mounted, I mean on the opposite side of the wall to his/my bedroom. When he'd asked if I wanted to slide into his secret hole, this wasn't what I'd been expecting, but I'm pleasantly surprised. The hatch is hidden so well in the shadow of the dresser I hadn't spotted it until Jasper pried out the splinter of wood that concealed a keyhole. Now I'm looking around with the assisted lighting I realize we're in the hollowed-out space beneath the bathroom's basin area.

It's like every teenage boy's fantasy in here; posters of naked women on the walls, a stack of porn magazines, shelves to hold out-of-date snacks, and a power pack with multiple extensions. There's not heaps of space, but enough for Jasper to stretch his legs out and jerk off if that's what he really wanted to do. I imagine it was more for the escape from the stubborn dickheads outside, and I must admit, there's no better way to waste time than to masturbate.

"Why would you share your secret spot with me? Now you can never escape when I'm being unreasonable," I roll my eyes. That word is usually passed around by most people I meet, although I have to disagree. If Angus tells me to do it, then it must be reasonable because he's the epitome of sense.

"Who said I want to? You're a source of entertainment at the best of times." I shrug, taking the compliment. I don't care for what I am or what I'm not. At least I can say I did life my way and have no doubt in my mind that I'll go out with a bang. What else is there?

Carvings in the wood beneath the shelf catch my eye, and I run my finger over the grooves. Some are initials, some symbols for Spade and Ace, and sitting at the top, the crown of a king. Slipping my penknife out of my jeans pocket, I chisel a bigger and better crown on top of the one meant for Malik, complete with a diamond in the middle. I intended for it to look superior, but the way Jasper beams with a strange emotion brightening his face, I realize the double meaning. If Jack was labeled Jack Diamond, then Jasper must effectively bear the same given last name, and I've just staked my claim.

Putting my knife away, I sit back as comfortably as I can in these circulation-permitting jeans, narrowing my eyes at him. The first Monarch I met, although I didn't realize it at the time. The tie between Jasper and I was forged as soon as he entered me in the bus cargo hold, and I knew from then I wouldn't ever have enough. Angus mumbles that I'm a greedy bitch, and I nod, not bothering to deny it. Still, the way Jasper is looking at me does something weird to my chest, both lifting and bulldozing it at the same time. Unlike the well-rehearsed smiles or cunning smirks I've grown used to, Jasper's current grin is pure and tugs at his scar. Crawling forward, I stroke my thumb over the raised mark until he pulls my hand away to kiss my palm.

"Candy, I..." Jasper breathes and then shakes his head. A lump rises into my throat, along with a foreboding sense that I'm about to feel very uncomfortable. "I never could have seen you coming. You're special."

"Special needs maybe," I dodge.

"And funny," he continues.

"Funny looking, more like."

"And unique," he growls.

"Uniquely retarded. I can do this all day," I roll my eyes. Jasper's hand shoots out, grabbing the back of my neck and hailing me towards him.

"Listen to the words I'm actually saying, Miss Crystal. I wouldn't change a single thing about you." Crashing his mouth against mine, Jasper silences any more arguments I had at the ready. The truth is it's easier to deny how Jasper's words make the butterfly fuckery start in my gut or how the serenity in his eyes makes my pussy pulse with delight. At least when it eventually all goes to hell, I can say I kept the illusion of dignity and didn't give a shit anyway.

Slipping past my defences, Jasper's tongue enters my mouth. He kisses me hard and deep, with enough vigor to dislodge the gum I stashed between my teeth and cheek. Drawing it into his own mouth, Jasper pulls back, chewing loudly with a smirk. I crawl forward to straddle him, attempting to take my gum back the same way but Jasper ducks his face away. Blowing a large, pink bubble, he pops it in my face and chuckles.

"You have no idea how long I've wanted to do that." Picking out the gum with his fingers, Jasper then pushes it into a crevice in the woodwork. Ignoring my protests, my sweatshirt is pushed over my head, and Jasper gives me something else to focus on. His jaw goes slack at finding me bare underneath, my pebbled nipples a breath from his mouth. Taking one in between his fingers and the other in his mouth, I drop my head back on a long, blissful sigh.

Bang. Jasper bites down hard, and I grind along the length of his dick through the roughness of our jeans. Bang. I shudder beneath Jasper's touch, growing wetter with every pinched touch. Bang. My ears prick up, an involuntary shudder running through my body. Frowning, I push a hand against the wall, and it happens again. My body isn't trembling but the actual building around us.

"Jasper," I hiss, regretfully prying him off my breasts. The banging comes again, shaking the dust from the wooden slats, and then all hell breaks loose. Distant sounds of glass shattering and the onslaught of gun fire ripping through the lower level of the bar. I dive off Jasper, dragging my sweatshirt back on as a thin layer of cotton armor. I can't have my lovely babaloons providing an easy target, although I have used them as distractions in several shoot-outs before. Probably best I assess today's threat before I start shaking my tits around, though - for all I know, they could be a bunch of nuns taking God's work into their own hands.

Reaching for the sliding panel, Jasper's hands grip my waist and yank me back onto my ass. "What the fuck?!" I cry out, wrestling him away. Using the advantage of his bulk, Jasper knocks me aside, hopping through the hide-out door before turning back to me.

"Stay here," he whispers harshly and switches out the light. Without waiting for a response, he slams the panel closed with me concealed inside. Yeah, fucking right. Grabbing the makeshift handle cut into the inner wood, I jimmy the door to find it's either been locked or barricaded from the outside. Motherfucker! Since when am I not an asset in war because anyone who attacks this stronghold is declaring just that - a war.

Throwing my weight against the panel, it doesn't shift, so I turn my focus on trying to pick the lock with my penknife. The whole time, Angus mocks me for getting trapped inside the damn walls.

"Only you would walk into such an obvious set-up," he laughs gruffly. *"Do you want to see my secret hole? You're too easy."* I grit my teeth and snarl at the little fucker.

"There's only so many pegging dreams a girl can have before it has to become a reality. And trust me, when I get out of here, I don't care how riddled with bullets Jasper is. I'm shoving my strap-on so far up his ass-" The door to my room crashes open on the other side of the wall, and I freeze, pressing my ear against the wood. Boots storm inside, and voices hiss, just barely audible for me to make out.

"Where the fuck is she? You said she'd be in here," a male

grumbles, although I don't hear a response. Shouts burst into the room, and words are replaced with the tell-tale scuffling of a fight. I remove my ear from the wall, not needing to listen that hard for the grunts, gunfire, and yells to reach me. Instead, I sit back, picturing the scene on the other side of the panel. The colliding of bodies and dodging of bullets, hopefully, my men are laying into the intruders with all the rage I wish I could take out on them. Malik's voice sounds above the rest, ordering one of the others to find me.

"Maybe it's best we lie low," Angus wonders out loud. I can't see him through the darkness, but I sense him dropping onto his jiggly butt beside my legs. Tipping my head back against the shelf, I sigh and wait for the final ring of bullets to sound. The thump of dead weights hit the floor, and I sincerely hope Jasper isn't one of them so he can let me out of here, and then I can shoot him myself for leaving me behind. Dragging the bodies away on a smooth slither, silence falls, and the darkness seems to get darker as my patience wains.

Eventually, there's a rattle of the key in the lock, and I lift my arms out wide. "There we fucking go! Was that so much to ask?!" I say as the panel slides open a crack. A metal can shines in the light, bleeding from the main room before it's thrown at my forehead and the panel slammed closed again. I jolt for the handle, but it's too late. I'm locked in with the dreaded hiss of gas leaking from the canister. Panicking, I raise my knees to my chest and slam my feet into the door, no longer staying silent.

"Hey! Get me the fuck out of here, assholes!" I scream with no particular asshole in mind. I'd take the intruders at this rate as the gas bleeds into my system. My throat seizes up on a string of coughs until I'm choking, the rawness of my chest burning with agony. Despite nothing to see, my eyes burn as I try to keep them open. Kicking the gas canister away, I pound my fist on the wood, unable to speak anymore.

Slumping against the hatch, I drift towards a mental image of Angus holding his arms out for me. A rainbow stretches across a crystal blue sky, the grass greener than Shrek in a sauna. Laughter bubbles from my lips, coaxing another cough from the base of my chest. In my mind, Angus' angry eyebrows soften into a look of concern which is how I know I'm really in deep shit now.

Suddenly, the panel slides open, and I drop outwards. Strong hands catch me before I smash into the floor, and a pair of muscled arms ease me out of the hole in the wall. Free from the confined space, my limbs sprawl uselessly as I'm scooped up into the comfort of a firm chest. Coconut seeps through the bitterness marring my senses, and through my blurred vision; a glimpse of green eyes and sandy hair allows me to breathe easily at last. He came back for me.

"Ja…"

"I've got you, Love," the husky voice tells me. Pressing a light kiss to my lips, his face moves to brush against mine, and I vaguely register the scar marring his smooth cheek isn't where it should be. The darkened daze fights to claim me, but I hang on just long enough for one last thought to penetrate my mind. Jack.

MALIK

I watch Ace drag the last of the men clad in black into the elevator after Spade has stamped down plastic wrap inside. Their blood covers my suit after I put a single bullet in each of their skulls. Whoever sent them didn't bother to train them. Every single one of their shots missed my men until I was able to get to my weapon stash. Jack steps out of Candy's room with her lifeless body flopped across his arms.

"You found her," I rush over, relieved to find she's breathing. Sweeping the pink hair from her face, I brush my thumb over her bottom lip.

"Who did this?" I growl, looking back to the heap of bodies. I've spent weeks drawing myself back from the dark corner of my mind I'd become comfortable in, but all of that work is about to go to shit. I won't rest until I've hunted down every fucker that means Candy harm and personally dealt with them. Jack deposits her into my arms just before Cherry appears from somewhere behind us; her face the picture of panic.

"It's lucky I did a second sweep of Candy's room. I didn't see who it was darting into the adjoined bathroom, but they left a key sticking out of the wall. Turns out there's a mini room behind the wall," Jack huffs. Cherry winds her arms around his waist, laying her head on his shoulder in comfort.

"She needs medical attention," Spade says on approach, taking her hand in his unrestrained one.

"Oh, don't worry. I've already called an ambulance," Cherry pitches in, and all eyes swing her way.

"You did what?!" Ace booms, joining our circle. "We can't have paramedics swarming to our place when there's a pile of dead bodies in the elevator. Don't you realize we've been attacked here-"

"Cool it, Ace," Jack snaps. "She's only trying to help." Drawing Cherry under his arm, she pouts her red lips. There's a tear in her vest, exposing a tattoo on her hip. Bruising handprints are starting to appear on her neck, showing she didn't escape the attack unscathed either. The last of us appears then as Jasper steps out of Jack's room, his eyes searching frantically until they land on Candy. Rushing over, he stops just short of barging past Cherry with his shoulder.

"Where the fuck have you been?" Jack barks accusingly. Jasper snorts in surprise, nudging his chin in Ace's direction.

"I could ask a few of you the same question. Caught this one sneaking out of your bathroom looking guilty as shit," he glares at Cherry. She rubs her neck, and I can gather the rest. Jasper took his interrogation into his own hands, literally. "Or perhaps Ace can fill us in. He seemed to know these assholes were on their way, headed them off in the kitchen." I frown, hiking Candy further up my body to rest her head in the crook of my neck.

"That true, Ace?" I ask. A bitter taste fills my mouth, and as much as I don't want to suspect my brothers, my need to protect Candy is stronger. Ace nods once, clearly not liking the turn of events happening here. "We don't have much time, so start talking. How did you know they were coming?"

"I was withdrawing from the dark web, like you asked," he scowls at me, "when the alert for Candy's hit popped up. It's still live, with a new clause stating the reward will be doubled if her head is delivered to Leicester's old mansion." I squeeze Candy tighter, sensing the mood shifting Jasper's way.

"You can't possibly think…" he trails off, taking a step back. Ace holds his hands up in an effort to stop his retreat.

"I didn't want to; trust me, I didn't. So I was hacking into the IP address right up to spotting those thugs on the surveillance cams. The new hit call came from the mansion a week after Leicester was killed." Jack scrunches up his nose, his brows tightening in confusion.

"If Jasper wanted Candy's head, he could have taken it a hundred times by now. What would be the point in coming here to play nice?" If what I'm hearing is true, I can only imagine it has something to do with me. I have to say I was dubious that Jasper returned so easily, and as much as I wanted to trust his intentions, I was going to be keeping a close eye on his anyway.

"Because that's what he does," I growl, stalking towards the stairs just to turn around and come straight back. "I really wanted to trust you'd changed, but it's too coincidental. The day you arrive back, we get ambushed, and you just came out of Jack's room, where whoever attacked Candy escaped to. This whole cat and mouse game is exactly your style, isn't it, Jasper? I may deserve it, but I won't let you hurt Candy. She's too precious to all of us." Ace grunts his agreement, and even Jack eases Cherry a sidestep away from his twin, seeming unsure what to think.

"Seriously, Jest? After she put her neck on the line for you," Spade shakes his head. The disappointment is palpable, but Jasper refuses to back down. Puffing out his chest, his fisted hands cause the knuckles to crack when my pocket begins to vibrate. Careful not to shake Candy too much, I pull out my phone and bark at the caller to speak fast.

"H-hey Boss. I've just arrived in the parking lot for my shift, and an ambulance has pulled up beside me. Should I send it away?" one of my employees asks. I'm not sure which as I didn't spare the Caller ID a glance, but I'm already shaking my head.

"No, Candy's hurt. Tell them to wait; we're coming down now."

"Not like that you're not," Jasper scoffs, pointing at my suit. The blood that coated me has now smeared across her delicate face, and I grimace. "I'll take her." Reaching out to take her from me, I twist Candy out of Jasper's reach. Her breathing against my neck has grown shallow with a gentle wheeze, her skin red and clammy to touch. Whatever gas she was exposed to can cause long-lasting damage if she's not treated soon, but I won't be giving her to a man I don't trust in any instance. Understanding the set glare in my eyes won't budge, Jasper suddenly erupts into a bitter laugh.

"I see." Every eye he meets regards him with the same allusive yet watchful stare. Finally, he settles on Candy and sighs loudly—Spade's body tenses, ready to fight off an abrupt attack one-handed if needed. "Well," Jasper claps, giving a half bow, "my time here before you turned on me again was even longer than I thought it'd be. No doubt it was a pretty fantasy, but you guys can all go fuck yourselves with rusty nails." With that, Jasper leaves via the stairs and doesn't look back. No one wants to speak first, but as a shiver passes through Candy's body, Ace moves towards me.

"He is right, though; you can't go to a hospital covered in all that blood. I'll go with Candy in the ambulance; you guys can follow right behind when you're more...decent." His brown, puppy-dog eyes plead for me to listen, and I finally relent.

"Don't let her out of your sight," I breathe, not in threat but in desperation. Not even I understand the way I feel about Candy, but I trust Ace with her life as much as I trust myself, even if handing her over seemed harder than it should have. Besides, a moment to cool off is probably best since the protective streak coursing through me will threaten to snap anyone's fingers if they dare touch her right now, even paramedics and doctors. Holding her with care, Ace disappears down the stairs with Spade on his tail. Jack remains in place, looking wistfully at the now-closed elevator door.

"Sending a group of untrained men to storm our home seems odd, even for Jasper. He could have done his own dirty work without such an elaborate distraction," he mumbles. I pause, spearing the gold door a quick glance.

"What are you getting at?" Cherry ducks behind Jack at my tone, impatient to change and get on my bike ASAP.

"Remember last time, we thought he wanted the flash drive, but he actually wanted me. What if this is all another ploy to get something else he wants? Possibly for you to leave and be occupied for a lengthy amount of time?" I mull Jack's words over in my mind, deciding it's not worth my time. If Jasper has an ulterior motive, we won't find out until he's ready to lay out his cards and gloat at his success.

"He can burn this entire building to the ground if that's what he wants, as long as none of us are in it." Ignoring his wide-eyed girlfriend, I clasp Jack's neck, pulling him into a quick hug. "We're a family; we can rebuild. Or we don't and decide to live on the road, hopping from town to town on our bikes. Whatever happens, nothing materialistic we own matters. Just each other." Jack smiles, at last, bearing his dimples in all their cocky glory. It was a close call this time, but I have a feeling it's only the start. Whatever crime vacation we were on has come to a swift end. We walk towards his room, pausing at the door after Cherry has gone inside.

"We're never going to be able to go straight, are we?" Jack asks in a low voice. His genuine disappointment cuts me deep since that's all I wanted to do for my men. I'm the reason we had to become criminals in the first place, in a bid to cover up my messes. I vow that we'll live a life free from crime, just not tonight.

"One day. Come on, let's get to the hospital. You can't hide your worry for Candy from me, even if you're hiding it from yourself." Jack rolls his eyes. From the window in his bedroom, red and blue lights flash across the ceiling, and I jolt into action. I have to change and get back to my girl before she wakes up before she realizes I left her side for even a moment. Being with Candy is strangely addictive, yet I know deep down, there's nowhere else I'm meant to be.

CANDY

A sickly green smoothie is placed in front of me, and I wince. Not another one. The moment Malik turns back to pour his own revolting shake from the blender, I throw mine across the kitchen. Glass and all. Sailing into the trash can, the glass shatters, and gloopy green liquid splashes upright. Still, hole in one - I'm happy with that.

"I could have kept that for later," Malik grumbles, not even bothered by my antics anymore. He's been my personal carer since I was discharged from hospital, not to mention overbearing, oppressive, and insufferable. These shakes, for instance, have got to go.

"I was cleared a week ago, so why am I still drinking my meals? Give me a double cheeseburger and loaded fries already," I whine. Malik gives me a look to say 'yeah right' and sits on a stool across the island.

Words aren't needed at this point when his eyes track the barely visible redness coating my arms. The doctor reckons I was lucky my baggy sweatshirt saved me from severe burns and gave me an extra day of oxygen at Malik's threat to come back if I had any long-term respiratory issues. It was the departing caution of sudden blindness that really sent him over the edge, though, forcing me to sleep in his bed so he could shine a torch in my eyes multiple times a night. Nope, I'm done.

Dropping from my stool, Malik's on me like a fly on shit all the way to the refrigerator. I reach for the bottom drawer where my stash of calories lives, but my wrist is snagged aside before I make it. After an initial pinch, Malik lightens his hold and eases me around to face him.

"I get you don't like being cared for, but if you just give me a few more days-" I whip my wrist out of his grip.

"No." The vein in Malik's temple pulses, and his eyebrows raise.

"No?" His tone is low, daring me to defy him again. Well, if you insist.

"Oh, I'm sorry - forgive me. What I meant to say was, fuck no with a triple sprinkle of screw you on top." A tempting darkness sweeps over Malik's eyes, his firm chest crowding me into the refrigerator. His hands drift to my hip, twitching as he reels himself back, and I grin. He wants to spank me, and that's something I could quickly get on board with. I bite at my bottom lip, a nasty habit I've developed since being banned from the gum. Don't ask me why just another restriction on my owner's part. The owner that I'm currently taunting by rolling my hips and smushing my boobs against him. On a warning growl, Malik slowly shakes his head from side to side.

"Not a chance." I sigh, slipping out of his hold. During our face-off, Jack and Cherry have entered the kitchen. Bending over the counter, scribbling on a piece of paper, Jack's hand runs over Cherry's ass in a floral skater dress and slips beneath the skirt. I look away, not interested in the sex show before me until Jack pockets the list they were working on and jiggles his truck keys in his hand.

"You're going out?" I suddenly perk up. Jack scoffs at me, taking Cherry's hand and continuing towards the door. "Wait! Take me with you! Please, fuck. I promise I'll play nice." Stopping in the doorway, Jack peers over his shoulder, a scowl etched into his features.

"I'm not taking you anywhere dressed like that," he snarls, and I look down at my outfit of choice. The more Malik treats me like I'm wearing a chastity belt, the edgier my clothing has become. A risqué swimming costume was today's pick; black with a non-existent back and a criss-cross pattern dipped low in the front. A gold belt pinned around my waist is attached to a floaty skirt that skims my ankles. The bunny ears on my head were a last minute addition when I didn't get the initial shocked reaction from Malik I was looking for. Despite his protest, Jack's green eyes keep returning to one particular part of my body that tells me he's not that concerned with my appearance.

"Stop staring at my tits, and I'll consider dropping the ears," I shoot back, catching him off-guard. Cherry's head whips around, outraged at my accusation, but she'd only need to see the blush coating Jack's cheeks to see the truth. As a goodwill gesture, I pick off the headband and pop it onto Malik instead. I grab his arms as he bucks and jerks to dislodge the white, fluffy ears, succeeding in knocking them aside.

"Look," Malik catches my eye with a serious look. "I've got to head out for a while, but I promise to take you to get food later. You can get at least…two sugary items," he tries to negotiate with me. Well, I am not a terrorist, sir. Spinning, I head for the door and scoop up the flat ballet shoes Cherry was about to put on. Jack's voice travels as I jump onto the back step, inhaling a lungful of fresh air. Sweet freedom.

"It's fine, Mal; I'll take her. She promised to play nice, and if she doesn't, I'll lock her in the ice cream freezer." It's my turn to scowl now. Just the thought of being locked in a confined space makes me shudder. Not that I'm scared, just my dreams have been extra vivid lately, and in each one, I'm locked in a tiny space, screaming to be released.

I lead the way to the garage, and after Jack's activated the automatic door, I hop into the back of his jeep. Sprawled across the back seat, I close my eyes for the whole journey in favor of watching the two up front stroke each other's thighs. What Jack even sees in her is beyond me. Her laugh is like glass being grated, and her nothing-can-phase-me attitude is highly annoying.

Luckily, the supermarket isn't too far away, and I've hopped out before the truck's fully parked.

"Don't go running off," Jack calls after me through his open window. "This is just a supply run for the bar before my shift starts. Someone has to fund your extravagant lifestyle." I snort. No one would ever describe my life as extravagant. Especially not the person whose fake girlfriend is trying to kill me.

Claiming a shopping cart just for myself, I hit the aisles with renewed vigor. There's no use moping around, wondering if Cherry might pop out from behind the juice cartons to throw another canister at me. There's no doubt in my mind it was her. She threatened me only days before, and I've heard enough of the Jasper debate this past week to bore me to death anyway. Jasper doesn't want me dead; he wants me very much alive and writhing in pleasure beneath him.

Heading off on my own, I load up my cart with every item that has 'full fat' printed on the side. A few people stop and stare at me, planking over the handlebars, skidding through the center of the supermarket, but I hop down when security takes chase. A bit of eyelash fluttering, and they let me off with a warning to do it again once out of sight. When my cart is overflowing, I head in search of today's cash cow, aka Jack. It comes as no surprise to find him in the international aisle. Cherry is hanging off his every word as he shows her something from the British section.

"What we looking at?" I ask, shoving my cart aside to budge in between the two. Cherry exaggerates stumbling back, clutching her chest, and I roll my eyes. Jack doesn't seem to pay too much notice either, too fascinated by the red box in his hands, covered in smiley faces.

"A biscuit tray," he mumbles, placing it in his basket. I pick it straight back out, popping the box open to see what's inside.

"Oh, you mean cookies," I say, turning the foil-covered tray around in my hands before ripping into it for a better look.

"No, I mean biscuits, you uncultured swine." Rude. Jack snatches it back, trying to fix the packaging, and I tut. Leaning over his shoulder, I poke a yellow, embossed square.

"What's that one?"

"A custard cream." I hum, mulling that name over in my mind before fingering the next.

"And that?" Jack shoves me away and sighs in exasperation. Scrunching up the foil, he tosses it away and relents to my curiosity.

"That's a bourbon. The one with the heart cut-out is a jammy dodger and this is a digestive. Not to be confused with the hobnob."

"The hobnob?!" I chuckle, shoving his shoulder playfully. "You're a fucking hobnob." Jack cracks a smile until Cherry's reddened face reminds him about hating me. Putting the 'biscuits' back in the box, he takes her hand and walks away. "A whipped hobnob," I shout after him. Sliding her arm around Jack's waist, Cherry looks over her shoulder to smirk at me. As if this bitch doesn't learn her lesson to keep her smirks to herself. Returning to my cart, Angus has appeared, taking up the baby seat with his jelly butt and stubby legs. Wheeling him towards the checkout, I push the cart into the back of Cherry. "Pack that lot up, Wench. I'll be outside."

I ignore Jack's shouts, the same way he ignored mine, pocketing a pack of gum on my way out the automatic door. Oh, sweet gum. Dropping onto a bench, I chew for my life, savoring the cavity-causing goodness Malik has been banning me from while soaking up the sun's rays. No doubt I'll be back under house arrest when I return home.

"Home?" Angus questions, hopping up onto the bench beside me. I tilt my head side to side, not having the evidence to deny it. For the most part, I've been welcomed in and given free rein to do what I like. I've got a decorated room of my own, although I choose to stay in any room I like. I even had a birthday party this year.

"What the hell is wrong with you?!" Jack booms, storming over. I spot Cherry struggling to push my cart over to the truck with her scrawny arms. The skinny high heels were probably a bad choice while I click her flats together on my feet.

"There's not enough time in the world to start that conversation, *Jackikins*," I roll my eyes, mocking the pet name I've heard Cherry call him.

"Get it through your thick skull. Cherry is staying, and nothing you do or say will change that." I knot my fingers over my middle, popping a bubble of gum. Flexing his fists, Jack begins to pace and tugs at his hair. "You may think you've got everyone fooled, but all it would take is one word from me, and you'd be out. I'm one of the OG's; you're just a side attraction." Wow, he must have been practicing that one while spending an ungodly amount of time sitting on the toilet.

"You sure?" I rise to my feet, closing the gap between us. Angus hops down and follows as my gummy bodyguard. "Let's be honest; if you weren't trying so hard to replace me, you'd be just as infatuated. News flash, I'm irreplaceable." It's Jack's turn to look cocky, folding his arms over his chest. His biceps bulge on either side of the white vest he's wearing, successfully distracting me from the malice seeping from his glare.

"You've found a group of men who are so broken; they can't see how much you're damaging us. Give it time. They'll grow bored of your drama and start to look for a Cherry of their own." I bristle, refusing to hear his words.

"I bring the fun. You guys wouldn't even be together anymore if it wasn't for me."

"All you have brought from day one is trouble," Jack spits back. My hands go slack by my sides. His green eyes glisten with a level of resentment that floors me. Joking aside, does he actually hate me that much? And for what - merely existing? He paces in a circle again, grumbling to himself before turning to stab a finger in my chest.

"I'm so sick of staying quiet when it's clear the only reason we're being targeted lately is because you're there. Not to mention you, yourself, have shot Spade twice. We've been beaten, open-fired at, attacked multiple times, all trying to save your ass when *you* are the problem. Destruction follows everywhere you go, and now it's bled through our home, leeching onto us like a cancer. No one can love a person who's addicted to causing chaos. That's the reason you've always been alone. Not even your own parents wanted you, so why the fuck would we?!"

Jack finishes on a shout, and the breaths saws out of me. Icy tremors consume my chest while my mind races with the words I didn't want to hear. Not just from Jack but from so many others I'd blocked out. Foster parents, teachers, Big Cheese, my mom, the local librarian. All reminding me just how insignificant I truly am. If I dropped down dead right at this moment, my funeral would have a grand guest list totaling four, if Jasper would even come.

A wave of dizziness catches me off guard, and I sway on my feet. My chest seizes up again, capturing the breath in my lungs. The voices grow louder, screaming inside my ears, taunting me with their false words. It takes a lot to dent my pink-tinted armor, but I'm pretty sure Jack has finally speared it. Not that I'll let him know the power he could have over me, in fear of what else he might say. Next, he'll tell me Angus isn't real and pink isn't part of the rainbow. Well fuck this prick; my rainbow is only shades of pink, laced with black and dripping in glitter.

Slamming my hands over my ears, I scrunch my ears closed, working on avoiding the panic attack rippling through me. I've felt like this once before but not in years. Since I was thirteen in fact. Back then, I put my reaction down to the fact my foster father at the time had been the only one I'd liked, the one I'd begun to trust. Is it possible Jack can hurt me so easily because…I care about him?

Hands grab my shoulders, shaking me, but I refuse to open my eyes. The shouting in my head blurs into one word; chaos. Over and over, it repeats. I drop to my knees, the breath leaving me in short pants. All of a sudden, the anguish churning from the depths of my being explodes, and I drop back on a gasp. Hands cup my face, a familiar voice calling my name. Fluttering my eyes open, I spot a pair of emerald green eyes hovering a few inches above. I smile, turning my cheek into his warm palm, and he whips it away.

"What the fuck was that all about?" Jack tuts, rising to walk away but not before I spot the concern in his returning gaze. Groaning, I push myself up, rubbing the center of my chest where a refreshing tingle has gathered. What the fuck, indeed.

"I'm gonna need a strong drink after that one, Angus," I mutter, hunting around for him. He sits before me, open-mouthed and his black eyebrows raised. I go to question him when a bagpipe melody fills the air.

"Ye need more than a drink, Lassy," the deepest rumble of a Scottish accent says. I jerk aside in time for a yellow gummy bear to hurdle over my shoulder and land in my lap. A mini tartan kilt circles his waist as he plants a flag on my knee, claiming his territory. "Let me introduce me'self. Name's Hamish. The hellish, the whorish, the hot...ish gummy bear aboot."

"Aboot?" I mimic, frowning at Angus, who is speechless for once. "Oh, you mean about."

"That's wha I said, aboot," Hamish nods. "Seems like ye have a wee problem with that there lad," he points a yellow stub at Jack. The 'lad' in question has finished helping Cherry put my shopping into the trunk, then lifts her skinny ass onto the edge and attacks her mouth. Her bare legs wrap around his waist, and her ugly talons drag down the length of his biceps.

"You're right, Hamish, I do have a wee problem," I nod. An old man looks at me like I have a pair of dicks growing out of my ears as he wheels his cart past, giving me a wide birth. Picking out my gum, I throw it in front of his wheel, so the cart locks up and squeezes. Ultimately, he abandons it and runs into the shop on rickety old legs. Some people are so weird. By the time I bring my focus back to Hamish, I find he's waddled over to Angus to check him out up close. And by check out, I mean he's taking a vast interest in Angus' fat little tail. Clicking my fingers, I bring his tilted black eyebrows back my way. "Tell me then. What would you propose we do?"

"Have you no' heard of post-nut syndrome?" he scoffs. The wind catches the skirt of his red, tartan kilt, revealing that he is a traditional Scot —no underwear in sight.

"You just made that up," I tut, dragging myself back up onto the bench. Hamish runs after me, kicking my ankle. Ow. I can tell he's going to be a little shit like Angus.

"I most certainly did no'! When ya bas empties his bawbag in a hoore, he has a moment of clarity whether she's the right fit for him or no'." His accent is so thick, I feel like my head is stuffed into a mound of jelly when he speaks. I'm going to need a translator at this rate. I huff out a relaxing breath.

"So what you're saying is…"

"Dinnae you unde'stand anything? Get rid of ol' fanny baws and fuck some sense into that dickheed. He'll realize who he should be with." Nodding, my eyes travel over to the pair dry humping in the back of the truck. That's right - the foreplay fivesome I had on the billiard table wasn't with Jack; it was Jasper. I can't unite the Monarchs with my magical pussy if they haven't all had a taste. A slow grin spreads across my face, my confidence fully restored.

"You know what, Hamish, I think you might be right."

JACK

"Has anyone seen Cherry?" I ask the bartenders upon entering. We were going to head out when she'd forgotten her water bottle and popped in to grab it and never returned. The staff shake their heads, so I head out back, across the games room, and into the kitchen. Having just made himself a protein shake, Malik's attention is centered on prepping his lunch. "Hey, have you seen Cherry anywhere?" He pauses, slicing a tomato for his salad, and points the knife towards the back door.

"There was a commotion between the girls. Something about jogging. Ace went to handle it." Returning to his precise cutting, I drop my forearms onto the island and hang my head.

"For fuck's sake," I huff. "Is it always going to be like this? Them at each other's throats while we fight to keep them separate?"

"Possibly," Malik shrugs unhelpfully. I roll my eyes, bracing myself for whatever carnage I'm about to walk into. "I heard about what you said to Candy," Malik's voice comes as I'm about to leave. I stop, scowling at his back. "You'd be careful to get your facts right before filling her head with doubt." I don't miss the intended threat and throw my hands down on the kitchen island.

"You wanted to be our leader, and there are four other people living under this roof. Either treat us all the same or step down. Candy's not the center of the universe, you know." Malik's knife stops mid-air, his jaw clenching. In the next moment, it's gone, and he returns to dicing his tomato into even slices.

"I don't control the Monarchs anymore. You're all free to make your own decisions, but the consequences are also on your heads. You brought another woman into Candy's domain; you'd better make sure she doesn't get murdered in her sleep." I suddenly glance at the ceiling, a whole number of images flashing through my mind of what could be happening directly above —shit on it. Dashing towards the staircase, I take them two at a time and race into my room. The lights are off and the blackout curtains drawn, but in the slip of light piercing the side gap, I see a figure lying across my bed.

"Oh, thank fuck," I breathe, closing the door. Not wanting to wake her if she's fallen asleep, I strip down to my boxers and climb beneath the cover. The bed rocks slightly on its suspended wires, shifting the slender body into my arms. Pomegranate sweeps over my senses, and I grit my teeth, really wishing Cherry would use different toiletries to Candy. It makes my cock twitch in defiance, and my mind wonders to places it shouldn't go. Especially in the dark, when it's all too easy to visualize who's lithe body is pressed against my dick.

"Hey," I coax gently. "You okay? Tell me she didn't lay a finger on you, or I'll-."

"It's not like you to give a shit, but the gesture sure is appreciated," a voice snips back, and I freeze. No imagination needed; that little bitch who is intent on ruining my life is right here. All illusions of wanting her have disappeared, replaced with loathing.

"What the fuck, Candy?! Get out of my fucking bed!" I shout, yet my arms don't immediately withdraw from around her warm body. Turning, Candy's nose brushes mine, and the scent of her raspberry flavored gum washes over my face. She's signed off cherry flavor for obvious reasons.

"I have a proposition for you," she wriggles back in an effort to get closer. "I recently learned about post-nut syndrome from a very reliable source. Tell me, did you have a eureka moment when you first screwed Bitchy McWhore Face?"

"Cherry," I grit out.

"Whatever. Either way, it occurred to me that we never actually got to fuck each other's brains out, and alas, you're searching for a substitute to me. Spoiler alert, there is no substitute for all of this." Candy rolls her body along the length of mine. I try to edge backward, so she doesn't feel my growing arousal, but it's too late. Her dry laugh tells me that. "You can't deny our chemistry Jack; it's so thick I could choke on it." A firm grip grabs onto the base of my shaft through the cotton, and an involuntary moan leaves my lips. I shake my head, trying to push her away as she body rolls against me again, singing 'bow chicka wow wow.'

"What the fuck have you done with Cherry? I swear to god if she's hurt, I'll-" Candy's mouth covers mine, and although I should, I don't pull away. Her lips are so soft, considering her spikey attitude, moving across mine like butter. When her tongue slides effortlessly in my mouth, I snap back and grab her by the throat. "Always such a fucking cock tease," I grit out. "Stop your games and tell me where Cherry is."

"Ace took her for a walk to calm down. Quite the temper your little skank has," Candy mocks, and I blow out a harsh breath. Just let it go Jack; she's only trying to goad you. Without any reason to stay now, I release Candy with a shove and attempt to leave. She's on me like an addict seizing her next hit, straddling my hips, and shoving my chest down with a force I didn't expect. My back pushes into the mattress properly now, settling uncomfortably on a crumbly layer coating my sheet.

"Are there crumbs in my bed?!" I force my way upright, tossing her aside. I bat my sheet clean, scraping away every last crumb I can feel. Ugh, why I'm still in this bed at all is a mystery.

"Helped myself to your biscuits while I was waiting. What did you call that round, oaty one? A hobnob," Candy giggles, twerking her ass against my hip. Dropping back onto the pillow with a sigh, I run a hand over my face.

"I'm not going to fuck you," I growl, elbowing her away. Just leave. Just get out of the bed and leave, I tell myself. But then that small voice in the back of my head asks why? Firstly, why should I because this is my damn room? But secondly, and this one is much quieter, why would I deprive myself of whatever Candy will do next. I'll only question myself over it, again and again, going insane with what-ifs. She must want something, and the reasons for me not to listen are waning.

"Yeah, you are," Candy coos, running her fingers over my chest. She's relentless. Actually relentless once something is in her sights, and for some reason today, it's me. I'd thought after I said all those horrible things yesterday, Candy would be off my radar for good. It wasn't my intention, but she just knows how to push my buttons until I explode. Yet here I am, lying in the dark with her lightly scratching my abs.

"This is ridiculous," I laugh to myself.

"What's that? You want to put your dick in my arse?" Candy mimics my accent, and I purse my lips. She may have the others fooled, and sure, seeing them all bond over her while I'm on the outside may infuriate me to hell, but I can't do this. I can't give her what she wants just because she's jealous. I have my own life to live, even if it's tied to her for the foreseeable future. "Come on, Jack Attack, just one fuck, and you'll realize you don't need anyone else."

"No."

"Nut me," Candy fakes a moan.

"I have a girlfriend," I grumble, squeezing my dick in my hand. He's throbbing, begging for release, but I can't. I can't be that type of guy.

"Nut me."

"I'm not a cheater." Shoving her hands off me, Candy rolls onto her front. I watch the silhouette of her ass tilt into the air. I hear the wetness of her pussy as she slides her hand between her thighs and enters a finger into herself.

"Jack," Candy moans breathily, rolling her hips in time with her hand. "This will prove to both of us if you're wasting your time with her or not. It's for the greater good. And if not, then at least prove you're a better lay than Jasper." I roll my eyes at her attempt to irritate me yet quickly bring my attention back to the quickening pace of her hand. She's going to cum, in my bed and not even scream my name while she does it. Fuck this.

Ripping off my boxers, I shove Candy's face into the pillow and slam home inside her. The following muffled cry is music to my ears, and I still drinking in the moment. She's finally silent, at my mercy, and I won't be giving her back the control. Arching back into me to fuck her the way she wants, I refuse. Pinning her flat with my hips, I roll myself impossibly deeper, rubbing against her G-spot.

"Say one word, and I'll leave," I warn. Releasing my grip on her hair, I draw her knees up beneath me in one, sharp motion.

"No, you won't," Candy whispers smugly, and I reach around, squeezing her throat in my hand. With my other hand locating her clit, I buck my hips and slam into her relentlessly. She struggles against my hand, but I only tighten my grip until she gives in. Whether she's conceded or passed out, I don't care at this rate. I've started this, and I'll see it through. Then she'll see; she means nothing to me. Circling her clit, soft mewls are drawn from Candy's lips, telling me she is, in fact conscious. My dick swells with each thrust, wanting to claim her in a way I shouldn't.

"Tell me you're on the pill or something," I growl, the last of my sanity fading fast.

"Sorry - not allowed to talk," Candy replies, pushing her own head into the pillow. I spank her for that one, hard. The connection of my palm cracks throughout the room like a shockwave that echoes back and resonates in my balls. With my fingers digging into the flesh at her waist, I fuck her with the intent of her not surviving. Let my dick snuff out her light and finally silence her smugness. She thinks she's winning right now, but it won't be long before her experiment fails, and she'll realize she's lost. Lost her mojo, lost me.

Muffled words grunted into the pillow catch my ear, and I slow to hear what she's saying. It becomes apparent straight away she's reeling off the names from my biscuit tray. "Bourbon me up. Custard my cream. Hob my nob. Oh yeah, just like that. I'm gonna crumb!" she screams while I do everything I can to tune her out.

Candy clenches around me, her whole body tensing on a strangled, muffled cry. Her nails imbed in my thighs, trying to still the roughness of my thrusts. No fucking way, this is exactly what she wanted. Her cunt threatens to cut off the blood supply to my dick as I slam inside her, relishing how she's quivering. Her screams seep through the walls, and at this point, I no longer care. Let the others hear how I can pleasure her better when I don't even want her. I slow long enough to part her hips wider, holding them open with my thighs.

What a stunning sight, even just in the drop of daylight leaking through the curtains. Perfectly rounded globes spread wide to expose her tight hole. Just beneath, my cock glistens with her juices. Spitting over her arse, I slide my thumb through the saliva and push it into her back passage. Splaying my hand over her cheeks, I hold her there, impossibly sheathed and crying for movement. I could give in at this point, both to her and myself. Make her cum a hundred times until sundown, fall into the trap of the fantasy she provides. But that goes against everything I've been trying to do. Head out on my own, discover who I actually am. I've come too far to backtrack now.

"I've never hated anyone as much as I hate you," I bend over to breathe in Candy's ear. She giggles in response, twerking to gain some much-wanted friction from my thumb.

"You sure Jacky? I can't imagine the man in the mirror is doing it for you right now." I frown at her reply. No matter what I do or say, she's impossible to rile. Straightening, I withdraw my dick and thumb from her openings. No longer in a rush to prove myself, I run my fingers through her juices, slickening a trail between her arse cheeks. She's an enigma, drawing on my hatred to fuel her pleasure. I find I have to please her as much as I need to hurt her ,and with that last thought, I push the head of my cock into her tight back passage.

CANDY

"Did you get what you wanted?" Malik asks as I step into my room after a glorious shower. His fingers are knotted over cargo-encased thighs, his face downcast from his position perched on the edge of my bed. Not that I'll let him bring me down from the bliss coursing through my veins. The scolding heat of the shower did nothing to erase Jack's touch from my skin and, if anything, has made the bruises deepen quicker. I ache in all the right places, and the smile on my face isn't going anywhere. Now that's what I call a good day.

"You can rescind your judgey tone. I agreed to belong to all of you. I was just taking back what's mine." I drop my towel in a heap on the floor, striding across the room naked to drop into Malik's lap. His eyes trail the length of me, and suddenly, the tension in his shoulders slackens. I push the leather jacket from his back and slip my hands up the fitted t-shirt he's wearing. Weird outfit choice, but I put it down to my influence.

"I have business to tend to," he mutters, although I reckon I could get him to stay if I wanted to. As it stands, I'm looking to curl up and binge Vampire Diaries again on Netflix, call in a pizza, and sleep for a few days.

"If you're supposed to be elsewhere, how come you're sitting on my bed waiting for me to come out of the shower?" I tilt my head.

"After Ace returned from the three-mile walk you requested, he took Cherry on," Malik narrows his dark eyes on me.

"I thought she could use the exercise," I shrug. Dropping onto the mattress, I lie back on the pillow with my legs still draped over Malik's lap. His hands wrap around my feet, kneading them softly on a low sigh.

"Mmmm. Well, after that, I guessed what you were up to and quickly sent her off to a spa for the night. Hopefully, that'll give you enough time for you and Jack to sort out…whatever it is you need to sort out."

"No need, my Honey Nut Cheerio," I smirk, stretching languidly. "Jack will be in there right now, realizing he's firmly on this Candy train, and there'll be no need for that homewrecker to return at all." I smile to myself until Malik's stern gaze sweeps the delight out from under me. Rolling my eyes, I throw my feet to the floor and go in search of clothes. He doesn't get to see me naked after bringing his moody mood into my room when I was ready to get my smug on. Wrapping myself in a thick, navy robe that's leftover from Jasper's old possessions, I tie the knot extra tight for good measure. Not that Malik is even looking. His attention is to focused on his black boots.

"Ace, Spade, and I really aren't enough for you. Are we?" he sighs. I scowl at the side of his head, bored of having to explain myself. Other than Angus, I'm used to riding the high's of life and steering clear of anyone who threatens that. Holding my head high, I head for the door and hold it open as Malik's cue to leave, taking his downer Dan attitude with him.

"I was promised five," I scowl as he rises from my bed. "And that's what I'm gonna get." Closing the distance between us, Malik pauses in front of me, his dark eyes sinking into the depths of jet black. His hand trails along the length of my outstretched arm pries my hand from the door, and slams it shut again. Opening my mouth to protest, he shoves my body against the wood, trapping me in place with his thighs. A forearm is postured on either side of my head, dousing me with the scent of an expensive cologne.

"You said it again," he growls in such a graveled tone; it's almost inaudible. I purse my lips, grabbing a hold of his biceps to pull my legs up and around his waist. Malik should know by now; he can't goad me for a reaction. I'm ungoadable.

"Five. You said five of us," he fills in the silence. I yawn widely, lying my head on Malik's shoulder.

"We're doing this again, huh?"

"I'm warning you, Candy. It's for your own safety. Stay away from Jasper." Jerking his shoulder, Malik forces me to look at him. A stare-down begins, neither of us going to be the first to back down. That's when I dig deep for my resolve and allow my smirk to resurface.

"Last time I checked, calling you daddy during sex doesn't give you parental responsibility over me. And therefore," I tighten my legs around his waist and buck off from the wall. We land in a heap on the floor, much to Malik's surprise. Straddling his hips, I run the pad of my tongue up the side of his face. "You don't get to tell me what to do," I say all breathily in his ear. On abated growl, Malik flips us over in one smooth move. It doesn't escape my notice how his hand rounds the back of my head, protecting me from cracking my skull on the lino floor.

"I promised I wouldn't give orders anymore, but this one is non-negotiable. Jasper is not to be trusted. I wouldn't be able to forgive myself if something were to happen to you. Again." A wave of vulnerability passes through his features, niggling at my chest. A part of me strangely yearns to give Malik whatever he wants, but I won't budge on this. Besides, he should have learned by now. I always do the opposite of what I'm told, especially when I'm being bossed around. Still, his dark eyes stare into the depths of my soul, stripping me bare of my defenses. Our breathes heave in unison, hinting at the depth of the connection we've created. Finally, he sighs and rests his forehead against mine.

"Get dressed. We're going out." Pushing himself up in one

sweeping motion, Malik heads for the wardrobe and starts pulling out hangers.

"Where?" I prop up on my elbows.

"I have some business in town, and I'm not leaving you alone to defy me the second I'm out of sight." He carefully removes the clothes from the hangers and then tosses them at me. I frown at the cargo trousers, long-sleeved top, hoodie and leather jacket, noting how it's all in black and practically matching his outfit of choice. Color me curious, but now I want to see where this is going. Abandoning all hopes of a cozy night in front of the TV and caked in grease, I quickly dress and move to stand before Malik. His eyes have not shifted from my body once, and on approach, he reaches out to zip up my Monarch jacket. Then he kicks my boots over, and once I've shoved my feet inside, we're out the door hand in hand.

No one is around to question our shady attire or rushed movements. On the way through the kitchen, Malik grabs a backpack from a random cupboard and throws it over his shoulder. He tugs me along while I wonder how many secret stashing places the kitchen really has, dragging me out the back door and onto his motorbike. The Harley Davidson is primed and ready, and within minutes we're flying down the dirt track and leaving the Devil's Bedpost behind.

I cling onto Malik's waist the entire way to some glitzy town at least an hour's drive away, if not more. All I know is it'll take just as long to flex some feeling back into my ass. Good thing I'm a master at entertaining myself, and I had Angus running 100 miles an hour alongside the road. His body jiggled so much at one point, he became a gummy bunny with long jelly ears in between, tripping over himself. We venture into a dark alley, skidding to a stop behind a dumpster. Malik hops off, peeling his backpack off my back in search of his black covering. Pulling his helmet from my head, I hang it over the handlebars before helping him stretch the tarp over the bike, concealing it in the shadows.

"You gonna tell me what we're doing here?" I ask, leaning against the brick wall. Malik steps into my personal space, drawing the hood over my head and tucking any loose, pink tendrils out of sight. Instead of answering me, he places a solid bundle in my palm.

"If anything should happen, take this and the bike. Get out of here and don't look back." I frown at my hand, catching sight of the metal keys as a vehicle passes the end of the alley.

"Is this...did you just give me a key to the bar?" The breath sawing out of my mouth puffs around us as the night's chill settles into the alleyway. I haven't felt much wind behind Malik's huge helmet and the bulk of his body shielding me, but now I'm glad he had the foresight to pick out multiple layers. Brushing his cheek against mine, I feel the twitch of his shy smile.

"It's long overdue anyway, and I'm not going in there without knowing you have an out." Pocketing the keys, Malik drags me down into the shadows at the sound of a fire door being shoved open. We peek around the corner at some burly guy sparking up a cigarette. He wanders towards the street, and on silent feet, Malik rounds the dumpster, catching the door before it slams closed. He ushers me inside, leading the way through corridors.

It strikes me as odd when I spot a logo printed into the tiles beneath our feet. A dollar sign in the center of a diamond, although the S is a snake with purple venom tipping both of its fangs. In a similar fashion, these back hallways are painted in shades of purple and green, so I can imagine the low beat pumping through the building stream from a club version of the Joker's lair. We remain low, creeping around even though Malik clearly knows where he's going. It's only when he moves towards a closed door and pulls out my old lock-pick kit that I connect all of the dots.

"Wait, is this a heist? Are we doing a heist right now?!" I ask, excitement bleeding through my tone. Feet scuffle nearby, and Malik whips me around the nearest corner, slamming a hand over my mouth.

"Shhhh," Malik hisses, putting a finger up to his lips. A crackle comes from a radio, and the guy stalking through the hallway mutters the all-clear before retreating. I keep on Malik's feet as he slinks back to the door, making quick work of the lock. We slip inside a darkened office, fresh with clogged smoke and cheap air fresheners.

"Spill the beans. You were going to do this heist by yourself. What's going on, and how many others have there been? Is that where you keep disappearing to?" I plant my hands on my hips, refusing to move from this spot by the slightly opened door.

"Will you close that?!" Malik growls. He's around the other side of a large desk already, checking drawers and switching on a monitor. I push the door closed with one finger, letting the click reverberate through the room just to see Malik's stern glare once more. He drops into the desk chair, pushing a flash drive into the side of the keyboard before him.

"Cutting all ties and going straight is a pretty fantasy, but I had to tie up loose ends first. Otherwise, the gangs I've spent years pissing off will come after not just me, but all of us." His face is firm in the screen's glow, with rows of digits flying across the reflection of his dark pupils. I drift over, dragging my feet and knocking a stack of papers off the desk. Steadying himself on a long exhale, Malik lifts his head to glare at me. "Are you trying to get us caught or just piss me off?"

"I'm bored," I pout. Malik beckons me over, holding his hand out for mine. After obeying, he places a kiss on the back of my hand.

"This is my last job, and then the Devil's Bedpost is free from any and all illegal ties. Please, allow me to get it done, and then I'll take you out, wherever you want to go."

"Wherever I want?" I double-check, and he nods. Fair enough. The screen pings as Malik's password encrypting software works, giving him full access to the desktop. The cursor flies around the screen, opening a range of windows, and that's where I tune out. A neon sign displaying the same logo as before hangs on the back wall, highlighting a pair of tall filing cabinets. I peer inside a few of the drawers, swiping a bottle of whiskey from amongst the files. A printer kicks into life, spewing out whatever evidence Malik has been hunting for. As he moves to hover over it, I drop into the seat and unscrew the bottle in my hand.

"So, what's the job?" I ask, necking the whiskey in long swigs. Malik keeps his back to me, his voice low and hoarse.

"I've done some shady shit in my time, but getting involved with the Diaz cartel was the stupidest. True, after Jasper slept with the leader's favorite girlfriend, the twins probably would have found themselves in shit anyway, but I saw an opportunity, and I took it." He takes his precious paper, folding it carefully and pushing it into his jacket pocket. I hand over the whiskey bottle, surprised when he takes it. Raising it to his lips, Malik snaps out of his trance and shoves it back in my hand.

"So what happened?" I ask, swiveling in the chair and planting my boots on the desk.

"At first, I was like an informant - keeping tabs on the twins and telling the cartel where they'd be. Then, when they became desperate, I paid the cartel a lot of money to lay off. The payments became regular, next thing I know, they're doubling their fee and paying visits to the bar as a low key threat. Everything with Jasper went tits up after he found out who they were, and I've been almost bankrupting the bar just to keep them off our backs."

"Makes sense. They had you backed into a corner and could ask for whatever they wanted." I nod to myself. "You said one last job. Does that mean you're getting out for good?" Malik finally breaks into a small smile, leaning his weight on the desk by my feet.

"After this job, they've agreed to call it quits. Except from the bar itself, I have nothing left to lose now, and thanks to you; I reckon the Monarchs are more solid than ever. We could move on and rebuild, but it is our home. I'll do whatever it takes to save it." Just then, the door handle rattles with the sound of a key, and Malik shoots upright. His eyes dart around, seeing no way out, so he pulls a gun from his waistband. Slapping his forearm, I tug him down to hide beneath the desk while I remain on the chair. As the door swings open, I spread my legs wide over the desk and grab a handful of Malik's hair.

"What the f-" the burly man from the alley starts, cut off when I roll my head back on a fake moan. Peering his way, I notice the hint of recognition when he flicks on the lights and grins. "Well, I'll be damned. That's not a face I thought I'd see again."

"Hey Cobra, how's life treating you?" I smirk, dropping my legs from his desk. Malik's expression beneath the desk is one of thunder, but I shove his face to stay down. The club owner opposite crosses his beefy arms and quirks a brow my way. He's never changed in all the years I've known him - a huge, bald man with more tattoos than I could count and a nasty habit for smoking that's stained his teeth and fingernails yellow.

"Oh, you know, same old." Cobra's smirk takes on a whole new level that tells me he's been up to no good. That much was obvious since we're here to steal information from him. Either way, letting on to Malik that the owner and I were old friends would have meant I missed out on the touching cartel story. "What's Leicester up to these days?"

"Decomposing." I take another swig of whiskey, feeling the burn all the way to my chest. Cobra mutters his apologies, but I wave him off. Doesn't bother me if Big Cheese is brooding in his mansion or terrifying worms in the ground. I snicker to myself, suddenly imagining the high-pitched screams of tiny worms when Malik clears his throat. Wheeling the chair back, I release him from the apex of my thighs. Cobra's eyes narrow as Malik stands and pulls me up from the chair, facing the boss side by side.

"Dare I ask what you and your friend are doing in my office?" Cobra asks, seeming guarded now. I snatch the piece of paper from Malik's pocket before he can stop me and wave it in Cobra's direction.

"Remember that favor you owe me? I've come to collect in the form of…" I open the paper to have a look at what I am actually using a valuable favor on. "Damn Cobe, you've been a busy boy. Laundering money from the account of Rodrigo Diaz through the club. Probably wasn't best to keep a paper trail," I wrinkle my nose.

"Candy," Malik says without actually moving his mouth. It was more of a guttural warning directly from his throat. "What the fuck are you doing?" Turning my back on Cobra, I tilt my head with a thoroughly amused look on my face.

"Wow, I didn't know you were a ventriloquist. Do it again," I beam. He doesn't. Whipping the paper out of my hand, Malik puts it back in his jacket pocket and remembers to do up the zip this time. Sighing, I turn back to Cobra, plastering my body to Malik's front like a shield.

"You know I can't let you leave with that information," the big man edges a step forward. "No matter how big a favor I owe you."

"See, the thing is," I halt Cobra with my hand when he gets close enough. Something hard presses into my ass, and either Malik is getting off on adrenaline from the heist, or he's preparing to use his gun. "This is a blessing in disguise for you too. Consider it a tip-off. The cartel are onto you, so as soon as we leave this room, you should get onto your computer and start erasing files. Stay one step ahead; let them make fools of themselves with information they can never prove. Be creative," I shrug. Cobra's pale eyes shift back and forth, the rusted cogs in his head grinding into action. As terrifying as he is to others, Cobra's not the sharpest tool in the shed.

"I suppose it's no use trying to offer you a higher price than the Diaz family to burn that paper and be done with this," he asks, already resigned to my way of thinking.

"Not this time. Money isn't the currency being offered; power is. But take my advice, this will be massively more entertaining. Give me a heads up; I'll come down for the show," I smirk, and Cobra joins me.

"Go on, get out of here before I change my mind. You're lucky I like you, Candy." Cobra raises a meaty fist, and I quickly pump it before Malik gets the wrong idea. Keeping him at my back, I scoot us around Cobra and shove Malik out of the door.

"Pleasure doing business with you," I call back, already halfway down the hall. Breaking into a run, laughter bubbles from my mouth as we barrel through the exit. The rush of the thrill makes me giddy, right down to my toes and not even Malik slamming me back into the brick wall quells my excitement. Conflicting emotions collide down the center of his shadowed face, resulting in an eye twitch he should probably get checked out.

"Next time you recognize the club we're breaking into, how about you let me know," he settles on. Releasing my shoulders, Malik makes his way over to the bike and proceeds to pull off the cover.

"Thought there wasn't going to be a next time," I grin with my tongue hanging out. Skipping closer, I drape myself over Malik's back and lick the outer shell of his ear. "Admit it; we make a good team."

"I never disputed the fact," he replies, all formal and shit again. I roll my eyes, shaking some of the tension out of his shoulders. It doesn't work, and in the next moment, a helmet is being stuffed onto my head. Stuffing my hands in my pockets, the coolness of the keys Malik gave me slip through my fingers, giving me an idea. There's no use in giving Malik a physical shake when it's a mental one that'll last longer. Much like the point of a shock collar, it's my job to remind Malik of what it feels like to be alive. Popping up the visor, I slide my leg over the bike while Malik faffs with folding his piece of tarp.

"Hey, what was that favor you and Cobra were talking about?" he asks, trying not to sound as interested as he clearly is. Scooting further down the seat, I slide the keys into the ignition.

"Oh, it was nothing really. I helped to prove his wife was cheating on him." Twisting the key and nudging the kickstand up with my foot, Malik lurches forward too late as the bike shoots forward. "And then I killed her," I smirk to myself, skidding onto the main road and heading in the opposite direction of the Devil's Bedpost. There's somewhere else I need to be tonight, and it's not waiting around for Mr. Stressy to find his own way home just to realize he doesn't have a key to get in.

JASPER

Laying back on the leather sofa, I drop the book onto my chest with a sigh. Wooden beams arch across the ceiling, interlocking in the center. In between the sections, hand-painted images cover every inch of space like the Sistine Chapel. Naked cherubs, angels, the odd Pegasus. Maybe a little over-kill for a library, but Leicester had an old-school type of taste. Mahogany shelving units built into the walls around an expensive, patterned rug bathe the room in a chocolatey richness. One that continually reminds me of Candy's eyes. For that and many other reasons, this has to be my favorite room in the mansion.

Although, I can't hide in here for much longer. The shower is calling, and I've thrown myself into so many different fantasies in a bid to avoid real life; my eyes are stinging just by staying open. Sliding my phone out of my lounge pants pocket, I find it's died, so I toss it onto the coffee table. Swinging my legs around, I place my book back into the box by the sofa's edge. This is my personal collection from the locker where all my stuff has been stored for too long now. It felt right to finally bring something of mine into the mansion since it seems to be the only place I can undoubtedly return to.

Heading over to the door, I flick the lock and pause to listen to the other side. Tanya tried to pound the door down multiple times with her insistent knocking, but as I told her through the wood, I just want to be left the fuck alone. After a lengthy silence follows, I slide into the hallway and quickly make my way to the bedroom I've claimed. I'm not worried about seeing her, but it's easier to avoid confrontation where possible. Lord knows there is enough of it in my life, even when I'm trying to mend the bridges Malik tore down and rebuilt on shaky foundations. Fucking Malik.

Deciding on a bath instead, I take my time soaking amongst the bubbles. Even though my playlist is bleeding from the speakers, certain thoughts begin to settle in. What the fuck am I going to do with myself now? What's the point of sticking around, and will I ever feel whole again? This is what I'd been avoiding, but I can't run from myself forever. I'd spent so long focused on my vendetta against the Monarchs; I just can't be bothered anymore. Lines have been drawn, blurred, erased, and re-established; it takes too much energy just to care. They're all welcome to each other, even Candy, if that's where she chooses to be. Running a wet hand through my hair, I close my eyes and drift off.

I jerk awake with a start, my head having dipped beneath the surface. My music is no longer playing, and the water has turned cold, pruning my skin. I drag myself out of the tub, wrapping a towel around my middle. My room is dark, the night's sky leaking across crumpled bedsheets and open dresser drawers. How long was I out for? Drying myself off, I leave the towel around my neck to don some fresh tracksuit bottoms when a light flashes from outside. Peering through the glass, I spot Tanya leaving in the Lambo with a woman in the passenger seat. Weird, I didn't know she had any friends. Shrugging, I thank fate that I don't need to sneak around and make my way back to the library.

The door is ajar and lights on inside after I specifically remember fully closing it behind me. I rush forward, the taste of venom seizing my mouth. If Tanya has touched any of my books out of spite, I'll-

"It's about damn time," Candy lifts her arms wide from the leather sofa. The lit candelabra behind her head highlights the pink hue of her wavy hair, and the color caricatures inked over her chest and arms. Sitting cross-legged in a pair of checked pajama pants and a grey, baggy vest, she mimes tying a lasso and throws it in my direction, coaxing me inside.

"How did…Are you wearing my clothes?"

"Well, I couldn't have a slumber party in my heist get-up, now could I?" My eyes fall on the crumpled black pile on the floor, then to the Chinese takeaway boxes on the coffee table. Candy dives in, opening one box after another and sampling each dish as she goes. Spotting my bed cover thrown over the sofa's arm, I sit beside her and draw it over the pair of us.

"To what do I owe this pleasure? Thought you'd have been warned off me by now," I edge, curious about what she's been told. I guess I should have learned by now; Candy doesn't listen to anyone except her instincts.

"Psh," Candy waves her hand through the air, dismissing my question. Wiping her sticky hand down my vest front, she makes a reach for my book box, and I lunge over to stop her. Gripping her wrists, she uses my hold to tug me over her body. Lifting our arms over her head, Candy pushes her chest into my face, distracting me enough to dislodge one hand. Her legs winding around my hips holds me in place as she picks up the book I was reading, giggling in success. "Didn't realize you were such a heavy reader, Jasp."

"Give it here!" Candy throws the book over the back of the sofa, and I dive after it with her thigh-grip still cemented around my waist. I can't let her find out what I was reading, or she'll never look at me the same way again. We fall hard onto the hard floor, and I shove the book underneath a sideboard. Candy's elbow lands in my ribs as I crowd her with my weight, refusing to let her get away.

"What's the big deal?! I just wanna see!" Twisting around to jam her ass against my crotch, Candy pushes herself up with a surprising amount of strength. I grab and yank her back from clawing at the sideboard feet like a woman possessed. We scuffle around on the dusty floor in a mess of limbs, ruining the point of having a bath. Somehow, Candy manages to twist her leg and knee me in the balls. I collapse, cradling my testies as she grabs my book from under the sideboard and runs across the room.

"Let's see what all the fuss was about then, shall we? Ooohhh, My Billionaire Baddie. A hate-to-love male on male romance," Candy leans over the back of the sofa to bob her eyebrows at me.

"Everyone wants to believe in a happy ever after," I groan, forcing myself into an upright position. My stomach rolls as I fight the need to throw up.

"Not me. I prefer a killer cliffhanger that leaves me wrecked," Candy shrugs, then vaults over the sofa to help me up. Despite all my efforts to stand straight, I hobble around and ease myself into the leather cushions. Candy drops down heavily, jarring my sensitive ball sack. When she doesn't stop staring at me with the biggest, knowing grin, I finally relent to the question burning in her eyes.

"Yes, okay, I'll swing whichever way will have me. Boys boarding school, remember? Kinda comes with the territory." I groan inwardly, running a hand over my face. Fuck, even playing it off sounds stupid. Sparing a glance Candy's way, her smile hasn't faltered, and I can only imagine what group sex scenarios she's conjuring up. "It's not a big deal. Love's love, no matter where it comes from," I shrug.

"Makes sense; that's why Malik's betrayal hurt you so hard then, considering you're in love with him and all." The earnest and lack of judgment in her statement knocks me off-kilter, and all defensive comebacks die on my tongue. With a sigh and a small smile, I pull her under my arm, sinking my fingers into her pink hair.

"There was a time we'd hang out much like this. Read side by side in silence, play pool, drink the nights away in his suite. Being such a tight-knit family, it became impossible to tell where my feelings started to deepen. But sure. I set myself up for failure wanting a man who'd never breach his own walls to show affection. Even in a platonic way." Candy sinks into my chest, running her hands over my abdomen. She finds a scar to play with, tracing her fingers up and down its length. Up until I received the one on my face, I wore my scars like battle wounds. Now I can hardly look in the mirror. It's not Ace's fault. I lost sight of my own end goal, and the reminder of that is cut from my eye to jaw.

"That's why you were hellbent on destroying him, and probably me at first. Jealousy is a wicked mistress," Candy muses, and I laugh.

"You should know," I snort. Halting her exploration of my naked torso, Candy whips those chocolate brown eyes on me with a harsh glare.

"I'm not jealous! That bitch is trying to replace me." That's laughable in itself, but it's the fact Candy actually feels threatened by some copycat that intrigues me. I'd have bet my life nothing could penetrate her outer shell.

"And I am jealous, but I'm not behind the hit on your life."

"I know," Candy replies instantly. She returns to her curled-up position, strewn across my body, gently flicking my nipple. My mind wanders as those two words sink in. She never doubted me for a moment. After years of being accused, blamed, and mistrusted, it's hard to digest, but deep down, I knew she'd come through for me. Candy gets me, plain and simple. We lay there, letting the takeout go cold, and the candles wither, but none of it matters. I relish her warmth, her feather-light touch caressing my chest and ribs, her presence after so many nights alone. Mourning for what could have been isn't my style, but I'd be lying *if I didn't worry I'd* missed my shot at re-entering the Monarchs. Now though, they can all get fucked. All I need is her.

"Come on, I want to show you something," Candy shoots upright, jolting me back to reality. Holding out her hand, she heaves me from the sofa and keeps a tight hold as she skips from the room. Passing my bedroom, I pull back so I can grab us both a hoodie and then continue on her course. Leading me into the last room down the hall, Candy announces it as hers before dramatically opening the door.

Just like the others, deep purple drapes hang over the windows, and a tall dresser looms over the four-poster bed. I can't help the curious sounds that escape me, even if Candy doesn't notice. I'm just surprised at how ordinary it all looks. I suppose it makes sense since she didn't spend as much time here but still. Candy not putting her stamp on everything she touches is unheard of.

Crossing the room, she pulls a long stick out from beneath her bed, a shining chrome hook fixed to the end. Angling it towards the vent in the top corner, Candy pops the cover and tugs down a hidden ladder inside. The rungs unfold and click into place until she's grinning at me to follow. There's no chance of me doing anything else when her round ass in my pajama pants is beckoning me up the ladder and into the hidden space behind.

Twisting to pull up the ladder via a thick looped rope and secure the vent back in place, we shuffle on our hands and knees until an opening allows us to stand upright. Candy's fingers relink with mine, and after remarking there's usually more cobwebs around, she drags me up a winding, wooden staircase to finally reach our destination. I don't even care at this point; I'm just happy to go along for the ride.

"You showed me your secret hideout, here's mine," Candy says into the darkness. Pushing a door open and switching on the lights, I make an 'ahh' noise. Here it is, Candy's stamp. In the apex of a tilted ceiling, a fake diamond chandelier hangs between plastic starfishes and seahorses. Glittery cushions are thrown against a stack of beanbags, and the walls are covered in random swatches of different wallpapers. All shades of pink and patterned, as if she spent years stealing them from a chain of decorating stores. An old-style rocking horse with an attached horn sits beside a hand-painted mushroom table, and from the beams, white nets hang low under the weight of a hundred stuffed teddies.

"Wow…it looks like a unicorn died in here."

"Don't be ridiculous." Candy scoffs, heading over to shake the dust from the beanbags. "I let him out years ago." Dropping down, she hugs a sequin heart cushion to her chest, and a rare look of vulnerability crosses her face. She's never brought anyone here before. Dropping onto a cushion by her side, something hard sticks into my butt, and I panic about what I'll find. Pulling on the remote control on a relieved sigh, I spot a small screen sitting in a carved-out hole in the wood.

"I'll admit, this makes my hole in the wall look pretty lame. At least you have a place to come when you realize Malik has you trapped," I mutter. The heart cushion smacks me in the face, and suddenly, Candy's straddling me with a frown.

"I'm not trapped; I have a key." Reaching behind her ear, she produces the brass key she stashed there with a wad of chewed gum attached. I huff a laugh, more interested in slipping my hands beneath the baggy hoodie she donned to hold her waist.

"That's cute." My stomach decides to grumble, breaking through the moment I was gearing up to with the slow circles towards Candy's chest. She whips off me before I can protest, taking her warmth with her. Crossing my arms over my middle, I slyly squeeze my gut to shut the fuck up and slide down into the beanbag. Candy circles the rocking horse and pops open a hidden cupboard door in the wall, never failing to keep the surprises coming. Pulling out a handful of snacks in individual packets, she starts to close the door, but I'm more interested in the huge gold block sitting further back.

"What's that?" I ask. Candy looks up as if seeing it for the first time, tilting her head. A section on the front is covered up, and there's a thick handle to the left.

"Oh, that's where Cheese asked me to hide his secret stash. When I did a job for him, I'd just add my haul in since the scanner is set up for my eyes only." Candy shrugs, closing the door. I jolt up from the beanbag, meeting her halfway across the room with long strides.

"Hold up. There's a retina scanner on the secret safe concealed in your attic hideout," I cock my question. Candy's brown eyes look at me like I'm the crazy one, shoving the cake bars and Oreos into my hands.

"Yeah...so?" Throwing her leg over the rocking horse, she casually swags back and forth while my head is reeling.

"So that seems like something someone might want your head for, Candy." I close the gap between us again, cupping her face in my hands.

"Only if someone were to find it," she shrugs in agreement but still not giving much of a shit. Maybe she's right. Most of Leicester's crew haven't stepped foot back in his mansion, and it'd be one hell of a coincidence to stumble upon the safe accidentally. Still doesn't make sense why he'd trust Candy with his fortune, but I guess there's no one more trustworthy than someone who doesn't care for greed. Candy gets by day to day, happy to have the clothes on her back and gum in her mouth. My anxiety quells, the threat of someone trying to hurt her easing from my system. Then again, what if hurting her is the opposite of what the hit is about. Is it possible I've been thinking about this all wrong?

"Unless..." I trail off, pacing in thought.

"Unless what?" I swing back to face her, dumping the snacks she gave me on the mushroom table. The signs all click together in my mind, and for some reason, the truth worries me more than if someone truly wanted to kill her.

"Unless the whole hit is fake, again. This could be a trap, just another ploy to work in Malik's favor. Isn't it a coincidence that Malik invites me over, then tells Ace to clear the hard drives, and your hit happens to pop up that very night? What about the gunmen being so untrained, they each held a machine gun, yet every single Monarch came out unscathed?" The more I think about it, the more I convince myself. It makes too much sense not to be true. Candy's expression doesn't falter, her features fixed in a stoic stare.

"What's the angle?" is all she asks, still rocking back and forth.

"Who knows with Malik, but my guess would be you. Did he use the attack as an excuse to move you into his suite? Watch your every move, control what you do and eat, stop you from going out alone?" She tries to hide the flicker of recognition, but I saw it. Fuck, that's what this whole ordeal is about. Blaming me so he can look like the hero. That's some straight-up savior syndrome bullshit. Laughing bitterly, I scrub a hand over my face, my fingers trailing the scar that reminds me just why the Monarchs can no longer be trusted. They're all corrupt, even if they don't realize it.

"That's how it starts. If it were anyone else, I'd say they're welcome to be controlled, but I can't let them do that to you. Your spirit is too wild to be caged, Crazy Girl."

"If what you're saying is true," Candy hedges, clearly not wanting to believe it, "what do you propose I do? Either seek revenge or be happy I finally have a place to belong? Malik may act stupid when he's desperate, but surely that just goes to show how much he wants me around." I sigh on a sad smile, holding my hands out to draw her off the rocking horse. Pulling her into my personal space, I stroke my thumb over her bottom lip and speak low in her ear, hoping she will listen to what I'm trying to say.

"Seeing the good in damaged people is your superpower love, but you don't need him to belong somewhere. We can't beat him when he's the best player in a game of his creation, but we can leave."

"Leave?" Candy jerks backward. The chandelier above floods her face with light, bringing forth the faint speckle of freckles covering her nose. Looking into her beautiful face that can bring so much wrath without blinking an eyelid, my decision is made.

"Runaway with me. We can fly solo, ride our bikes into the sunset and never look back. Hit a new town every day, sleep under the stars. Whatever you want, we'll do it." My hand slides around the back of her hand, clutching on a little too hard. Fuck, who's the desperate one now? But separating from her isn't an option. She's wormed her way into my heart, always seeing the real me others refused to acknowledge. I've been waiting years for that gut-churning realization I've found the person for me, just like in my books, and here she is —insane, spontaneous, and mine.

"Hmmmm, I've never had to choose between lifestyles before. I usually just go with whatever I'm given, but I haven't had to steal from day to day lately or search for a shelter when the cops are storming my basement apartment, and it's been…kinda nice. I've even got a pet; I can't just leave him behind." Candy clicks her tongue, dousing my excitement at the fantasy I'd built up in my mind.

"Bring him," I say instantly. I vaguely remember the hairless cat I spotted around during our false meeting. No doubt another trick by Malik to keep her housebound. One day he'll learn you can't contain a bird born to fly, and losing Candy might just teach him that lesson. "We'll take the Lambo. Loads of room in the back seat for whatever you want to bring. Hair like this deserves to fly in the wind of freedom," I wink, shaking her wavy lengths. A small smile pulls at her rose-pink lips as she toys with the strings to my hood.

"And how do you propose we get by? Being poor isn't fun, not even with me." My eyes trail from her face to the closed cupboard that hides the safe. Her safe. Leicester isn't here to make use of his riches anymore; why shouldn't we? Plus, for some unknown reason, he practically set her up for life by gifting her free access. Twisting her head to follow my gaze, the face that turns back to me doesn't bear any trace of a smile. Instead, tightly pitched eyebrows and pursed lips assess me before she withdraws from my hold. "Ahh, I see. You find out I have access to a fortune, and you suddenly want to run away with me. Funny thing is Malik wants me, even though I have nothing to give him. I thought you did to."

"Wait, no! That's not-" I stutter, reaching for her, but she backs up too fast. My chest squeezes, my words not forming as I rush to find the right thing to say. "Candy, wait, listen, please. I just want what's best for both of us, and fuck, all I want is you." I hold my hands out uselessly, trying to bring her back to me without being forceful. That'll only push her further away, even though the small voice in the back of my head is telling me it's too late.

Her chocolate eyes sink in misery as they drop to the floor, and she shakes her head. Without saying another word, Candy is out the door and running down the steps. I run to the door jam, throwing my hands into the wood, and the entire roof shakes. I fucked it. She's fallen for Malik as much as I'm sure she has for me, but in trying to pull her away, I've just become as much of a selfish bastard as he is. Hanging my head low, I hear the smash of the vent door being kicked clean off its hinges, and my heart sinks.

"The offer is always open. When he snuffs out your light, you know where to find me!"

CANDY

I rise early, slipping out of my bed on silent feet. Despite getting back last night after everyone had already turned in, I felt the need to sneak into my room and be alone with my thoughts. I've never had to think so much in my life. Normally I act on instinct and don't consider it twice, but now all the voices in my head are shouting — all except the two gruff ones I'm used to. Looking around, I hunt for Angus and Hamish with no success. Grabbing some sweats and sneakers, I pass through the bathroom to lock Jack's adjoining door. It was all arguments in there last night for some reason, this is why relationships are pointless — *the drama.* Once I'm sure I won't be interrupted, I switch on the light.

"Holy twat crumpets," I gasp, covering my eyes. Now the image of Hamish bending Angus over on the countertop is imprinted in my mind; I can't help to hear the squeaking their bodies make rubbing up against one another. "On the counter, guys? Really?!"

"Is it too much ta ask for a little privacy?!" Hamish's thick accent cuts through their screechy butt sesh. I duck out of the room, closing the door but not before Angus cries 'spank my balls' at the top of his lungs. I'm never going to be able to forget that now.

Dressing in my room instead, I creep downstairs to use the customer toilets in the bar. I leave, feeling much more refreshed, having washed in the fancy hand soap and managed to shake a chewable toothbrush free from the wall dispenser.

The bar is dark and still, cloaked in shadow with the scent of artificial fumes filling the air. I sniff around, unable to place the smell when movement on the bar, and a sharp hiss make me lash out. My fist connects with Sphinx, sending him skidding across the bar counter. I jump forward, grabbing him before he drops off the other side and crush him into my chest. "You stupid little shit," I soothe, stroking his wrinkly back. Sure, he shouldn't have snuck up on me, but it's not his fault I'm on edge this morning. My mind is confused, causing my actions to be erratic, and that's not good for anyone.

"What am I going to do with myself, Sphinx?" I ask, setting him back onto the counter. Long claw marks have been etched in the wood from where he skidded, which I try to patch over with beer mats. "I don't think either of us should be around for when Malik finds this, do you?" Sphinx lets me tickle the underside of his chin while peeing on the beer mats and kicking them to the floor with his hind legs. I have to say, I like his style, but now I definitely don't want to be here for when Malik finds this mess. Grabbing him by the collar, I tuck Sphinx under my arm and carry him out back.

"Stay out of the way," I tell him, popping him into the middle compartment in a high, straw, scratch tower. I'm not sure who bought it, but Sphinx seems to like it, curling up inside to go back to sleep. Grabbing my keys from the hook behind the door, I leave in the light of the rising sun. It's already balmy in the promise for a sweltering hot day, so now is the perfect time to go for a ride, clear my thoughts and just feel the breeze on my face. That's one way to stay out of trouble and avoid being on the Monarchs bad side. Again. In the light of a new day, all I can depend on is that Cherry is a goner, Malik is going to be super pissed about being ditched last night, and Jasper's confused me to shit.

"Trouble in paradise?" Angus quirks a brow, barring the way to the garage. I freeze, my eyes widening.

"No, not at all. Living my best life over here." I glance away and then swing my narrowed gaze back to him. "Anyways, Mister. We need to talk about what I just saw in the bathroom. After all your big talk and ballsy attitude, Angus, *you're* the bottom?!" He stutters, rubbing a patch on his ass that must have taken quite the spanking, and I'm over this conversation.

Pressing the automatic beeper to start elevating the door, Angus' body flops forward and flails on the ground like a beached whale. I step over him, ducking beneath the door as it continues to rise. Skylight spills over Jack's truck, the row of bikes beneath water-resistant covers, and then my quad. My fucking quad! Used cans of paint have been tossed aside in a hurry, the last remnants leaking beneath my slashed tires. The brakes have been cut, hanging uselessly over the handlebar. In between the vibrant, red paint poured all over my beautiful quad, 'slut' has been scratched into the body, and the leather seat has been slashed.

That's it. If that bitch is stupid enough to still be around, she's going to learn today why messing with me is a bad choice. I once followed a barista home and filled his bed with the contents of his trash can for screwing up my coffee order. Leaping over some spilled paint, I grab my faithful bat from the middle shelf on the rack. The Candy Crusher. I inhale the smell of her pinewood, feeling her heavyweight in my hand. She radiates vengeance, and I'm here for it.

Stomping back across the parking lot, some assholes wolf whistle my skin-tight leggings and crop top. I swing my bat over one shoulder and flip them off, too preoccupied to curse them out properly. I'll come back later when covered in blood and buzzing with the rush of a recent kill. Malik's double, Gabriel, opens the revolving bar door just before I shove my way through it, nearly knocking him off his feet. Ignoring his protests, I rear back my bat and take a swing at a small vase holding a single white rose in the center of a table. It shatters on impact, spraying tiny shards across the room and against the bar.

"Motherfucker!" Gabriel shouts in unison with the lookalikes who have ducked behind the bar. Spade's double pops up first, scowling at me like I just shot his dog.

"What? I needed some target practice before I knock this trashy whore right back into her mother's cunt." I exit, trailing my bat behind me up the staircase —Clunk, clunk, clunk. Imma get payback, then Imma get drunk. Throwing my foot down on the top step, I bend my knees and brace myself. This has to be a death to remember so she makes sure to stay dead. Releasing a warrior cry and holding my bat up high, I turn the corner and break into a run, straight into the clothesline of Ace's solid arm.

"I don't think so, hot stuff. You're coming with me." Dragging me up off the floor, he snatches my bat before manhandling me down the hall in the wrong direction.

"Get the fuck off me, Ace! I have to see if she's in Jack's room!"

"Yeah, I got that from your suicide strut on the surveillance cams. What you really need is to vent." Not stopping until he chucks me into the gym, Ace slams the door shut and stands in front of it. I launch myself at him, trying to unfold his crossed arms and budge him out the way, but he's like a fricking statue. I whip my bat out from beneath his chunky bicep, raising it in threat.

"I'll do it!" I say to him. Ace cocks a brow, the trace of a smile playing about his lips. Well, he can't say I didn't warn him. Rearing back a little further, the bat is suddenly torn from my grip, along with a menacing laugh.

"Nice try," Spade chuckles. I spin, preparing to shove him, when I notice he's not wearing the sling. His arm is still pinned against his bare torso, the white dressing visible over his shoulder and a pair of sports shorts hanging low on his hips. I glance back, noticing Ace is also dressed for a workout. Seems I caught him on the way for his usual morning routine.

"You didn't see what she-"

"We don't need to see," Ace interrupts me. "You were loud

enough with Jack yesterday for the whole bar to hear. Whether you like it or not, you screwed her boyfriend. She deserves to lash out, and you need to let it go. Now get down and give me 20 push-ups."

I laugh bitterly, putting my hands on my hips. No fucking way am I burning valuable murder fuel on giving myself cramp. Ace doesn't get the memo somehow, his hands lashing out to toss me around and put me into the plank position on the floor. I try to resist, but Spade plants his foot on my back, applying enough pressure to make me lower enough to quiver.

"One," Spade counts, and the pair share a laugh at my expense. "Two."

"I have a better idea," I grit out. "Let's vent my frustrations another way. Namely, a way that ends in us all being sated, sweaty and sssss-ahhhh!" I buckle under Spade's shoe, kissing the lino floor. That's it. Rolling away, I hop to my feet. "Fine, you want me to work out my anger? Let's do it the good old-fashioned way." I raise my fists in front of my face, keeping my guard up.

"You want to fight me?" Ace seems highly amused.

"Well, if you won't sink your dick in me, there's really no other choice." Spade takes a step back, sitting on the weight bench to tie his sling back into place. Ace helps him do the knot, keeping his back to me.

"I don't hit girls," he grumbles. "anymore."

"Okie dokie," I lower my guard, no longer needing to keep it up and throw a fist at the back of Ace's head. He spins in a flash, grabbing my wrist before I manage to land the punch. Applying force, he twists me around and wrenches my arm behind my back in one swift move.

"I said I don't hit girls, doesn't mean I won't defend myself against psycho bitches," Ace taunts in my ear. Struggling against his hold, my heart racing in my chest. I know Ace would release me if I just asked, but that goes against my nature. Stomping my shoe into his shin, I buck wildly until he wrenches my arm back that bit more, making me scream. Red covers my vision, sending me down a dark path I should know better than wander down.

Leaning back on his chest, I raise my leg and swing at Spade's head.

"Hey!" Spade shouts, dodging my kick but jarring his shoulder in the process. He pulls himself to his feet and orders Ace to release me. I thought it was for a fair fight, but when he strokes my cheek, I still. Confusion washes over me, and I look for Angus, hoping for a clue how to react, but he's nowhere to be seen. "What's really got you all hyped up like this? Surely it's not just the quad you know we can fix."

"That's not the point," I jerk out of his hold, shoving back for Ace to give me some breathing space. "You guys gifted me that quad. No one has ever given me anything that wasn't sexually transmitted or for personal gain. It proves I'm one of you." Ducking away, I walk over to the pull-up bar. Maybe Ace is right; some physical exercise might be just what I need. Jumping up, I grab the bar and attempt to pull myself up to chin level. My arms shake and buckle, landing me back on my feet. Maybe not then. My back bumps into a firm chest, and one arm wraps around me.

"You don't need a bike to be one of us, although I vow to see it back to the exact condition it deserves to be. But it's this notion of fucking or fighting that concerns me more right now." I shrug but don't try to leave his hold. Something about Spade's protective hold and gentle tone after I just tried to kick him in the head strikes a new chord with me.

"That's all I know," my voice comes out too small. Another hand links into mine, Ace stepping in for solidarity purposes.

"Then it's time we change that," Spade states, and the pair share a nod over my shoulder. "Promise us you'll let the quad bike thing go and stay out of trouble for the rest of the day, and tonight, we're having a date."

"A date?" a third voice echoes from the doorway, and we all turn to see Malik standing there. Sharply dressed, ready for whatever meetings the day will bring, he takes one look at the vulnerability in my eyes and starts undoing his tie. "I believe that's a fantastic idea and long overdue. I'll stay with Candy today; you guys do whatever you need." Holding out his hand for me, I don't hesitate to move from Spade's hold and cross the room to take it. Jasper's words echo around my head, reminding me of the reason I needed to get some air in the first place, yet I don't feel constricted. Placing my hand in Malik's, the stress of the morning evaporates, and I finally feel free.

SPADE

Sticking a sign to the revolving glass door, I smooth it flat before triple checking the lock. Ace announced on all our business socials earlier this afternoon, but no doubt, people will still turn up just for confirmation. The Devil's Bedpost hasn't shut its doors a single night since opening, but it's official. We are closed for a private event. A fresh shiver of nerves rolls the length of my spine. Why I have no idea. I'm a fully fucking grown man, and women aren't difficult to please. But Candy's not just any woman.

"Are you sure this is the direction we should be going in?" Ace asks, setting down a vase of pink roses. "Candy's not really the flowers and fine dining type." Yep, that's what I'm worried about. Sighing, I cross the bar to the table we've spent all day fussing over.

"Maybe that's because no one's ever done it for her before," I grumble, really hoping I'm right. This rollercoaster ride she's taking us all on just keeps getting better, and I'm desperate to pin her down. But I find with every passing day; I can feel my anxiety levels rising that I'll wake up and she'll be gone.

"Fair enough," Ace shrugs. He tweaks with the cutlery and straightens the table cloth before crossing his arms. "Let's run through this again. The gourmet chef is already prepping in the kitchen, our doubles are tonight's waiters, and the playlist is ready to go from my phone. All that's left to do is light the candles and pour the wine."

Nodding, I grab a box of matches from behind the bar and throw them to Ace. He huffs but strikes one off, lighting the wick of each candle placed around the central vase. Following a mad rush to town, we've pushed together four square tables and covered them with a white and rose gold trim cloth. Four places have been set with circular mats, silver cutlery, and a wine glass. After pouring for each of us, I place the wine bottle back in its ice bucket beside the window. Twisting my lips, I sense something is missing. Picking a head from one of the roses, I sprinkle the petals in any white gaps to complete the look. There.

"I still think we should have had a backup plan in case she's feeling reckless. Like axe throwing or some shit," Ace snorts and tosses the box of matches onto one of the nearby low tables.

"We are not handing Candy an axe while there's another female in the house. Jack's intent on keeping Cherry around, so the least we can do is make sure she keeps her head." Ace shakes his head at the ridiculousness of it all, and I have to agree. Whatever Jack is trying to prove, that he can make a functioning relationship work or just to make Candy jealous, it's making life impossible for us all. Worse than that, he's putting Cherry at risk by keeping her here. I don't condone Candy's irrationality, but we've welcomed her into our domain and given her free reign. It's too late to take that away now, even if we wanted to.

I step back from the table and exhale deeply. It's done. Ace heads out back to connect his phone to the speaker system, leaving me to wander aimlessly towards the mirror at the back of the bar. My blue eyes catch the light, sparkling with apprehension. I've gone all out in wearing a black suit and tie, forgoing the sling for tonight. I'm healing quickly and just a little sore after the daily physiotherapy workouts. Shiny dress shoes feel uncomfortable on my feet, and I twist my neck against the tightness of the collar. How does Malik do this every day? Scratching a hand over my jaw and the neatly trimmed stubble there, I then trail my palm over my braids which are tied back in a lengthy ponytail.

The door to my right opens, presenting the pink-haired bombshell in all her glory. A gold satin dress hugs her every curve. My jaw drops at the shimmering material that flares slightly by her high-heeled feet. The neckline dips low to her sternum, just about hiding her pebbled nipples with a slip of fabric head in place with spaghetti straps. I wonder how long Malik's had this number stashed away. Her pink waves are loose, and the movement of her jaw hints at her chewing gum. At least she hasn't completely changed. Looking around, Candy's eyes ensnare mine, and she beckons me to her.

"Fuck Candy," I breathe. A hand winds around her waist as I close the gap between us, Malik stepping in at her side with a smirk. I pay him no mind, sliding a hand around Candy's slender neck and pulling her in for a kiss. There's no chance in hell of resisting her when she's this stunning. Her lips welcome mine, quickly dominating our kiss with powerful strokes of her tongue before pushing her wad of gum into my mouth.

"Hold onto that for me," she winks. Ace has appeared at her back, ushering her past me while I spit her gum into the trash can behind the bar. Yeah, thanks, but no thanks. I rush to catch up with the trio, wanting to witness Candy's reaction myself. Moving to the head of the table, I pull out the chair intended for her.

"Oh," Candy mutters, staring at the flowers. Her eyebrows twitch, and dread knots in my stomach. Her chocolate eyes scan the entire length of the table before lifting them to rest on mine. "You guy did all of this…for me?" she asks softly.

"Of course we did. You're worth this and so much more," I reply honestly. Voicing our feelings is obviously not a skill the Monarchs possess, but Candy must know at this point she's not some fleeting fascination for us.

"I don't think so somehow," she laughs, and I notice Malik's grip around her waist tighten. "I once sold my soul to Spanish Jesus for 50 cents and a stick of gum." Ace, Malik, and I share a look until I clear my throat, signaling for Candy to take the chair I'm holding out. She drops down with a tilt to her naturally pink lips that melts my heart. Brushing my fingers across her shoulder, I move for the seat Malik is trying to take and nudge him again.

"You've had her to yourself all day. It's my turn to be close to her," I warn him in a low tone. Maybe I'm slightly pent-up from nerves, but Malik doesn't react. Instead, he pulls me in for a one-armed hug.

"I must say, I'm surprised, Spade. I'd expected a massive movie projector with some pizzas and popcorn," he tilts an eyebrow, and my face drops. Shit. That's a much better idea – we should have done that! Chuckling, Malik moves to the other end of the table, and I relax in my seat.

"First date of many. There's always next time," I smile easily back. Behind that smile, I swallow past the lump in my throat, hoping I won't regret those words later. Until then, though, I need to dig deep and find that careful guy Candy likes me for instead of this Malik copycat I've become.

"So," Candy leans her elbows on the table to lie on her hands. "What do people do on these kinds of dates?"

"Not throw axes," Ace mumbles beneath his breath, and I kick him under the table.

"Drink good wine, eat good food, share a conversation," I list off. "Then we're going to take you upstairs and shove a dick in each of your holes until you're a living cum dumpster." Malik chokes on his drink while Ace whoops in agreement, and just like that, order has been restored.

"Sounds perfect," Candy grins, taking her wine glass in hand. Nick and Gabriel appear with our first courses, serving with the timed precision only employees hired by Malik could. Setting our plates down, we fall into silence to enjoy our artistically presented scallops. They're divine, perfectly cooked with a slight crust. We should dine like this more often.

"Oh, my baby beluga," Candy gasps. "Is this what food can

taste like? I always refused Leicester's family dinners because I thought they'd eventually turn into skeleton rabbits from their fancy, tiny portions." Her small moans are music to my ears, and my chest puffs out proudly. Sure, the chef was Ace's idea, but after all the snarky comments about this not being the right type of date, I think I've pulled it off. We made Candy our queen, and it's damn time we started treating her like one.

After finishing every spec of food on her plate, Candy pushes to her feet. "I need to learn how to make this," she declares. I'm unable to form an argument before she's moving across the bar, and we all scramble to catch up to her. Passing through the games room, the lookalikes flinch as if they weren't just helping themselves to Malik's sideboard. Guess we'll be looking for new staff in the morning. Candy enters the kitchen first, gushing over Chef Mitchell and his incredible food.

"Well, thank you very much," the burly man beams. It's not the first time Mitchell has cooked for us, and it won't be the last; the man's a food genius. He's not a typical chef with his rosy cheeks, ginger beard beneath a hair net, and heavily inked arms, but not only is he incredibly skilled, we genuinely enjoy his company —a rarity in this household.

"Do you mind if I watch you work?" Candy asks, hoisting herself up on a spare bit of counter. Her gold dress strains around her chest, not that she notices. Candy's too busy swinging her legs back and forth; Ace and I share a shrug. If she's happy, we're happy.

"Not at all," Mitchell smiles, but his eyes keep trailing back to the spot where Candy's sitting. Malik takes the hint, lifting her off the side and placing her onto a nearby stool.

"Spoilsport," Candy smirks. Fascinated by Mitchell's movements as he creates our main course, we fall into easy conversation until something collides with the back door, followed by the undertone of voices back and forth. I share a look with Malik, and the bang comes again.

"Excuse me," I press a light kiss to Candy's forehead and turn away before she sees the unconcealable anger fall over my face. My back is ramrod straight as I keep my strides even, slipping out of view into the night. Jack's blonde hair whips around the side of the building, his face strained.

"What the hell is going on back here?" I demand. He grunts and disappears again, so I circle around to see Cherry fighting against his grip. Oh, hell no.

"You are blowing this way out of proportion," Cherry struggles, wriggling free of his hold and rushing over to address me. "I just want to let Candy know I didn't go near her quad. I swear I didn't." Cherry's large eyes are pleading, her red hair rumpled from scuffling with Jack. Considering the blouse and skinny jeans she's wearing, I reckon she just got back from her night away. I sigh, not having time for this right now.

"We're in the middle of dinner," I state coldly. Not just dinner, but the best date Candy will have ever had if I have anything to do with it. A small voice in the back of my head reasons that if we can just show Candy, she doesn't need to live in fight or flight mode, she might balance herself out. And Cherry interrupting at this crucial moment will send all of that to hell.

"I know, I know, I'm sorry," Cherry nods. "I just…I need to clear the air. I'm not interested in starting a war with her. Why would I even attack her bike in the first place?" I frown, pointing towards Jack, who rushes forward.

"Because she and J-" I start, but he barrels past her and elbows me in the ribs. I shout at the jolt of my shoulder, grabbing my bicep to hold my arm in place. Jack's green eyes promise death, and the understanding dawns. Cherry doesn't know about Candy and Jack. Then it's true, she wouldn't have the motive, but now's not the time to discuss it.

"Like I was trying to say," Jack tells her. "I appreciate you mean well, but now's not the time. We can sit down together tomorrow and talk, but only as long as all of us are there to detain Candy if need be." I grunt in agreement, and we stare at Cherry, urging her to go back to Jack's truck for the evening if need be. Just to stay out of here for a few more hours, and I'll do whatever intervention bullshit is needed tomorrow.

"Are you guys scared of her?" Cherry narrows her eyes and folds her arms.

"Pssh, what? No," I shake my hand, and Jack forces a laugh. "No, no. Not at all. But I'd better get back before she realizes I've been out here talking to you during our date night. I'd like my balls to remain attached." Cherry rolls her eyes, and Jack swoops in to lead her away. Ducking back inside, I return just in time to see Candy leaning over a saucepan. She gasps upon lifting a ladle, fully immersed in the wobble of her egg.

"Look at me, Spade! I'm poaching!" she cries. Her smile is everything at that moment, and I never want to see her without it again. "Can you grab my phone from the bar? My old crackhead friend Simon bet if I could poach an egg, he'd summon his grandma's spirit to tell her poaching isn't a form of witchcraft." I'm pretty sure I don't want anything to do with that but walk through the lower level of the building anyway. My hands are in my pockets, and my head dipped low as I muse to myself how innocently joyful Candy looked over her creation. I reckon my hunch was right - Candy is a creation of the life she's had to lead. Her experiences have molded her. Now she's ours; we can give her a reason to smile like that more.

Pushing the metal door open, I step into the bar. Heat floods my face, pulling me to an instant stop. Sphinx sits beside a smashed bowl on the floor, licking it clean and remaining completely oblivious to his surroundings while my heart jackhammers in my chest. Upon the table above his head, the candles have been knocked over and ignited the table cloth in flames. That I could deal with, if it weren't for the tendrils of flame that have dripped onto the nearby rug beneath the coffee table. Almost in slow motion, I watch the flickering element climb the leg of the coffee table and stroke the edges of the matchbox on top. Shit.

"Fire!" I yell over my shoulder and rush inside. My hands hover uselessly in front of me while I think of what to do. Ducking behind the bar, I fill jugs of water with one hand and attempt to throw them at the flames, but it's no use. The fire has seeped into the wooden floor and taken a fancy to our handcrafted wooden furniture. It's spreading quicker than I can contain it, so there's only one thing to do. Get out of here.

Candy's phone lights up on the chair where she must have left it, and I divert in my tracks, keeping my right arm pressed against my mid-section. Flames lick at my shoes as I grab the device and turn back on myself when a mewl catches my ear —damn cat. Unsurprisingly, Candy's phone doesn't have a lock, so I locate her call app, finding only four contacts. At the top, I tap 'Emergency Services' and sandwich the phone between my ear and shoulder whilst looking for Sphinx.

"9-11, what's your emergency?" an operator asks, and I quickly relay the details, followed by the address to the Devil's Bedpost, and hang up. Spotting the hairless feline beneath the table, I kick the closest chair aside and try to call for it. When that doesn't work, I grab for his collar and miss. Fucking cat is going to get me killed. A cough erupts from my throat, burning a trail of ash all the way down to my lungs. Covering my nose with the crease of my elbow, I'm forced to drop onto my knees amongst the flames and reach out with my right arm. Agony slices through my shoulder at each jerky movement, but with fire pressing in on me from all sides, I manage to grab Sphinx by the scuff of his neck. He hisses, sinking his teeth into my hand, but I don't let go, pushing up and running out of there as fast as I can.

"Fire!" I shout again. This time my voice is hoarse, and I stagger into the kitchen, coughing heavily. Everyone bursts into action, with Candy taking Sphinx and Ace ushering me outside. "Why didn't you guys come when I shouted?"

"We thought you were joking," Ace shrugs sheepishly. Malik stays behind to make sure everyone is out and safe before joining us in the rear parking lot, although I reckon he needed a moment to look upon the flames consuming his beloved bar. Jack jumps off the hood of his truck and runs over as Cherry appears from the side of the building.

"It's okay," she says quickly. "I've called the fire brigade. They're on their way." I frown, shooing Ace's hands off me.

"That was fast. How did you even know the bar was on fire? It's not visible from back here." The others don't seem too worried about my question as they rip the jacket from my pocket, drawing a pained cry from me. Cherry, however, glares at me with the force of thunder.

"I needed a walk to clear my head and saw the flames through the glass door." She purses her red lips, drawing on an attitude I've not seen from her before. I wonder what else she's hiding. Luckily, Candy pays her no attention and makes a point of ignoring Jack completely.

"Spade, you're burnt. We need to get this shirt off you," Malik says as he removes my tie with too much care. His hands are still and precise, yet his dark eyes swim with concern. It must be bad. I stand still, allowing him to unbutton my shirt, and together, he, Ace, and Jack peel the cotton from my body. I grimace at the slice of melted fabric tugging at my skin, asking the world once again, why is it always me?

Sirens blare in the distance, growing closer as we make our way around the building. The red flashes light up the darkened dirt track, and within minutes, two trucks are pulling up side by side. Three men and a woman hop out of the first, getting to work by unraveling the hose and releasing the jet spray against our smashed-out windows. Whereas the first is clearly well used, the second truck sits there, shiny and red like a movie prop. The contrast in upkeep between the two strikes me as odd but not as much as the two men who jump out of the cab and rush towards us.

"Erm, guys? The fire's that way," I point my good hand towards the building. Neither seems concerned, tipping their yellow hats in my direction. Both men reach 6ft, fill out their fire suits with obvious muscle, and have freakishly straight teeth in their chiseled smiles. Their eyes sweep over Candy with too much familiarity, who's too concerned with comforting Sphinx to notice their predatory gazes.

"Candy, Candy, Candy," the first male says. Candy's head whips up, and her concern is forgotten as she tosses Sphinx to the ground. "As usual, you always know how to heat up a party." The other removes a strap from his shoulder, revealing an old-style boom box that had been concealed behind his suit. Shoving it into Jack's hands, he presses play for 'Buttons' by The Pussycat Dolls to leak from the speakers. The first fireman takes Candy's hand while Mr. Boombox snares Cherry's, drawing the girls away from the crowd.

"What the fuck is happening here?" Ace seethes, and I shake my head.

"I have no idea." Right up until Mr. Boombox rips his uniform in half, revealing a set of washboard abs. He draws Cherry's hand down the length of his torso, hooking her fingers into his waistband while he body rolls and stretches his biceps behind his head. They're fucking strippers.

Candy's well acquainted with hers, rocking her pelvis against his in time with the music. Ace is the one to rush forward, whipping Candy off her feet and hoisting her over his shoulder.

"Wait, wait!" Candy pounds her fist on Ace's back. He pauses just beside me so she can crane her neck to meet my gaze. "Best. Date. Ever!" Her lips crash against mine, nipping and sucking playfully. Fuck it. I step into her kiss, taking every ounce of pleasure I deserve for saving Sphinx. Our tongues swirl, creating an inferno of our own until a sharp jerk from Ace's shoulder tears us apart. "Oh, by the way, the call-out fee alone for this type of emergency service is $300, so I'll leave you to deal with that."

Without sparing us a second glance, Ace retreats to Jack's truck and locks Candy behind the blacked-out windows of the backseat with him. Jack just stands and stares at his so-called girlfriend rubbing against the stripper, indecision clawing at his features. As far as I know, Malik spoke to Jack after he got down and dirty with

Candy. I figured since he'd clearly sought out Cherry afterward, he'd made his decision. The tension between his eyebrows now, though, show not even he's sure what he wants anymore. My head swims, and I blow out a steady breath, trying not to pass out from the pain consuming my arms and thighs.

"Hey Malik," I reach out. His hand grips mine so I can use his weight to lower myself to the gravelly floor. "Next time, we call it quits at pizza and popcorn."

CANDY

The house is buzzing with life from the minute my eyes open. I stretch on a yawn, my fingers grazing the metals bars of Malik's headboard. Flopping onto my side, I already know I'll find the mattress cold and empty as I can hear his barked orders from the floor below. Credit given where it's due, he remained rather calm last night, despite the vein threatening to blow a vessel in his head. Today, however, I can already tell I'll need to bring the full Candy charisma to remind him why a bit of charred wood and broken glass doesn't really matter.

Rolling out of bed, I head to the bathroom first, returning with Malik's toothbrush hanging from my mouth. I brush lazily whilst searching for something to wear. The gold dress I had on last night has moved from the crumpled floor tile I left it and is now hanging in a see-through bag on the wardrobe door, ready for dry cleaning. Rummaging around inside the wardrobe, I take two hangers off the rail and hook them on my index finger. That'll do nicely.

Emerging from the bedroom a short while later, I straighten the tie hanging over my cleavage. I was pleasantly surprised at the drawer full of rolled ties I found, and most of all that there was more than one shade of pink in the mix. I selected a pale shade in smooth satin to pair with the white shirt I've rolled up to my elbows and left open the top four buttons. A soft grey pair of slacks are pulled up to my waist, cinched with a belt to make my ass look dreamy. I've even gone the extra mile to tie my hair in a high, messy ponytail with a few waves framing my face.

Trotting down the stairs, I make a pit stop in my room for my latest purchase, custom white high-tops with a hot pink stripe. Perfect. I leave the laces undone, so the tongue hangs over the front of the slacks. I swing my door open as a giant filling the frame lifts his hand to knock.

"What the...Woah," Ace breathes. His eyebrows disappear beneath his floppy brown hair, his stubbled jaw hanging open. "What's all of this?"

"I'm taking over. Malik can't stress about what he doesn't control anymore," I shrug, taking Ace's hand. He chuckles roughly, closing his huge fingers over my small palm.

"I wouldn't be so sure about that." Ace and I walk down the hall with me turning his hand over in mine and my mind wandering. They really are girthy fingers. Without realizing, I'm drawn into Ace's room, and he's released me to rifle through a drawer in his desk. "If you really want to mean business, you should wear these," he grins, providing a pair of reading glasses. The frames are circular and big enough to swamp my face, not to mention making my vision all blurry.

"Do I look hot?" I strike a pose, almost toppling over. Ace catches me, winding his arms around my back for his growing erection to stick into my hip. I'll take that as a yes. "That's all that matters. Come on; there's a big bad wolf I need to blow before he threatens to burn the rest of this house down."

"I'm not sure that's how the story goes," Ace muses, his stubble grazing my cheek as he plants a longing kiss there. I will definitely be revisiting this scenario later when the crashing and banging downstairs has been resolved. Glasses, tie, and everything.

"It does when I tell it." Drawing Ace into the hallway, another body bumps into me. Hands capture my waist before quickly whipping away but not before I see the flare of desire flash through Jack's hazy green eyes. His hair blends into a mess of yellow, quickly joined by the flash of red that is Cherry.

"Just keep moving. We'll deal with this situation later," says Ace, guiding me towards the elevator. I don't need my eyes to sense the tension in the air, just like I didn't need ears to hear Jack grilling Cherry last night. In direct contrast with how angry I was about my quad yesterday, this morning presents a new day and hence, a new mindset. Seems like Cherry is intent on ruining her own chances with Jack, so I'll sit back and let her get on with it.

The doors close us inside with the smell of bleach that still hasn't faded. I'm not sure who disposed of the bodies that were heaped in here not so long ago, only that they did a fantastic job at covering all bases. I inhale deeply, allowing the fumes to douse any rising fury I have for Jack, the lying bastard, and his desperate groupie, not lying to me, but to himself. He knows I rocked his world, and he's treating me like a stranger. More fool him.

Introduced with a ping, the doors slide open, and I stride into the chaos with confidence. After all, remaining calm in the face of danger is my whole niche. Malik's voice can be heard from the bar, yelling for someone to be careful and others to get out of the way. I spot his fuzzy outline through the mirror before pushing the dividing door open with Ace's hands steadying me from behind.

"Stop panicking, everyone. I'll be taking over from here." No one stops or even pays me attention, other than Malik. Through my skewed vision, I mostly see the color black, and the taste of cremated dreams hit the back of my throat. The funeral director himself, dressed in a depressing black suit, strides over to me with a frown pinching his features.

"What are you up to?" Malik asks tentatively. I reach out, using his arm for balance to walk further inside. The majority of the damage is in the center of the room, outlined by a black smear across the wooden floor. The tables, sofas and front wall are the biggest victims, but luckily, the actual bar isn't in too bad condition.

"I'm taking over business for today. You're relieved of your duties," I say absentmindedly, releasing Malik to shoo him away. Ace is right behind me still, and a gasp in the doorway announces Cherry and Jack's arrival.

"Erm," Malik hesitates, his head swinging around a mile a minute. "Do you know the first thing about renovating after fire damage?" I scoff at his tone, holding a hand up to his face.

"I know everything. And first things first, you need to go. Your negative stress levels are going to kill the morale of my team."

"She's not wrong there," Gabriel mutters, passing with a lump of ash-coated wood in his hands. "But then again, please don't leave us alone with her." Rude. I flip him off, returning my attention to Malik. He's already shaking his head, a rejection on the tip of his tongue.

"Am I as much a part of this team as everybody else?" I challenge, popping my hip.

"Yes but-"

"So shouldn't I get a say in the bar as well?" I take a step closer, daring him to deny me.

"Of course, but..." Malik sighs, hanging his head. "You're going to make everything pink, aren't you?"

"Believe it or not, Malli-moo, pink doesn't suit every occasion. I liked the whole modern-day western vibe, and with me controlling things in here, you can have time to build new furniture in the garage with the other Monarchs. Wouldn't you prefer to get back to your roots and bond with them like the good old days, rather than shouting around orders in here?" I sense his defeat before his shoulders sag, and Malik pulls his tie loose.

"How do you always see what's best for me when I don't even realize it myself?" He pulls me into a kiss instead of letting me answer, transferring his sense of longing and wonder through his touch. I revel in it, feeling wanted and confident in only the way a woman with the complete faith of her man would. Releasing me,

Malik draws my attention to Spade, who has appeared on a stool beside us, his body more bandage than skin right now.

"Spade. You should be resting, but we all know you're a stubborn mule about taking care of yourself. I'll head out back with Ace to look at what tools we have. You stay here and don't let Candy out of your sight."

"Wouldn't dream of it," Spade drawls, his piercing blue eyes resting on me. I remove the glasses, stepping in between his legs as Malik leaves us to it. A part of me is stunned I managed to get him to agree. Power of the magical pussy, bing, bang, bosh.

"How are you feeling?" I ask, carefully stroking the areas around Spade's bandages. He's only wearing a pair of cotton shorts which loosely hang over the dressing disappearing beneath. In addition to his shoulder, there's now patches of white tape along the length of his bronzed biceps and one covering his left ribs and pec. I lean forward, pressing a feather-light kiss to his collar bone, and remain there. Not touching him but close enough for his heady scent to embrace me.

"Same as the day I met you like I've been hit by a truck." I glance up into Spade's oceanic eyes, losing myself in their sparkling depths. His full lips are set in a hard line, and a thread of niggling doubt worms its way through my gut.

"Do you regret it?" I breathe, scared of the answer but needing to know. "Meeting me? All you seem to do is get hurt when I'm around." I return my lips to his left shoulder, gently moving them back and forth over his soft skin.

"If I could do it all over," Spade grunts, tilting my chin up to return to his face, "I wouldn't change a thing because then I wouldn't get to see you look at me like that. It shows you care, and I don't think that's a privilege many get often." I can feel it, the hint of worry seeping from my eyes and the slight frown dragging around my mouth. I do care. The bar staff continues heaving away chunks of dead wood around us, but the moment Spade and I have created is untouchable. I smooth my fingers over his solid jawline, drinking in his beauty.

"You were the first one to show me love, you know. That day you found me in the basement after Jasper stuffed me in the barrel, and you just held me. You don't have to say it; I felt everything shift at that moment. I wouldn't still be here if it wasn't for you, Spade." My voice is sore, and my heart opens a crack, just enough to let this gorgeous man slither in and stake his claim. I didn't even know I felt that way until the words came out. Now the truth hangs between us on a shared smile and brief contact of our lips.

Clearing my throat, I turn in the cage of his body, careful not to push back against him. "Okay, everyone, stop what you're doing and come in for a team meeting." The staff share an unimpressed look, all six of them, but slowly wander over anyway. Both the lookalikes and the female waitresses have been provided matching blue overalls to wear, most of which are already covered in soot and ash. Their hands are filthy with more than a few smudges over their faces, and the ladies especially seem highly unimpressed.

"It just so happens; I'm in charge now," I start strong.

"A horrible decision," someone mutters, but I don't catch who.

"So we need to revise our game plan and make sure everybody knows what they need to do. First order of business, does anyone know the Muffin Man?"

"The Muffin Man?" Spade's double, Greg, asks.

"Yes, the Muffin Man." I nod.

"Yeah, I know the Muffin Man," Max raises his hand at the back of the group. His beach blonde hair needs a touch-up and he's making a habit of leaving his green contacts out, but otherwise is a perfect match of Jack's. "He owns the coffee and pastry cart on Dury Avenue. I've got his number on speed dial."

"Perfect," I beam. "No one can work on an empty stomach. Give him a call to come on down here; breakfast is on Malik. Greg, can you handle the socials to let people know we'll be closed this week, but there will be a grand reopening of The Devil's Bedpost on Friday, hashtag under new management." I wink, popping my collar like the boss I am. "The rest of you can work with me on planning the party of the century, starting with new uniforms.

You're bar staff, not funeral directors." Excited murmurs break out amongst the group, and I turn to Spade, brushing my hands together for a good job well done.

"What about clearing the debris?" one of the waitresses asks as we all head in the direction of the revolving door that's missing its glasswork. I want to say her name is Debbie, but I wouldn't put money on it. I tend to ignore other straight women since there's nothing I can gain from them. "Malik said we need to clear as much as possible because this afternoon deliveries begin to arrive."

"Are you kidding me? We're not a freaking removals company. The deliveries can be stored in the basement for now, and we'll hire the professionals to handle this mess," I kick over a chair that had nothing wrong with it; I just didn't particularly like it.

"Are you sure about this? I'm in my final year of uni, and I really need to keep this job. There's nothing else for me around this area as well paid." We all step onto the porch via door frame and bask in the mid-morning sun. A few other pairs of eyes are staring nervously at the side of my head, suddenly unsure of my decisions, but I just smile.

"Malik has a tendency to get caught up in his own head and devise unrealistic expectations. I see it as my role in his life to shatter those expectations and prove to him the world is still going to orbit the sun, regardless of how shiny his shoes are or how tight his collar is. It's not going to be pretty, but it'll be worth it for all our sakes." The staff seem satisfied, and Max gets on the phone to call our coffee cart. Leaning over the porch railing, Spade steps in behind me and places his hands on either side of my arms.

"You should consider motivational speaking as an alternative career," he murmurs, clearly amused. I twist and push myself up on the railing, meeting his blue gaze.

"Issue is, that'd take up valuable time that I could be rocking your world, and wouldn't that be a shame?" I smirk, playfully licking my top lip.

"A crying shame," Spade agrees, lashing out to take my tongue into his mouth and dominate it with his. Injuries forgotten, Spade's straining crotch rolls against my core, riding the power trip I've started. His fingers dig into my sides as his mouth assaults mine, leaving me marked, bruised, and oh so impressed. Like his brothers, Spade has become addicted to the flavor of Candy and I'm not complaining. I reckon I stumbled across the jackpot the day I decided to break into the Devil's Bedpost, and this is a prize I refuse to squander.

ACE

Thanks to my morning eyeful of Malik's balls, quickly followed by an impromptu fall down the stairs, I've taken to hiding in the garage for the rest of the day. It's where I was headed anyway, needing to meet with the mechanics who came to take Candy's quad to the shop for repairs, but now there's no need for me to resurface. Sweat pours down my forehead, and my arm is cramping from the vigorously waxing of the dark maple slab beneath me.

Malik was supposed to be working on this new table centerpiece with me since Candy ordered him to, but unsurprisingly he had some business calls to make on the first day and never came back. Fine by me, I've seen too much of him this morning anyway. I'm quite happy, losing myself to the rock music streaming from my phone and relishing the sweet burn in my muscles. I'm so caught up; in fact, I don't notice the side door open and another presence in the room until a hand slams down on my shoulder.

"Hey man, how's it going?" Jack smirks, nudging me playfully.

"All good here, just finding my zen amongst the carnage." We share a dry chuckle before Cherry appears, totting over on skinny heels. Skin-tight jeans grip her long legs, and a large knit jumper in pale grey hangs from one shoulder. I'm pretty sure I've seen Candy in something like that before. Beneath huge framed shades, her lips are painted red and tilted up in an easy smile.

"Oh hey Ace, looking good." Both Jack and I straighten, raising an eyebrow her way, and she stutters. "No, sorry, I meant - the wood. The wood you're polishing, it looks really good-"

"Do me a favor," Candy's voice sounds as she also appears around the corner. *Great*, the whole gangs here. "Stop talking to my man about his polished wood." She pays Cherry no mind, striding over to me in the exact same outfit minus the heels. A pair of badass biker boots hug her feet and lace-up past her shin. I hold my grimy, oiled hands away, but Candy grabs my wrists and winds them around her body anyway. Hooking her arms around my neck, I forgo the rising tension clogging up my pace and sink my face into the bend of her neck. Her pomegranate scent fills my senses, giving me a better high than any drug on the market.

"We're heading out," Jack's voice breaks through my daze. Whatever playfulness I caught a glimpse of moments ago has died a sudden death, leaving him grumpy in its wake. After hitting the button on the wall to release the automatic garage door, Jack gestures for Cherry to get in his truck. "I'm running errands, and then Cherry wants to get her nails done. You need anything, Ace?" It doesn't go unnoticed that he acts as if Candy isn't in the vicinity, but she doesn't seem to care.

"No thanks," Candy replies with a mischievous grin. "We're coming with you."

"We are?" I ask. Her fingers dive into my hair, combing the overgrown brown length at the back of my neck.

"Yeah, we can be all coupley and shit too. Don't you want to see my nails all pretty when they're wrapped around your cock?" Now there's an invitation that's impossible to refuse; especially now the mental image is making my dick twitch.

"Well, I can't argue with that," I smirk but then catch the flash of red climbing into the passenger seat. Whatever Candy's planning, it doesn't end with a simple double date but denying her won't work either. She'll just steal a bike and go anyway. "You will...behave right?"

"Why do people keep asking me that? I'm impulsive, not a ticking time bomb." Candy kisses my cheek, moving towards the truck. I twist my neck, sharing a look with Jack, who's now behind the wheel. He shakes his head, and I sigh, grabbing for a hand towel to wipe my hands clean. I reach for my t-shirt and follow Candy's tight ass into the back of the cab. I should have learned to control myself better by now, but every time Candy is nearby, I'm like a stud panting after his bitch. She crawls over the leather seats on her knees, and my hand flexes with the urge to spank her. She drops down and wriggles to pull her jeans a little looser around the crotch while I wish I could rip them off completely.

"This is a terrible idea," Jack mutters from the front seat, putting the truck into drive. I slide over into the middle, carefully securing Candy's seatbelt in place and then wrapping my arm around her for extra measure. Not from the fear of a crash and not even for her own protection, but for Cherry's, just in case the redhead says something that might set Candy off. Contrary to her invitation, I'm under no illusion that I'm accompanying Candy today as her bodyguard instead of her boyfriend. Although my role is to guard the world from her rather than the other way round. I hate to sound like Malik, but it would all be so much easier if she'd just stay home where we can keep watch over her.

The truck guns its way down the open freeway to the closest town, in as much a rush to get this trip over with as Jack and I. His green eyes meet mine in the rear-view mirror often, mentally conveying that I'd better be on top of my game. Swinging into a parking lot, he pulls over to let me usher Candy out of the truck first. I manage to wrangle her onto the pavement before he speeds away to find a space.

"What the fuck?!" Candy shoves out of my arms. "If you wanted me to hop out the cab, you could have just asked nicely." I cock my brow at her, knowing she wouldn't have listened. There's a plan brewing behind those brown eyes, and her reaction is enough to confirm it. Standing on her tiptoes, Candy looks around for a sight of Jack and Cherry. Spotting them across the other side, she grabs my hand and drags me along to intercept them at the exit. "That was lucky. We almost got separated," Candy says.

"What a crying shame that would have been," Jack drawls sarcastically. Cherry clings to his arm, purposely avoiding looking our way as we move forward in an awkward unit. Pedestrians are forced to step onto the road to get past, not daring to challenge our authority. The sheer tension radiating from Candy and Cherry alone is palpable, while Jack and I act as their bodyguards.

"Didn't you say you guys have errands to run?" Candy asks after a short while of walking. "Us ladies can head to the salon, and you can catch up with us there later."

"Not a fucking chance," Jack stops abruptly to growl. Cherry's eyes widen, silently pleading him to stay with her.

"Oh, don't be a second-rate cock-wrangler your whole life. The nail bar is right over there," Candy points across the road. The 'Pinky Blossom' is alive with female customers sitting before a row of tables behind the huge windows. Each station has a clear divider separating the clients from a beautician wearing a face mask, pretending to listen to their gossip while using mini drills and other strange appliances on their nails.

"I do want to get in before it gets any busier," Cherry mumbles, unsure of herself. "And it'll take a while to fix this hot mess." She glances at her nails which I can't see anything wrong with, but it's not my forte. My nails are currently soaked in varnish and chipped to shit. "Don't worry, Jackikins; I'm sure it'll be fine." Her brown eyes slide to Candy's, and for a moment, it's like a mirror has been placed in between them. Long, blinking lashes, a slight upturn to their noses, heart-shaped faces. It still freaks me out how Jack managed to find a woman so similar in looks yet so different in personality.

"Well, it's settled. Come on then." Candy grabs onto Cherry's forearm and drags her out into the road. A car skids to a stop, drawing a scream from Cherry, but Candy drags her onwards, not releasing her until they reach the other side. I'm too caught up in my sense of foreboding to realize Jack has stepped into my personal space.

"If anything has happened to Cherry by the time I return," he glares at me with his face contorted in rage. "I'm holding you personally responsible." Jack gives my chest a shove and turns away until I grab his t-shirt in my fist. Spinning him around, I scare a pair of old ladies walking by as I slam Jack's back into the closest building.

"The concern you're currently feeling is on you." I give him another slam into the brickwork. "You moved another woman into the house where a possessive psychopath now lives. Don't threaten me because of your bullshit choices." Jack's face is thunder, his eyes so full of anger, I barely recognize him. Where is the relaxed, unshakeable guy I used to rely on the mellow me out?

"If she's such a psychopath, why have you allowed yourself to fall in love with her?" Jack spits, pushing me a step away. I release his t-shirt roughly, the scowl embedded in my features.

"For the same reason, you're pretending you haven't. She speaks to the demons living deep inside, and instead of pretending they don't exist, she embraces me. Just the way I am. You should let her in some time, or was it you who is desperate to be in her?" I chuckle to myself, dodging out the way of Jack's incoming fist. His swing was slopping because he's all over the fucking shot, acting on impulse instead of logic. That's what got him into this state in the first place when he couldn't resist Candy and is now living with the consequences. Keeping the smirk plastered on my face, I leave to catch up to the girls before Candy gets herself into trouble.

Inside the nail salon, the fumes of polish hit me tenfold than any varnish I was using in the garage. The place is heaving, with every seat taken and a line of ladies queued along a bench to the left. Above their heads, wooden hearts hanging on the walls contain mini shelves for all of the nail polishes. Every shade of color imaginable, and then again in neon or glitter. A couple of those waiting lower their magazines to drink in the sight of me, then nudge their friends to do the same. I suppose to anyone else, my battered jeans would seem fashionably distressed, and the grease mark that's seeped through into my t-shirt could be mistaken for a sweaty workout. Soon every eye in the place is on me, standing in the doorway as if I'm lost. All except the two pairs I'm looking for. Where the fuck is Candy and Cherry?

"Err, 'cuse me miss," I ask the approaching woman on her way to the exit. "Have you seen-" Candy's fuchsia pink hair darts from the furthest booth and resumes her place on the bench before Cherry appears from a rear bathroom. Pretending not to have seen the redhead, Candy catches my eye and waves me over. "Never mind," I grumble to the woman still waiting for me to finish my sentence, making my way through the crowded space. Spotting everyone staring after me, Candy leaps off the bench and pushes me down between a jumpy blonde and Cherry. Then, she proceeds to straddle me and lay claim to my mouth for all to see. Her raspberry flavored tongue enters my mind, and I let her have her possessive fill, no longer surprised by anything she does.

After an unnecessary display, although I'm not complaining, Candy swivels and drops down into my crotch. I catch her in time, preventing the complete annihilation of my dick, and ease her onto me gently.

"Never a dull day with you, is there?" Cherry comments, reaching out for a magazine from a side table.

"Not if I can help it," Candy shrugs against my chest. "You'd be wise to stay on my good side. Who knows, maybe there's hope for a friendship out of us yet." Okay yeah, Candy is definitely up to something. I nudge her, catching sight of those large brown eyes when she peers over her bare shoulder. How someone can look sexy in an oversized sweater is beyond me, but Candy owns everything she wears, touches, sees. Including me.

"Thought you didn't want any friends," Cherry scoffs, faking interest in some article. Candy doesn't break my stare, passing some silent communication I can't read. I reckon Candy is always thinking about one of two things, sex or revenge, and at this present moment in time, she's alluding to both.

"Honestly," Candy smirks, glancing at the side of Cherry's face. "I just didn't think you'd be around this long. It's my job to protect the Monarchs, even from their own stupidity." I bark a laugh, jolting her off balance with my thighs. I know she's referring to Jack, but she has a way of making it feel really personal when I'm sitting right here, eavesdropping in a conversation I'm not a part of. Honestly, I didn't realize Candy took her role as our queen so seriously, and it's slightly disconcerting how she's starting to sound like Malik.

"And now what? You've realized I'm here to stay, so you're ready to bond?" Cherry rolls her eyes. It doesn't escape my notice how the worried female clinging to Jack's arm outside has seemed to vanish, and the woman beside me is sitting ramrod straight, ready for a fight. Candy loudly pops a bubble of gum, snatching the magazine from Cherry's hands to fake read it herself.

"Sure, we'll go with that. It occurred to me you're still a complete stranger to all of us. We don't know the first thing about you. What's your real name, where did you come from, who hired you?"

"Who's next?" a nail technician thankfully interrupts wherever this conversation was going. The last booth on the end has opened up thanks to a lunchtime swap over; the same booth I saw Candy darting away from when I first entered. Candy doesn't move other than to stick a thumb in Cherry's direction.

"No, no, I wouldn't dream of keeping you waiting. You go first," Cherry replies, all sweet as pie. Her smile is too forced and there's a knowing tilt to her eyebrows.

"You go. I insist. Ace will keep me company while I wait." Candy wriggles her hips against my crotch to prove a point.

"Really, it's fine."

"Oh, I'll go," the woman to my right shoots to her feet, throwing her magazine down on the floor. "Some of us have places to be, you know." The blonde stomps over to the technician, who then guides her into the booth. Candy turns in my lap, planting her feet on the bench's vacated spot and muttering *'shit'* over and over. I can practically hear the cogs turning in her brain as a crowd of ladies exit a hidden room around the back. The leader of the group has her hair in curlers and a sash hanging over her satin robe to declare her the 'bride-to-be.' After the group has vacated, a handful of technicians follow them into the main area to announce the foot spas are now free.

Candy jumps up, grabbing my hand and hauling me into the back. Tall, leather recliners with bubbling pools of water at the base curve in a semi-circle around the room. Oceanic tunes soft play from small speakers in the corners, separating this area from the noise outside.

"Shoes off and sit," Candy orders, clicking her fingers at me like a dog. I laugh bitterly, crossing my arms. There's no way in hell she's getting me to sit in one of these pedicure chairs. I've seen Legally Blonde; I'm not totally oblivious to the things women get up to in their spare time. A pedicure becomes a bend and snap, and next thing I know; I'll be applying to Harvard. Candy's stubborn posture weakens, and she glances backward, clearly worried about something.

"Candy," I breathe beneath the low hum of music. "What did you do?" Other ladies file inside, and Candy lashes her arms out, claiming the two chairs on the end as ours.

"Get in the chair, and I'll tell you," she growls. The women and technicians are all staring at me, wondering if I'll obey my woman. I'll only look like an asshole if I don't, and I'm not in the business of being an asshole anymore. Grumbling that I don't like my feet being touched, I kick off my high-tops and socks before dropping into the chair. Out of nowhere, a male technician appears. A pure white streak has been added to his combed-back hair, and he winks at me above a blue face mask. You've got to be kidding me.

The male takes a mini pair of shears to my toenails, making me cringe with each cut. I squirm in my seat, trying to find that inner man that could look down the barrel of a gun and not flinch. Alas, that fucker has deserted me. He then eases my feet into the warm water and leaves to let them soak a while.

"Start talking," I tell Candy. She rolls her head over on her bare shoulder, looking at me through a thin veil of her pink hair.

"Just some basic sabotage, nothing that bad." I sigh, having figured as much.

"To what end? Maybe if you stopped seeing Cherry as the enemy, it might be easier on all of us." I didn't mean to hurt her feelings, but the frown I receive shows I did anyway. Words aren't my strong suit, so I reach out to take her hand, but she shrugs me off.

"Easier doesn't mean better. It just means thoughts go unspoken, and emotions are buried until they break free. Better to weed out the weak than to wait for her to strike again. Her oh-so-innocent act might have Jack, and the rest of you fooled, but I don't think with my dick." Ahh so this is either still about the quad bike or Jack's rejection. Just at that moment, a scream sounds from the room next door. Then again, followed by a pained hiss.

"Basic sabotage, huh?" I ask, and Candy hums in agreement. "Such as?"

"Standard shit. An extra sharpened nail file, some watered down varnish." This time, the cry of anguish is bordering a scream, and the ripple of glass shatters suggests the nail polish bottles have hit the floor. Candy pops another pink bubble of gum, staring at the ceiling as she hunts for patience to answer the question burning in my gaze. "I replaced the topcoat for ammonia. Causes chemical burns when it comes into contact with the skin."

"Candy!" I whisper shout, trying not to grab the attention of those around us. "You can't just burn some innocent woman." I'd meant the poor blonde now taking the brunt of Candy's grudge, but she clearly mistakes my meaning for Cherry. Removing her feet from the foot spa, Candy jumps onto the towel stretched across the floor, splashing water everywhere.

"Strange how you guys are quick to remind me of my downfalls, yet I've been tear-gassed, threatened, and had my property defaced since she arrived. If it'd been the other way around, I'd have been under watch 24/7 without privileges. You might as well take these as well since obviously, I'm too much of a liability to be around." Shoving her hand into her jeans pocket, Candy tosses me a handful of tiny screws. Grabbing her boots and striding away, I'm left staring at them in confusion until the mother of all crashes sounds through the wall. I jump up, patting my feet dry on the same towel and rushing around the corner to see the blonde heaped on the floor, next to the collapsed chair I'm holding the screws to. Fuck this.

High-tops in hand, I go in search of Candy. She didn't leave out the front, so I start opening random doors. A few are bathrooms, one of which was occupied without putting the lock on, I might add; the next several are set aside for massages or waxing. This place is like a house of mirrors, small on the outside but never-ending once trapped in the maze of corridors. Approaching a door that's slight ajar, I clock onto a set of female voices and pause outside to listen in.

"Bet you think you're real sly with the stunt you just pulled," a voice says that sounds too much like Cherry's to not be. It's hard to tell since I've never heard her tone quite as harsh, but it's definitely her.

"I take pride in my creativity," Candy replies, and my guts drop. "Unlike you. It doesn't take a genius to lead someone into a cleaning cupboard."

"Yet you fell for it anyway. It's about time you realized, I'm always going to be one step ahead of you," Cherry says. I can practically hear the smirk through her tone. Pulling out my phone, I hit the voice record button. Is it possible we've all been wrong about her? Maybe we should have listened to Candy instead of presuming she was being her usual, irrational self. "Jack's right. It really is pathetic watching you try so hard to get his attention."

"Oh, I have his attention," Candy responds. "The only pathetic one here is you, thinking you're the shit because you're screwing my Monarch. He's only using you to make me jealous." Cherry's responding laugh is hard and cold.

"Actually, I'm screwing *my* Monarch. Get it into your head; Jack chose me. Your nutcase routine doesn't work with him."

"It will when he realizes you're just a second-rate version of me. What's the point in keeping a copycat around when the real deal is right here?" I imagine Candy doing some kind of body roll, pointing at her chest and biting her lip. Cherry grunts, and there's a scuffle of someone being shoved.

"Bring it on bitch. I'm not scared of you, and I'm not going anywhere."

"We'll see," Candy replies. Another scuffle sounds, and I can foresee this becoming a full-on catfight in the cleaning cupboard. Switching off my phone and pocketing it, I prepare myself to yank the door open when Cherry's voice stops me.

"Oh, by the way, it's a shame your bike was sent off to be repaired. I, for one, thought it suited you much better when it looked like a piece of trash. Maybe next time, the damage will be permanent." My movements still as I curse myself for putting my phone away. Shit, that was practically an admission of guilt, but Jack won't take my word for it. He'll say I'm pussy whipped when it's obvious he's the one guilty of that particular crime. I retreat back to the nearest corner, throwing my voice along the length of the hallway.

"Candy? You back here?" I call out. A dull thud sounds from behind the door, swiftly followed by a heavy weight collapsing onto the floor. Fighting to open the door, Candy steps out with a wide grin.

"Oh, hey, Ace. I was just looking for the bathroom and got lost." Slipping into the hallway, Candy shoves her boot into the bulk slumped against the other side of the door and then slams it closed. "I'm over this place. You ready to go?"

"Er…sure. Have you seen Cherry anywhere? Jack will have my head if I leave without her." I push my hands into my jeans pockets, forcing myself to keep her eye line.

"Ummm not recently, maybe she already left," Candy shrugs. Walking over to me, I ignore the redness covering her knuckles and allow her to crash her lips against mine. Wrapping my arms around her, I allow myself to fall into Candy's aura. Her sugar-coated words and dangerous kisses. The sweet taste of revenge sweeping across her tongue and the hands that could do so much damage caressing my biceps. Whether she feels my regret at not believing her through our connection, I'm not sure, but I can at least prove I'm on her side from now on. Pulling Candy under my arm, I place one place kiss on the top of her vibrant colored head.

"Come on, let's go," I draw her away from the hallway, leaving Cherry firmly behind.

CANDY

Malik's bedroom door opens, and Mr. Sleepy Head himself strolls out. I sit back in the chair, enjoying the rare view before me. Ruffled hair, stubbed jaw, crinkled t-shirt. As he passes the dining table on the way to the kitchen, he pushes a hand into his super-tight, black boxers and rearranges his junk. If anyone were to see him now, they'd have no idea he was the bar's owner, and it leads me to wonder what it'd take to get Malik comfortable just being himself. No hiding behind his suits or orders, just at ease with his brothers.

After entering the kitchen, the coffee machine splutters to life, hissing steam into the mug below. Malik clatters about, bumping into the side and passing the doorway with his palms pressed into his eyes. My guess is he drank himself to sleep last night after I refused his nightcap. Mumbling away, Malik strides back through the dining area until his dazed eyes sweep over the table and find me sitting behind it.

"Jesus Christ, Candy," Malik jolts to a stop. "What the hell are you doing sitting here in the dark, and how have you stayed quiet for so long?"

"Quite flinchy this morning, aren't ya?" I muse, ignoring his questions. Gesturing to the chair opposite, Malik frowns and slowly eases himself down. Using an app on his phone, he switches on the overhead light, casting a glow over the two boxes sitting before me. I gift-wrapped and hand-tied the stupid, fiddly bows myself somewhere between my sixth Red Bull and passing out on the tabletop.

"Is that…drool?" Malik points to the glistening puddle by my arm. I wipe it up with my sleeve, not questioning why I felt the need to wear the hoodie I stole from Jasper for this particular talk.

"Or as I like to call it - free lube. We could bottle this shit and make a fortune. Anyways, concentrate. We've got serious business to discuss."

"Can I at least get my coffee first?" Malik asks, and I shake my head firmly.

"Pick a box," I demand, shoving them closer. It's do or die time, and I'm done waiting. "Pink is for me, obviously, and red is for *her*." There's no need to explain any further; the reference is clear enough. Like the colors before me, Cherry and I clash, and there's not enough room for the two of us here. Malik reaches out for my box without hesitation, and I slap his hand away. "Wait for it; you haven't heard the rules yet. You like rules so you'll appreciate the time I've put into this."

Standing, I carefully tuck my chair under the table and begin to pace. "At exactly, 2:07 am this morning in his bedroom, one Jack Diamond removed the back door key from his Ducati keychain and gave it to Cherry McBitchface. He said it was *'to help her feel safe'*." I finger quote in the air, turning a sarcastic glare to the man across the table. "But the only one in any danger of her being here is me."

"Rewind. How did you know what Jack said in his room?" he asks, frowning in concern. I sigh since that's beside the point but indulge him with an answer anyway.

"I was in the wardrobe with my nail clippers at the ready to chop her talons off when they fell asleep. On my way out, I stole it back from the bedside table. But all of that's irrelevant. She doesn't deserve to be here, she's done nothing but try to kill me since she arrived, and I won't stand for it!" I finish strong with my index finger pointed high in the air.

"I'm not dismissing the fact Jack should have spoken to me first, but we can't interfere with his relationship." I gag at that word, hating to think of Cherry as any more than a minor distraction. "Besides, other than your word, which I'm not discounting, there's been no evidence of Cherry trying to kill you. If anything, she's only tried to be your friend." Malik quirks a brow.

"A common tactic of distraction from a member of WAWA!" I shout, and Malik pinches the bridge of his nose.

"Nope, I'm not doing this without my coffee." Malik disappears into the kitchen, leaving me to pace once more. It's not a usual trait of mine; I must be harnessing Jasper through his hoodie. My mind trails off on the thought of my scarred twin and the way he looked before I ran. Ran from him and any feelings of uncertainty that I left behind in the attic. After a few minutes of brewing a fresh coffee, Malik returns with a steaming mug in each hand, placing one down for me. "Okay, I'm ready. What the fuck is WAWA?"

"The Women Assassinating Women Association," I sigh, slapping my hands against my jean-clad thighs. I haven't gone to bed and therefore am still wearing mostly the same clothes from yesterday. Plus, watching Jack and Ace throwing fists at each other in the parking lot was far too entertaining to walk away from. True to his word, Jack held Ace responsible after finding Cherry unconscious in the cleaning cupboard, and that possibly could have spurred the whole key-giving situation. Grunting, I take my coffee and down the steaming liquid. Big mistake now that I've burnt the living shit out of my gums, but it'll draw the caffeine into my body quicker. Probably.

"So, here's the deal," I continue, retaking my seat. "In my box is my key, and in the red is hers. Keeping all of your macho bullshit in check is a full-time job, and I can't do that while she's here fucking with my mind. But on the other hand, Jack is your family, and he's been here longer than I have. With tensions still running high, you should probably take his side. I know when it's time for me to hit the road find a new place to settle for a while. I've done it before, I can do it again, but the decision is yours. Take back the key of the person you decide should leave."

My breath sticks in my throat as my body goes into preparation mode for what Malik might say. This is the ultimate test. Will he toss me aside like yesterday's trash or keep me close? All the while, Jasper's words ring through my mind if he'll keep me too close, confusing the shit out of me. What's the lesser evil, and what do I really want? Malik's blank stare holds mine long enough to make me squirm before he grabs the red box. My mouth drops open, but that has nothing on how my heart plummets inwards my ass. I guess the truth of my desires is evident now in my reaction. Fuck, I wanted to stay.

Rising from the table, Malik strides away, leaving his coffee to go cold ,and I conclude that I've been dismissed. Yet I can't bring myself to move. My limbs have gone numb, and an unwelcome tingle claims my chest. Am I having a stroke? Tracking Malik's back in his crumpled t-shirt, possibly looking hotter to me than usual, he unlocked the balcony doors. Shoving them open with a powerful heave, he then rears back and throws the red box in his hand across the parking lot below. My eyebrows rise, and by the time he turns a furious glare on me, I'm utterly stunned.

"Soooooo, does this mean you chose me?" I ask, a smug grin taking residence on my face. In fact, I think it's going to stay for so long; it might as well start paying rent. I stand to meet Malik face on after he's stormed over to me, his temple vein-popping like it's at a disco. "That was a tad dramatic. Anyone could find-" Malik lurches forward, slamming his mouth on mine. Unlike the expensive cologne that usually tingles my nostrils, a slept-in scent hits me that's all man and all Malik. Hot damn. He takes ownership of my mouth, spearing me with his tongue in a rushed, haphazard vow. In effect, he's claiming what's his, and I don't resist.

"If you doubt my intentions for even a moment," his raspy

voice growls against my swollen lips, "then I'm obviously doing something wrong. What else will it take to prove this is where you belong?" My eyes hold his, staring into the abyss in his inky irises. He really wants me and for more than just my body or dazzling charm. Just for *me*. His wild hair hangs limply, framing his face in a boyish way I need to see more of. Glancing at the old t-shirt twisted in my hand, an idea hits me. A genius idea I could pat myself on the back for, but I'll wait until after he's agreed.

"Give me control," I tilt my chin, daring him to decline. His eyebrows twitch, so I carry on. "Let me break you, crumble you down and then rebuild you back up. You'll be surprised how freeing it is." I stick out my tongue, licking a trail across his bottom lip, and he lets me. That's a start in itself. A long breath saws out of his mouth, dousing me in a gust of mint. Luckily Malik's sloppy morning routine doesn't go as far as ignoring his dental hygiene.

"And who broke you?" he mumbles, tucking a strand of pink hair behind my ear. Nope, too personal. I take a step back, clicking my fingers and pointing to the bedroom.

"Conversation over. Go strip." On a nod, Malik does as he's told, wandering into the bedroom sluggishly. I spank his ass, hurrying him along. His room is immaculate as usual, not a speck of dust on the expensive mahogany furniture with his handkerchiefs anally folded on the dresser. Grabbing the corner of his bed cover, I toss it aside and kick Malik when he tries to pick it up. "Tell me you didn't throw out all of my sex toys," I bark, wondering where they disappeared to. Malik points to his wardrobe, reluctantly easing down his pajama pants.

"Perfect," I beam. Skipping across the room, I find the bulky trash bag he must have collected them into and stuffed in there. I swear that sex factory was one of the luckiest hauls I've stumbled across in years. Grabbing the bag and hoisting it over my shoulder like a naughty Santa, I turn back to see the look of pure terror claiming Malik's features. "Relax, and you'll enjoy it. Stay tense, and you'll bust a ball before we've even got to the best part," I shrug, tipping the contents across the dresser top.

"What's the best part?" Malik asks, crossing his arms in an effort to retain his dignity. I don't respond because I haven't thought of it yet myself. I trust that when the time comes, my instincts will pull out something epic. Walking over to Malik, I use one finger to push at the center of his chest, dropping him back on the mattress. It's time to break this bad boy and teach him a lesson in crossing boundaries.

Turns out, I'm quite the sadist. Tightening the strap on Malik's ankle, I jostle the iron bar forcing his legs to stay in place. Stretched from corner to corner, a strap pulled taut beneath the mattress connects the cuffs restraining Malik's hands. His muscles flex as he tests the durability, and I bring a flogger down on his upper thigh, so close to his balls it draws a hiss out from between his teeth.

"Snap those restraints, and the next strike will be across your dick." Malik's eyes bulge out of his head, and he opens his mouth to protest. "Na ah," I tease. Ripping a stretch of black tape from the roll and placing it back on the dresser, I press it over Malik's mouth, silencing his mumbling. From there on, it's basic torture techniques. Scraping my nails over the bottom of his feet, licking up the inside of his thighs but totally ignoring his dick. Leaving teeth marks all over his chest and sucking on his neck to make him look like a cheap whore. Just the way I like him.

He's stunning like this. Quivering, submissive, furious. The way his torso ripples with each flex of his abs. How he emanates power even though he's under my rule now. Skimming my fingers across his hard chest, I soak in his throaty growls and the heady sense of dominance that comes with it. Finally paying attention to the incessant bucking of his hips, I grasp the base of his solid shaft tightly in my grip.

"You're going to shatter for me before I permit you to cum," I tell him. Keeping my hold firm to the point of pain, I stroke his shaft slowly, all the way to his smooth, bulbous head. His balls clench upwards, and I lean forward to draw my tongue over his tip before releasing him completely. The anguished groans behind the tape gag are music to my ears while Malik's eyes spear me with the threat of murder. Game on Malli-moo.

Lifting my leg over his middle, thanks to the flexibility of my skinny jeans pants, I ease the hoodie up over my chest, securing the hem between my teeth. With them on full display, I tease my nipples and massage my breasts, all the while grinding my ass back on Malik's cock. Then it's his turn. Dropping the hoodie back into place, only to restrain myself from rushing this sweet torture, I take Malik's nipple in my mouth. Nipping with my teeth and flicking my tongue back and forth, I twiddle the other, trying to guess if he's naturally this smooth but then deciding he clearly plucks —no judgment here for male grooming.

"You're not nearly screaming loud enough for me to consider fucking you senseless yet," I tell him when he nudges his dick against my ass again. Scraping my nails through his hair, I pout, wondering what will make this man buckle and break, before begging for it all over again. Conjuring up my best porno ideas if I ever had the chance to shoot one, I hop up before fully making my decision. "I've got it. Be right back." This makes him really scream, but I'm already halfway through his suite after leaving his bedroom door wide open. Opening his freezer and dropping to a crouch, I riffle between the carefully organized tubs of frozen meals.

"Huh, no ice," I mutter to myself. I'll just have to go downstairs to get some. Jogging down the stairs, I bump into Ace coming the opposite way down the hall.

"Woah, where's the fire?" he asks, genuine concern flooding his puppy dog eyes.

"No fire," I smirk. "Just ice." I laugh to myself all the way down the next flight of steps, skidding into the kitchen. A yawn pulls at my mouth from my all-nighter, but I can't be deterred now. Pulling open the freezer door, I reach for the bag of ice when a voice travels my way.

"I can't believe you'd misplace it the morning after I gave it to you," Jack growls in a low but audible tone. "You know that was my only copy, right? Now I'll have to tell Malik I need two keys cut, and he'll want to know why."

"He's not the boss of you, remember?" Cherry's follows a moment later. I shiver at her voice, remembering now how angry I was this morning. Why she'd want to muscle in on a turf that's clearly already taken is beyond me. I've come to the assumption she's a gold digger, whereas I'm driven by dick. I'm a dick digger. The two of them enter the kitchen, too engrossed in their row to notice me. "Just borrow a key from someone else to get ours replaced. Besides, I didn't lose it - it was stolen."

"How would your key get stolen within hours of me giving it to you when there was no one else around?" Jack holds out his arms and Cherry spots me. Her brown eyes narrow, and I return to the freezer drawer my hand is hovering on. What did I come down here for? Shrugging, I grab a tub of ice cream and kick it closed. Placing the tub on the middle island, I wriggle between the two of them to fetch a spoon from the drawer and return to sit at the island for my show and calorie-filled breakfast.

"Don't you have somewhere better to be?" Cherry says with a bitchy tilt to her head.

"Nope," I pop the tub's lid and wave them on. "Please continue." Making the sound of a disgruntled rhino, her red hair whips back to Jack with enough force to give her whiplash.

"Isn't it obvious she stole my key?!" Cherry points my way, stamping her barefoot. Seems like the two of them just got up, wearing his and her flannel pajamas and some serious bedhead.

"Candy's a raging psycho, but she wasn't there. If you didn't want it, you could have just said so," Jack sighs, walking past Cherry towards the back door. His fist tightens and loosens, showing he needs the release of working in the garage to cool down. I'm sure someone else needs a release, but for the life of me, I can't remember who.

"So you're taking her side?" That screech comes again, drawing a hiss from Sphinx as he enters the door Jack has just opened. I fold in half to grab the scruff of his neck and put him on the counter.

Stroking his wrinkled back, I praise him for being a good boy and let him share my ice cream.

"Of course, he's taking my side," I interject with my mouth full. "He didn't take a boat ride down the Candy rapids and bathe in my sherbet fountain just for the fun of it. Can't beat a Monarch connection, babe." I wink at Jack. Cherry's jaw slackens, her face turning the same shade as her hair. I tilt my head the same way she did before, cocking my eyebrows. She really shouldn't take it to heart, there's just no competition when I'm involved. The magical pussy strikes again. "Maybe if you take a break from trying to kill me, you'd have realized that."

"For the last time." Jack steps in between our stare-off. "Cherry is not responsible for any of those attacks. There's enough enemies on your tail to make your own version of Guess Who. Try looking for Colonel Resentment in the basement with a drain pipe."

"That's Cluedo," I roll my eyes. "If you're trying to insult me with game references, at least get it right."

"Hey, anyone seen Malik?" Greg, the bartender, interrupts our stare off as he strolls into the kitchen. I glance at the clock behind his head, noting he's super early for his shift. "The Ejaculating Unicorn delivery needs his signature, but he's not responding to my calls."

"Oh shit!" I shout, smacking Sphinx away from my ice cream. Grabbing the tub, I run as fast as my legs will carry me with the spoon still hanging out of my mouth. I make it halfway up the second staircase when Ace's bellow rings through my ears. He runs from Malik's suite with his hand covering his eyes and barrels into me, sending us both flying. My ribs smack a few steps, but for the most part, the blind brute takes the brunt of our fall. I land on top of him in the 69 position, my forehead slamming into his dick, and he cries out again. A strong hand helps me to my feet as Spade looks me over, checking for injuries with his one hand.

"Do I even want to know?" he asks when satisfied I'm not hurt.

"Probably not, but it'll make a good story later," I grin. With Ace writhing around on the floor, clutching his junk, another yell comes from the suite above. This one sounding distinctly like my name. "Motherfucker," I grumble. Malik broke the restraints, so now I'm gonna have to flog his dick standing up. Funny how not only an hour ago, I thought I was ready to leave, but then who'd bring the morning mayhem? Not Cherry, that's for damn sure.

JACK

Cherry hasn't moved from her spot next to the kitchen counter. Her hip is resting against the marbled countertop while she drums her jagged fingernails across the surface. Doesn't take a genius to figure out who really took Cherry's key and cut her precious claws during the night, but I saw an out, and I took it. My head is a minefield; one wrong step, and all my hard work has exploded around me. As usual, Candy has fucked everything.

"Well? Is it true, you slept with her?" Cherry's voice is full of venom to match the barely concealed anger alight in her brown eyes. If it weren't for current circumstances, the flare of her nostrils would be cute. Not when I'm in the dog house and not sure if I want out. A bartender appears in the open doorway, glancing between us curiously on his way to the basement.

"We should go somewhere more private," I grumble. Ignoring her protests, I shove my feet into a pair of nearby boots and walk out of the back door with Cherry on my heel. My strides are long and hurried, desperate to put space between me and the drama that hangs over this building like the impending storm. I don't stop when passing the garage, I just keep going until my boots feel the crunch of the forest floor that frames the dirt track. Heavy rain clouds rolling across the morning sky permit the canopy of the trees to block out any lasting light and send a sweeping chill through my t-shirt. Still, I keep walking.

"Where are we going?!" Cherry shouts, struggling to keep up. I peer over my shoulder, spotting the flats and hoodie she must of grabbed in a rush. Frilly, blue pyjama shorts poke out of the bottom, but instead of feeling bad, I just want her to head on back without me. Every instinct I have is screaming to start groveling, to make Cherry believe that Candy means nothing to me, but I can't. A shack comes into view, trapped between the hunched trunks surrounding, just in time for the rain to begin falling. I duck inside, holding the door open for Cherry as the first crack of thunder sends her bolting forward. Closing us inside, I switch on the lights and check the windows are secure.

"What is this place?" Cherry asks with a shiver in her voice. The single room is bare in appearance until I pop one of the floorboards to reveal a secret stash hidden within.

"It's our rendezvous point if there's a serious attack on the Devil's Bedpost. We're made our fair share of enemies over the years, and god knows how many more Malik has hidden away. Don't even get me started on..." my voice trails away. Probably best not to mention Candy and the chaos that follows her around like a bad smell. Fishing out a pair of thick sweatpants, I toss them over to Cherry before grabbing myself a hoodie.

"Does that happen often?" Her brown eyes bulge as she pulls the sweatpants on over her pajama shorts. I shrug, dropping down in the corner. I hunch my arms over my knees, pulling the hood low over my head. Why did Candy have to open her big mouth? Or even prior to that, why did she have to lure me into my own bed and refuse to let me leave? But none of that is really what I'm pissed about. I'm furious with myself for giving in. A fully grown man, finally finding his feet in this world, falling straight back in the trap of being told what to do. A pair of hands touch my legs,

Cherry's soft voice penetrating the demons threatening to consume me.

"Jack?" I sigh again, dropping my arms aside. Despite putting on the sweatpants, I can still feel Cherry shivering through her light touch. I reach for her, both for warmth and to stop myself from doing something stupid. There's a whole case of weapons stashed beneath the floorboards at my feet, and one sure-fire way to make sure Candy couldn't manipulate me again would be to blow my dick off completely. Cherry obeys to the plead in my grip, winding her arms around my neck and laying her cheek upon my head.

"I fucked up." I don't know who I'm talking to, her or myself. It doesn't matter either way. But for the sake of the record, I don't want to look back and regret not fighting for Cherry at this moment. She was my way out. The first decision I made all for myself. "No doubt you'll be leaving after this, but I need to explain. Need to tell you I'm…"

"Sorry?" Cherry supplies. I nod but fuck; it's a lie. Deep down, I'm not sorry. I knowingly sabotaged myself and the reinvented life I was trying to achieve. I hated Malik for taking my decisions out of my hands, but it was so much better than hating myself. There's no one else to blame this time except Candy because just fuck her. "There's obviously a lot going on in there," Cherry pokes a finger at my temple. "Why don't you start at the beginning? Talk to me; you'll feel better for it."

"You should be slapping me or something, not listening to my sob story."

"Well, let me hear the story first so I can judge how shitty it is before I decide if you deserve this slap or not." Despite myself, I finally smile. A simple jerk of my lips that cracks through the ice block seized in my chest. I gasp in a breath, shaking off the chill in favor for what Cherry is giving me. A chance to voice the thoughts I'd never shared with anyone else, not even Jasper.

"I've always known my role in the Monarchs. I was the easygoing one that made everyone laugh. I hid behind my smile while on the inside, I was choking on the stress that radiated from the others. Everyone had a reason to be there, something they were running from, even though the real issues were themselves. It got even worse when Jasper left, despite how much that simple action broke me. They expected me to keep smiling, keep laughing, keep joking, and if I didn't...well, I couldn't bear to lose any more of my brothers."

"Sounds like a lot of pressure," Cherry strokes my hair through her fingers. With each word I spill, the crack slicing my core in two opens into a gaping chasm.

"I don't dispute Malik and Ace have issues of their own, but not even Spade took the time to look a little closer. They hoped I wouldn't falter after Jasper left because that'd mean there was someone else to look out for, so I didn't. I didn't say a word about the twin who had been with me every second of my life. The one who fought off every bully at boarding school, who relayed the news that we were orphans instead of the social worker, who just walked away without so much as a goodbye or a phone call. The worst bit was that he never even wanted me to go with him, so for the first time, I was utterly alone. Betrayed, struggling, and alone."

"Is that what I am? A reason for you not to be alone?" There's no accusation in Cherry's voice, her tone remaining soft and gentle. It's a fair question and one I wish I could answer. The least I can do is continue to be honest, and if she sticks around, it won't be based on a bed of lies. It'll prove if our relationship is worth saving, taking it a step beyond infatuation.

"I can't give you the best of me, Cherry, because I have no fucking clue what that would look like. You're the one person I refuse to give an idyllic version of me. So I will fuck up, I'll let you down and hurt you on the route to finding myself. You should probably leave now, find someone who knows what they want and where they're going. I'm not that guy, and I can't promise I ever will be."

Quiet settles between us, leaving the wind whipping against the shack to fill the silence. It's not lost on me how the storm outside perfectly represents the tornado of misery batting around inside my chest. It was so much easier to quiet the screams of the doubt when Jasper or even Candy were there, being twice as loud. But now, even with Cherry sitting on my lap, I can't help to spiral into their truth. On my own, I'll never be good enough. A hand softly grabs the side of my face, drawing my gaze up to Cherry's brown gaze.

"Everyone gets lost on the path to discovery, but it's not one I'll let you walk alone anymore. You chose me for a reason, and I don't believe it was just to find a gap. So I'll make you a deal. We're going to head back to your room, pack up your stuff and get the hell out of dodge. This place is poisonous for you, and not just because of her. If Malik and the others can't recognize you at your worst, they don't deserve you at your best. And needless to say, I'm only interested in an exclusive relationship. If you want to sleep with someone else, have the decency to break up with me first." I nod, hanging on her every word to give me a sense of direction. I am but a slave to coincidence, needing destiny to guide the way.

"I want to go, I really do. But without the Monarchs, I don't even know who I am," I breathe, hanging my head forward on her shoulder. Why I had to tumble into an identity crisis just when I was starting to move past all this is beyond me. Jasper was the popular one, the smooth talker. I was his shadow, not enough to stand up on my own, but I met Cherry. Nudging me upright, her full red lips tilt into a small smile.

"Let me tell you exactly who you are. Protective, caring, considerate. Loyal to a fault with a tendency to overthink." We share a smirk. "I'm not the kind of girl that will be taken for a ride, but your situation isn't normal, to say the least. So, get your ass up, and let's get out of here." Drawing Cherry up to her feet, I brush the red hair back from her pale face. Shadows from billowing branches leak through the windows, closing in on us from all sides. I brush my lips over hers, exhaling the weight of my stress against her cheek.

"I hope at the end of this; it turns out I'm worthy of you because the biggest tragedy would be for you to have wasted time that you could have been out there, finding Mr. Right."

"Promise me there'll be no more lies, and that's all the Mr. Right I need."

"That I can do." Smiling, our fingers interlink, cementing this moment as the change in the tide. I can be better, will be better, and I won't let some pick-haired psycho persuade me otherwise. This is my life. My choice. My decision, despite the consequences.

CANDY

Skipping through the bar, I fist pump the bartenders and high-five the waitresses. This whole boss thing is swinging in my favor, and for once, I feel like I'm really making a difference. Sure, not in a feed-the-orphans kind of way, but I'm officially placing down roots and putting my stamp on the Devil's Bedpost. I'm fucking home, baby.

The storm passed quickly, thanks to my naked rain dance in the back parking lot. Malik made a chivalrous show of carrying an umbrella out, but I reckon that was just a ploy to get me into his shower. I rub my ass absentmindedly, grinning at the swollen patch where his hand has spanked a permanent mark into me. Wet, unsatisfied Malik is a moody Malik. Least he's not unsatisfied anymore, and the bar staff won't feel his wrath today. You're all welcome.

Movement through the empty revolving door catches my eye, but it's not the arrival of a glacier truck like I was expecting. Red hair bobs up and down, a baggy sweatsuit that doesn't fit above flat shoes splashing through the puddles. Not that any of those things matter when the dog-faced whorebag heading this way is smirking like she just ate my last mars bar. By the way, her fingers are interlocked with Jack's, his arm brushing hers every chance he gets, it looks like they've been playing a game of hide the mars bar of their own. Greedy bitch.

"Hey Candy," Max calls out from his place at the top of a ladder. His long arms are stretched out, moving an abstract painting back and forth. It's my latest guilty purchase; an explosion of blues and purples covering the canvas which some old guy painted with his dick. The art of self-expression at its finest. That bitchy smirk catches my eye again, causing a red mist to descend over my mood. "Where would you like this hung?"

"Why don't you hang it from your balls so I can use you as a human pinata?!" I shout, stomping over to throw my boot into the bottom of the ladder. Gabriel jumps into action, diving aside to catch Max just before he hits the ground. The pair give me a weird look, muttering that I'm a crazy bitch, but I don't have time for that. Jack and Cherry step through the glassless door, spotting the metal ladder laying horizontal across the games machine it smashed on the way down.

"You really should have someone holding the base of the ladder when you're up there," I scold Max. "Workplace accidents are no joke." Gabriel puts him down for me to brush off the shoulders on his fitted t-shirt. There you go, no harm done. Keeping my head held high, I pick up the shattered buttons and pieces of glass from the game's machine. All the while, my eyes keep tracking back to Jack's hand in hers, much to Cherry's amusement.

"Something wrong?" Cherry smirks, knowing all too well her mere presence irks me. Standing, I toss the pieces into a nearby trash can and clap my hands together.

"It's been a full-on morning, that's all. But there's work to be done, so off you fuck."

"Malik is training you well," Jack comments, and the pair share a laugh as they leave. Scooping Sphinx up from the floor, I drop down in one of the leather sofas, losing myself in thought as I stroke his wrinkled skin. Why do these types of Egyptian cats not have fur anyway? Is that the trick of evolution - you originate from a hot place, so you lose all your fur? I wonder if their men are the same, bald right down to the balls.

"You're distracting yourself," Angus states from beside me. I hadn't seen him jump up, need mind recline and crossing his chubby cankles.

"What do you expect? I can't risk killing off another employee by pacing and seething." Conversations stop behind me, and feet shuffle backward across the wooden floor. Pussies.

"Would be an ideal time to go for a ride right about now," Angus pipes up. "It's been quite the emotional rollercoaster this morning." I don't know if he's only referring to me or if Hamish's lack of appearance has something to do with Angus' resigned tone. I let it slide, not wanting both of us to wander down depression avenue together.

"Nice thought, but my quad is still in the repair shop. I'm stuck here." A fresh wave of resentment rises up at those three words. I churn them over in my mind, and suddenly, they echo back in a deeper voice. Jasper's voice. 'You're stuck there,' he mocks me.

"Sorry to interrupt," Angus cuts through my thoughts. He wriggles his giggly ass up my thigh and hops onto Sphinx's back. "But I said go for a ride. I didn't say it had to be on your quad. There's a whole row of bikes out there; the old Candy would have taken what she wanted and not stopped for a moment to question it."

"What's the point?" I shrug, shuffling further down the sofa. Sphinx is forced to claw up my body in an effort not to fall on the floor, curling up on my sternum to go to sleep. A heavy sigh deflates my chest, my morale feeling uncomfortably limp. Angus is right. A few months ago, I'd have been on a bike and out of here as soon as shit got real, even if it was just to circle right back. Considering they were all 'your wild side makes life exciting', shit got boring around here real fast. Now all I hear is Candy behave, Candy, be good. Don't do anything reckless, don't hurt anyone. I guess they got their wish; the gust has well and truly left my sails.

"I refuse to believe that," Angus growls. He climbs up my body, heaving himself over Sphinx, and lands on my boobs. Then, quick as a whip, he slaps me across the face. "You're Candy fucking Crystal. Your ship is unsinkable, like the Titanic."

"I'm pretty sure-" I start, but Angus raises his chubby arm again. My eyes widen, but instead of being gummy-slapped again, he reaches over and smushes my cheeks in his paws.

"The pure fact Hamish isn't here shows you're slipping. Soon enough, you'll be wearing a turtle-neck and jeans day in, day out, baking for fun, and taking up knitting. You know what comes then," Angus raises a thick black eyebrow at me, and I swallow hard.

"Motherhood," we say in unison. My ultimate fear. That I'll become so ordinarily bored, the only source of entertainment I can have is baring children. A flock of feral little boys that I have to cart to soccer practice in my minivan. Fuck. That. A hand touches my shoulder, and I shoot upright, flinging Sphinx a mile across the bar. Spinning with my fists balled, a shocked-looking Spade stands stock still.

"I will never bear your children!" I scream, running at the revolving door.

"Candy, wait!" Spade shouts, but it's too late. I jump through the doorframe, discovering too late they've replaced that glass panel while I was having my pity fest. Shattering on impact, shards of glass rain all over me and slip down the sweater's neckline. Other tiny splinters become trapped in the cotton, itching me, and I continue to run. I rip it off over my head, tossing it into the puddles that my boots are splashing through. This is why anything aside from leather and corsets are inappropriate forms of clothing. Why I ever wanted to change my style is beyond me; I can't even remember when that happened. Just another reason to put distance between me and the domesticated pit I'm sinking into.

Heavy footfalls are right behind, alerting me to Spade's presence. If he thinks he is going to stop me from taking this time to myself, he might just find himself with another critical wound. I head toward the back of the garage, finding the rear door already open. Ace is hunched over his precious slab of wood that is supposed to be the centerpiece for the table at Friday's grand reopening. With the amount of time he's taking waxing it, everyone's drinks will slide right off the end. But that's not my problem. He twists his naked torso my way, rippling with muscle and thickly corded veins flowing the length of his arms. Spade jumps into the garage right behind me, reminding me of why I ran in here.

Keeping both in my eye line, I tread sideways carefully. Goosebumps line my flesh from denim waistband to the black and pink lace bra covering my tat-tas. Since when did I start wearing underwear, for that matter?

"Trying to stop me will make this so much worse," I warn them both, and Ace's eyebrows furrow. I raise my hand, pressing the release button for the garage door, and lift Jack's keys from the hook. No one moves; the breaths sawing out of me are low, controlled movements. Then, all at once, I unlock the truck via the fob, and all hell breaks loose.

I dive for the truck door, ripping it open and throwing myself into the driver's seat. Slamming the door closed, I hit the locks, but it's already too late. Spade is halfway in the passenger door, Ace rushing into the back. Lifting my knees to my chest, I swivel and kick wildly at Spade's bad shoulder. He grabs my legs, yanking my boots clean off and tossing them at Ace one by one.

Relentless, Spade pushes forward despite my punches and kicks until he's sitting on my shins. Grabbing me by the waist, an anguished groan leaves Spade as he heaves me from the leather seat and tosses me to Ace in the back. Strong arms slick with grease and sweat band around me like iron, taking the brunt of my struggles with ease. Spade closes his door and slides behind the wheel, kicking the truck into drive with a roar of the engine. We fly out of the garage, almost mowing down one of the glaciers I stop struggling, sharing a confused look with Angus as he pops his head around from the passenger seat.

"What…why…I thought-"

"You thought," Spade grumbles, flashing a cold blue stare at me in the mirror, "after everything we've been through, you couldn't just say 'Hey Spade, I need some space.'" He grunts, rubbing a hand over his shoulder.

"You really shouldn't be driving," Ace chastises him.

"Well, if you were quicker, you could have got to the passenger door first. All that muscle is useless if it's just for show and not practicality."

"I could practically give you another reason to visit the hospital if you'd like," Ace quips, turning his stare to the landscape passing at 80 miles an hour. Thundering down the freeway, Spade doesn't respond, and I just sit there, in Ace's lap. Thankfully, Spade hits the radio, filling the awkward silence with some Post Malone. I don't question where he's taking us, at ease with the confidence in his directions. Without a map in sight, Spade must know his destination, and it'll have to be somewhere you don't need a shirt or shoes in Ace's case. Not even when we pull away from civilization and fly towards an abandoned-looking building on some beat-up back road.

It's begun to rain again by the time we pull up, the automatic windscreen wipers swiping steadily back and forth. Spade hops out without a word, making his way towards the building with long strides and leaving Ace and me to follow. Ace tries his best to shield me from the rain, but I shrug him off. It'll take a little more than a few drops of water to dampen my curiosity. Approaching the main entrance, Spade bangs his fist on the door and yells out for someone called 'Tater'. I shift from foot to foot, accepting the warmth of Ace's hug now that the cold has settled in.

A rounded man with an unkept beard and straggling hair yanks the door open from the other side, grumbling to Spade about remembering his key. He leaves us to it, retreating inside before we get a chance to see where he's gone. Gripping my wrist painfully, Spade drags me in out of the rain. The lights blink on as we pass underneath, and the smell of chlorine hits me before we make it to the center of the building. We come to a stop on a balcony, looking down at the swimming pool below.

"You have personal access to a pool, and you're just showing me this now?!" I ask. My voice vibrates around the vast space, so I make a string of nonsense sounds. "Halabaloloo! Hallie Berry's bouncy babalooooons!" Spade nudges me and then hisses, massaging his injured shoulder.

"The pool was shut down years ago due to health and safety. I pay Tater to keep it running for any time I need a break, and you, Candy, need to take a fucking break." He's pissed for the way I acted back at the bar, shouting in his face and making a run for it. I've obviously hurt his shoulder too, but instead of looking for revenge, he's giving me an outlet. I hang over the railing, marveling at how inviting the water looks, considering it's solely maintained for Spade's personal use.

"How high up do you think we are?" I wonder out loud. Ace leans forward, brushing me with his arm, and tilts his head to the side.

"About thirty feet? Give or take," he shrugs. Almost the height of an Olympic diving board, I muse to myself, picking up on some of the useless knowledge I have stashed away. Spade finally releases his hold on me, sighing on a long exhale, and I take my shot. I throw myself over the balcony, feeling the scrape of fingers that try to catch me. Bellowing roars fill the space, causing me to smirk as I stretch out my arms and plunge into the water. It's. Fucking. Freezing. Clearly, the money spent on upkeep is not being put towards the heating.

Still, I roll my body like a mermaid, twirling around in the water for long enough to make the guys up above sweat it out. More than that, the pressure of the water beating in on the sides of my head manages to cancel out the noises in my head. Having left the weight of my stresses above the surface, I sway back and forth, revealing in a rare moment of freedom.

Breaching the water, I find only Spade overhead, gaping at me as a movement to my right announces Ace. He dives into the water, colliding with my body and dragging me down. Bubbles stream from his mouth and nose, his eyes wide and erratic. Closing his hands around my throat, he shakes me vigorously before dragging me back up to the surface.

"Don't you ever fucking do that again," he barks, slapping his palm against the water to splash me. Submerging the lower half of my face in the water, I blink at him with my best puppy dog eyes. Ace huffs, swishing his arms to close the distance between us. That's when I bop up, spraying my mouthful all over his face, and use the soles of my feet to kick away from his abs. If Ace wants to punish me, he's going to have to catch me first. And please fuck, let him catch me.

MALIK

The red dot on my phone continues to flash, leading me directly to Jack's truck abandoned sideways across three bays in a derelict parking lot. I wipe down the waterproof case concealing my phone from the rain before removing it from the handlebars of my motorbike. It's not strictly legal to use the 'track my iPhone' app while hurtling down the freeway, but it was necessary. Peering through the truck's window, I see Spade's phone sitting on the driver's seat with no indication anyone is still inside. Which can only mean the three who suddenly went missing from the bar and garage must be in the shabby building behind me. I cross the parking lot in a rushed sprint, yanking the helmet from my head to bang on the door.

"Spade, Ace, Candy! You in there?!" I shout, surprised when the door actually opens, but it's none of the three I was expecting standing there.

"Can I help you?" a man with one of the biggest beer guts I've ever seen asks. It's hard to tell where the hair on his head ends, and his facial hair begins, the tangled mess draped all over his shoulders. There's an old sauce stain on his dirty t-shirt and the smell to accompany the fact he mustn't have showered anytime in the past year.

"I'm looking for someone. Three someone's in fact. Are they here?" The man begins to shake his head, so I sidestep, jerking my head towards the truck. I must have the air of 'don't fuck with me' because he sighs and nods, stepping aside to let me enter. Straightening the labels of my jacket, because fuck changing when I don't know where Candy is or what she's up to, I pass, careful not to let his gut or body odor touch me.

I don't need a map to know where to go since Candy's laugh can be heard throughout the entire building. Wherever she is, at least she's amused. That doesn't ease me as much as it should, though, since I'm now picturing a room covered in plastic sheeting and a machete in her hand, dripping with the blood of her enemies. At least it's not Cherry; I saw her and Jack on the way to his room looking closer than ever.

"Did my invite get lost in the mail?" I ask, causing Spade to flinch. He's shed his t-shirt, draping it over the seat he's perched on. Beneath the hand kneading his shoulder, I finally see what's he's so carefully kept covered up to now, and I don't like it one bit. A heavy bruise still surrounds the barely sealed gash on his shoulder blade. The scar itself is puckered and raised, but there are also the tender patches of skin that's re-growing over his recent burns. I'm sure he should have a dressing on all of them, but knowing Spade, he wouldn't have listened to the doctor's care advice in favor of getting out of hospital quicker.

"It wasn't exactly a planned outing," Spade grumbles, gesturing to the seat beside him. From this vantage point halfway back in the bleachers, we have a clear view of Candy and Ace splashing about in the pool below. Unbuttoning my soaking wet suit jacket, I peel it off to drop in to the plastic seat.

"So, tell me, why exactly we're here then."

"What does it matter?" Spade quips back without pause. "She's happy for another day; let's just leave it at that." I shift in my seat, taking my attention away from the pair splashing around below to focus on Spade. His jaw is tight, his blue eyes razor-sharp. Out of all the Monarchs, Spade is the one I could have relied on to back me up. Sure, he's prone to his moods, but this feels different.

"What's that supposed to mean?" I ask carefully. My shoulders flex uncomfortably in the wet shirt, and I strain my neck against the collar.

"Don't worry about it," he mutters, keeping his gaze away from me.

"No need to be shy, Spade. You've got something to say, get it off your chest." He doesn't respond other than a frustrated tap to his foot. "Spade. How am I supposed to better myself if you're still keeping things from me?"

"Maybe by not making everything about you!" Spade's shout catches Candy's and Ace's attention, putting an end to their playfulness. Both pairs of eyes swing my way, filling with concern before they make their way towards the ladder. Spade stands, pacing up and down the row. Clearly, something has him rattled, which doesn't resonate well with me. I struggle to level out my emotions at the best of times, but when my men are hurting, I tend to get erratic. Scrubbing a hand over his face, Spade whips back around to glare at me.

"You didn't see her face, Malik. Something freaked her, and she was seconds from bolting if I hadn't brought her here. We can't keep her contained in fear she'll get in trouble without losing her completely. We're not her minders-"

"Everything okay up here?" Candy appears, dripping wet in jeans and a bra. Ace is at her back, shivering from the cold and shaking droplets of water from his shaggy fringe. Spade's blue stare holds my gaze, slowly nodding his head.

"Everything's fine. We'd better get going; our keeper has come to bring us all home," Spade says, his voice laced with venom. I don't react to his attitude, keeping my face impassive, even if I don't understand it. Maintaining my newfound calmness was much easier before the attacks on Candy started again, and try as I might, being the boss and a brother is a hard balance to get right. Mission failed thus far.

"Who said anything about taking you home? Perhaps I decided to take a day off from the bar to join in with your spontaneous swim."

"Yeah, right," Spade scoffs, grabbing his t-shirt. He walks towards Candy, planning on leaving until she slams a hand into the center of his chest. Spade coughs, taking the blow with less resilience than usual.

"Hang on now. You brought me here for a good time. Surely there's more on offer than catching hyperthermia." Spade spears me with a glance over his shoulder, curses, and walks on, leaving us to follow.

I pocket the conversation I need to have with Spade for later. Clearly, he thinks how I'm handling Candy is wrong, and old habits of not speaking openly with me are still an issue. I know my faults; even though half the time I struggle to change them, but I am trying. I thought they'd have given me a little more credit than I'm currently receiving. But then again, forgiveness can't come before retribution.

Pushing to my feet, Candy watches me carefully after Ace and Spade have wandered off. The pink length of her hair hangs limply over the colored array of caricature tattoos covering her chest and shoulders.

"Why are you really here?" Candy pops her hip to the side. Her nipples are pushing against the lacey fabric of her bra, taunting me. There's a test held within her brown eyes, one I refuse to fail. Instead, I hold out my hand with the palm facing up.

"Because I didn't want to miss out on the chance of an adventure with you." Seeming pleased with my response, Candy takes my hand and pulls me along behind her. Noting the goosebumps lining her arms, I yank her back and draw her beneath my arm. It still puzzles me how my anger can shift from blinding rage to non-existent with a simple touch. Only her touch, though.

Winding through the corridors, we follow the sound of Ace and Spade's voices to a male changing room on the lower level.

Like the rest of the building, this room has been neglected. Abandoned benches, limescale between the tiles. A row of lockers appears unused for so long rust has seized the hinges. Moving further inside, we round the shower area to spot a sauna, steam room, and hot tub all hidden at the back. The swimming pool is visible through a thin walkway to the left. By the time Candy and I have closed the distance between us and the hot tub, we're both shivering.

"Tater knows to keep the hot tub up to temp, just in case," Spade winks at Candy. His body language switches as he looks from her to me, all traces of humor vanishing. Aside from the obvious, what the fuck I did to receive his icy reception is anyone's guess. Ace strips out of his sodden jeans with no shame then helps Spade to lift the hot tub lid with his good arm. Steam pours out of the clear water, the temperature gauge showing it's all full heat. Candy's next to wriggle out of my hold and strips off, undeterred by the three sets of eyes that are transfixed to her body. Her curves, her tatts, her confidence. She's the most beautiful sight I've ever seen.

I don't hesitate to follow suit. Where I used to keep myself distanced, watching my men from afar, I no longer want that separation between us. Experiencing their experiences, laughing along with their jokes. That's the only way Candy can fully connect us in the way I hoped —the way we need. I join Ace in the hot tub, surprised when he fist pumps me as I slide into the steaming water. Fuck knows how we'll bring ourselves to leave but that is a problem for later.

When he doesn't move, Candy unbuttons Spade's jeans next, pushing them down his hips. I get an incredible view of her ass, slightly tilted upright as she gets the material to his knees and leaves him to do the rest. Holding out both hands, she waits for Ace and me to accept them and draw her into the water. Spade quickly shakes off his jeans in time to grab her ass, hoisting her the rest of the way despite the grunt of pain he releases. Sliding in after her, he's careful to keep the wound on his back clear of the water and sighs contentedly. They all do, in fact, except for me. Words that need to be said are on the tip of my tongue, and although I don't want to ruin the relaxed atmosphere, I also can't be the one to withhold information anymore.

"I passed Jack in the hall before coming here. He's leaving." I announce. All eyes flick my way, and postures tighten, but it's only Ace who responds.

"What? When?" Running a wet hand over my hair, I slump back into the wall of the tub.

"I've convinced him to stay for the reopening party tonight. This was supposed to be our fresh beginning. The least we can do is start it off as a team, and hopefully, he'll still visit," I reply solemnly.

"Wow, look at the master of optimism over here," Spade mutters under his breath. Candy punches him in the arm, uncaring that it's his bad side. I merely shrug, catching his icy blue gaze with earnest.

"I'm trying."

"I can see that," Candy responds. Scooting her way over to me, her ass happens to fall into my hand, and I react without thinking. My fingers slide into her pussy, catching her off guard for once. It's more than just sexual appeal; she has always seen the best in me. Have I always deserved it? No. Have I given her the same opportunity? Also, no, but she seems patient enough to wait around until I figure out how. Slowly, my fingers slip in and out of her, twisting with controlled flicks of my wrist. Her pink hair rolls back against the tub, and her legs widen, unashamed of the others opposite. Spade's eyes flare with heat while Ace shifts, moving around to join us. Beneath the water, Candy lays her leg lazily over Ace's thigh, and her brown eyes tease Spade.

"Thought you'd have had enough of just watching by now," she smirks. I ignore their back and forth communications and the way Spade's eyes roam over me every so often. I'm here to be one of them like we all agreed. Maybe the practice is harder than the theory, but I'm not holding myself back anymore. Instead, I focus on wringing small moans of pleasure from Candy's lips. Ace covers her breasts, massaging and plucking at her nipples in turn. Breathy moans turn desperate as we work her body like a well-tuned instrument.

A warning growl from across the tub is my only indication before Spade wades over and silences Candy's sounds with his mouth. His grip on her throat is as possessive as the strong strokes of his tongue. His jaw works as he devours her like his favorite treat, and I don't blame him. I should look away give them their privacy as much as possible given the situation, but I can't. Seeing one of my men with Candy lights a fire in my veins. To be included in the scenario is something else completely. Adding a third finger into her and twisting hard, my chest swells when Candy's groan explodes free of Spade's kiss. Her pleasure may be our only goal, but a healthy, albeit twisted, competition is good for morale. Swinging his blue eyes my way, a challenge is obvious, one he quickly backs down from.

"I shouldn't be soaking my back fully yet," he grumbles. Standing, Spade makes a move to leave until Candy catches his thighs.

"Don't then, you moody bastard," she grins. Pushing him to sit on the edge of the tub with his feet still in the water, she moves between his legs to kneel on the bench seat. I avoid the sight of Spade's hard-on, too preoccupied with lifting Candy aside, and placing her in my lap. She doesn't protest, spreading her thighs over me while leaning across to take Spade into her mouth. Fine by me. I slump down, trailing my lips between her cleavage as she lowers onto me. Like every time, I hit home in one thrust. I know Candy's body better than she does at this point, attuned to each of her responses. The flush on her neck the way her nails pierce my skin tells me I'm doing something right. Water laps around us as she rolls her hips, and Ace moves in my peripheral vision.

"I'm taking the back this time," he mutters. Candy releases

Spade with a pop to share a coy smile, and I get the feeling I've missed something. Returning to deep throat Spade, she doesn't even flinch as Ace's hand winds around her stomach and his cock presses against her back entrance. On each of her steady bounces on my dick, Ace's eases in bit by bit until I feel his thick pressure pushing against mine. Candy takes us both like a pro, and I wonder if I don't know her body as well as I thought.

Grabbing her hips and holding her in place, I take back the control of thrusting up into her. Slowly at first, but then at an increasing rate to make her muffled moans around Spade's dick louder. The dull weight of both Ace and I shifting against one another fills Candy until there's not a space inside her untouched. We equally own her at this moment, drawing the start of an intense orgasm closer with each movement. At one point, I don't know who out of the four of us is groaning louder.

"Slow down," Spade grits through his teeth, clutching the back of Candy's hair. Scraping my fingers up the front of her body, I smooth my fingers along the underneath of her jaw out of curiosity. The next time she takes Spade all the way to the back of her throat, I feel it. Anyone on the outside looking in would think we're dominating Candy when in reality, it's the other way around. She has us at her command. She holds the power to let us all cum or hold us off indefinitely. My only demand is that when we go down, she's sinking with us.

Ace's fingers brush my abdomen as he hunts for her clit, rubbing frantically. He must be feeling the impending urge like I am. Her cunt is impossibly tight around my shaft, causing my eyes to roll back in my head. My body relaxes, even with Ace's hips rubbing against my inner thighs. Nothing else matters except breaking Candy's resolve before I break for her completely. Light tremors running the length of my dick suddenly intensify as Candy's sweet pussy clamps down, taking me over the edge with her.

"Holy fuck," I grunt, my fingers digging into her flesh. Ace roars just after, Candy's pulsating walls having a domino effect on us all. If only we weren't always wound so tight for her, we might be able to prolong these sessions. But there's always the next time. With my balls drawn up, my cum pumps into her cunt while hers fights to escape the air-tight vacuum we've created. Ace's dick throbs in her back passage as we continue to draw out her orgasm.

The water splashes over the lower half of my face, and I slam up into her. Again and again, drawing cries from her mouth when she takes to pumping Spade's dick in her hand. Using his hand on her hair, he angles her head in the perfect position for him to explode all over her beautiful face. Somehow, it's even more glorious, marked with the evidence of a fellow Monarch. I fall into the trap of marveling at her once more when Ace slowly retreats, causing us both to gasp. Easing her off my lap slowly too, I lower Candy onto the bench seat. She slips right down beneath the water, scrubbing her face clean and resurfacing with a grin.

"The magic pussy strikes again!" she beams, forcing us all to high-five her in turn. I can't help but laugh, feeling more relaxed than I can ever remember. This is how it should be – playful, spontaneous, and united. Convincing Jack he belongs with us is my next job, but that can wait until later. For now, I link my fingers with Candy's and thank whatever strange twist of fate sent her our way in the first place.

SPADE

"This feels stupid," I grumble as Candy strangles me with a black tie. When she offered to do it for me, I figured she knew how. How wrong I was.

"I thought draining your blue balls would have rekindled your sense of fun," Candy smirks. She gives up on the tie, unraveling and leaving it loose on either side of my collar. My shoulder strains against the sling Malik is forcing me to wear again, leaving me helpless against Candy's tie-knotting abuse. The slacks feel rough against my thighs, too tight in the crotch, and this formal button-up shirt isn't doing it for me either. "I'd be so much more comfortable in jeans and a t-shirt."

"But then I wouldn't get to spend all night thinking about ripping these buttons off and gagging you with this tie. Besides, you think I want to look like this?" My eyes trail the length of her body. The satin dress clings to her body from the strapless neckline down to her studded heels. Shimmering in silver, the material splits from the hem to her waist, exposing a glimpse of her hip that shows she's not wearing any underwear. "It's a few hours; then we can hibernate naked together for a few weeks."

"Deal." With that incentive, I hold my free arm out for her to take, and we exit my room. Ace, Jack and Cherry are waiting for us outside, similarly dressed. Only the best for our grand re-opening, according to Malik. He insisted this will be a reinvention for the Monarchs, too, solidifying our new dynamic as partners, not his minions. Keeping her gaze diverted from the others, Candy leads the the way to the elevator, taking me down to the bottom floor. Stepping out, we can see Malik through the two-sided mirror, leaning his hands on the bar to oversee the final adjustments.

"Hey, hot stuff," Candy addresses him the moment we enter the bar. She withdraws from my arm, sauntering away in the dress he bought her. I choose to ignore the chill that settles in my chest; listening to the voice in my head that says just because she's naturally drawn to him doesn't mean she's rejecting me. Jack pours a round of beers, handing them out to the rest of us. The calm before the storm takes hold as the overly large clock on the wall shows five minutes before opening, and the queue of people waiting to get in stretches towards the dirt track across the parking lot and out of sight. Malik calls out to Gabriel in his new bartender's uniform, passing his phone over the bar.

"Hey guys, come over for a photo. This is our moment," Malik beckons us over with his hand.

"So you keep saying," I mutter, moving with Ace to stand with the group behind the bar. Jack reluctantly joins on the side, and Cherry cleverly remains out of shot. I can't imagine Candy would have let her take the spotlight in our reopening snapshot. Gabriel holds up Malik's iPhone, telling us all to smile. At the last second, Candy grabs me, dragging me into the center, and plants a sloppy kiss on my cheek. I can't help the responding boyish grin that sweeps across my face, no doubt now cemented into Malik's camera roll.

"To a fresh start," Candy whispers in my ear. She reaches around, giving my crotch a hard squeeze, and then addresses the waitresses on standby. "Unlock the door. The Devil's Bedpost is officially open for business!" The DJ takes his cue, flooding the room with the latest dance music as the customers push through the revolving door. There's a booth set up outside to handle ticket sales and trays of champagne ready for the bartenders to carry around.

That leaves the six of us to handle the bar, just like the old days, except minus a Monarch and with the addition of two eccentric women. No matter how hard Candy tries to involve me with her sly smiles and flicking droplets of glittery unicorn gin my way, I can't shake the feeling Jasper should be here and that, just like last time, this isn't going to end well. Especially with the death glares being passed between the women and Jack's useless attempt to stay in between them. This dynamic, this bar, it was always doomed to fail long before it started.

"Right, come on," Candy says, grabbing the back of my shirt. She drags me away from the bar, all the way to the center of the dance floor. "I'm sick of looking at your moody face. Remember my birthday party? Find that version of Spade and bring him back to me." I smile for her benefit, but she is right. I need to get out of this funk and start enjoying myself. Worrying isn't worth missing an opportunity to grind up against Candy in the midst of a busy crowd. The music is booming, the people all around laughing and having the night of their lives. We've had such a good turn-out; the dancers are spread from the DJ booth to the back wall and amongst the tables. Candy drops down low, lifting her ass to wiggle against my crotch like the minx she is. Fuck it.

Spanking her sharply, I wind an arm around her waist and draw her back up to me. We move as one, rocking our hips, vibing to the music. Songs bleed from one to the other until a layer of sweat coats our skin from the sheer body heat enclosing us in a world of our own. This is my zen place, with her plush against me in an impenetrable bubble. Twisting in my hold, Candy winds her arms around my neck.

"There he is," she says in my ear before hunting for my mouth. I throw myself into her kiss, coaxing the same emotion from her that's threatening to consume me. A burning need I can't deny. An irresistible attachment I don't want to lose. Her tongue battles mine, taking what she needs and leaving me raw in its wake. I'm exposed, vulnerable, and hers. Our lips connect over and over in a string of lustful kisses that send an arrow of pleasure straight to my cock. And just like that, all notions of misery and hatred are a distant memory.

"You're all I'm ever going to need," I tell her in between the change of another song. Candy's back goes rigid beneath my hand, even if her smile is as sweet as sugar. Pushing herself impossibly closer against me, her hand rests on my shoulder. She exhales, long and deep, allowing the tension to escape her body. At that moment, I know she's given in. She's accepted her fate, and from here on out, a part of her will belong to me. I don't need her pretty words to confirm it, just the knowledge of her by my side each day.

"Cut Malik some slack. He's doing his best," Candy looks at me knowingly.

"His best isn't always good enough," is my only reply. Just because Malik hasn't scared Candy away today doesn't mean he'll be able to keep her around long-term, and that's what worries me. Although it shouldn't, because wherever she goes, I go. My alliance to the Monarchs is sat solely on Candy's shoulders.

A pair of bodies bump into ours, jarring my shoulder. I groan, alerting Candy to the intrusion. Shooting upright, we glare at none other than Cherry and Jack, locked in each other's arms and taking up more room than necessary. They pretend not to notice us, swinging their hips side to side with Jack's thigh firmly between Cherry's center. She grinds against him shamelessly with a smile that says she knows exactly what she's doing.

"Get a fucking room," Candy shouts over the pounding bass. "If it's yours, Jacky, make sure you've changed the sheets. Unless rolling around in my dried cum does it for you." Cherry stops still, even though Jack tries to tell her to ignore us. Her brown eyes glare at Candy with a challenge before she shoves Jack a few steps back.

"You wanna go?" she asks, confronting Candy head-on. The flare of anger in her expression is foreign to me, and suddenly, I'm doubting all of my previous beliefs involving Cherry. Ace tried to convince me she had a mean streak, but with no evidence until now, it was hard to imagine. Trying to keep a hold of Candy, she twists out of my grip, never one to back down from a fight. Reaching into the chest cup of her dress, Candy pulls out a stick of gum. Unwrapping and shoving it into her mouth, she chews vigorously to blow a large bubble and pops it in Cherry's face.

"Let's do this, bitch tits," she growls, lowering her stance. Many of those dancing around us have clocked on to what is about to happen and take a step back to give the girls a wide birth.

"Uh oh, ladies and gentlemen," the DJ announces into the headset hanging on his neck. "Make some room. Looks like we have ourselves a dance-off!" The strobe lights overhead shift into a collective spotlight, circling the room to land on the center of the dance floor. Kesha bursts to life from the speakers, and the smirk on Candy's face takes on a new level of malice. Smart move. I catch the DJ's eye, nodding my appreciation for the distraction. He salutes me until Jack moves to stand beside my shoulder. He balks at the mere sight of Jack's face, pushing the headset over his ears and busying himself on his old-school turn-tables.

"What was that about?" Jack asks, his eyes glazed and breath stinking of tequila. He always was a lightweight compared to the rest of us. Focusing on his question, the memory of the last time we hired this particular DJ returns to the forefront of my mind.

"There was an incident when Jasper was here. Some pissing contest over Candy that the DJ clearly lost." Jack grunts in response, focusing on the two females circling each other in the middle of the dancefloor.

Candy is first to break, falling into a slut drop and twerking her way back out. The crowd goes crazy, cheering her on with deafening roars. Slinking her hips to the beat, she then moves into a running man/moonwalk combo. It's as hilarious as it is ridiculous, and the audience hangs on her every move. In other words, it's utterly Candy. In some version of capoeira, Candy spins and kicks out, her heel coming within an inch of Cherry's face. The redhead screams, falling against the crowd. Hands shove her forward, and even Jack is unable to stifle his laughter. Candy stomps the same heel on the ground, beating on her chest like a gorilla.

"Yeah, and what?!" she shouts at Cherry, blowing a large bubble of gum. The crowd swarm in, not even waiting to see if the woman opposite would be able to beat her. I lose sight of Candy, but her laughter can be heard through the beat of the music, telling me she's just fine. Cherry wriggles her way through the bodies, coming to stand before us. She puffs out her cheeks, which have turned as red as her hair, and looks to Jack for backup. When he doesn't immediately move, she whips out her hand for him to take.

"I'm not sticking around to be humiliated. It's time to go. You coming?" her voice asks, sharp as a razor. I swallow thickly, realizing she means go as in leave, for good. So soon after, we've all come back to give it another shot. But it's Jack's life, and he needs to live it for himself, not a sense of duty. Jack looks at me with uncertainty, then to Candy who's now body surfing over the crowd.

"I think I'm going to stick around. Enjoy the party for a little while longer." His eyes drag over the length of Candy's barely concealed body floating above, the hunger in his green gaze blatant. It's not her dance moves that will have swayed him, but her spontaneity. How any situation can be turned into one of those unexpected moments that he won't want to miss. Cherry gets the hint, striding away after bashing into Jack's shoulder. I whistle low under my breath.

"Good luck with that one," I slap him on the back, and to my surprise, he smirks.

"It's my last night. Can't let you guys have all the fun," he smiles sadly. It goes without saying 'all the fun' is referring to Candy. Perhaps he's finally come to realize Candy isn't the enemy she's the one uniting us – for the most part. I can't shake the tension between Malik and me, even after the hot tub. Not until he's proven, his manipulative ways are truly a thing of the past. The woman in question is planted back on her feet with her dress ruffled around her thighs. I straighten the satin material, noting the split has ripped up to her waist from her vigorous dancing.

"That was literally...top three of the best moments of my life," she beams, eyeing Jack curiously. Returning her attention to me, I'm swept into the playfulness in her large eyes.

"Oh yeah? What takes the prized place of first and second?" I ask as Candy leans into me, licking her tongue over my bottom lip.

"I'll tell you later, alone, in your bed." She winks at me, and I wind my arm around her waist with the intent of carrying her off this dancefloor right here and now.

"Not so fast," a gruff voice sounds from behind me. A hand slams over my good shoulder, and the meaty hand I recognize as Ace's clamps around the back of Candy's neck. He drags her forward, delving his tongue into her mouth while I'm sandwiched in the middle. Whatever magic he's performing on her mouth leaves her grinding her chest and hips into my front while I feel the tell-tale hardness growing against my back.

"Seriously, man?!" I shove backward and then slip out of the Spade sandwich I got caught up in. "At least pull her aside before your cock accidentally falls into my ass."

"Accidently?" Candy quirks a brow. "That's the whole idea, right Ace?" He doesn't deny it, and I fake a gag. We may be sharing a woman, but my boundaries are iron clad when it comes to who's entering who. Spotting Malik approaching, I make to break away, but Candy grips me by the belt, holding me in place. "I don't know what's happened between you and Malik, but avoiding him isn't the answer. He's really trying," Candy blinks those large brown eyes my way. I remain in place, pressing a kiss to her cheek. Call me whipped, but I'd do anything to see the resulting smile from her full lips.

"Everything okay over here?" Malik asks, sliding his dark eyes over our group, looking for an opening where he can join. Candy gives it to him, slipping away to loosen his tie. He lets her, his face impassive but his eyes sparkle with amusement. I wonder how much of the champagne he helped himself to while watching our girl dance her way out of a fight.

"Never better, right boys?" Candy peers over her shoulder, jutting out her shimmering ass. The three of us shake our heads, halting a passing waitress to grab flutes of champagne. I have a feeling to participate in the cat and mouse game of who's going to end up with Candy tonight or to find the courage to share her with *all* the others, at last; I'll need to be blind drunk.

"Okay then," Malik raises an eyebrow. "I was just coming to let you know we're out of Pinot Grigio, so I'm going to head out back and grab some. Not that you'd have noticed, but no more running off without an explanation, right?" He aims his words at Candy, and she screws up her features.

"I have a better idea." Sliding her hand inside Malik's suit jacket, Candy pulls an oblong box from his inner pocket. She pushes the bottom for a row of cigars to slide into view. "You guys should head up to Malik's suite and celebrate. Not just the bar, but the fact you're all here, back together and closer than ever," Candy whips me with a quick glare. "That's the main success of tonight. I'll grab the Pinot and hold down the bar." I notice Malik tense at the mere suggestion, as does Candy. "Trust me. I can handle overseeing a party. I am the fucking party." Trailing her mouth along his jaw, she moves to leave, but his grip on her waist doesn't relent. Candy gives Malik her sternest glare that dares him to disobey her, and like the rest of us would, he crumbles.

"We won't be long," he tells her, pressing a kiss to her forehead. Jerking his head, he takes a step away, waiting for the rest of us to follow. Ace kisses her cheek, then I capture her lips for a swift peck, and that just leaves Jack. The two stare at each other, unsure of whether to kiss, shake hands, or have a punch up. Jack raises his hand, settling for a fist pump that Candy accepts. If actions could speak, that one would have screamed with unravelling tension of a truce. I physically feel the promise of an easier tomorrow filter through the air, beating in time with the DJ's heavy bass. Thank fuck for that.

CANDY

Leaving the party behind, the Monarchs cram into a shared elevator while I move into the games room and take a moment to stand behind the two-way mirror. I should get myself a plaque to hang over the bar - 'Candy Crystal. Queen of Monarchs and Fixer of Rifts.' And I thought I was meant to be the difficult one. The party is a hit, from the packed out dancefloor to the non-stop flow of drinks. There's not a frown in sight, and a rush of pride bursts to life inside of me—the artwork on the walls, the glittery cocktails, the sea of pink boas. Angus pops up in my peripheral vision, hand in hand with Hamish on the poker table.

'Hope you're enjoying the party boys,' I say through our mental connection. *'Look what I was able to make happen with just a little dick-based motivation. With the right incentive, I could take over the damn world.'*

Through the crowd of dancers, some shithead with a red mohawk kicks his feet up on Ace's prized maple oak table. My smile drops until the girl with him boots his legs aside—my kind of girl. I kick off my heels, giving my feet a much-needed rest from totting around like an expensive stripper. That was my mom's deal, and I honestly don't know how she did it. Not when the shoes hurt this much and the dresses are this tight. It's no wonder she took to a life on her back instead.

A line of bartenders pass through the room, carrying trays of canapes on their palms. I grab two for myself, giving Gabriel a wink when he scowls at me. I wonder if we're going to re-train Malik's double now that his personality traits are changing faster than any of us could have foreseen. After rolling my ankles, I pad from the kitchen to the basement in search of the Pinot. Tugging the light cord, I welcome the cool stone beneath my tired soles. A chill rushes through my spine, and I wrap my arms around myself, a yawn pulling at my mouth. It wasn't so long ago I could have partied through the night, blending one night's drunkenness into the next. Either I'm getting old, or I've become too comfortable lying around, being waited on hand and foot.

Turning at the bottom of the steps, the wine bottles are easy to locate on a shelving unit beside the chest freezer. Carrying them, however, might be slightly trickier. Grabbing six bottles, shoving one into each of my armpits, I wrangle my way up to the steps with my arms full and use my elbow to navigate the door handle. Stepping back into the kitchen, a flash of red catches my eyes, but it's not the bimbo I danced out of the bar. It's something so much worse. Dropping the Pinot bottles, they shatter around my feet, but I don't care. Treading through the glass, I near the sight that has halted the beating of my heart and solidified the blood in my veins.

Sphinx. Or at least the outline of Sphinx. Hanging upside down on the refrigerator. His tail has been jammed in the close of the door, his body coated in a slick layer of glistening crimson. I can't look, turning away to throw up in my mouth. A pool of blood has dripped onto the tile floor, trickling through the granite borders, so no matter which way I turn, I can't escape it.

My Sphinx, my pet. The little shit that hissed his way into my heart. I grab my chest, gasping at the weight of emptiness filling the space between my ribs. How can emotional pain physically hurt this much? I didn't realize I even cared for the wrinkly fucker, but now I can't avoid the sobs racking the length on my body. I drop down, clasping a hand over my mouth. Candy doesn't cry, and for this very reason, I remember now why Candy also doesn't love. Because a jealous red-headed bitch couldn't bow down and admit defeat. Pushing myself back onto aching feet filled with glass splinters, I rise up taller than I have ever stood before.

This is it. The last fucking straw. Taking the stairs two at a time, I don't stop until I'm flying into Malik's suite without bothering to announce myself. He's felt enough shockwaves radiating from my pussy that he should be in tune with my emotions by now. That's how coupley shit works, right? You transfer a piece of your soul through your genitals as easily as making a deal with the devil, and suddenly those individuals merge into the same person. Talking the same, only eating the same foods, matching interests until your spending every fucking day together and want to blow your fucking brains out.

"You're ranting internally again," Angus deadpans. He's hanging onto one of my shins and Hamish on the other, both jiggling along with each of my bloodstained stomps. I kick him aside, and he skids across the lino with a cringe-worthy squeak.

"No fucking shit Sherlock. How about instead of clinging onto me like a chlamydia-ridden koala, you offer me a realistic solution to kill that bitch?!"

"Candy?" Malik steps in from his balcony with the rest of the Monarchs trailing behind him. I narrow my eyes at Jack in particular, seething through my teeth.

"You," I point a finger directly at his forehead. "You're next." His green eyes widen, and he has the audacity to look confused. The group take a cautious step closer, trying to distract me with their loose ties and untucked shirts. The glazed sheen to their eyes suggests they either swapped out the cigars for some joints, or they've all been banging one out together on the balcony. Either way, I will not be deterred from my mission. Focusing on Malik's stoney glare, I dig deep for the resolve he'd have in my position. I must remain calm for a steadier shot. "Where's your gun stash? I know you have one."

"What's happened?" Malik answers my question with a question, and I flip his side table. The fancy vase that lived on top smashes against the floor beside Angus, sending chunks of gold and ivory porcelain skidding from the dining area to the kitchen.

"That...would be my parents," Malik fills the silence when everyone else freezes up. I roll my eyes, not having the patience or time for this.

"Well, now you know how I feel! His trashy whore killed my cat! Gutted him up, desecrating the little bastard's ugly face." A tear gathers in the corner of my eye, and I wipe it away so viciously I slap myself in the face.

"Yes Candy, that is totally the same thing," Angus deadpans in his gruff voice. Narrowing my eyes at him on the ground, I hold up my index finger and thumb reallllll close together.

"I am this close to ignoring you for the rest of my damn life." Ace and Spade shift uncomfortably while Jack ignores me and Malik just stares at the ashes on the floor. Clenching my fists, I make the noise of a strangled coyote at the ceiling.

"I'll vacuum this shit up later. Right now, you need to give me a machine gun so I can deal with the bitch who's somewhere in my house!" Malik looks up now, a question hitched in his eyebrow. "Yeah, you heard me - my fucking house. I assembled the fucking D-team, I have each and every one of you by the balls, and when I said this hoe needs to go, you should have kicked her straight out. Now, look what's happened. I threatened her, she tear-gassed me. I fuck her boyfriend; she ruins my quad. Beat her in a dance-off and she kills my fucking cat. So now, I'm going to make her into a human colander."

"Are you done?" Malik asks calmly when I come back down from my rant for air. The stoney expression on his face is a remnant of the man I thought we'd left back in the woods.

"Am I bathing in her blood?" I gesture to myself. It'll be a shame to ruin the satin dress he gifted me, but needs must.

"You didn't even like that cat," Jack pipes up, although I don't miss the nervous twitch to his eye. That's right motherfucker; you should be nervous. You'll be hunting for a spot to dig a six-foot hole tonight, wishing you'd never tried to challenge Candy Crystal. Realizing none of the guys opposite are going to willingly show me to their armory, I take to hunting for myself. Darting into Malik's bedroom, I slam the door shut and lean my weight against it. Then I notice the lock, twisting it into place as bodies collide with the other side of the door.

"Candy! Don't do this!" Malik shouts, telling me I'm on the right track. There's definitely weapons in here. Heading for the mattress first, it takes some strength to drag it from the king-size frame and flop it over. Taking the penknife from where I hooked it in my thong, I drag it down the center, yanking out handfuls of foam. When satisfied the mattress isn't hiding a stash of firearms, I turn to dissect the pillows as well. "Candy!" Malik roars again. "If you just slow down, we can talk this through!"

"Tell me where they are, and I'll stop destroying your room!" I yell back. To prove my point, I rip the lamp from the wall and throw it at the door. The crash gives him pause, and I still, their silence causing me to doubt myself more than the bellowing. Angus shares a shrug with me, and I go for the headboard, feeling down the back of the leather for hints of a concealment. Standing with my hands on my hips, a body slams into my side. I scream, being thrown onto the hollowed-out mattress with a bundle of muscle pinning me beneath his weight.

"Get the...fuck...off me!" I struggle, going for a knee to the balls. A flash of green catches my attention from Jack straddling my hips, his beach blonde hair swishing all over the place with my persistent bucking. A separate pair of hands to the ones pushing down my shoulders grabs my ankles to yank my legs straight. The bite of a zip-tie pinches my skin above the ankles as Ace manages to do the same to my wrists. Only then does Jack sit back on my thighs with a satisfied grin.

"Traitor!" I scream as Ace stands to join Spade a few paces back, regret marring his brow. I don't care for his sympathy; I just want revenge. The truth sinks in as my brain clears, and I drop back, relenting. Sphinx is dead. Mrs. Smithers entrusted him in my care, and like everything else I've ever grown attached to, someone slashed up his face. Not just someone, a prissy copycat bitch who's about to skip town thinking she's won. "She killed my cat," I whisper. My eyes cloud over, and I close them sharply. If I refuse to cry over that wrinkly cretin alone, I'm definitely not doing it in front of the Monarch's pity-filled gazes, but damn it. I want to.

"Candy," Jack calls out to me, stroking my cheek. "Cherry is leaving. Alone. She texted me while I was on the balcony, she's packing up, and there's a taxi on the way to pick her up. She thought she could handle my baggage but..." he trails off, although not with as much regret as I'd have presumed. My eyes fly open, not wanting to believe his words. Malik nods in agreement, and that only fuels my flames of anger further. She's leaving now? With her spine intact. I don't fucking think so. Bucking wildly, Jack fights to keep me pinned under his thighs.

"If Cherry was the one to hurt Sphinx, Ace will be able to check the surveillance cams, and then we can deal with it properly. If it wasn't her, I guess ultimately you've got what you wanted." There's a bitterness to his tone and a blame in his green eyes I don't appreciate. I wasn't the one who told Jack to prove to himself he was man enough to date outside of the Monarchs.

"Get off of me! I need to get to her before she goes," I scream and twist. The zip wires cut my flesh, slicing bands of fresh blood into my wrists and ankles. "She's not leaving this building with both her eyes. I'm going to stuff her eyeball into Sphinx's mutilated face so he can clearly see the white light at the end of the tunnel." Jack's hand falls away from my face, and he pushes to his feet, drawing Malik and the others in for a hushed meeting. I drop still, my chest heaving and ears ringing with the rush of adrenaline, so I strain to overhear their conversation.

"-can't have been her. It doesn't make any sense."

"Someone did."

"Who then? There's a bar full of strangers downstairs, but only the bartenders have the code to the door."

"There's been caterers, delivery men, the DJ, people in and out all day. Anyone could have-" I stop listening to their pointless conversations. After everything I've told them, they still don't believe me. Instead, I focus on wriggling off the mattress and locating my penknife. The cool blade presses against the top of my back, and with some careful navigating, I manage to do the backward worm up the tile until it's gripped in my hand. Bending my legs backwards like the flexible bitch I am, it only takes a minute to cut my ankles loose. On a low breath, I prep myself for the party move of the century.

Leaning all of my weight onto my back, I lift my legs and butt off the floor and launch myself forward. Landing heavily on my feet, I ignore the stab of pain and run. Just fucking run. Ducking into the bathroom, I spot a secret open door decorated like the rest of the walls—the one the guys must have used to sneak up on me. Flying through Malik's suite with my arms wrenched behind my back, I can taste sweet freedom when a hand wraps around my neck.

"Do you ever do as you're told?" Jack curses, hoisting me backward. Using his chest, he takes the brunt of my weight until my legs are kicking wildly.

"If you don't want me to kill her, one of you had better get there first." And with that, I topple myself in half, heaving Jack's weight over my back and throwing the pair of us down the stairs. Twice in one week, my ribs slam into the steps, exploding a shot of agony through my mid-section. I crumple to a stop, my vision swimming from the emotions and severe pain cutting through my wrists and torso. It would be so easy to just give up now. To lie here, accepting my fate. Jack will continue to pretend I mean nothing to him, and his replacements will continue trying to kill me. A mini giggly hand slaps me across the face, and I blink myself back to clarity, finding Angus' thick eyebrows as vexed as ever. He's right. Giving in is never an option.

I attempt to regain my footing, despite sliding around from the blood now seeping from my heels. Somehow, Jack is already upright a few steps below, foreseeing me launching myself at him. Using his grip on the railing, Jack heaves me backward into Malik's hold before vaulting down the rest of the staircase. I scream, sinking my teeth into Malik's arm. Another hand flashes out, then another. With one on each ankle and a solid arm around my torso, the three men I considered to be on my side awkwardly navigate me down the final steps. I flail, screaming like a crazed banshee, cursing Cherry's name to all hell.

"Just…stop and…listen," Malik grunts, fighting to keep me contained. I manage to dislodge one of my legs, smashing a bloodstained footprint across Ace's face. I vaguely register Spade's arm retreat, and he disappears just before my bedroom door is kicked open by one of the others. I'm wrangled to my bed, tossed on the mattress, and before I regain my composure, both mine and the adjoining bathroom doors are slammed shut and locked from the other sides. Limping with Angus and Hamish on either side of my ankles, we make it over to my door and ram our shoulders on the wood.

"If you don't let me the fuck out, I'll never forgive any of you for this! Someone will pay for Sphinx's life, and so be it if it's one of you!" I scream at the top of my lungs. Stupidly, Ace tries to respond by telling me to calm down. Like a red flag to a bull, my temper flares to an inferno of malice I can't pull myself back from. Throwing my weight into the door, the walls, the wardrobe, I kick and scream louder than I ever had. No one has the right to rile me up this much. I've never let it get this far before, usually opting for a bullet to the head and a victory cheeseburger. But with the strength of newfound rage, I'm starting to scare even myself. Angus and Hamish are hiding behind the pillows, peering out every so often.

"Just…stay in your room and let us take care of this," Malik bargains with me through the wood. "Once you've calmed down, we'll let you out, but for now," a short silence follows. "It's best you don't interfere." I stand stock-still, gaping at the door. Is he serious right now? Someone killed my first pet, and I shouldn't interfere? I wonder where the Monarchs would be right now if I didn't interfere. Not standing United as they lock me up, that's for sure. No one was complaining when I single-handedly emptied their ballsacks.

They seem to have forgotten this is who I am. I create chaos and leave behind a trail of enemies. I live for the now and fuck what comes tomorrow. No matter how much Malik has tried to convince me otherwise, it's clear I'm not a house cat. I'm a wild cat who's overstayed her welcome. Just when I thought these guys might be able to handle me, it's becoming all too clear that no one is. Except maybe one. Hopefully.

With my contortion skills, thank you reject circus, I manage to navigate my tied wrists beneath my feet to step over them. Using the corner of the dresser, I scrape the cable ties back and forth until they snap. All the while, Angus and Hamish sit on the bed, watching me. Their black eyebrows have dipped into an expression of pity, reminding me of exactly who tied me up in the first place.

How could the Monarchs do this to me? They were supposed to be on my side like I was on theirs. I'd have done anything they asked without question, yet my own revenge is too outlandish? I was wrong to think we were a team. I was wrong to depend on others to deal with my vendettas. I should have killed that bitch the minute I laid eyes on her, and my instincts screamed she was bad news. Fool me once; shame on the whole fucking world because I'm Candy motherfucking Crystal and I always get my own way.

ACE

"Okay, so what's the plan?" Spade growls, refusing to hang back and guard Candy's door as Malik asked. Asked – not ordered, even in this stressful situation. In Malik's defense against whatever grudge Spade is carrying against him, that has to count for something.

"Find Cherry before Jack has the chance to get her out of here," Malik states, his strides eating up the hallway. "She has a lot to answer for."

"You really think she's capable of murdering Sphinx? What about the other stuff; the quad, the tear gas attack?" Spade asks, but Malik doesn't answer him this time. The vein in his temple is fit to burst alongside the tooth-grinding clench of his jaw. If only he'd listened to Candy and then myself the multiple times I tried to caution him following the nail salon, but now doesn't feel like the time for 'I told you so'.

We descend the stairs and stand before the two-way mirror. The party is still in full swing, thankfully drowning out Candy's screams from upstairs. I'd go as far as to say it looks busier, although we were previously at full capacity. The bartenders can't keep up with those hanging over the bar to get their attention, and the DJ booth has been hijacked by women in their underwear. If Cherry and Jack are hiding in plain sight amongst the chaos, we can't see her.

Heading out back, I freeze at the sight of bloody footsteps leaving the kitchen before remembering Candy's blood-crusted mark is still smeared across my face. Scrubbing my cheek with my jacket sleeve, we move as a unit towards the kitchen, taking in the scene. Smashed bottles, blood embedded in the granite framing each floor tile, Sphinx hanging on the refrigerator. The way he's been slaughtered is in no way a retaliation to some dance battle humiliation; it's a full-out declaration of war. No wonder Candy was so pissed. In all honesty, I've never seen her so erratic, which caused alarm bells in itself. A woman's scream comes from out back, sending us in a rushed frenzy towards the rear door.

Spade gets there first, despite the cries of agony leaving him at his jaunted movements. No injury in the world will keep him from avenging Candy, and I wholly concur with that notion. Leaping over the back steps, the light from inside the kitchen briefly shines over a redhead, disappearing into the surrounding woodland. Jack is right on her heels, also being engulfed in the tree line before the door behind us slams shut. We take chase, blind in the dark as our dress shoes slam against the forest floor. Sticks slide beneath my heel, the occasional pine cone almost rolling my ankle. Our invasion forces birds to scatter from the branches overhead, masking the undertone of what sounded like a pained yell.

Keeping up pace with the huffs from Malik and Spade, I'm barrelling forward when my shins connect with a heavy mass. Sailing through the air, my face breaks my fall before the rest of my limbs catch up. A flash of light in my eyes burns my retinas, adding insult to the injuries until I spot Jack in the phone's flashlight. He's the obstruction in the footpath, and for good reason. A thick blade is sticking out of his ribs, barely protected by the cage he's made with his body. Slumped over, his head shifts towards me, but his eyes are unfocused.

"She's heading for the shack," he raises a finger in the direction we were headed. His voice is hoarse as if he's unable to draw a full breath.

"It's a dead-end, we can trap her in there," Malik replies, but the rattling sound vibrating from Jack's chest dashes any hope I may have briefly had.

"She knows where the guns are stashed," he mumbles and sinks lower onto his other side. Collectively, the three of us reach out to slap the back of Jack's head for being so stupid but manage to refrain. We haven't even shown Candy the shack, and for a good reason. She could open fire on the lot of us for misplacing her gum stash.

"Spade, get Jack back to the bar. Ace, follow me," Malik states, slipping into old ways, and I welcome it. Briefly, I pause to crawl over to Jack and cup his cheek. I don't know what to say, and even if I did, it would sound super gay, so I leave my well wishes at that. Then I join Malik's side and don't look back.

The forest seems quieter this time as if the surrounding wildlife dare not move, never mind breathe. As if each carefully placed footstep from now on is being watched. Malik keeps his phone's flashlight close, just highlighting the area in front before withdrawing it against his thigh again. We've trekked this path many times in the dark for practice, but knowing there's a knife-wielding redhead with a vendetta is loose on our land puts me on edge. She's had no formal training as far as I know, but then again, it turns out we didn't really know Cherry at all.

Nearing the direction the shack should be, light suddenly bursts through the bullet-proof windows. Dropping low, we crept the rest of the way, molding ourselves to the wooden panels. Soft footfalls pace inside as Malik and I skirt around to the front door. Without a direct plan in mind other than to detain her, we burst through the door.

Skidding across the floor towards the redhead in the center, I only get one foot on the floor when several red lasers shine in my eyes. Sparing a glance at Malik, similar red dots decorate the center of his forehead. His posture would insinuate he doesn't realize but I know him better than that. The woman in the middle of our shack spins, feigning surprise before pulling the red wig free from her brunette locks. Armed men in black fatigues step out of the shadows, keeping their guns raised while she laughs in our faces.

"I know you," Malik states, and I look a little closer. Brown hair hangs in manufactured curls on either side of her try-hard catsuit that I'd imagine Candy in with much more ease. Blue eyes sparkle with triumph, and the cruel smile on her painted lips slips as Malik continues. "Tanya, isn't it? From that night in the woods. You were with Jasper."

"Yeah, well," she snips back bitterly. "I'm not with Jasper anymore. He wasn't man enough to get the job done, so I've taken over." This time, Malik meets my eye with uncertainty.

"The job as in…the hit on Candy?" I question playing catch up with someone who's clearly bored of the game. "You're the reason it is still live after Leicester died." The realization sets in that we've been missing the clues all along while Tanya taps the toe of her ankle boot and indulges us further.

"Ha. Leicester didn't know about the hit in the first place. He'd never have knowingly put his *little girl* in danger," Tanya spits. A trickle of unease prickles at the each of my awareness, too aware of the barrel ends of snipers in my peripheral vision to focus. Tanya checks her phone and huffs, beginning to pace around again. "She killed my brother; you know that? And guess what Leicester did. Absolutely nothing. Yet the old man was furious when he found out Nigel tried to hurt her and had him executed in front of all the others to send a message. It's how we lost half our numbers in one night. Favoritism is difficult to contend with and impossible to break. Luckily, he didn't figure I'd been the one calling the shots, even before that."

"It's been you from the start. Leicester never wanted Candy dead," Malik responds. That venomous look from earlier is back with a vengeance. His dark eyes are pitch black beneath the shack's single bulb, his breath sawing out in measured heaves. Jack is out there with a knife in his side while we're kneeling here, helpless because of the trap we stupidly walked into. In my mind, I can hear what the old Malik would be saying about letting our emotions blind us. But this new version of the boss we desperately need right now, I haven't got a clue what he's thinking. Tanya kicks over a crate to sit on with a sigh.

"Killing Candy would have been kinda counterproductive for what he was trying to rear her for. He wanted her contained, sure. But very much alive." Tossing one leg over the other, Tanya peers at her phone again, fully invested in the screen.

"And here I was thinking Leicester had managing his crew down to a fine art. It never ceases to amaze me what people will do for a little attention," Malik tosses my way, and I grunt in agreement. Tanya flicks her leg back over and stomps her boot on the floor. Giving us the reaction we were going for, she lets her cool mask slip. Anger rises to the surface of her reddened cheeks and spiteful glare. Sensing her mood shift in the air, the gunmen take a menacing step forward, and I just refrain from sniggering. If they need to get that close with snipers, they obviously aren't very skilled. Although I'm sure if we knew what tonight entailed, it'd be Spade in here with a firearm in each hand, and I'd be the one ushering Jack to safety.

"The mansion and legacy are all I have left. I'm going to build my crew back up, better than it ever was," Tanya seethes, pointing a pointy digit my way. "But first, I need the riches and then Candy out of the picture so she can't lay claim to any of it."

"Why would she?" I frown. Not answering me, Tanya smooths her hands over her hair, carefully adjusting the curls back into place. Whatever chord we just struck has been quelled by the ruse of control in her favor. The roar of a motorcycle echoes through the trees beyond the shack, disappearing into the night. Tanya chuckles to herself, sashaying her hips as she paces back and forth between us and the crate.

"You know nothing she says is true, right? It's all bullshit spewed from the loopy bin in her head." Tanya chokes off a laugh, spinning her index fingers by her temples. I shouldn't let such a stupid taunt get to me, but an insult is on the tip of my tongue to defend Candy's honor if Malik didn't get there first.

"I figured," he states calmly. "But anyone who needs to create such narratives must do so for a reason. I have no doubt Candy's been through more shit than the lot of us combined, and I'm going to make damn sure she never has to suffer again." His words weren't as sharp as mine would have been, but the threat is there, clear to all. She's our girl, and collectively, we'll make damn sure she's protected.

"Good luck with that," Tanya snorts, peering at her phone again. "When she's not even here." My gut drops as it becomes all too obvious now. Tanya's impatient twitching, her addiction to her phone's screen. She's been stalling.

"What's that supposed to mean?" Malik asks, catching on too late. Flicking her phone to face us with a malicious grin on her face, my own surveillance cams stare back at us—specifically, a view of Candy's room from the top corner. The pillows are dented, the dresser on its side. At first, I don't understand why until I realize a string of knotted sheets are secured to it somehow, leading towards the open window. Candy is nowhere to be seen.

"It doesn't take a genius to figure out if you can hack my surveillance system; you've no doubt been listening into our conversations too," I drawl, trying to sound as unimpressed as possible. Power-hungry people like Tanya thrive on their effect to make others squirm, which would seem to be the only card I currently hold.

"Like my new favorite sofa opera," Tanya beams. "Seriously, you all made it too easy. Not believing her delusions, favoring Jack's side piece, trying to bring Jasper back into your fold. All it took was one gas canister and a goon pile to make you turn on him in the same night," she bursts out laughing. Malik's shoulders tighten in his suit jacket. "Pathetic effort, gentlemen. You were going to lose your precious Candy either way, but this has been much more entertaining than I'd anticipated." Tucking the phone into a hidden pocket of her catsuit, Tanya pulls her hair over one shoulder. Noting whatever signal she just gave off, the snipers take another step closer, surrounding us from all sides.

"Well, as fun as this has been, I have a safe to crack and a psycho to finish off. Fortunately, you guys have played into my hand yet again and already sent her back to where I need her to be." Walking around Malik, his hand whips out to grab Tanya by the ankle. A sniper presses into the back of his head, but he doesn't retreat.

"Candy could be sitting at the bottom of the ocean with her arms wrapped around an anchor, and you still wouldn't be able to drown her. She doesn't need any of us to hold her own." Keeping her head high, Tanya shakes off Malik's hold and strides out of the shack. I peer over at my brother, finally able to call him that by the vulnerability in his blank stare back. Malik is no longer my boss or puppet master; he's my equal. And he's right; Candy never needed us, but we've quickly learned to depend on her. So much so that as soon as the door clicks shut, Malik and I instantly dive in opposite directions.

I sweep out the legs of the gunman closest, quick to grab his gun on the way down. Diving at the next, I shoot wildly amongst the chaos erupting around the shack. Bullets fly with the crackle of gunfire, and I can't be sure if I'm hit, the adrenaline spurring me on until the two men on my side have a bullet hole in their foreheads. Malik's side is silent as he approaches me, patting a hand on my shoulder. Keeping the guns in our possession, we take off after Tanya, who no doubt heard the ruckus.

Uncaring of who sees anymore, Malik wields his phone's flashlight like a weapon in itself, spearing the trees with light. Footfalls crunch heavily over the woodland floor, drawing us in the direction of the bar. Thumping music pours through the walls, growing louder as he breaches the tree line. People have swarmed the parking lot, filling the gaps between the vehicles as the inside of the bar appears to be beyond capacity. A prickle along my spine says that's no coincidence.

Hunting for Tanya, my eyes catch on a glimpse of red hair. From the real source this time. Across the lot, a taxi is lying in wait at the entrance of the dirt track. Cherry struggles against the male holding her; the one I'd have been convinced is Malik if he weren't standing at my side. Gabriel. His hand clamps over Cherry's mouth as he navigates her from the bar's entrance and into the sea of people. Appearing around the side of the building closest, Jack hobbles towards the taxi, his bellows of Cherry's name only audible to those who would be listening out for it. The scene plays out in slow motion; even though my feet are moving, I know I'm already too late.

Malik bulldozes through the crowd, elbowing people aside slamming them into their vehicles. Using the path he's created, I'm right behind, catching glimpses of the taxi headlights. Tanya appears, skidding to a stop as the passenger door is opened for her from the inside. Disappearing from view, my eyes track Cherry instead as Gabriel drags her to the taxi where Nick is holding the rear door open for them. My own lookalike, as if that makes the deception cut even deeper. The pair shove Cherry's gangly legs inside, ignoring Jack's roaring shouts coming from behind. Tanya notices, though, twisting around in her seat. I catch a glimpse of her malicious smile before a group of bearded bikers gets in my way. They don't seem impressed by Malik's aggression as he tries to barrel through the center.

Wobbling on their feet, one of the bald men with a bandana tied around his neck is holding Malik's decanter from his personal sideboard. The group lazily searches for more of us, telling me their position here isn't by chance. A fist is swung at my face, which I dodge, only to catch another one in the side of my jaw. Their movements are slow, thanks to the free alcohol, and within moments Malik and I have the lot of them writhing on the ground in agony. But it was long enough.

Tires skid, and a dull thud rings through the heavy bass. I know what I'll find, to the point that I don't want to look. Malik drags me up by the back of the shirt, though, pulling me over to where Jack lays limp on the floor. His body is contorted from the taxi reversing into him, his blonde hair seeming duller than ever before. Dropping on my knees at his side, my hands hover, unsure of what to do. The area where the knife had been is covered with a makeshift bandage, but now it's pissing out with blood again. Ripping my shirt off, I hold it over the wound while Malik checks his pulse. Spade skids down at Jack's other side, his blue eyes wide and panicked.

"Candy's gone. I told him to stay in the games area while I checked in on her. It was only a small knife, I-"

"It's okay Spade," Malik says, but his grave tone implies it's anything but okay. Dropping his fingers from Jack's neck, he hangs his head, and my stomach drops. A lone tear trickles down my cheek. It's over. We lost, and I can't for the life of me understand where it went so wrong.

JASPER

Wrapping the thickly corded rope around my wrists, I give one final heave, pulling the safe free from its hidden confines. Sweat coats my t-shirt even though I'd planned this to be a short diversion. It took the best part of an hour just to shimmy the metal box forward enough and loop the rope around the back. Then I had to remove the cupboard door that once concealed it since the hinges stuck out too far. I meant what I said to Candy, I couldn't give a shit about the money. But it's obvious she's gone and has no interest in claiming the riches herself, so one of us might as well enjoy them. It's not like I have much else going for me anymore.

Not bothering with the retinal scanner, I drop down on my hunches, reaching for the duffel bag I brought to the attic with me. Not knowing what might work, I'd grabbed every power tool I could see in the garage, but with the safe on its side, the answer seems obvious now. Lifting the grinder and donning a pair of plastic goggles, sparks fly all around. Maybe I should have put down some sheets to protect Candy's hideout if she ever were to return. After seeing her reaction to Cherry threatening her social standing with the Monarchs, I can only imagine what she'd do if I burned down her unicorn cave.

The noise is deafening as I draw the grinder back and forth, slicing a deep ridge from corner to corner. Soon enough, the safe's side drops to the ground with a heavy clang. Tipping out the contents of the duffel bag, I drop to my knees to refill it —bags of diamonds and cash, Rolex watches, a handful of keys. Then there's a stash of paperwork and a large brown envelope with an official-looking stamp across the unbroken seal. Pushing the bag aside, I drop onto a glittery, heart cushion to read some of the documents. I shouldn't snoop, even if the owner of the files is dead. Then again, most of these have Candy's name on, and she wouldn't give a shit either way.

Popping the seal, I pull out a page covered in random numbers. The key information stands out, though, and the results are all too clear to decipher. With the mother untested, Candy's column stands along with the 'alleged father', aka Robert Leicester. A statement in bold states the obvious after so many of their numbers match up. **'The alleged father cannot be excluded as the biological father of the tested child. Based on the analysis above, the probability of paternity is 99.99%.'**

Well, damn. As if being the spunky wild child that stole my heart and refused to give it back wasn't enough. She had to be the secret heiress of a crime gang too. I only knew Leicester as an old, bitter man but hiding this information was smart for multiple reasons. A key one being that Candy doesn't care for riches or labels. If she'd known the heists she did were for her own future security, I have no doubt she'd have flushed it all away, literally, down the toilet. There's no excitement and spontaneity in a life that's been designed for you. Stuffing the letter back inside the envelope, I add it to the pile of riches in the bag, zipping it up tightly.

Strolling through the mansion, my eyes drag lazily over the lavish décor I'd strangely become accustomed to. At first, I thought I'd never feel comfortable with the knot of nausea in my gut at just how much money people waste. The excessive of aged clocks, the dusty tapestries that belong in a museum. But it was a place to hang my coat, and all good things must come to an end. With no sight of Tanya, I toss my keys into a dish on the kitchen side and leave via the back door. No point locking up since keeping the estate secure is no longer my problem.

Hitting the fob on the Lambo keychain, because fuck leaving that behind, the garage door slides up, and a wash of déjà vu halts my footsteps.

"Room for one more?" Candy smirks. Stretched across the backseat, the dirt caked over my favorite hoodie, and a pair of old sweatpants aren't the only reason alarm bells blare in my head. Hanging her bare feet over the side of the vehicle, I can't tell where the mud ends and the blood begins. Her pink hair is ruffled, filled with leaves.

"What the fuck," I mutter. Making my way to the trunk, I dump the duffle bag amongst the others I stuffed in there earlier. Then I pop the back door, carefully lowering Candy's feet, and crawl over the length of her body. Prying the Candy Crusher from her grip, I take her shaky hands in mine. "What happened, Crazy Girl?" The cocky smile on her face falters and for once, for the first fucking time, I see her crack. That in itself is all I need to know.

"I'm going to get you out of here, and we're never looking back." Pushing upright, Candy's hand lashes out. She grabs the collar of my t-shirt in her first, dragging me back down. Pretending I didn't see the crimson bands sliced into her wrists, I scoop her into my arms and just hold her.

"I have a condition," Candy whispers into my ear. I'm already nodding, eager to get on the road. To get her the fuck away from whatever the Monarchs have done because if it wasn't them, she wouldn't be here. She'd be curled up in Malik's arms instead, thanking him for being the hero as per usual. He can screw us all over but still come out victorious as the almighty King. Realizing she's yet to tell me the condition, I raise my head enough to brush my nose over hers.

"You look like shit."

"Abseiling from a second-story window with knotted bedsheets isn't as easy as it looks in the movies. Neither is wearing sneakers or riding a bike when there's still glass in my feet." She cancels out my barrage of curses and promise of retribution with a heated kiss. A connection filled with longing that takes my breath away. Passion and something deeper explode between our mouths, sinking lower to resonate in my chest. Possessive strokes of her tongue, impatience tugs at my t-shirt. The taste of desperation held on her lips spear my soul with the need to fix it. To patch her up good as new and bring back the psycho chick I fell for. And fuck if I haven't fallen hard.

"Tell me the condition, now. We're stopping by the ER before our new adventure begins," I try to smile, but it's really fucking hard.

"There's a reason I don't trust people, but I'm trusting you. If I tell you someone is trying to kill me, I want to know you'll believe it. If I say I'm going to chase this Cherry bitch to the ends of the Earth, I want to know you'll be at my side."

"Where else would I be?" I reply immediately. Her body deflates beneath me, and I'm rewarded with another kiss, but my mind is in overdrive. Reaching over, I buckle Candy in place and draw myself away from her warmth. Dropping into the driver's seat, I spot an empty hole behind the fuse box on the wall. Nothing surprises me anymore, and my concern is firmly on the woman in the back. She's clearly had a rough night, but at least she's here now. Dully, as I peel the Lambo out of the garage, a tiny voice in the back of my mind isn't quite drowned out by the roar of the engine. She came back to me in her time of need, and I won't let her down. But at the risk of sounding like Malik, she's mine now, and I also can't let her go.

ACKNOWLEDGMENTS

Thank you so much to you all for taking a chance on the 'I Love Candy' series. This book was so much fun to write, and I absolutely loved letting my crazy run loose with Candy and Hamish. I hope you had as much fun reading as I had writing it. This is a dark reverse harem romance which will ultimately (eventually) have a HEA at the end of the trilogy…so hang in there!

There are so many people that helped me make this book a reality, and I have them to thank.

Morrigan McKay, Avery Stone, Maya Morrison, and Unlikely Optimist - My Sprint Room Team - I can honestly say that they are the people who kept me motivated each and every day to write this book. If you haven't had the chance to read books by these amazing authors, I highly recommend you giving them a chance.

Sam - not only are you an amazing PA, who I would be lost without, you have now helped make my words even better. You are a great editor and I'm so proud of you for completing your course. I don't ever want to share you!

To my Street Team - thank you for pushing so much and telling people how much you love my books. You're all amazing and your hard work is much appreciated.

Emma Luna - every time I challenge you to create a new masterpiece, you make it even better than I imagine. Thank you you helping to make my book pretty.

To my beautiful children - thank you for being so patient with me, and being so understanding when I don't have as much time for family time. Every word I write is for you. I love you.

To my amazing husband - Not only do you support me and encourage me to follow my dream, you are there by my side while I do it. Thank you for all your help and support. We make a great team, and I love you.

ABOUT MADDISON COLE

Maddison is a married mum of two, and a serial daydreamer. As a huge fan of all romance troupes, from RH to Omegaverse, she finally decided to put pen to paper (finger to keyboard doesn't sound as poetic) and write her own.

As a child, life was moving around the UK and a short stint in the Caribbean, before Maddison has found herself back in the south east of England where she is now happily settled. With a double award in applied arts and an A-level in art history, Maddison is an average musical-loving, Disney-obsessed, jive- dancer with a dark passion for steamy fantasy books.

FOLLOW MADDISON COLE

If you have enjoyed getting to know me and my books, please do reach out to me via social media. I love chatting about my books, so don't hesitate to contact me.

My social media is where you can find out all about reveals, announcements, giveaways and more!

Sign up to my newsletter here:

http://eepurl.com/hx3Zqr

Make sure to join my Facebook readers group:

Coles Reading Moles

- facebook.com/maddison.cole.314
- instagram.com/maddison_cole_author
- amazon.com/author/B086ZQ6SW4
- bookbub.com/authors/maddison-cole
- goodreads.com/authormaddisoncole
- tiktok.com/@coles_moles

ALSO BY MADDISON COLE

ALL MY PRETTY PSYCHOS

Paranormal RH with ghosts and demons

Queen of Crazy

https://amzn.to/3O4biQt

Kings of Madness

https://amzn.to/3HzvBCY

Hoax: The Untold Story (novella)

https://amzn.to/3xAJhcA

Reign of Chaos (pre-order)

https://amzn.to/3b95PcI

·

I LOVE CANDY

Dark Humor RH - Completed

Findin' Candy (novella)

https://amzn.to/3bcueOp

Crushin' Candy

https://amzn.to/3n0TASf

Smashin' Candy

https://amzn.to/3Oniuai

Friggin' Candy
https://amzn.to/3QwlmUb

The Complete Candy Boxset
https://amzn.to/3t2dqiW.

·

THE WAR AT WAVERSEA
Basketball College MFM Menage - Completed

Perfectly Powerless
https://amzn.to/3OqHTQp

Handsomely Heartless
https://amzn.to/3tMoRfu

Beautifully Boundless
https://amzn.to/3MYiiNG

·

MOON BOUND
Vampire/Shifters Fated Mates Standalones

Exiled Heir
https://amzn.to/3OtlqSD

Privileged Heir
https://amzn.to/3mYwQ5g

·

WILLOWMEAD ACADEMY (CO-WRITTEN WITH EMMA LUNA)

Sexy Student - Teacher Taboo Age Gap Standalone

Life Lessons
https://amzn.to/3tL8eAX

·

A WONDERLUST ADVENTURE: A DERANGED DUET
Retelling of Alice - twenty years on

My Tweedle Boys (pre-order)
https://amzn.to/3wRIqVd

Our Malice (TBC)

·

VICES AND HEDONISM SHARED WORLD
A Reverse Harem MMA Romance

A Night of Pleasure and Wrath
https://amzn.to/3Rgg0fC

·

FINDING LOVE AFTER DEATH (CO-WRITTEN WITH EMMALEIGH WYNTERS)

Haunted by Desire
https://amzn.to/3BaTlvI

Printed in Great Britain
by Amazon